THE LEGEND OF TRIQUETRA

TARA REWA

Copyright © 2023 by Tara Rewa

All rights reserved.

This book or any portion thereof may not be reproduced or used in any manner whatsoever without the express written permission of the respective writer of the respective content except for the use of brief quotations in a book review.

The writer of the respective work holds sole responsibility for the originality of the content and The Write Order is not responsible in any way whatsoever.

Printed in India
ISBN: 978-93-5776-918-1
First Printing, 2023

The Write Order

A division of Nasadiya Technologies Private Ltd.

Koramangala, Bangalore

Karnataka-560029

THE WRITE ORDER PUBLICATIONS.

www.thewriteorder.com

Publishing Consultant – Priyanka Lal

For my mom, my rock.

CHAPTER 1

A February Night, New Delhi

My grandmother, Naani, found it rather unfortunate that I could transform into a twig snake. She said that my animal side was weak. That I ought to be extra careful in matters that were slightly dangerous for others. For me, the same situations could be life-threatening. So I studied the back door in the boundary wall of our condo for any movement. The back door opened into a village. The rendezvous was fixed for midnight at the banyan tree in the village, a couple of hundred meters away.

Gurgaon was unique in that way. There still existed some villages within the city, like unwanted pulp in clear juice. Some people liked the character these rural pockets added to the city; others hated having to live with the country folk.

Personally, I wasn't very fond of the village. But since Naani had forbidden us to visit it, from time to time, I would stop by a tuck-shop in the village for snack packs. Mohan, my baby brother, generally followed me, and I let him. I liked to think I was disobeying Naani. On one occasion, a group of bullies surrounded Mohan, and when I intervened with a fist, Mohan screamed at me to stop hitting them. How annoying is that! What did he expect? For me to organize peace talks? He could be so aggravating. He acted as if he did not have an animal side to him at all.

Thunk. Thunk.

The sound of the guard's thick wooden staff hitting the tarmac road that bordered the condo towers echoed near me. Of the two guards on duty, one remained at the gate while the other did the rounds. Once the guard disappeared, I sprinted to the gate and waved the access card across the reader to slip unnoticed into the village.

I tiptoed my way through the gate when I heard a voice. "Where do you think you are headed?"

Great snakes! I had not expected the second guard to be walking around too. Worse, I hadn't heard him approach.

One of the main drawbacks of having a snake silhouette was that unless I was barefoot, I was practically deaf. If I wore regular branded shoes, I ended up bouncing on my toes taking my oddball image to a whole new level. So Naani had a pair of ugly, bulky orthopedic shoes designed for me. I abhorred them. But I'd worn them today, as there was no way of crossing the uneven and cracked village roads in bare feet.

Without looking back, I hopped over the threshold, pulling the door hard behind me. It did not click shut. Much to my horror, I realized the guard had managed to block the door with his thick wooden staff.

I stood rooted to the ground as the door opened and the guard appeared in the doorway with his staff raised for an attack. I searched for an excuse: *Naani needs medicines… Mohan is hurt, and Naani sent me to get medicines…*

You can't even lie properly, Naani's voice sounded in my head. It was common knowledge that the pharmacy in the village would be shut at this hour. If there was a snake saint, he or she had to help me now.

"Sorry," I mumbled, still trying to fish for an excuse when the guard receded into the doorway, confusion writ on his face. Either he had not seen me, which was impossible since I froze right before his eyes, or he had decided to go tell on me to Naani.

I patted my body and felt my clothes, face, and eyes just to make sure I had not silhouetted into a timid little twig snake. Except for Naani, no one knew about my silhouette. Not my classmates, not even my brother.

Naani said that twig snakes were mildly venomous, and in a face-off with me, a king cobra would die of boredom first. These are hard words to hear for anyone, let alone a fourteen-year-old boy who pops into animal form at the merest provocation.

A pack of street dogs was napping all around a bench on my right. Like a queen surrounded by guards, a fluffy stray cat the color of dirty snow was sleeping on the bench. When I turned around, the cat's tail twitched.

I tiptoed away, praying the cat wouldn't wake up the dogs, who would rouse the village with their barking. How had it managed to plonk itself right in the middle of dogs, anyway?

I hurried on the beaten track, expecting the guard and Naani to burst in at any time through the door behind me. Lining the lane were pennant flags bearing the smiling face of a candidate for the municipal elections that year. In the moonlight, the same face peered at me from the walls of the houses. It was a standard political poster in bright colors on cheap paper.

Vinay Chaubey
Your leader, Your friend

Vinay Chaubey's face was printed in a circle in the middle of the poster. A staff-bearing hippie stood on one side of the circle, a turbaned man with light-green eyes in a pathani suit on the other. Despite their smiling faces and folded hands, these men had a threatening air about them. They seemed to be saying, "If you don't vote for Vinay Chaubey, you're dead meat."

Still, I found Vinay Chaubey's face, with his trimmed mustache and sincere smile, quite pleasant.

As I moved on, I stumbled a few times, unable to see clearly. Perhaps my glasses were dirty. I could not take the risk of fumbling the delivery, so I removed my glasses to wipe them with my shirt but was shocked to find I could see perfectly without them. I wasn't sure what was happening. Perhaps it had to do with my approaching birthday tomorrow. But now was not the time to figure that out.

I stuffed the glasses into my satchel and bent to touch the ground out of habit to check for noises around me. I heard the soft patter of feet and turned around to find that the cat had followed me, apparently for the lack of anything better to do. There was no sign of the guard.

The wind had picked up even more and was causing a bustle

in the trees and bushes. Could someone be hiding in the thicket? Would anyone want to intercept the parcel that Batty, the school janitor, had assigned me to deliver? What if it contained something valuable like jewelry, or something illegal like drugs?

Naani's voice returned in my head: *You will bring disrepute to your forefathers' name one day.*

It isn't as if I'm smuggling anything into the school, I reasoned.

Thankfully, I was distracted from my negative thoughts by a black nightingale fighting the strong winds. It finally perched on the roof of a nearby house. The presence of the cat and the nightingale was reassuring. Instinctively, I felt closer to animals than humans.

The delivery point was the humongous banyan tree with a cement parapet built around it for sitting. Countless red threads, similar to the ones Naani kept in the temple at home, were wound around the tree trunk.

People said the tree was haunted, and that the holy threads kept the dark spirits away. When you've lived the life of a snake whose worst nightmare is being stepped on or crushed, ghost stories sound ridiculous.

I could see the shadow of the banyan up ahead. It was so close to my condo that if not for the two-storied houses that had sprouted up all over the village, I could have spotted the tree from the balcony of our flat on the seventh floor.

For a place that was so noisy during the day with kids creating a ruckus or the chatter of old men puffing away on their hookahs, it felt unnaturally quiet at this hour.

I felt a pinch on my upper arm. It was the amulet that Naani had tied on my arm the day I silhouetted. It had suddenly tightened.

Was it warning me? Nah! My immediate hunch was that when I got twenty-twenty vision a few minutes back, my body, too, had undergone a change. I had buffed up somehow. I felt myself grow a little taller, and my muscles become taut. Perhaps that was why the arm band felt tight. I hoped it wasn't just wishful thinking.

I clutched the parcel to my chest; I ran my left hand over my right arm until I felt the amulet through my flannel shirt and the t-shirt beneath it. I had half a mind to pull the amulet off before I remembered Batty's warning to be on time for the delivery.

Stepping into the shadow of the tree, I moved toward the darker interior of its trunk. An outline of a man in a jacket standing on the cement platform became visible. My amulet tightened some more.

Could it be due to this man?

I shook off the wild thought, blaming it on the stormy night, which was getting more ominous with every second. But then all my birthdays felt like doom to me.

"Look for a baton in the man's hand," Batty had directed me earlier in the day.

When I told him that the delivery location was in my condo's back yard and that I was familiar with the banyan tree, Batty had said, "That's good, but if for any reason you get delayed, be sure to leave within an hour."

That was too precise. I wanted to ask him what would happen if I didn't leave on time, but I couldn't bear to see Batty more nervous than he already was.

Unlike a janitor, Batty had a learned look about him with his balding head, just a few strands combed over the crown, and half-moon glasses that rested on a round blunt nose. He always wore a faded old safari suit, and I had never seen him without a book in his hand. Mostly, he was a cool cucumber as he trundled about the school with a mop.

I guess I'm the only person who ever saw him anxious. Like when he gave me directions for this delivery. His nose had twitched repeatedly. His left hand had moved in and out of his shirt pocket as if he were searching for something but forgot about it by the time his fingers reached the pocket.

"Hurry up, boy. I don't have all night," the man standing on the parapet said to me in a voice that was impossibly scratchy, like the scrubbing of a vinyl record. He stood statue-still.

I tried to see the face of the receiver, but the dense shadow of the tree added another layer of darkness to his hooded head and shoulders. Suddenly, he moved, crossing his arms. In one hand, he held a baton. Check.

In order to exchange the passwords, I had to see the man's face to read his lips. I said, "Strike the iron while…"

"…it's soft," the man finished, emphasizing the "f" in soft, lifting his face enough to reveal half of it.

The good part about this conversation was that I had heard him perfectly and that the password exchange was over and done with. For when I saw the man's mouth, my voice caught in my throat.

Two sharp canines rested just over his lower lip like in the mouth of a wild animal. At that moment, I understood why Batty had been anxious about this delivery.

Every delivery I had made for Batty in the past seven months had been protected by a mysterious password formed by the nonsensical twisting of proverbs or wordplay.

"Twice in a blue moon, thrice in the sun."

"Blood moon stalls the wheels of history."

"Two stones, one bird."

Disinterested couriers would turn up, twirling their keys or scrolling on their phones to receive the deliveries at pre-appointed locations. These men would mutter the remaining half of the password, grab the parcel, and jump into their vehicles without a single glance at me. All deliveries had been for Gargo D'Souza.

Something told me I was finally meeting Gargo D'Souza himself.

"Let's have it, then," the man said. He tucked his baton into his belt and stuck out his hand. I did a double take when I saw the sickly, calloused, and warty skin on his hand. It was not human skin.

My hands fumbled with the flap of my satchel, and I hurriedly pulled out the parcel, holding it up with both hands in case I dropped it, like an offering to a fearsome deity.

"What is your name, boy?" the man said, gently lifting Batty's parcel out of my hand. His unnaturally long fingernails grazed lightly against my hands.

"Adi," I said, trying my best to sound confident.

"Adi," he repeated. He sliced the cling film with a fingernail and upturned the packet. A gold dagger fell into his hand. The hilt was sculpted into a horse's head, neck, and torso. The rest of the blade was covered with a leather sheath. A black stone shone in place of the horse's eye.

So, Batty dealt in smuggled antiques. *Antiques that are also weapons,* Naani's voice echoed in my head.

"Dusht Uchchaihshravas," the man said in a satisfied whisper as he examined the item. He gripped the hilt with his right hand and attempted to pull out the dagger, but it remained stuck. He faltered, bent his leg, placed the dagger on his thigh, and pulled in both directions, grunting. The dagger did not budge.

Afraid he might complain about the item being damaged, I flipped back the satchel's flap and stepped back. My job was done. It was time to leave.

"Wait, boy," the man hissed. "Where did you get that bag?"

The question was so unwarranted that for a moment I thought my hearing had failed me again. I expected him to say something about the dagger's condition since it was jammed. But my bag?

"It carries the Naga seal. Who gave it to you?" the man said and moved forward. I looked up into yellow eyes under a bumpy, rough-skinned forehead. The yellow of the eyes was so bright and inhuman that if I hadn't forced myself to break my gaze, I wouldn't have noticed the sunken eye sockets and lack of eyelashes. He had shiny black stubble. He looked like an evil panther.

"B-B-Batty," I lied.

My feet remained rooted to the ground as my attention returned to his eyes. I realized the man was not looking at me—

rather, his sight was fixed on the snake logo on my satchel.

When I was six, my mother gave me a used brown leather satchel. The flap was embossed with a logo: a serpent shaped like the infinity symbol, the tail of the serpent ending in its mouth. The symbol had grown hazy owing to use. I remembered Mother mentioning that the mark was the insignia of our family's rich history. She said it would look snazzy on me once I became a teenager and that it was a gender-neutral bag that had been a gift from her own grandmother. I found the bag too girly for my taste. I hung it in my cupboard and forgot all about it.

When Naani came to live with us, she discarded everything that carried that symbol. I hid the bag from her and used it whenever I could for the satisfaction that came from doing everything that Naani forbade.

"This is nothing," I said to Gargo D'Souza, rubbing the mark with my thumb, hoping the faint embossing might even out. My heart felt like it was aboard a rocking boat. Nothing snaky had ever brought me luck.

"What is your name again?" the man asked. His voice had a menacing edge to it, and his body had grown alert like a panther ready to pounce on its prey.

"Adi," I said in a voice as low as I could manage. "Adi Yoshi."

The man hissed. "Yoshi? Are you sure?" He grunted, much like a jungle cat. He moved his head closer as if studying my face to see if it was familiar. Did he rise in the air a little, or was it my imagination?

I didn't reply. I had always hated my middle name, Nagaraj,

and even though my birth certificate carried it, my school admission card didn't. Naani made sure my middle name was dropped from all records. I wondered if Batty had told the man about my deafness. Perhaps I could play along.

He must have read the conflict on my face, for he whispered, "But that's not possible. With my own eyes, I saw the clan slaughtered."

The cat I saw near the condo gate had taken a prime seat for the unfolding drama. It got up suddenly and started to move away from the parapet. Lucky cat, it could just walk away. Had I been stupid in accepting this last-minute delivery? Had Batty trapped me?

I reminded myself of the journey I would undertake tomorrow to Goa and the freedom from Naani. A step closer to my dream.

The dream had taken seed in my head when I read *Bud, Not Buddy* by Christopher Paul Curtis. Ten-year-old Bud leaves home to find his father with a flyer as a sole clue.

My clue was my Aunty Padma's letter that I had chanced upon last year on my birthday when I tried on the brown leather satchel. The letter was written to my mother by my dad's sister, Padma Yoshi, who lived in Goa. There was no phone number or address. The letter was vague except for the sentence where Aunty Padma called me her favorite nephew. I liked the thought of being loved by a family member. This was how the plan to escape to Goa caught my fancy.

After numerous letters sent to random strangers who went by the name of Padma Yoshi, I received a return letter containing a phone number. In her high-pitched singsong voice,

Aunty Padma told me she'd tried to look for me after my parents' death, but Naani had hidden me and Mohan from her. Naani threatened to report Aunty Padma to the police if she stepped anywhere near us. That was why Aunty Padma had stopped looking for us.

This wasn't strange for me. I knew Naani. Her distrust of people was legendary. Aunty Padma and I decided that I would leave for Goa with her. Once I got settled at her place, I would call Naani and let her know.

I just have to get out of here, I reminded myself, ignoring the towering monster man who stood before me. But try as hard as I might, I couldn't shrug off Naani's voice in my head: *You are a child, Adi. Children cannot have grown-up dreams.*

"How long has Batra known you?" the man asked me.

I pretended not to hear. I took a step back when the man growled. I stood rooted to the spot as I stammered, "About two years," hoping that was the answer he was looking for. So Batra was Batty's proper name.

"Two years! We should have squished that dimwit when we had the chance," he said as if Batty were a cockroach. "How did you keep your silhouette concealed for so long?"

I returned to my deaf act. This had "silhouette trouble" written all over it.

One fear I always carried with me was being told, "You snake!" The phrase was offensive to my silhouette and had shameful connotations. It got my temper soaring every time I saw someone use it in a movie or on TV. I had a feeling Gargo D'Souza would use it today. If he did, I would fly into a rage, silhouette, and get trampled.

You think too much. You are not ready, Adi, Naani intoned in my mind. I tried to imagine the beaches of Goa to keep the anger from getting to me.

"Where do you live?" the man asked. "Tell me about your family."

I stared back. There was no way I was going to share my address with this monster man. It was true I hated Naani and Mohan, but if I wanted them dead, I would have killed them myself.

Before the man could prod further, a shrill birdcall and a cat's meowing erupted behind me. The man looked at the nightingale and the cat in alarm, then his chin set in the determination that comes from realizing an omission. He held out his baton, but instead of striking the nightingale with it, he twirled the baton as if he were performing a rite that made the threads wound around the tree light up like neon red hula-hoops.

The nightingale launched an attack on the man, pecking at his head and arms. The man snarled in pain and stopped twirling the baton. The dagger fell from his hand and landed on the ground next to me. Thunder cracked down on the banyan tree, but it did not reach us.

I tried to back away from the tree, but the man caught my collar. I was done for. In desperation, I grabbed the dagger. I wondered why Batty, if he was my friend, had sent me here. Had he known this man's identity?

"I am Gargouille, Rahu's mount, his panther ride, and you will make my lord very happy," the man whispered in my ear, holding my hands behind me with one hand and pulling my head back with the other.

The nightingale and the cat were throwing themselves at the man, but he stood rooted to the ground as if numb to the blows by the cat's claws and the nightingale's sharp beak.

I am not violent by nature, but my silhouette is unpredictable. I felt animal rage rise within me, and for the first time in my life, I let it boil. It was liberating to not have to quieten it like I did at school or around Naani.

I bit Gargo's hand with all my might, but my teeth couldn't dent his hard, scaly skin, which had the thorny feel of raw pineapple. Still, I felt my hands go free.

I pulled hard at the dagger, expecting it to be jammed. To my surprise, it slid out easily. This did not go unnoticed by Gargo.

I now stood facing him with the nightingale and the cat on either side of me.

I swiped the dagger at him, nicking his arm. The nightingale went for his eye, and the cat jammed its teeth into Gargo's leg.

As Gargo tried to smack the nightingale with his baton, missing it every time, he lifted his hand and snapped his fingers twice. What happened next was so unexpected that my brain refused to believe what my eyes saw.

The trunk of the massive banyan tree began to shed its skin like a pineapple being peeled. Pointed, scrappy edges and flimsy layers of bark flopped over the holy red threads, leaving dents in the tree's trunk. The hollows were disproportionate to the thin layer of bark that had fallen off. This mystery solved itself when the bark straightened and expanded into shapes with bat-like wings, the small sharp horns of an antelope, and a panther's tail. The creatures started to climb over the red threads as if crossing a park fence.

Taken in by the sight, I didn't see Gargo's baton coming down on me. My head exploded in pain. Everything blurred around me; the ground rocked under my feet while the goblin-like creatures surrounded me.

I had promised myself that I would never take Naani's help, that I would prove all of Naani's gloomy predictions about my future wrong, and that there was nothing dark about me or my parents. But I was not vain enough to deny that it was time to use a lifeline, no matter who had thrown it to me.

With blood dripping into my eyes, I whispered the chant Naani taught me for emergencies such as this one. As my eyes shut and my knees buckled, I caught sight of the nightingale flapping its wings over me.

CHAPTER 2

I opened my eyes at the same moment my hand moved to the back of my aching head. It was soaked in blood. I felt the spot where the skin had split. "Rats on a stick!"

"He's coming around," said a soft voice close to me.

A whiff of oranges and caramel candy jolted me into a sitting position despite my throbbing head. The floor I was sitting on was hard but velvety to touch. Wait a minute! I was sitting on our living room carpet. Naani's carpet.

Oh, no, no, the blood from my injury would be all over the carpet. Though it was a delicate five-by-three-foot Persian carpet, it was also the only thing Naani had brought with her and ferociously guarded all her life. Oh, the things she would say to me.

Before I could check for bloodstains on the rug, I detected movement followed by the tapping of boots. The sound boomed in my head, bringing a fresh tide of pain.

I took a deep breath and braced my head against the wall. That felt better. The storm clouds had scattered by now. I shielded my eyes from the sharp glint of the moonlight just a week shy of the full moon and looked up to find a girl dressed in a purple kurta and black jeans. Her jeans were tucked into worn-out and patched calf-high Doc Martens. Dark, wavy hair with red tints framed her petite face. The face drew closer to me. Her flawless caramel skin and sharp nose made her seem unearthly, like a stone sculpture or an angel.

"Is it true?" the girl asked me, dropping to one knee so she could look me in the eyes. "Do you belong to the Naga clan?"

From my encounter at the banyan tree, it was clear my father must have had something to do with this clan business since my middle name indeed was Nagaraj. Also, Naani hated my silhouette, which further strengthened my hunch about my father's history.

I shrugged. "I'm just a delivery boy."

"You can tell us. We are Maruts too. We can silhouette," the girl said.

"I have no idea what you're talking about," I said. "How did you find me? I've never met you before."

"I was the nightingale at the banyan tree. I hail from the Pakshi clan. The important question is who are you?"

"My name is Adi." Despite the blood on my hands and the blinding pain in my head, I cracked a smile. Batty had told me once that I had a charming smile.

"That is… nice," the girl said without returning my smile. "I mean, what is your identity as a Marut? Why did Gargouille not feed you to his Yechs?"

Gargouille, Gargo D'Souza's actual name, evoked images of gargoyles and ancient beasts. It fit him like a glove.

"Surp, he's bleeding badly," the first voice came from behind me.

I turned my body around so my head wouldn't hurt. A small, mousy girl peered at me through glasses. Her hair was pulled back, probably in a braid, and tiny silver hoops swung in her ears. She also wore a nose ring and an eyebrow piercing. She looked younger than me.

I had never met these girls before. While I didn't get along with the boys in my school or our condo, my classmate and class bully, Ayesha Saini, had taught me not to trust girls, either. Both of these girls seemed far from street thugs. They showed signs of a cultured background with their clean clothes, radiant faces, and fine manner of speaking. The younger girl even wore monogrammed sneakers that read AM.

I took stock of my surroundings. Circular, unpainted walls, splotched with water stains and grass growing through the cracks, suggested I was in a shed of sorts. It was infested with cobwebs and littered with snack packs. Old Delhi ruins, perhaps? The stains on the wall grew hazier with every blink.

"I wish we had intervened sooner," the girl called Surp said to the younger girl.

If you find yourself in strange surroundings, lie low. Don't try to get back home, as it could put your brother in danger.

Naani's words rang in my head. Usually, my motto was to never follow her advice. But I could not return home with a blood-soaked carpet. Too badly wounded to make a run for it, I was at the mercy of these girls.

"Could you bring me to a doctor, please?" I said. My voice came out as a croak.

"There are no hospitals here," Surp said, tucking a lock of hair behind her ear. Her bracelet tinkled. She craned forward to look at the wound on my head. I felt her warm breath on my neck as she examined the wound. Even in my injured state, I was conscious of her proximity. I had never been that close to a girl before. Many boys my age had started dating, but I had never even had a decent conversation with a girl.

"At least we escaped Gargouille's death pike. We launched our attack just in time," Surp said and examined the wound on my head again. "This is nothing. Jambukita tincture will heal it in a jiffy. We should bring him to the shivir."

"What's a shivir? Unless you take me to a hospital, I will not move from here," I declared.

"He will get us killed. Perhaps we should let him go," the younger girl said.

"If Adi is a Naga Marut, then he is not safe all by himself," Surp said. "Especially now."

Nothing these girls were saying made sense. Batty had asked me to leave the delivery spot within an hour. I checked my watch. I still had twenty minutes to get back to the gate. I wasn't keen on facing Naani with a bloodied carpet, but I had no choice.

"Where are we?" I asked. I considered using Naani's chant once again. But given where I'd landed, there was no telling where I would wake up next.

"This is Wantra. There are no hospitals here," the younger girl said.

I had never heard of a place called Wantra. It could be another village in Gurgaon, given there were so many.

"I have twenty minutes to get back home."

"The only way out of Wantra for you is through the condo gate. They will follow you and kill everyone in your family. You have no idea what you're dealing with, do you?" Surp said.

"I will be fine," I told her. It felt good that my safety worried her, unlike the other girl who wanted to get rid of me.

"How did you come to be in possession of the Dusht Uchchaihshravas?" the younger girl said, nodding toward the dagger lying on the carpet next to me.

"Dusht what, now?" I asked, picking up the dagger. It was an exquisite piece of weaponry, definitely a collector's pride. "I didn't know the package contained this dagger. I was just making a delivery."

"Was the dagger entrusted to you because you are a Naga? Who gave it to you?" Surp asked, intent on getting me to reveal my identity.

I shook my head. "I don't know what you're talking about."

"Perhaps he's right. Nagas went extinct a hundred and fifty years ago," the younger girls said. "No silhouette can stay hidden for so many generations." She hesitated and asked Surp to step aside for a word.

Once they were in a corner, the younger girl cupped her hand around Surp's ear and said, "If you ask me, he looks quite ordinary."

Surp replied, "He has a celestial dagger that Gargouille could not unsheathe."

Even though they were whispering, owing to my newly acquired hyper-hearing, I caught every word of their conversation. I detected another sound somewhere outside the shed:

loud flapping like wet laundry on a clothesline on a windy day.

"Look at him, Surp. If *he* is the Naga heir from the prophecy, then we're all doomed."

Surp looked over at me. I smiled back at her and realized what a loser I must look like. I didn't have to try to look ordinary. I just was.

"Right now, we need to keep him safe," Surp said firmly. I was really beginning to like her.

The younger girl tsked. "Our plate is full. He is dead weight."

"He has a dagger that might be of some interest to Dakini." That seemed to shut up the younger girl, whose name I still did not know.

What caught my attention was the word "Dakini." Mythologically speaking, a Dakini was a combination of a witch, a vampire, and an evil vindictive ghost. I didn't believe in any of these.

Both girls walked back to me. "Gargouille is merciless with kids," Surp said. "He sends them to Dakini's lab or hands them over to his Yechs. He wanted to present you to Rahu. That means you are important to Rahu.

"Look, I'm telling you. I don't know how I got here. I am an average student." At this point, the younger girl snorted. I ignored her and continued to speak. "My parents are dead, and my grandmother thinks I'm scum," I said, looking as defiant as possible. "If you don't help me, I'll find my own way out."

A crunching sound behind the girls startled me. Surp and the younger girl spun around. Each snatched a keychain hanging from the belt loop of their pants. The younger girl swung her keychain on her forefinger. In keeping with the tenor of the night, I wasn't surprised to see it unfold into a mace. The mace was as long as her forearm and was dotted with ruthless spikes. Surp's keychain grew into a spear.

As they stood poised to pummel the intruder, an upturned wicker basket in the corner stirred again, crunching the dry leaves. The younger girl sighed with relief.

Surp walked over to the basket and brought it to me. "I had forgotten all about this. It rolled off when we landed here," she said, handing it to me.

Did she just say "landed"? I took the basket made of colorful wicker and embroidered with gossamer silk threads. This was the snake charmer's basket that Naani kept for emergencies, like when I silhouetted in a fit of anger or from excessive joy. It felt heavy, as if it were occupied.

If I admitted this basket was mine, there would be no escape. I thought of my planned trip to Goa and said, "Never seen this before."

"Go on, then. Open it," the younger girl said.

Before I could, a bird flew in from the window of the shed and perched on Surp's shoulder. It was the koel from the banyan tree—a small black bird with purple-tinged feathers and red eyes. The resemblance between the bird and Surp was uncanny. It cooed softly in her ear.

Surp murmured something to the koel and turned to us. "He's here," she said. "It's Gargouille. We must leave immediately." The koel flapped its way out of the window.

"Why did you send her away? You might need her for your warrior silhouette," Anku said.

"There's no time. Gargouille is on our tail," Surp said.

"Fine," I said, "let's leave." I tried to sit up, but pain and dizziness punched me in my head, and I stumbled.

Surp and the younger girl quickly got under each of my shoulders to help me up. When I started to step off the carpet, they did not move.

"You must fly Kaleeni," the younger girl said.

"Kaleeni?" I asked, puzzled. Literally, "kaleen" meant a carpet. It couldn't be… "You're joking, right?"

The younger girl's eyes narrowed. "Yes, Kaleeni, this carpet."

"You mean this rug has a name? And it flies?" I stammered.

"Yes, *it* does have a name," the younger girl said. "The Mayanis of Akashganga, also called the witches of the Milky Way, combine rare silk and divinity to create Kaleenis." She regarded me with a mix of curiosity and arrogance.

"This is not the time, Anku," Surp said sharply, admonishing the girl for showing off.

"I don't care what you know about me, but this carpet belongs to my grandmother, and I can't make it fly!" I said.

Surp shushed me. "Try to remember. Did you say anything before Gargouille hit you? Perhaps a word your grandmother taught you?" she whispered urgently.

I faltered. How did she know? When I turned thirteen, Naani had instructed me to ask for Vasuki's help only in the gravest danger. "Unless it's a question of life or death, do not utter the mantra," she had said.

"Adi," Surp said, snapping her fingers before my eyes. I came to with a start. I heard the flapping again, closer this time.

"Vasuki Upakritam," I whispered as Naani had taught me.

No sooner had I uttered the words than the carpet started to shake and ripple as if a ghost had taken possession of it.

I bolted off, my head injury forgotten. Surp and Anku came to stand next to me as the spasms in the rug settled. The carpet rose a few inches above the ground. The sound of its rustling tassels merged with the stirring of the leaves as the edges of the hovering carpet rolled up inside and turned into richly embroidered bolster cushions.

Footfall and scraping on the ground moved closer to the entrance of the shelter.

"I'll handle him," Surp whispered to Anku, who nodded back.

Surp let go of my shoulder and stepped away from the carpet. I felt Anku sag under my weight. We stepped on the floating carpet. I braced myself, expecting my feet to sink in, but the carpet was as hard and flat as a tar road.

Kaleeni had not completed its transformation yet. Upholstered satin seats and curtains emerged from the pattern in the carpet's weave as if in a pop-up book. Together, Anku and I shimmied, dipped, and bumped into each other to make room for the furniture and the ornamental trimmings.

Silent as a grave, a sleek, black, silk roof rose from the back of the carpet and set itself over our heads. A frail golden tassel dropped like a chandelier from the center of the roof. All of this took five seconds, the time it took Gargouille to reach the threshold of the shelter.

Anku asked me to fly Kaleeni. I shrugged. If the carpet or Kaleeni had indeed saved me from Gargouille, then it did that completely of its own accord. I didn't have an inkling about how to fly it; I didn't know how.

I mouthed my exasperation at her. In reply, Anku held up her mace and turned to face the entrance. I drew the dagger, but I froze when I saw the shadow that loomed at the threshold—a beefy body with gigantic bat wings and tiny horns. Surp seemed dwarfed by the massive shadow.

A small part of me wanted to jump off the carpet and throw myself at the beast to save Surp. It was a new feeling. I generally took pride in slinking away from conflicts. After all, what was the use of my silhouette if I didn't use its biggest strength: to blend into the surroundings.

Naani often shook her head in disappointment when she heard about it from Mohan. "You're not ready," she would say to me.

For what? I would think wryly. She wanted me to stay hidden from the world but at the same time expected me to turn into a superhero when somebody needed help. Over the years, I had never let Naani's paradoxical expectations override my safety instinct. But today, something stirred inside me. I could not bear the thought of watching Surp being butchered by a monster.

For a girl! Naani's disgusted voice echoed in my head.

But I didn't care for it. My senses were alert from danger. I could hardly feel the pain of the wound on my head. In desperation, I moved my hands around, hoping the carpet might follow my lead.

Just as a paw with retractable claws entered the threshold, the carpet rose toward the ceiling. It had responded to a hand mudra we'd learned early on in life: forefinger joined to the thumb, palm facing up.

Gargouille's panther-skinned body with membranous wings struggled through the doorway. He was sneering at Surp. He seemed to have morphed into a more monstrous version of himself with a hunched body that made his spine stand out.

I felt my skin prickle. As if sensing death, the scurrying and chirruping of insects faded into silence. Kaleeni rocked gently in the air, a hair's breadth away from tickling Gargouille's bald head with its tassels.

A chain attached to a spoked ball the size of a winter melon hung from Gargouille's baton. The ball was dripping with a green, gooey liquid that gave off opaque fumes. The ball trailed on the floor, clunking against the broken concrete.

Gargouille cackled. I caught a glimpse of a blood-red tongue. Surp stood her ground with her spear pointed at him.

"Deserted by your friends?" he rasped like an old and evil witch. "That boy is a Naga. What did you expect?"

I glanced at Anku. What the heck was that supposed to mean?

CHAPTER 3

I had never flown before. I mean, like a normal person in an airplane. Naani hated holidaying as far back as I could remember. All our school holidays would be spent taking care of the animals at her pet store. We were also active volunteers at the local animal shelter. It was the only social activity approved by Naani. But we never left the city. Sleepovers were out of the question.

I yearned for a holiday, but Naani would hear none of it. No amount of pleading could get her to plan one. She stuck to her pet store like a queen bee to her hive, surrounded by an army of animals. Had I known that we possessed a flying carpet, I could have holidayed anywhere in the world.

Surp's voice drew me back to the present. "You can't catch him. He is a Marut," she said to the cackling beast.

"Silly girl, he can run all he wants. He can't outrun his destiny."

"Maruts make their own destiny," Surp said.

"Lying to ourselves now, are we? You will become a Dakini

one day, and you can do nothing about it," Gargouille said.

Surp, a Dakini, a witch? That was impossible.

"Where is the boy? Tell me, and I'll let you walk," Gargouille cackled.

My heart hammered. If I were given such a choice, I would blurt out the information, not risk my life to save a stranger! Did that make me selfish? Perhaps less of a Marut, or whatever I was supposed to be.

You are not ready, Adi.

"I will never desert one of my own, whether a Marut or a Dakini," Surp said and spat at Gargouille.

Gargouille held up his chain and mace menacingly.

"Your death pike doesn't scare me," Surp said.

Gargouille snarled. That Surp was undaunted by the danger his chain mace or death pike presented seemed to miff him more than her spitting.

There was something so confident and infectious about Surp's words and manner that it nudged me into action. It was as if a boulder of self-doubt and unnecessary caution had been dislodged, releasing repressed confidence and energy in me. A few moments spent in her company had cast a spell of boldness on me. It was like being introduced to a different Adi.

I wanted to thump the daylights out of Gargouille. I felt the urge to let go and embrace the animal inside.

"All Maruts will be part of Rahu's army one day," Gargouille hissed as he wiped away the droplets of Surp's saliva that had sprayed his arm. "And you will make a fine general in Rahu's army."

Naani loved to narrate stories from world mythologies. I

recalled her talking about the deity of death and disease called Rahu. Was it possible they were talking about the same Rahu?

I placed the wicker basket on the seat and joined the fingertips of my hands to guide the carpet toward the window.

The moment Kaleeni slid out of the window, it would block the moonlight, and its shadow would alert Gargouille. That was exactly what I wanted. As Kaleeni flew over the windowsill, I reached out and dislodged the broken and empty bird nest that lay spilled over the ledge, causing it to tip and fall on Gargouille's head.

Gargouille screeched in delight when he saw Kaleeni leave through the window. Pushing Surp out of his way, he leaped toward the window. I caught sight of his chain and mace as they swung up and smacked him in the head, causing him to emit a high-pitched, spine-chilling howl.

I pointed my hands toward the entrance of the shed with the skill of someone who'd been navigating this carpet all his life. The new Adi had hidden talents! I could get used to this new version of me if only I could be sure all of this was really happening.

Kaleeni zoomed toward the entrance and halted long enough for a fuming Surp to hop aboard. Her nostrils flared, and her teeth clenched. She glared at me. What was she upset about?

I pointed with my hands to have Kaleeni fly up at a steep angle, its underside grazing an ancient iron pillar in the compound. I looked around at Gargouille. He sat on his toes on the windowsill of the shed like a terrifying cross between a goblin and a bat, his death pike hanging over the shed wall. He shrieked and jumped into the air, his wings flapping. His body merged with the black night.

As Kaleeni rose, the ruins around the shelter became visible, including the splendid Qutb Minar, smaller broken buildings, and the ancient metallic column, one of many famous pillars of King Ashoka. I didn't remember traveling from the banyan tree to Qutb Minar.

The broken ruins of the Qutb complex, which looked harmless by day, were downright terrifying in the night with their crooked shadows and latticed stone screens.

I checked my watch again. I still had ten minutes to reach the gate.

Anku had started overturning cushions, flipping curtains, and looking under the seats, mumbling, "There's a button. I've read about it."

"Why did you do that?" Surp snapped at me. Before I could answer, she turned to Anku. "Why did you let him alert Gargouille? You should have flown to the shivir. You know I would have handled Gargouille. We'll have an army of Yechs tailing us now."

"He did not ask me," Anku replied curtly. "Nobody ever does."

They glared at each other. I sensed emotional baggage in their conversation. This was one thing about girls I did not get. They "felt bad" about things no one gave a hoot about.

Meanwhile, Kaleeni zoomed ahead, sending me sliding to the back of the flying carpet. My spine flattened against the soft fabric frame of Kaleeni.

I looked over my shoulder through the back window to find

that Gargouille was in hot pursuit after us.

On catching my eye, he grinned, a smile so terrible even brain damage wouldn't make me forget it. Cracked lips were caked with blood on a hungry, fanged, and leathery mouth.

"He's catching up," Surp said. "I'll distract him." The koel flew off Surp's shoulder. Surp walked to the edge of the entrance and said, "Two bodies, one mind."

The koel flew away, and Surp vaulted into the air at the same time before I could do anything. I rushed to the edge of the doorframe to find that Surp's fingers were drawing the bird into her body. As she plummeted toward the ground, Surp's body transformed midair, starting with her hands and feet turning into wings and claws. Her face was last, and it changed quickly. As a gargantuan koel in body armor, Surp flapped her way toward Gargouille, causing tidal waves in the air.

I turned to Anku. "You can do that too?"

Anku shook her head. "That's a warrior silhouette. Through training and practice, the animal inside the Marut becomes so strong that it can be separated from the body and harnessed at will to form the warrior silhouette."

I turned to look at Surp. Kaleeni was receding from the scene at a fast pace. The sharp-edged metallic wings of the koel glinted in the moonlight as they fanned out, creating a formidable barricade protecting Kaleeni from Gargouille. The koel rose to block Gargouille.

I gripped Kaleeni's frame and leaned out for a better view when I lost my foothold and slipped out. *Rats on a stick!*

Kaleeni tilted like an unstable boat flipping over. I slipped out, but I managed to hook my hand in the base of the doorframe. Anku, who had been looking out the other window, also lost her balance and slipped. As she slid past me, I caught her wrist in the nick of time.

There was no way I could have saved the wicker basket that I had placed on the seat. It dropped out, its lid flying open. In alarm, I saw Patches, my pet chameleon, still sleeping soundly inside. I cried out his name with no regard for attracting attention. My hands tied, I watched helplessly as the basket fell into the maw of the night.

Why had the wicker basket appeared with Patches inside when I used the chant? Perhaps it was Naani's way of punishing me for landing myself in danger.

Anku and I hung onto Kaleeni, which had turned on its side. Some ornaments and cushions spilled out.

Thunder rolled in the distance. In the flash of lightning, I saw Gargouille and the fearsome gigantic koel engaged in battle, their weapons locked. The koel was resisting him with a spear held in her claws. Her wings slapped the beast, slashing his body and face.

Even though I hadn't checked my watch, I knew that time was running out for me to get back home. I couldn't command Kaleeni, as neither of my hands was free for flying the carpet. Kaleeni dangled in the air like a leaf caught in a cross-current of wind.

Something brushed my arm. It was the decorative tassel that hung from the center of Kaleeni. I could catch the tassel and pull myself up. That would steady the carpet, but since I couldn't let go of Anku's hand, I would have to let go of Kaleeni's doorframe.

"Hold on," I cried out to Anku.

Thunderous clouds had gathered in the sky. A bolt of lightning and thunder drowned out my voice. Praying that the tassel wouldn't snap from our combined weight, I caught it. Immediately, the tassel lengthened, and I felt a tingle in my spine that comes from the fear of having made a bad decision.

Anku and I sank in the air, but the tassel did not snap. It had taken our weight. I hauled myself up. Kaleeni evened out just a little, making it easier for me to hook my foot on the frame and crawl up.

I let go of the tassel and pulled Anku up. Kaleeni was still slightly unsteady, but once Anku was in, it finally flattened out.

"It wobbles. I guess that's a safety feature that the Mayanis of Akashganga forgot to add," I said for Anku's benefit. If she knew so much about Kaleeni, she could have warned me.

Anku's brows snapped together, and in a chilly voice, she said, "Kaleenis are fitted with laces and buttons that perform many functions. It's your carpet. You should have known."

If I had known I had 20/20 vision and a flying carpet, I wouldn't have been making deliveries. I sighed and plopped onto the seat. Twinkling lights visible through Kaleeni's floor caught my eye. These lights were moving. *Car headlights!*

My heart stopped just for a moment. I could see wispy tufts of clouds under my feet. Through the storm that was now raging around us, I detected the contours of the Rashtrapati Bhavan and the vibrant Mughal Gardens below, which were flooded with roses.

"I knew it! Kaleeni can turn invisible!" Anku exclaimed. "The marvel of the witches."

I shook my head. Did she really believe the witches of Akashganga wove carpets as they floated in the Milky Way? "Next you'll say the carpet has feelings."

"I wouldn't be surprised—" Anku began, but I cut her short.

"That was my pet chameleon in the basket," I said.

She bit her lower lip. "I'm sorry." Then, after a few moments of silence, she burst out, "You can deny it all you want, but the fact that you have a flying carpet at your command is proof you are a Marut. You also have a pet reptile. You must be a Naga."

"*Had* a pet," I corrected her. Chameleons could survive falls surprisingly well, but I doubted they could live through a drop from the sky.

"If he remains in the basket, he will be unhurt," Anku said.

"How can you know?"

"Because chameleons are hardier than some humans."

"I never asked for your help."

"It's easy to say that now."

"Fine, then spill it out. Why did you save me from Gargouille? Why is Surp risking her life for me?"

Anku looked taken aback. "Because," she stammered, "no Marut kid has ever been spared by Gargouille. We can't afford to lose another Marut, even one with a death wish." She had skirted the issue of the Naga heir and prophecy I'd heard them whispering about.

"How many of you are there?"

"A dozen, including you," she said.

This was a sad number, but I didn't say it out loud. "I'm

sorry to burst your bubble, but I am not a Marut," I repeated.

My headache returned as my body woke to its battered condition. I checked my watch. It showed five minutes to the end of my delivery window.

"I need a hospital now," I said, hoping she would understand the urgency. I commanded Kaleeni to fly us to the condo gate.

"I can't stop you from leaving," Anku said, "but know that this is just the beginning. You have been discovered by none other than Rahu's closest aide. Gargouille will get to you eventually. And you won't have anyone around to help you."

"I'll take my chances," I said.

"Your family—" Anku began.

"You don't know my family."

"True, but at least you have one," Anku said, looking at me meaningfully.

She was not going to give up easily. I decided to ignore her. What would I do when I got back home battered, bloodied, and with a torn Kaleeni? *One bridge at a time,* I told myself.

Anku started pacing on Kaleeni in a huff. Was she preparing to jump? Perhaps that would be good riddance. I could not stand know-it-alls.

I realized I had slid to the floor of Kaleeni, my head supported against the seat.

Anku gripped me tightly by the shoulders. "Surp and I can't leave Wantra without your help," she said desperately. This was new.

"What do you mean?" I asked.

"You have one of Indra's twin daggers," Anku said.

"It's not mine. I must return it to Batty," I said.

Indra? The God of thunder? She must be off her rocker.

"Also, I don't know how to use it. Heck! I don't like to fight," I added in desperation.

"You don't have to fight," Anku said hurriedly. "In order to leave Wantra, we need a celestial object to give to the gate-keeper."

"Didn't you hear me? This dagger is not mine to give to anyone," I said, though every cell in my body wanted to flee with the dagger and get back at Batty by selling it elsewhere, in a thieves' market perhaps. Not only had he put me in danger, but he could also be responsible for Patches' death.

I felt my heart squeeze at the thought of Patches. A few tears escaped my eyes that I quickly rubbed away with my sleeve before Anku could notice. The entire business of making deliveries without Naani's knowledge had been a huge mistake.

We reached the banyan tree, and I could see its vast and thick canopy. I held out my hand like a traffic policeman. Kaleeni responded by stopping short.

I glanced at my watch. I had two minutes to breeze through the gate. I wasn't sure if Kaleeni would even fly once I crossed the gate.

We approached the gate on Kaleeni, my access card in my hand, when something moved in the shadows near the gate. Two creatures—smaller, thinner, and pointier versions of Gargouille—stood guarding the back gate of our condo. Did they know my home was just across the gate?

"Yechs," Anku said.

"Look," I said, "I can give the dagger to you for free if you help me get back home."

"Adi, only you can wield the dagger. Even Gargouille could not unsheathe it."

That was true. It had surprised me, too. Anku crossed her arms and sat on the plush seat in Kaleeni. It was clear she wouldn't help.

I got ready to run to the condo backdoor, the dagger in my hand to ward off the Yechs. I didn't know what would happen to Anku once we crossed the door.

"You are not trained to fight with the dagger. If the cursed rasa on their death pikes touches you, you will turn into a pile of ash by tomorrow morning," Anku said, holding my arm.

I brushed her hand away. "I could ask Kaleeni to take me through some other route."

"You can't leave through any other gate without appeasing the gatekeeper," she said.

"What about this one? I entered through here and I didn't see any gatekeeper." One minute to midnight. I couldn't waste any more time.

"Your friend Batty must have bribed the gatekeeper for the delivery."

"I could go over the wall."

"It won't work. It has to be through this door."

This was my only chance to get back home, to somehow leave for Goa the next day.

"If you want your chameleon back, you must stay in Wantra," Anku said.

"He's probably dead," I said. The thought somehow

worsened the pain in my head wound.

"Chameleons do not die that easily," Anku insisted.

I considered her words. There had been a thick tree cover where Patches had fallen. Trees and foliage were like a safety net for chameleons. There was a tiny chance that Patches could still be alive.

She must have figured she finally had my attention. "I can help you look for Patches," she said eagerly.

"The only reason you want me to stay is so you can use me as bait for the Dakini."

"What are you talking about?" Anku said, confused but wary.

"I heard you and Surp talking," I said.

Neither of us moved or said anything. As the seconds ticked their way to the completion of an hour, my spirits plummeted at the thought of the wasted chance to meet my aunt.

Tomorrow, Naani would wake up to find me gone; the school would be alerted. Batty could get caught, and he might spill the beans on me. Aunty Padma would write in vain. What if Naani found her letters?

We watched the Yechs take to the skies. They must have known about the one-hour window.

"It's true," Anku said. "Surp has a plan, but I can tell she has taken a shine to you." If her goal was to have me relax, she had succeeded. At that moment, I wanted nothing more than to see Patches alive and ask Surp out on a date.

"There goes Goa," I whispered to myself.

"Ask Kaleeni to take us to the shivir," said a visibly relieved Anku.

CHAPTER 4

I was walking toward a wooden door at the end of a corridor. I tried to stop, but my feet kept moving. I felt like a puppet being made to walk in an unfamiliar place. The door at the end of the corridor was shut. Portraits of regally dressed people with high foreheads and aquiline noses, painted in matte colors, lined the corridor. I heard a sound behind me. Perhaps it was Mohan, who had followed me to this corridor, which was in all probability an aisle in a museum. Mohan followed me everywhere. I spun around to find an empty corridor. Something didn't feel right. That was when I smelled fire.

The door at the end of the corridor was on fire. Run! I said to myself, but my feet refused to listen. I was rooted to the floor, which had started shaking vigorously. I screamed, but I couldn't hear myself—only the crackling and popping of the raging fire that now surrounded me.

The orange flames morphed into the fiery red of a setting sun on the horizon. I was standing on the roof of a boxy house in the village with Mohan. We had dreamed of flying kites and battling them with boys in the neighboring village. Finally, the day had come.

"Let go of the thread!" I cried out to Mohan, who was so intent on *watching the kites battle in the sky that he didn't feel the tug on the spool in his hand.*

"Sorry, bhai," Mohan said, letting the spool unreel in his hands. He liked to call me "bhai," which meant brother. Everything he did was a desperate attempt at getting my approval.

I moved forward to loosen the stretch on the kite's thread and take away the advantage from the rival kite flyer, but I felt it lighten. We had lost the battle. Our kite went loose in the sky, vulnerable to pillage.

Playing to the tug-and-easing of the wind was the trick to flying kites. One slip could cost you the battle. All kite flyers knew this rule. I looked around to find Mohan standing with his hands folded against his chest.

"Never mind," I replied curtly. "Let's get our kite back, at least. You go down the stairs and head for the pond. I'll take the roofs."

Mohan sprang up like a buck, wiping his tears and winding the spool at the same time. I ran over the low walls of the busy rooftops, keeping an eye on Mohan in case the boys of the rival kite-flying gang cornered him. If Mohan got beaten up while he was out with me, Naani would go bonkers.

I ran into the fluttering wet laundry hung on clotheslines, and tripped over stray bricks used as tables, pegs, or stools. Still, my eyes didn't leave Mohan's fleeing back. I wished I'd been flying the kite alone.

I could now see the kite tangled in the branches of the peepul tree by the dirty pond. The rival group of boys was nowhere around. I was a few paces behind Mohan when I spied two boys holding a string end-to-end across the street. Before I could shout out a warning, Mohan tripped over the string, landing facedown in the muddy path.

The burly leader of the group towered over Mohan.

My head was pounding with anger and fear. That never ended well. I bounded off the parapets and landed before my brother, my arms held out across my chest. I was not wearing my eyeglasses, and even though I had my shoes on, I could hear everything with crisp clarity.

"Bhai, let it go. I'm not hurt," Mohan said, trying to calm me. Why did he have to act preachy toward me? I was four years older than him.

"Ah! The wimpy brothers," the burly boy said, rubbing his hands together. His voice, unlike a child's, was heavy, and he spoke with a drawl. His face was red and shiny from ample consumption of milk and ghee.

I knelt to let Mohan climb piggyback and then charged the boy, sending him toppling backward and causing a ripple that brought down the other two boys behind him.

Jumping over the bully, I dropped and ducked through the aimless punches of the other boys and slipped into the narrow adjacent lane.

As soon as I whispered, "Vasuki Upakritam," a strong gust of wind and sand blinded me. When the wind died down and I opened my eyes, I found myself back at home standing on Naani's carpet. But Mohan wasn't with me.

My heart was racing, and my face was dripping when I opened my eyes to find Anku's anxious face peering at me. It was still dark, and trickling clouds hung around us like water balloons ready to burst. My face and clothes were soaked as if someone had dumped a bucket of water on me. Before I could block it, another mug of water splashed on my face. I put up my hand to stop Anku as I gasped for breath. Was she trying to drown me? I planned to tell her off for her lack of sensitivity as soon as I could speak.

But I forgot my protests when I saw that, once again, I was sitting on Naani's carpet. *Drat!* My back was propped against a lamppost with a ladder leaning against it.

"We must get inside the shivir," Anku said. She moved my arm around her shoulder and tried to help me to my feet, but we both fell back.

I got hold of the ladder. It was made of wooden logs; its rungs were tied to its rails with rope. The rope was frayed and falling to pieces. It looked like someone had discarded the ladder but had left it leaning against the lamppost, which itself belonged to another age.

The flickering light from the lamppost revealed two curtain flaps fashioned from gunny. The flaps were so taut and dirty that the rainwater was rolling down their surface in rivulets.

Anku wedged her shoulder under my arm again and said, "Adi, only Maruts can enter the shivir. It has a layer of protection around it that Kaleeni can't breach. You have to try and walk."

I pulled myself up and tumbled forward, my feet refusing to comply with my brain. Anku held the curtain flaps aside to lead me into a cave-like room. She lowered me into a rundown armchair and wrapped me in a red-checkered blanket.

"I'll get the restorative tincture for the wound on your head," she said and disappeared into the dark interiors of the shivir.

Now that I was here, I had no other option but to play along. Cool dabs of ointment on my head lulled me to sleep. I resisted it. I tried to keep my eyes open, attempting to find something, anything familiar in the surroundings. But I found myself sinking into numbing darkness.

I wasn't sure how much time had passed when I woke to the sound of chirping birds. Sure that last night had been a nightmare, I opened my eyes, expecting Mohan to land on me singing the "Happy Birthday" song.

It was my fifteenth birthday today. I had my own little ways of celebrating. It generally began with Mohan's singing, followed by Naani's half-hearted birthday wishes and reminders for me to stay out of trouble.

The rest of the day would be spent in hopes of not being picked on. You may call it a silly way to spend one's birthday, but it was my way, and I found comfort in it.

Like a cheerful song grinding to a halt, my enthusiasm ran out when I registered my surroundings. I was alone, and Mohan was nowhere to be seen.

I was sitting inside a cave-like structure with old, dirty, stiff burlap curtains hanging at the entrance. The space around me was bare except for two weatherworn wooden cupboards and a bed next to each cupboard. I heard the scuffing of feet overhead and the purring of cats playing outside.

We were under a bridge!

Given the increasing number of highways in the city, I thought this was a rather innovative solution to living on the pavement. Doors, drainage, and ventilation were all that was needed to cozy up.

My hand traveled to my head. It was wrapped in a tight bandage. Last night's events came rushing back to me.

The wound on my head had been a nasty blow from Gargouille's baton. I was sure it would need stitches, but even without removing the bandage, I could tell it had healed completely. How was that possible?

If last night had indeed happened and I hadn't escaped from

the place called Wantra, then how could I hear the birds and the cars?

My leather satchel sat next to the armchair. I turned over the bag, and the dagger, my mobile phone, and Aunty Padma's letter fell out.

I snatched up my phone and found its battery had run out. I knew no one would be worried for my safety, but at least with some battery power I could have googled my location. I returned the contents to my bag and looked around.

Of the two bunk beds on either side of the room, one was tidy, and the other one was messy with books scattered across it. It was easy to tell that this was Anku's bed. I caught the title of one book: *The Wrath of Shani*.

I flipped through the book's pages. It contained pictures of Shani, a deity known to bring bad luck to people, or that's what I'd gathered from watching Naani fuss over keeping Shani happy over the years. She would often break into a sweat every time she saw a crow. It was also the one bird she said could never be a pet.

"As crooked as its master, Shani," she would say. "And an ally of Rahu!"

An underlined paragraph in the book caught my eye.

His gaze can reduce a person to ashes or ruins. He wears metal glasses, which contain his gaze. He is feared by all, deity or not. He lives all alone in his garden, the Shani Nandana, with only crows to keep him company. One must learn to fight one's impulses to win his favor. In the margins, someone had jotted: *A misunderstood deity?*

Shani and Rahu were considered dark deities. I put the book back. Had I been hoodwinked into joining a cult?

A cool breeze blew in from the gaps between the curtain flaps. I drew my shirt closer around me. What was I doing here? Why had I decided to stay back instead of going back home to Naani for help in looking for Patches?

The thing was, Naani had never given me a reason to confide in her about anything. In fact, my dislike for my younger brother was owing to Naani's blatant harshness toward me. Though Mohan's cloying behavior was annoying in its own way, he was more family than Naani.

In my dream, Mohan had disappeared. Did that mean anything? I didn't believe in superstitions or premonitions, but the dream gave me the heebie-jeebies. Mohan had to be kept safe.

Now that I had a flying carpet, I could pop in to let Mohan know what was happening. He could inform Naani and the police about Batty's underhanded dealings. But first I had to find Patches. I sprang up to look for Kaleeni.

The idea of Naani's carpet flying was dreamy but not farfetched. Naani was a mysterious and frightening woman. Our family album contained pictures of my father's side only. I had not heard of Naani until the day she announced herself after my parents passed away. She never shared information about herself or told stories about my mother's childhood like most grandmothers did. Some nights, she would disappear, saying there was an emergency at her pet shelter, Jantu House. What emergency could possibly happen at a pet shelter at midnight? If all these years she had managed to keep Kaleeni under wraps, I wondered what else was in Naani's closet of secrets.

I found Kaleeni rolled up and propped against the wall. I flung it over my shoulder and tiptoed toward the burlap curtains. Some part of me still hoped the events of last night had not happened. But once you've seen sinister monsters peel themselves off a tree, it's hard to forget them.

A thick cover of fog greeted me when I stepped outside the curtains. The lamppost and the ladder were barely visible. Strangely, the fog ended abruptly near the road, as if an invisible barrier were stopping it from spreading out.

Across the road, a tea seller poured ginger tea into tiny glasses. His cast-iron pan had omelets sizzling on it. The appetizing smells made my stomach growl. I fished in my pocket for the fifty bucks I carried for emergencies and sauntered toward the tea cart.

As I crossed the road, I missed a speeding car by a hairsbreadth. The car had turned around a bend, and the man had sped up as if he hadn't seen me.

My heart was still hammering in my chest when I approached the tea seller.

"Can I have a glass of tea?" I said to the man behind the cart.

He kept pouring the tea into the open pot on the stove like a competitor in a tournament for producing the thinnest strand of chai. I knocked on the metal container. While I heard it, the man didn't.

I felt a tingle in my toes. I wondered if I should just pick a packet of milk biscuits to get the man's attention, but I chose not to. This wasn't the time to get into trouble for stealing.

I shook out Kaleeni on the pavement in preparation to leave. To avoid an audience, I planned to pull the invisibility tassel as soon as the transformation of the rug into a flying carpet began.

Finding Patches would be like looking for a needle in a haystack, but I had no option. I couldn't imagine life without him. Naani had never been fond of Patches, but if she disliked him so much she would have never gifted him to me as a pet.

Why had Patches shown up along with the carpet, anyway? Could he have some connection with the chant, Vasuki Upakritam?

There was a steady stream of people stopping at the tea seller's cart or going about their work on cycles, cars, and buses, but no one showed any interest in me. Not even a glance my way—a boy standing on a fancy carpet spread out on the pavement. This was unsettling.

"No one can see you," Anku's voice carried to me. She stood next to the tea seller. In daylight, she didn't look as tiny and childish as she had last night. There was a smug fearlessness about her. She came from the same mold as girls like Ayesha Saini, a school bully who operated with the slickness of a world-class criminal.

She picked up two glasses of tea from behind the metal box, a packet of glucose biscuits, and a bag of potato chips. The tea seller didn't react to Anku treating the cart as if it belonged to her. I came around the cart to find that the tea seller's glasses and snack packs were intact.

She handed me a cup of tea and chips and walked over to the huddle of cement slabs that had been thrown on the ground to create a makeshift dining area.

"How did you do that?" I asked, trailing her.

"It's one of the laws of Wantra. Maruts can help themselves

to the food they want from the real world without being seen."

"Super!" I said as I tore into the packet of chips, food that was forbidden in our house as "the curse of progress."

Anku sat looking at me for a few seconds. As she drained her cup of tea and set it on the stone slab, the glass disappeared, as did the empty packet of chips.

"No trash, no pollution," she said.

I could live with that. The whole world could.

"It's dangerous to wander alone in Wantra," Anku said. "It was once under Marut control, but now Yechs hold power here. No one respects rules anymore."

"What are you talking about? We're in Delhi. This road is Lodhi Road." I pointed to a road sign. I felt silly even as I said it because it was as plain as daylight. Still, a tiny corner of my mind screamed that something was off.

"You are invisible to them, Adi. For them, you're as good as a ghost," she said, pulling open the packet of biscuits and offering it to me.

"It doesn't make sense."

"See for yourself," she said, waving toward a hungry crowd that had gathered around the tea seller's cart.

I walked up to the throng and patted lightly on a man's shoulder. I could feel the coarse cotton fabric of his shirt but got no response, not even a brush-off.

I used a harder touch and followed it with a punch on the man's arm, but I withdrew my hand in agony. It was as if I had punched a wall.

All of a sudden, the man turned around and walked right through me as if I weren't there.

In shock, I backed over the curb of the pavement, only to have a car zoom right through me.

Naani's prediction had come true.

Your silhouette is fraught with rotten luck. If you don't toughen up, you will die.

CHAPTER 5

Anku was watching me closely. I corrected my expressions. I didn't want to look frightened.

"So Wantra is a land of ghosts," I said with a fake chuckle, which came out as nervous laughter.

"No, it's the shadow reality of the real world, or Samsara. The same way Maruts have silhouettes and humans have shadows. Wantra is accessible only to Maruts and celestials, not humans."

"That is as good as being dead."

"You can travel back to Samsara from Wantra, but once you're dead…" She moved her forefinger across her neck. "You're gone forever." I figured she had a knack for painting a dark picture.

"If humans can't enter Wantra, then why have a gatekeeper?"

"So you *do* remember our conversation from last night. I feared the wound from Gargouille's baton may have caused memory loss."

"Well?" I said. She had still not answered my question.

"When Wantra was run over by Boors a hundred and fifty or so years ago, the celestials appointed a gatekeeper to stop Boor infiltration into Samsara. It was also to protect other celestial spots like Kalpavriksha and Amravati."

Her words were beginning to sound like gobbledegook to me. She had struck a deal with me last night. Surp and Anku needed the dagger that apparently only I could wield, and they would in return help me look for Patches.

"We should look for Patches," I said. Her story seemed too far-fetched to be true.

Anku nodded and said, "We'll look for Patches, but not yet."

I could not believe that she was playing for time with me. She had chosen the wrong silhouette to mess with. Delay tactics were second nature to me. "Patches is dead, isn't he? You lied to me to get me to stay in this tomb," I said.

"Chill. Animals are safe in Wantra. Yechs don't harass them. That was why Gargouille didn't recognize Surp and me at the banyan tree last night. We both know chameleons can survive falls." She checked her watch and got up. "It's time," she said and walked back to the shivir without a care for the cars.

As I followed her, a tremor passed through the ground. Could a shadow world experience an earthquake? I had a feeling I would know soon enough.

"Hurry up," Anku said. "We'll have no cover if we miss the shift." She plucked a chipped and peeling mirror from the wall next to her bed and exited through the curtains.

I placed Kaleeni gently by the armchair in the shivir and returned to find that the ground had started shaking, and although there were no clouds in the sky, I heard the rumble of thunder and the crack of lightning.

"What's the shift?" I asked.

Anku leaned against the lamppost, hugging the mirror to her chest. "Every Monday before the full moon, the location of the shivir changes," she said. As she spoke, a fog began to form and thicken around us. "That's when it mists up. The next full moon is on Saturday, and it is a special one, too. The blue blood moon falls on that day."

"A blue blood moon?" I repeated to check if I'd heard right.

Anku nodded. "It happens once every hundred and fifty years."

The fog was growing denser, and soon it started swirling around us. The light shaking of the earth turned into vigorous wobbling, the mist billowing below and around us.

Anku stood with one leg bent, her foot propped against the lamppost.

I tried to mimic her nonchalance but ended up hugging the pole when the ground beneath my feet zipped up like an elevator in the open air. And then the world around me blurred as the lamppost started to spin.

I screamed, and my body twirled like a spool of thread on a spindle.

I couldn't understand how this strange and torturous churning would help me find Patches, but I had no other option than to trust Anku.

After what seemed like an eternity, the ground landed with a thud. I released the lamppost and bolted away toward a brick wall, my gait unsteady and my head dizzy. The mist cleared up in seconds to reveal a dank and musty underground hole lined with bricks.

This time around, I heard a cacophony of shoes scraping and horns blaring overhead. The spot looked like the site of abandoned road works. While the pedestrian bridge overhead seemed to be in working condition, the side railings had never been installed, explaining the light rain of debris and litter over the edge of the entrance. The clearing under the bridge, which must also have served as a channel for rainwater, was devoid of light and life.

The lamppost was now planted outside this Underbridge, with a relaxed Anku leaning against it, studying the new location.

"Chandni Chowk," she said, frowning. "I wonder why." She pushed her foot off the lamppost and walked right into the cobwebbed belly of the relocated shivir. She placed the mirror carefully on a rusted iron post, adjusting it as if that was just the touch the place needed to become livable amid spiders, drain rats, and piles of rotting cardboard boxes.

I pointed at the lamp, which was still lit and seemed like a waste of precious energy in the daylight. "Isn't there a way to turn it off?" I asked, squinting at the lamplight.

"The glow of the lamp conceals the shivir in both Wantra and Samsara," she said.

"The broken ladder is a nifty camouflage too, I guess," I said with a smirk.

"No," she replied crossly. "The Akashi Ladders connect Wantra to Amravati and other celestial cities. Devas," she paused and added, "also called celestials, use these ladders to visit Wantra."

"Maruts can visit celestial cities?" I was amazed at the travel options that had opened up for me in the last few hours.

"Maruts are forbidden from climbing these ladders," came Anku's curt reply. "Eons ago, it was our job to guard them."

The story about devas and celestial cities still sounded far-fetched, but in light of recent happenings, I pointed out the more pressing omission. "There weren't any Maruts guarding the ladder last night."

"After Boors from Boorlok invaded Wantra under Rahu's command, the celestials bestowed the lampposts with the eternal light of the sun. It casts a protective glow around the shivir. If a Boor approaches the lamppost, he or she will be unable to see anything in this light. If they stay longer, they could lose their sight or their mind."

I observed the rickety old ladder held together with tattered ropes. The glass in the lamp was so dirty that it was hard to pinpoint whether the source of the light was a bulb, candle, or oil lamp wick. For something so important, its maintenance was hardly top-notch. Still, the idea of an impenetrable protective barrier against Boors was reassuring.

Though the morning sun had arrived in full force, the alley was dark and cool. It contained a pile of rotting empty cartons and a broken shopping cart. The air was dank and devoid of movement. I covered my nose with my sleeve and hoped we wouldn't have to stay for long in this place.

"How will Surp find us?" I asked Anku.

"Her silhouette will know the location of the shivir." She tapped on the mirror, causing a ripple of light inside it. As the glow mellowed and evened out, the image of the Underbridge we'd just left swam before our eyes.

"Chandni Chowk is a long way from where Patches fell," I said, taking a step back just as a cupboard moved inside the mirror and fell toward us.

Anku was about to say something but was interrupted by a loud squeak. "At least get out of the way if you can't help!" A loud huffing and puffing was followed by the corner of the cupboard poking through the mirror. As the cupboard moved into its new home, the mirror grew to the size of a door.

"We must wait for Surp to return," Anku said just as the cupboard tumbled out through the mirror, causing a cloud of dust around us. It was followed by the table, the beds, other furniture and kitchen sundries, and finally an array of shiny metallic parts that looked suspiciously like an airplane's body.

Once everything lay in a huge pile before us, a short woman with the face and tail of a squirrel walked through the door, muttering angrily to herself. The mirror snapped back into its original, tiny, dilapidated photo-frame size behind her.

I was aware that Maruts could silhouette into animals, but this woman seemed to have stopped midway in the process of transformation, as if her squirrel silhouette had got stuck in her human body. She didn't seem much concerned about it, though, and didn't even bother to look my way. She had the brisk manner of a professional who was there to do a job.

"Hasn't Mothy Maddy asked you not to make a mess every

time we shift, Chinni?" Anku said with a loud sigh.

"Where's the fun in that? I like to think the shift mirrors life. There's the mess, and then there's cleaning up the mess," Chinni said and gave the space around us a hard, disgusted look. "Looks like we're running out of clean Underbridges. This one will take special treatment to make it livable."

She grabbed the dusting cloth slung over her shoulder and heaved the wardrobe with her tiny frame dressed in denim dungarees and a shower cap. I was about to assist her in pushing the wooden almirah when Anku held me back. "She doesn't take kindly to help," she whispered, ushering me toward the Underbridge curtains.

"If we're in Wantra, where is the shivir located?" I asked.

"It lies in both worlds," Anku said mysteriously. "Ever explored Chandni Chowk?" It was a clear attempt to change the subject. But I was not done asking questions.

"What if Surp gets captured by Gargouille and his Yechs?" I said and realized I had crossed a line when Chinni stopped working and Anku grew cross.

A pull at my sleeve drew my attention to Chinni, who was standing with two cups of tea and a plate of sandwiches in a tray, as if conjured out of thin air. "Vibhaga silhouette is impossible to trap, unlike regular animals," she said, but her forehead creased with worry lines.

I finished my sandwich and turned to find that the furniture was arranged. The metallic scraps had joined to form a crude cabin wall with a propellor for a window!

Before I could inquire about the wall, a screech resounded in the alley. At first, I thought it was coming from the discarded wooden cabinet. But Anku, in the middle of braiding her hair, moved to stand before the mirror. Like CCTV high-speed chase footage, the mirror showed a wounded and bloody Surp running in fright.

"Where is she?"

"Very close," Anku said and asked me to take out my dagger and stand by. She stood facing the shivir entrance, her mace held high, her half-braided hair forgotten. The picture in the mirror had faded.

The tense silence was broken by a koel flapping its way into the alley, followed by the familiar sound of tapping boots. Surp staggered in.

"What happened?" Anku cried as Surp toppled forward. Both Anku and I reached to catch her. We led her to the armchair.

"Rudra," Surp mumbled, her faint voice breaking.

Chinni handed Anku a jug of water, and she sprinkled some on Surp's face. It woke Surp up ever so slightly.

"We must save him. He doesn't have time," Surp said and passed out again.

"Surp. Wake up," Anku said, lightly slapping Surp's face.

The wounds on Surp's face, thin and crisscrossed as if a vicious cat had been let loose on her, had missed her almond-shaped eyes. If Gargouille's claws had touched her face, it would have been unrecognizable.

When I could not bear to look at the graffiti of nasty scratches anymore, my eyes traveled to her arm, where a web of dark-blue veins was spreading rapidly. "Look," I said, holding up her arm.

Anku drew in a sharp breath. "Cursed rasa, the evil serum from the depths of Boorlok, the green goo on Gargouille's death pike."

Boorlok was the place where all evil forces of the universe resided. I recalled Naani telling us that Boorlok was different from Hell or Naraka. *Souls repent their actions by serving a sentence in Naraka, but the spirits that live in Boorlok are beyond saving.* I felt a shiver travel down my spine.

"You are responsible for this," Anku said, pointing a finger right at my nose, her facial features contorted in anger. "You should have let her fight Gargouille in the ruins last night."

She pulled back her accusing finger as if reigning in her rage and grabbed her backpack.

Unbelievable! Last night was the first time I'd stepped out of my comfort zone and helped someone.

"I saved her," I said. "That beast would have captured her. He said she would turn into a Dakini or whatever."

From her backpack, Anku brought out a vial that contained an oily liquid and some herbs in addition to dried orange rind. The fragrance was extremely familiar. She dabbed the ointment on Surp's face. The cuts and scratches began to mend immediately.

"Gargouille can easily be defeated when he is on land. His death pike weighs him down. But once he takes to the air…" Anku said, breathing deeply as she dabbed the ointment on the blue-webbed wound on Surp's arm. "His wings, provided by Rahu, make him powerful, and the iron ball turns weightless."

How was I supposed to know that? *Some people are just not meant to be heroes,* Naani chimed in my head. Even though Surp and Anku had come to my rescue last night for their own selfish reasons, I did owe them my life. Especially Surp, who had jumped off to fight Gargouille without hesitation.

I looked at Anku, her mace lying by her side, brave despite her tiny size, annoyingly arrogant for her age. She would take care of Surp. I had to get Patches and leave before I messed things up further. Didn't Naani say that we were all born with our roles spelled out? If Naani believed I had no hero-like qualities, then who was I kidding by assuming I could help?

The wound on Surp's arm had not responded to the tincture. It was spreading at an alarming pace. I shook off Naani's voice, removed my shirt, and rolled it up to form a pillow for Surp's head, which was rolling to one side as if devoid of life.

Something clutched in Surp's hand caught my eye. It was a roughly torn piece of paper, a sepia parchment with blue ribbon-like strokes. "What's this?"

Anku took the paper and spread it on the ground. "It's a map. Looks like the sacred rivers. Ganga and Narmada," she said, pointing to the thicker lines. Squiggles and crosses were drawn all across the parchment.

"What is this place?" I asked.

"This is the Aravali Ridge," Anku said, running her hands along the length of hills marked as red slanted lines. "An ancient and mystical spot on the planet."

She pointed to the five hand-drawn symbols on the east, west, south, north, and center of the map, four of which had been crossed out with red ink that looked brighter than the old, faded markings on the map. "These are the five gates connecting the three worlds of Boorlok, Bhuvahlok, and Swahalok."

The gates were represented by animal heads: a horse in the west, an ox in the east, an elephant in the south, and a lion in the north. In the center of the map was the fifth symbol, an empty box. This was the only symbol that had not been crossed out.

I studied the map. "The crosses could mean that the gates don't work anymore. Isn't that good news?"

"Not if someone is plotting a trap," Anku said, growing somber. "This one portal is then the only source of celestial help for Samsara."

While Anku pondered over the map, I noticed a tiny symbol in the rightmost corner: a flower with a snake looping through its three petals, and a small dot on top. The tail of the snake, like the etching on my bag, ended in the mouth of the snake. The mark was stamped in the lower right corner of the map.

Anku had not noticed the mark.

"The Akashi ladders are connected to celestial cities," I suggested.

"Can you see an army climbing down that ladder, Adi?" came Anku's snarky reply.

"It was just an idea," I said.

"Ladders are limited, like picket gates into a park. The gates are large openings into Swahalok."

"Swahalok?" I asked.

"It's where the deities live," Anku said, engrossed in reading the map.

We spent some time ruffling through Anku's books, trying to find any reference to the map and the incantations. But my mind was riddled with a million questions. Most importantly, if Rahu was a deity, why had he set up camp in Wantra?

"I think we're losing her." Chinni's voice diverted me from my thoughts. The purple veins on Surp's arms had turned solid like frozen blood.

"We need shrapmukta tincture for this wound," Chinni said, moving stray hair away from Surp's face. "If we wait for Madhav or Pilot Roy to return, it might get too late."

"But I've never visited Aunty Tara alone," Anku said.

"The shift brought us to Chandni Chowk for a reason," Chinni urged Anku. "Moreover, you have a Naga Marut with you." She glanced at me as if I were the lucky charm they'd been waiting for.

Naani never missed reminding me that I brought bad luck to myself and others. So I sat down slowly on the floor next to the armchair.

"What do you think you're doing?" Anku said in exasperation.

"I'll wait here in case Surp needs anything," I said.

"What she needs is medicine, and I've never…"

Her voice trailed off as she stood wringing her hands, at a loss for words. Clearly, I had touched a raw nerve.

"Chandni Chowk is crawling with Yechs," she mumbled lamely.

It was hard for some people to ask for help, especially those who thought they knew everything.

"If you think my presence will somehow make things easier for you in Wantra," I said, "you're mistaken. Even if for argument's sake I *was* a Naga Marut, I don't have a clue as to what that means. I can't fight, and as you've witnessed already, my attempts to help often go the other way."

Anku sighed. "No one needs to know you are the much-awaited Naga heir. We must work together to save Surp."

"What if I refuse?" It would be for Surp's sake for sure.

"Then good luck finding Patches on your own," Anku said over her shoulder as she strode out of the Underbridge.

I turned to find Chinni glaring at me, her brows knotted. I grabbed my satchel and followed Anku out of the shivir.

CHAPTER 6

We emerged to find the lamp's light flickering in the sunlight.

"Stay close on my heels," Anku said and set out down the street to the left.

Chandni Chowk was made of numerous lanes lined with shops, cart sellers, and even mats spread out with a mind-boggling variety of wares. During the day, it would be jam-packed with people and was known for pickpockets and petty thieves. The colorful pottery, traditional costumes, and range of mouth-watering street food were so alluring that the place drew its share of international tourists and photographers.

Naani had been such a nervous Nelly that the only shopping complex Mohan and I were allowed to explore was the one near her pet shelter.

I hurried after Anku. As we passed a fruit seller's cart, she plucked two bananas and tossed one to me. In the blink of an eye, the bunch of bananas returned to their original number in the basket.

"We need the energy," she said, gobbling up the banana and reaching for an orange.

A concoction of fresh floral offerings to the deities, chants of morning prayers, and aromas of sizzling buttered paranthas created a heady air of early morning optimism. I found that mornings generally had a positive note to them because one woke up with a blank mind, the unpleasantness of the previous day at school and home forgotten. That morning high always dissipated as soon as Naani started with her list of do's and don'ts meant specially for me without any regard for how humiliating it was for me to be lectured every morning as my younger brother looked on.

I reminded myself that today was my birthday. This morning, I was invisible, and the rules of Samsara did not apply to me. I started patting whatever I could as we crossed various stalls— the rough grain of a stone sculpture, the crispness of a cotton scarf, and the wet and cool watermelon skin. The familiarity of touch soothed my frayed nerves.

As I relaxed a little, I saw a man wearing a black turban approach. He was a big man in pathani kurta pajamas and leather juttis, the traditional footwear in northern India. He had dark-green eyes, and his bushy mustache stretched to his sideburns. He was walking slowly with an arrogant sneer and a lengthy stride as if he owned the street. Anku had disappeared into the crowd.

With my confidence running high, I stopped and started walking backwards next to the man whose sight was set ahead. Suddenly, the man stopped and looked around.

Feeling invincible, I reached out and pulled his mustache

lightly. To my horror, instead of walking on, the man jerked toward me and peered into my face, recognition dawning in his eyes.

I called out for Anku frantically, backing away from the man to have people walk through me. It seemed to please him.

I whirled around and dashed into the scanty stream of people on the road. I ran for my life, without a care for whether I was moving through the bodies of people, or around them.

In the rush to get the shrapmukta tincture for Surp, I had forgotten to carry Kaleeni. "Vasuki Upakritam," I muttered, hoping for Kaleeni to come to my aid despite the knowledge that the Underbridge was immune to divine magic. "Vasuki Upakritam," I tried again and again.

The turbaned man was just a few steps behind me, a sword in his hand!

The chant Naani taught me had failed me, but then she would never have expected me to wind up in Wantra. It also meant Naani knew all about Maruts and Wantra. Why hadn't she told me?

I glanced over my shoulder. Naani's wrath at my actions would be worse than this man's sword. Would silhouetting help?

My mind muddled from lack of options, I was blindsided by the curve to the left of the road and ran right through several multicolored dupattas displayed on a clothesline by a dupatta seller.

I instinctively shut my eyes and brought my arms together, expecting to crash into a wooden door inset with wrought iron bars, rusted spokes, and a heavy lock. Instead, I felt my feet touch the ground. I had landed in the courtyard of an old, dilapidated house.

Even though Anku said that Wantra was not a ghost land, I couldn't have felt more like a ghost than at that moment. Horror movies showed spirits walking through people, walls, and closed doors.

I was standing on the porch of what must have been a grand house many years ago but was now a cluster of broken walls carrying swatches of roof. The first floor had dipped to one side, and a winding staircase was visible from where I stood.

A flock of sparrows sat chirping on the branches of a tree that had shrunk and grown crooked over time. Nonetheless, it was covered in baby green leaves. In the narrow strips of vacant land around the house, wild grass, tussocks, and bushes were growing rampantly. I crept to the passage on the far end and waited there. Any minute, the turbaned man would burst through the door.

A minute turned into five. After my fear subsided, anger took its place. If there were men walking about in Wantra who could identify Maruts, why hadn't Anku warned me? Something told me Anku was hiding the truth from me. She reminded me of Naani, who controlled my life by withholding information.

I hopped over the rubble to find a comfortable stone to plonk myself on as I waited for her. I wiped the stone and was about to sit when I nearly lost my balance. Etched on the large stone was the same symbol that was printed on the map: three intertwined petals with a snake looping through them.

I looked around in alarm. A gentle breeze and chirping birds worked as a reminder to calm myself and think rationally.

The one feature common between that symbol and the mark on my bag was the looping snake. Could there be a connection? Was it possible there were clues hidden in Wantra about my family, the family that Naani had gone out of her way to hide from me?

I kicked at some stones, which sent the ants and insects beneath them scurrying. My eyes fell on something jutting from a heap of rubble. I scraped the soil stuck to the piece of wood to uncover the corner of a frame.

Getting down on my knees, I scooped out the earth around it and then tried to tug it out. I had to jerk it back and forth a few times before it came loose, sending me tumbling on my back. The painting landed on top of me.

"Get me off your body!" someone said loudly.

I pushed the painting off and stood up in a huff, looking around for the source of the voice. At the same time, an apparition arose from the painting. I tried to back out and away from the ground, but as usual, my feet had turned to lead from terror.

I watched the apparition begin to take shape, starting with the outline of a curvy body, followed by broad strokes of facial features, and finally clothes. Then the colors started to flow from the surroundings into its body and clothes, from its toes to the belled tassels of the dupatta covering its head.

I wished Anku were here so I could prove her wrong about ghosts. For here was the scary ghost of a lady complete with a veil and anklets.

CHAPTER 7

"What's your name, boy?" the woman asked, stretching out languidly, her glass bangles jingling.

"A-A-A…" I tried to say my name but couldn't get my shocked mouth to follow my lead.

"What's the matter with you?" she said, catching the edge of her dupatta and throwing up her veil. Naani generally wore her dupatta around her neck. I had never seen her cover her head, let alone her face with it.

I shut my eyes in case the lady's face was a skull or if she turned out to be a rotting zombie. On a whim, I slipped my hand into my satchel to grip the hilt of the Dusht Uchchaihshravas. I wasn't sure if the dagger would work on a ghost, but if it attacked me, I would lash out with all my force.

The sound of anklets and bangles got closer, and I felt icy-cold breath against my ear. "You are a Naga, aren't you?" she whispered. I closed my eyes even tighter. "All skin and bones, Manasa must be pretty disappointed in you."

My eyes flew open. Manasa was Naani's name. How could this ghost possibly know Naani? Before me stood a woman who looked like she'd woken fresh from a long slumber. Still heavy-lidded from sleep, her face was flushed. She wore a long red shimmery skirt and a short green silk blouse with an orange organza dupatta on her head. Her large nose ring was a thick gold wire threaded with a red bead resting close to her lips.

"You're a-a-a bhoot?" I said, my body tingly with pins and needles. Bhoot was another word for ghost. I found the term bhoot creepier than ghost.

"Preposterous! In what way do I look like a bhoot to you?" the lady asked, emphasizing the "p" in "preposterous" and "w" in "what way" like an educated person particular about enunciation.

"You're alive?" I asked.

"Get a grip, boy. I can't be alive. I was buried with this godforsaken painting for over…" She paused and cocked an eyebrow. "What year is it?"

"2022," I said.

"Well, over a hundred and fifty years, then!" she said.

My heart pounded inside my chest as I studied her, a lady busting all clichés surrounding ghosts. She had appeared in broad daylight and had no telltale signs like feet turned backwards, bloodshot eyes, or fangs dripping with blood. In fact, she had striking looks with a high forehead that had a snake tattoo in the center, proud arched eyebrows, lotus-shaped eyes, and a dainty chin.

"Oh, would you stop staring?" she said to me, a smile playing on her lips.

I apologized. "How do you know Naani… er, Manasa?"

"You mean Shesh's know-it-all wife?" she said with a smirk. "I warned him not to marry her, and look what it brought him." She turned around to face the ruins of the house. The dupatta on her head billowed in the absence of a breeze. I checked the leaves of the trees and grass blades for a draft that could have caused the swirling in the dupatta but found no movement.

"Marrying her was a bad, bad idea," she repeated with a vacant look in her eyes as if mentally she were somewhere else.

I had never heard of Shesh Nagaraj. It had never occurred to me to inquire after my grandfather. I had been too busy hating Naani.

My presence in Wantra was beginning to make sense. Contrary to my previous belief that my father had something to do with Marut business, it was clear that Naani was the reason I was here. But why had she kept me hidden all these years? Was she embarrassed by me like this lady suggested?

"Isn't Manasa the worst?" the lady asked, as if the conclusion explained everything that was wrong with the world.

I nodded out of understanding. Finally, I'd found someone who shared my hatred for Naani. The only problem was that it was a ghost who believed Naani had been alive a hundred and fifty years ago.

I decided to be direct about the matter. "You've been buried for over a hundred and fifty years," I said. "We must be talking about different Manasas."

She drew back, wonderstruck. "She hasn't told you, has she?

"Told me what?"

"She's a shrewd one, your Naani," the lady said, fuming. "But too over-smart for her own good. Had it not been for her la-di-da ways, Nagas would have been prominent politicians or noblemen, or what do people do nowadays?" she asked, snapping her fingers.

"There are scientists, engineers, sportsmen, and sportswomen," I said.

"Yeah, all of that. Nagas would have been all over the place. Instead, she threw open the Haveli doors for the radical clans. She wanted to reform Marut laws since most Maruts had married humans. She should have known Swahalok would never allow that." She stretched the word "never" and rolled the "r" for emphasis. "With the devas' support gone, Maruts became vulnerable to attack by Boors." After a few seconds of silence, she burst out, her nostrils flaring, "Manasa and her charity!"

Naani and charity? I was getting more and more convinced that the lady was referring to someone else. Also, Naani could not have been alive a hundred and fifty years ago.

"Naani runs a pet shelter," I said in an effort to clear up the misunderstanding.

"She does? Well, it's all good but a little too late to save young Maruts," she said with a sigh.

"I mean, she can't be the same person you're talking about," I insisted.

She looked at me sideways. "Boy, your Naani is a pure Marut, an immortal. There must be a handful left of them."

The ghost was off her rocker, but she got me thinking. Could that be the reason for the secrecy regarding our family?

But immortality was a myth. Naani frequently made fun of mankind chasing it.

"Why would she hide it?" I asked.

"That is a head-scratcher, I'll admit."

"Are you a pure Marut too?"

She looked at me for what felt like a long time. When the silence threatened to grow uncomfortable, she said, "In my day, every child knew me. What are they teaching you in schools nowadays?"

This was rich. Even dead, the woman was all arrogance.

"My name is Ulupi. I'm a Naga princess. I am not a Marut, but I am neither a deity. I am what people call a Deva. A celestial," she added for my benefit. She must have read my blank expression because she continued to speak. "I chose to dwell here, in Shesh's house, though now I feel it was not one of my brightest decisions."

"Why?"

"Because of this." Ulupi held up her left hand, palm facing toward herself. She seemed to realize that there was nothing to show on her hand because she cursed aloud. "Where has it gone?" she said, examining her fingers closely.

"What are you talking about?"

"The ring of Kundalini."

She started pacing over the stones and the rubble, completely flustered. She picked the sides of her long skirt with both hands and hopped over to her portrait in her silk shoes. She dusted the painting and put her index finger on her hand in the painting that held a hand fan.

"It's gone," she said, her shoulders drooping.

"We could look for it in the rubble," I said. I never got female obsession with jewelry.

"You don't understand. As long as it remained on my finger, no one could touch it. Only Shesh knew the incantation to access the sacred jewel."

"Maybe he shared the incantation with someone," I suggested.

"A Naga would die before revealing the chant. It amounts to divine betrayal." As she uttered these words, Ulupi's humongous eyes grew larger, as if a realization had dawned on her. She turned to me. "That is why she went under. Your Naani. She must have betrayed the divine trust."

That sounded closer to Naani than the charitable image Ulupi had sketched a few moments earlier.

"Why does it matter?" I asked.

My indifference seemed to touch a raw nerve in her. Her nostrils flared, and worry lines crowded her flawless forehead. "Because that ring was entrusted by the deities to the Naga clan. That ring," she said, pointing to the symbol on the stone, "is responsible for the circle of life. If it went missing in the attack on Naga Haveli in 1862, that means Gargouille managed to secure the ring of Kundalini for Rahu. We're doomed."

I wanted to point out that the "circle of life" had continued for a hundred and fifty years after the ring was looted, but in consideration of Ulupi being buried in rubble for a century and a half, I kept my thoughts to myself.

"Gargouille tried to capture me last night. He said he would gift me to Rahu," I said, hoping she could shed some light on the matter.

She nodded, then whispered, "He needs you to wake up the ancient spirit of snake Vasuki that sleeps inside the ring." Her eyes darted around as she figured things out in her mind.

Was Vasuki an ancient spirit of a snake? And if Vasuki was in Rahu's possession, how had the chant with Vasuki's name brought me a flying carpet?

"A few drops of your blood, the Naga heir, on that ring will bring Vasuki to life. It's all making sense now," Ulupi said, intent on solving the puzzle.

Naani insisted that the basic nature of the world was predictable and silhouetting was not natural in this world.

I got it. I was a freak. However, she was petrified of voodoo.

Shadows are not as innocent as they used to be; evil spirits lurk there.

In keeping with my cynicism for all she said, I believed voodoo was hogwash, and any ritual involving blood and sacrifice had voodoo written all over it.

"Even if for a moment we assume what you're saying is true, there would have been many heirs before me," I said.

"But none of them walked into Wantra, did they?" All of a sudden, she turned around. "I never met you."

"Excuse me?"

"You are wanted by Rahu for your blood, and by the deities for the betrayal. To go on living in Swahalok, I have to be unaware of this truth."

"The ring was taken from your finger. Won't the devas know you were involved in the matter?" I asked.

"I was not responsible for its safety. There's nothing I can do."

"We could look for the ring together."

Ulupi considered my words, then shook her head. "Not unless I steal an identity, and after having been buried in the muck for over a hundred years, I am in no mood for all that hard work."

It seemed fair. I would have felt the same way. "What will you do, then?"

"A long holiday in one of Swahalok's celestial gardens, or a celestial city, perhaps," Ulupi said, tapping her chin with a finger. "The real question is: what will *you* do?"

"I am not a Naga heir," I said with conviction that comes from hours of self-reflection. I knew my worth.

She made a humming noise, which could have meant either agreement or displeasure.

"Dear boy. If you are Shesh Nagaraj's progeny, then you don't have many options," she said, straightening her dupatta.

I caught movement under her dupatta. Disconcerting.

"Moreover, Gargouille has discovered you. Either you can spend your life running from Rahu, or you could steal the ring back." She gave me a once-over. "Which doesn't look like a rock you can climb."

"Or I could ask Naani," I said. "Since she is a pure Marut and immortal."

Ulupi gave a light chuckle. "I like you. You are a survivor. Pity you will die so young."

"But Naani—" I began.

"Have you seen her silhouette lately?" she said, raising an eyebrow.

"Not with my own eyes—"

Ulupi cut me short. "To hide herself from the Yechs and the deities, she would have given up her silhouette," she said, scrunching her eyes.

You could do that? Why hadn't Naani ever told me?

"It's called Chalvesha. By now, she must have lost touch with the animal inside her."

Oh, Naani still had an animal inside her, alright. Probably a mean-spirited bat!

"It means she's not a Marut anymore, but a mere human," Ulupi added. How I envied Naani at that moment.

At the risk of another judgmental battering, I said, "So giving up the silhouette would solve all problems."

Ulupi's scathing look proved my gut was right. "You're a half-Marut. Only pure Maruts have the power of Chalvesha."

She must have sensed my disappointment, for she said, "Chalvesha takes many years to manifest. You don't have much time." She shaded her eyes and peered into the powder-blue sky. "On the eve of the blue blood moon, in a few days' time, it will all be over." She walked toward the house and spread her arms to feel its outer wall. Her face contorted in pain and longing.

"You said the deities would get me for betraying them," I said as Ulupi got ready to bid the place a final adieu.

"Yes, I would be wary of trusting anyone. The forgotten deities, also known as the Fallen Ones, walk amongst humans. They've taken to guerrilla tactics to foil plans by Boors. I doubt they'll think twice before sacrificing a boy for the greater good of mankind. If mankind perishes, so will the deities."

So I didn't even have gods to turn to!

A high-pitched shriek startled us. We turned together to find Anku at the gate of the Haveli. She was holding her mace up, ready to strike.

"Step away from Adi," she said, addressing Ulupi.

Ulupi snorted in amusement and snapped her fingers. Anku's mace flew from her hand and struck the tree, its spokes sinking into the tree's bark. Ulupi moved deftly toward Anku. In that instant, Ulupi's dupatta slid down from her head to reveal a braid that was unnaturally alive. It was when it crept along Ulupi's back that I realized it was a snake!

I didn't follow Ulupi, who started to examine Anku up close. "What do we have here?" Ulupi said. The braided snake reared itself over her shoulder like a nosey neighbor.

"Are you a Dakini?" Anku asked, clearly harried. "You can't hurt us. It's written in the peace charter of 1995."

"Peace charter?" Ulupi exclaimed and emitted a throaty laugh. "They forgot to send me a copy of that!"

"What do you want with Adi?" Anku said, glaring at Ulupi.

"I'm glad you're not alone," Ulupi said to me over her shoulder. She brought her face close to Anku's and appeared to sniff her. "You hide secrets, don't you?"

I had shut my eyes out of fright when Ulupi examined me. But Anku's eyes darted around, her body ready to attack. I was surprised she hadn't struck Ulupi yet.

While she eyeballed Anku, Ulupi's braid snaked its way to Anku's neck. Would she strangle Anku? I was about to protest when Ulupi said, "Aha!"

Ulupi's snake braid pulled out something from under Anku's collar. It was a necklace with a single wooden bead on it. It was the size of a marble and had a face etched on it—a bead-sized voodoo doll.

"How dare you," Anku said and swiped the necklace back.

But Ulupi observed Anku with a knowing smile. "We have a little Yech-slayer here," she said to me, raising her eyebrows. "It's not a bad career option, if I've read the direction of the wind right."

"Who are you to make such statements?" Anku said.

"I'll let Adi make the introductions after I've left. I haven't been alive as many minutes as the number of words I've spoken." Ulupi picked up her feather light silk dupatta and extended it to Anku. "A trophy for your courage. Kill the brutes and collect their heads. This dupatta will hide them for you."

Warily, Anku took the dupatta and muttered her thanks.

Ulupi turned back to leave but stopped short before me. She gave me a small bow and said, "Thanks for saving me, Adi. You are a brave boy."

I shifted uncomfortably on my feet and glanced from Anku to Ulupi. Anku's eyes narrowed with suspicion.

As she passed me, Ulupi whispered in my ear, "Now this one, you can marry." She winked at me with a slight jerk of her head toward Anku. With that, she disappeared into the dark interiors of the crumbling Haveli.

At Ulupi's remark, I felt heat rise in my cheeks. It was highly inappropriate to suggest something like that to a fifteen-year-old. At the same time, I wished Surp had been here with me and that Ulupi had given us her blessing to marry.

"You saved her?" There was disbelief on Anku's face and a flicker of admiration in her voice.

I was about to tell her that all I did was dig out the old painting, but, on second thought, I let her believe I'd saved Ulupi. I liked the look of awe on her face. Perhaps it would help impress Surp when Anku narrated the incident to her.

"So this is the famous Naga Haveli that was attacked in 1862? I never knew it was right here, so close," Anku whispered.

I turned to look at the ruins with her. There were faded frescoes on its walls that I hadn't noticed before. The wooden panes of the doors and windows hung, broken and defeated, from their hinges. Sturdy columns ran around the main house.

The top half of the Haveli looked like it had fallen in an explosion. The column heads were all etched with dragon faces, though you could hardly tell from the worn-out edges. The Haveli felt familiar, as if I had been here in my dreams. I shrugged off the feeling.

We left the place through the wooden door. "I searched the entire path three times over for you. Then I went from house to house to find you," Anku said. "I thought Yechs had got you."

"They almost did," I said and narrated the chase by the turbaned man.

"That is Kabeela, one of Gargouille's Yechs. While ordinary Yechs can't snatch identities, Kabeela has been awarded that freedom for the heinous crimes he committed for Gargouille. He can exist both in Wantra and Samsara at the same time. He must have only sensed your presence, not seen you clearly," Anku said, as if that made up for the near-death fright I had experienced.

"Are there any other kinds of monsters in Wantra I should look out for?" I asked.

Anku turned thoughtful. "There are the Dakinis, Chamruks, and Yali," she said, sticking out the fingers of her right hand one by one. "Most of them live in the Kalpavriksha."

"How does one tell them apart?" I interrupted her.

"You just know," she said, winding Ulupi's dupatta carefully around her neck. Her necklace, which I could not take my eyes off now that I'd seen it, disappeared from plain view. "I've read about this scarf," she whispered. "Nagakanyas wear this fabric to hide their serpent body parts. It's called a guptikr, an oblivion scarf."

"You mean an invisibility cloak?" I asked with affected incredulity. I was still getting used to the idea of a carpet flying.

Anku pretended to ignore my remark. "Well, it's more than that. This scarf hides only what you want to be hidden," she said.

She believed that an invisibility scarf could read your mind and a flying carpet could have feelings? Boy, was she gullible! I shrugged.

Technically, the dupatta belonged to me since I'd saved Ulupi and she was related to me. But I was not the one to ask Anku for it, nor was I ready to admit to being a Marut.

We retraced our steps toward the lanes of Chandni Chowk, crossing many alleys until Anku stopped short outside a spice store called Tara's Attars.

Pulling me aside, she said, "Don't be alarmed by what happens inside. When I ask you to leave, retrace your steps back to the shivir. No matter what, do not turn back."

"But—" I began to say. She cut me short.

"Give the shrapmukta tincture to Chinni. She will administer it to Surp. Then wait for Mothy Maddy or Pilot Roy."

"What about you?"

"Mothy Maddy will sort things out," she said as if trying to convince herself.

How could she possibly rely on someone called Mothy Maddy?

CHAPTER 8

Without waiting for me to reply, Anku sauntered into the shop. I followed her. Chimes made of hollow coconut shells clopped dully when the door opened. Someone had scratched faces into the coconuts. I shook off the creepy feeling.

Even though the shop was eerily silent, overall it had a warm and welcoming ambience. Sunrays seeped in through windows in the roof and bathed sacks of dried spices in a comforting glow. I took in a deep breath and caught a whiff of black pepper, dried red chilies, cinnamon, cardamoms, and many other spices that I didn't know the names of but that brought about a bout of sneezing and tears streaming down my cheeks.

As a snake silhouette, my olfactory sense was overwhelmingly strong; I detected the flavors with both my nose and my tongue.

Naani had been very regular about rapping my knuckles every time she found me flicking out my tongue. "You look like a toad," she would say hurtfully. But it was a natural reflex for me. Even if not entirely in good taste.

I pursed my lips to stem the sensory assault of the spices. I stood next to sacks heaped with dried herbs, flowers, and roots held in smaller gunnysacks. These were less intense. Behind us, opposite the counter, multi-hued bottles and jars crowded the shelves. Something scurried across the counter and made me jump back. It was a brown recluse spider the size of a tarantula.

Naani had given me a reference book on insects of all kinds. "Don't go about eating poisonous insects in your silhouette form," she had said, handing me the book. I lapped up the information contained within.

The earthy color of the spider on the counter blended with the wood. Six eyes arranged in pairs looked at me. "Haven't seen you in a few centuries, Shesh," the spider said in the gravelly voice of someone half asleep.

I had never communicated with anyone while in silhouette. Naani would rather I slip into a wicker basket and sleep until the effects of silhouette wore off in five to six hours.

When the spider spoke to me, it felt natural. Any other kid in my place would have freaked out. But I found it fascinating, and I wished I had someone to talk to when I silhouetted. I had assumed the life of a silhouette to be a lonely one.

What was intriguing was that the spider had mistaken me for Shesh, who according to Ulupi was my ancestor.

"She can get nasty. Play along," Anku whispered in my ear.

"Uh, hello," I said to the spider.

"Did you manage to solve the riddle, then?" the spider asked me.

I glanced at Anku sideways. She shrugged.

"Er, there are so many riddles I've worked on," I answered, spreading my hands.

"Is spirit the home, or the circle it lives in?" the spider said mysteriously. "Only a fool would try it. On the other hand, only a Marut with unique genius could solve it." The spider's voice had a tingly note to it, like the hypnotic resonance of a tuning fork.

I pondered her words. Perhaps by "circle" she meant the circle of life. In that case, the words in the riddle probably alluded to a spirit changing itself as it moved from one life to the next. By this logic, the circle was the real home. The spider felt that only a Marut with unique genius could solve the riddle, and I knew well that I was no genius. I kept mum.

The spider started swaying as if in a trance. It stopped suddenly. "Couldn't crack it, could you? I knew it. You got too cocky."

Anku cleared her throat to catch the spider's attention. "We're in a hurry, Aunty Tara."

"How can I help you today?" the spider said, its voice growing formal all of a sudden as she scurried toward bottles containing whole nutmeg and chicory.

"Ancient Maruts lose track of time, especially in their silhouette forms. She must have mistaken you for someone else," Anku whispered.

I was about to tell her that I knew who she'd taken me for when Anku placed a finger on her mouth.

A fragile lady bustled forth from behind the huge jars of spices on the counter. She wore a traditional salwar kameez, and her straw-like hair was stretched into a bun. Still, a shocking amount of it had escaped and stood out like the petals of an ornamental onion flower. As if bulging eyes on a thin frame were not unsettling enough, she also sported bushy eyebrows and a dense upper lip. Aunty Tara looked ancient yet spry, fragile yet menacing.

"Shrapmukta tincture, please," Anku said, the hint of a tremor in her voice.

Aunty Tara must have noticed it too for she looked up sharply, raised her thick eyebrows, and said, "Shrapmukta tincture is used to heal cursed wounds."

"I know that. We're just stocking our medicine cabinet at the shivir," Anku said, adjusting her glasses and grinning. It was a nervous grin and completely unnecessary.

I glanced at Aunty Tara for a reaction. Her right eye had started to twitch.

"Do you have Pilot Roy's letter or Madhav's authorization?" she asked Anku in a hoarse voice.

"Mothy Maddy left on an urgent mission, so he sent us," Anku said in a fake pleasant voice.

An unconvinced Aunty Tara turned to look at me. Her eyes settled on my bag as she started sorting the herb packets in the basket before her. "Where's the other girl? The one who generally hangs out with the boy with a lion silhouette," she asked, sticking price tags on the cellophane packets of herbs.

"She is back at the training camp," Anku said. Lying came easily to her.

"I heard someone went missing at the camp." Aunty Tara had still not moved to get the medicine.

"Maruts who live under bridges are under paladin protection. Boors don't dare enter," Anku said, deftly evading the question.

Aunty Tara stood still, her gaze fixed on Anku. She was waiting for Anku to answer her question.

"A handful of Maruts were playing a prank on Pilot Roy. All is well," Anku continued, waving away Aunty Tara's concern.

Was all of this true, or was Anku making it up just to get the medicine? As they chatted, I turned around to look at some of the labels on the bottles in the cabinet.

Shatam Amnesia. Brahma's Duality. Immortal's Dissonance.

The names just grew stranger and more improbable as I read on. In another glass cabinet on one side of the shack, perfumed oils in dreamy reds, greens, and blues were held in fancy bottles. They were all labeled "Tara's Attars" and had gold caps and tassels around their necks. The lowest shelf held a jar with a handful of live brown recluse spiders.

I caught movement in the reflection in the cabinet's glass. With horror, I watched as two more pairs of arms sprouted from Aunty Tara's back. These arms moved at a frenzied speed, extracting herbs and remedies from various bottles and boxes to add to a jar like an improbable alien bartender.

When the bottle was stuffed with dried herbs and condiments and swimming in clove oil, she paused, and all of her arms came to rest by her side.

"And now to add the water of Meru," she said. "You wait right here."

I noticed that some spittle had trickled down the corner of her mouth. She picked up the tincture bottle and moved toward an old crumbling ladder that went up through a tiny hole in the roof.

"Did you hear the name she called me?" I whispered to Anku.

"Yes. But she's not all there. Many Maruts were traumatized by the death of Shesh Nagaraj and the invasion of Wantra by Rahu," Anku said. "The loyalists believe that Shesh Nagaraj will come back to restore Wantra to Maruts."

In spite of Anku's reassurance, I felt something was off about Aunty Tara. She seemed haggard and hungry yet cautious like a starving animal who suddenly comes upon food and is wary of appearing elated about it. "How can you be sure she's not a spy?"

"Her family has been dealing in tinctures for centuries. If she were a spy, Maruts would have been wiped out long ago."

"Then why didn't you tell her about Surp?"

"Aunty Tara is a makadee silhouette. They may not work for Rahu, but they are vindictive and vicious," Anku said.

Did she ever pause to hear herself? She just said Aunty Tara was loyal, and in the same breath, she told me Aunty Tara's silhouette could not be trusted.

"Actually, brown recluse spiders can be extremely docile," I said, picking up a clove and flicking my tongue to smell it right.

At that moment, Aunty Tara returned and handed us a vial with a light-green translucent liquid dotted with herbs and seeds. A fabric tied with twine held the cork in place.

Anku dug into her pocket and retrieved some money, but Aunty Tara shook her head and said, "You know the cost for controlled tinctures."

Anku hesitated. "Why don't you add it to our account?"

"I can't make a living out of granting favors," Aunty Tara said and opened a wooden cabinet behind her. The shelves in the cabinet were lined with empty half-liter bottles. Only the bottommost shelf contained a half-full bottle of blood. "My supplies are running low as you can see. Marut blood is in great demand nowadays."

"How can you sell Marut blood, being a Marut yourself?" Anku said.

"Don't judge me, girl! You have to do what it takes to feed a family. I've had to hunt in Samsara, setting traps for stray humans. I will never say no to free food."

She collected Marut blood and ate humans. I glanced at Anku in the "I told you so" way.

"Pilot Roy has never sent for shrapmukta tincture without its cost in blood," Aunty Tara said.

Anku looked at me sideways. She handed the tincture bottle to me and said, "Fine, but we will have to check it for authenticity first." She nudged me toward the door.

If I had known that a spindly hairy arm of Aunty Tara would grow and barricade the door, I would have sprinted out of the shop the moment Anku handed me the tincture. But I didn't, and so I studied her arm that ran right past my nose and looked like an unbreakable vine, sinewy and knobby, devoid of bones. I gripped it with both hands, but no amount of pushing or pulling made it budge.

"I will need a bottle each from both of you," Aunty Tara said, smiling for the first time, revealing a set of crooked and crowded teeth that seemed to be layered on top of one another. Two pincer-like curved ends were visible just behind the incisors. Her smile was not wicked but hungry.

"Duck, Adi!" Anku cried and pushed some bottles off the counter toward Aunty Tara.

The warning was a second or two late because Aunty Tara had already added two more arms to the blockade. Her left arm caught Anku by her waist.

As Anku struggled to push the arm off to retrieve her key ring, I placed the tincture carefully in my satchel, my hand lingering on the hilt of the dagger in my bag.

I looked at Aunty Tara's arm again. It was reedy but definitely not an old lady's arm. Would the dagger work? What if the dagger was a mere antique, a trinket for Gargouille's drawing room? It was hard to depend on my memory of the night before, but I had a faint recollection of having nicked Gargouille with the dagger.

"Aunty Tara, if Mothy Maddy gets to know about this, you will be in trouble," Anku warned.

"You know what I think?" Aunty Tara said. "Madhav would never send underlings to collect shrapmukta tincture. If I'm not mistaken, you kids are up to something nasty, and I will not let you get away with it without my gallon of blood."

A gallon of blood! That was probably all that Anku had in her. I unsheathed the dagger while my hand was still inside the satchel and felt the sharp blade of the dagger.

The Adi I knew would have liked to silhouette and slither

out from under Aunty Tara's arms. The Adi I had become overnight was not ready to abandon someone, even Anku, to a bloodthirsty spider.

I imagined curing Surp with the help of the tincture. She would feel indebted to me and would accompany me to school, where I would feast on the perplexity on Ayesha Saini's face and the envy of all the boys who had bullied me for so many years.

"Perhaps," I said, causing both Aunty Tara and Anku to look at me, "you would like some of your own blood."

I jabbed Aunty Tara's arm with the dagger, expecting resistance, but the dagger tore into her arm in one go and sliced through easily. I pulled it out. I had planned to injure her so she would allow us to leave, but I had never intended to delimb her. Now her arm was hanging by a few strands of muscle. *Yikes!*

"Fiend, snake in the grass, Manasa's spawn!" Aunty Tara screamed as I slashed at the other two arms. She let go of Anku.

Manasa? In addition to Ulupi, Aunty Tara also knew Naani? I would have given that more thought had I not seen her aim at me with the two pincers that appeared between her lips.

The pincers squirted a jet of blue liquid that fell on dried rose petals beside me, instantly reducing them to powder. Steam rose from the scalded gunnysack.

Anku was free of Aunty Tara's grip now. We jumped through the gap that Aunty Tara's injured arm had created and rushed out onto the streets.

Her remaining arms wriggled after us like the tentacles of a giant squid. She squirted more venom our way. The venom of brown recluse spiders was not known to be fatal, but Aunty Tara's venom turned everything it touched into ash or vapor.

Anku tripped while ducking from a jet of venom. I lashed out at Aunty Tara's outstretched arm to cover Anku as I screamed, "Go! Go! Go!"

Anku bolted, and I backed away, waving my dagger at Aunty Tara's hands, which were swiping at us as if trying to collect scattered coins. My clothes were covered in blood now.

I felt a tug on my t-shirt as Anku pulled me back and out of the reach of Aunty Tara's wormy arm, which was inching toward my ankle.

Together, we dodged another jet of venom that charred the weeds on the sidewalk. "Run, she can still hurt us!" Anku cried and rushed down the road, away from Tara's Attars.

When we couldn't see her waving tentacles anymore, we slowed down. "For a moment, I thought we would be Aunty Tara's cocktail today," I said between pants.

"It's strange. She's generally not sociable," Anku said, leaning against a wall and taking deep breaths. "But she has never been aggressive."

"You have to agree her pantry was quite empty," I said with a cheeky grin. "On a related topic, Mothy Maddy brings her blood?" I asked. It was a nugget of information Anku should have shared with me before we set foot in that vampire den.

"From the butchers," Anku said. "Most Makadee silhouettes are cannibals. Their favorite food is spiders, especially the spiders they manufacture in their webs by trapping humans. Mothy Maddy is doing his bit to save humans."

"If Maruts are celestial soldiers, isn't it against the rules for Aunty Tara to hunt humans?"

"Those Maruts who continue to live in Wantra are survivors," she said with a shrug.

"Still, I feel it's highly inappropriate to send kids on an errand of this nature."

"Mothy Maddy is investigating children's disappearances. He hasn't had time to visit," Anku repeated, her brows creasing. She hadn't lied to Aunty Tara after all, but then how could I tell she wasn't lying to me too?

Anku continued, "A makadee silhouette must leave a human body in a web for over a month before it morphs into a spider. Aunty Tara prefers Mothy Maddy to fetch her food rather than hunting for it herself."

That was one sordid silhouette detail I could have done without. I wondered if Naani had been shielding Mohan and me from such influences of the Marut world. *Naani is incapable of such a thoughtful gesture,* my mind replied. "Why didn't you pull out your mace on her?" I asked Anku.

"She was too swift," she said, wringing the corner of her kurta. When I didn't reply, she threw up her hands and said, "Fine, I didn't want her to complain to Mothy Maddy. I was trying to be diplomatic. You don't plan on staying in Wantra, so using Dusht Uchchaihshravas doesn't count. It's not a foul until it's found."

"Aunty Tara will tell on you anyway," I said, scrunching up my nose and wiping the stains of blood and muscle off the dagger blade with a leaf.

"No, she won't. She will be as worried about us

complaining about her," Anku said with satisfaction, eyeing the clean and glinting blade of the Dusht Uchchaihshravas. "You are lucky to have that."

She extended her hand, and I let it go in her palm. She ran her hand over the intricate work on the horse's head and rubbed her thumb over the onyx in the eye. "Did you know onyx is a Boor stone?" she said. "That must be the reason why Kabeela did not sense you right away. You had to try and touch his mustache!"

She rolled her eyes. Even though the joke wasn't funny, we broke into giggles. Our weariness tipped into hysteria, and we laughed until our sides ached.

I had never experienced this kind of relief before. My tense muscles settled into the frivolous comicality of touching a Yech's facial hair, and just for a moment, I forgot all my past and future worries.

Anku wiped away tears as she sobered up. "You've got the shrapmukta tincture?"

I nodded and handed the vial to Anku. Now that we had shared an adventure and laughter, perhaps Anku would share information without acting like a snob.

CHAPTER 9

As we hurried to get the tincture to Surp, I decided to make the most of Anku's good mood by gleaning as much information as possible.

"Have you ever heard of the Fallen Ones?"

Anku paused in her stride and glanced at me. "Why do you ask?"

"Just something Ulupi mentioned."

"Fallen Ones are the deities that are not worshipped by humans anymore. Over time, as their powers became irrelevant, they lost their deity status."

"Are they dangerous?"

"They're still celestials, but the Fallen Ones are a bitter and sore lot. They envy deities and blame Maruts for their fall from grace."

"Why Maruts?"

"Maruts decided to settle in Samsara, thus diluting their own powers by sharing them with the humans. That was how major discoveries, from fire to nuclear power, happened. The stronger humans grew physically and intellectually, and nature gods like Agni, Varuna, and Indra lost stature."

Agni, the god of fire, Varuna the god of water, and Indra the lord of thunder had been the first deities to be worshipped.

"Is there any reason the Fallen Ones may harbor a grudge against Shesh Nagaraj?"

"The Naga clan was entrusted with the ring of Kundalini, which is said to have been looted in an attack on Haveli. If the ring falls into wrong hands, the Fallen Ones will be the first to vanish into oblivion." Anku stopped to watch me closely. "Ulupi warned you, didn't she?"

I kept my gaze fixed on the broken tar street ahead of us. There was no doubt in my mind that I was a Marut. I could silhouette, command a flying carpet that belonged to the Naga clan, had met the ghost of a celestial ancestor, and even Aunty Tara had mistaken me for Shesh Nagaraj. The question was if I was ready to admit it to Anku.

I had loved my father, a gentle soul far removed from adventure. Even so, in my wildest dreams, I could not have connected my mother and Naani to the fantastical events unfolding around me. The prospect of finding out more about my mother's family excited me, but I had a choice to make. I could find out more about Wantra, my silhouette and heritage, or I could leave it all to live a normal life with Aunt Padma.

I touched my satchel, which held Aunt Padma's letter. Anku must have read the conflict on my face, for she said, "If it helps, I believe you're not a Marut. It's not uncommon for a silhouette to appear randomly in humans. Just shows the extent to which Maruts mingled with them."

Though she had expressed sympathy, I felt snubbed once again. I sighed and followed her.

When I fell into step beside her, she said, "They say that Rahu already has the ring of Kundalini and is waiting to take over the three worlds on Rahu Amavasya or the blue blood moon."

"Isn't anyone worried that he might?" I asked.

"I am not," Anku said, self-important as ever. "The ring of Kundalini is part of fable now," she said with a shrug. "The more urgent matter is the rising Boor numbers in Samsara. Rahu, Ketu, Gargouille, and Dakinis all lead double lives in Wantra and Samsara."

We had reached the lamppost, but Anku didn't rush inside to administer the tincture to Surp. Instead, she frowned as she looked at the blinking light of the lamppost.

"We have a visitor. That's never good news." No sooner had she said these words than a pair of leather boots appeared on the top rung of the ladder, the upper part of the body missing as if sawed clean. As the boots descended, the body of a man appeared and leaped off carelessly, bumping into me and sending me crashing to the ground. It felt as if I had been knocked over by a massive rock.

"For the love of Indra!" the man said. He wore a thin and flimsy beige overcoat and a red bandanna on his bald head. Hefty and rugged, he reminded me of the bouncers who manned the doors of discotheques.

"Hey, be mindful of where you step," Anku said to the man, unfazed by his size and ruggedness.

"You think you are talking, but all I can hear is meow,

meow," the man said and chuckled.

Was this a reference to Anku's silhouette?

"Thank your stars my meowing isn't as bad as my bite," Anku said and pushed the man hard on his shoulder. What was she doing? I would never engage with someone who was looking to pick a fight.

Another pair of legs appeared at the top of the ladder and started moving down the rungs. A man dressed exactly like the first one—jeans, a striped t-shirt, and a red bandanna—hopped down the ladder and demanded to know what was happening.

"The kitten is alone today," the first man said.

"I am not alone," Anku said, squaring her shoulders. Both men turned to look at me.

"Got a new sitter today? Where is Surp-a-nosa?" the second man said to Anku.

The two men guffawed. Each wore a gold chain with a pendant made of three petals that jiggled on their stocky chests. Their floral bandanna and lack of eyebrows took my attention straight to the men's beady eyes. Hardly any white of the eye was visible. The effect was so terrifying that I almost missed the fact they had rhino horns for noses.

"What are you doing here, anyway? Isn't Wantra beneath the station of Gandaks?" Anku said, using air quotes for "beneath the station."

"Don't mind us, and carry on with your guerrilla warfare against the Boors. We're here to attend the ARAC."

"Ah! A big change from all the eating and sleeping, which is what Gandaks do best," Anku retorted and pulled at my arm.

"We can do plenty more," the first Gandak said menacingly. "The thing is, you are just not important enough to be trusted with a mission. And correct me if I'm wrong, but your mother thinks so, too."

Anku drew back, stung. "How dare you?" The necklace she wore with a wooden bead carrying a Yech's face flashed before my eyes.

"Er, Surp needs the medicine," I said to Anku, bringing her attention back to the more pressing matter. My words seemed to knock her out of the lull that anger can create.

"Why? What happened to her?" the first Gandak asked, turning sharply toward me.

"Nothing happened to her. You will meet her soon enough, and you will live to regret it," Anku said. She tried her best to sound vicious, but the threat sounded so empty that I tugged her sleeve to pull her back.

"Tell your toffee-nosed friend we know what she's up to. If she has anything to do with the robbery at the Bank of Karma, she will either be banished to Naraka or sent to Boorlok," the second Gandak remarked.

Naraka was the mythological hell where the river of blood and bones was said to flow through lifeless lands inhabited by spirits in repentance. But the Bank of Karma was not only new; it sounded made up.

The first Gandak tapped his mate and gestured toward two men approaching us. These men were dragging their feet, lost in thought, a layered steel lunchbox in each of their hands.

The Gandaks skipped off the pavement and stood facing the pedestrians, who seemed oblivious to the rhino men blocking their way. The moment the pedestrians got near, the Gandaks lifted their pendants and placed them on the chests of the approaching men. The Gandaks' bodies grew mist-like as they stepped into the bodies of the pedestrians. Without a pause, the men kept walking, their trudge now a confident strut. They nodded at each other and swaggered off in different directions toward the bazaar.

I must have looked aghast, for Anku said, "Rinca and Gilli. Less celestial, more oaf! They used the triquetras for identity theft."

"They're celestials?" I had assumed they were rhino-silhouetted Maruts.

"Gandaks," she said. "At one time, deities relied upon them heavily for spy work. When these deities fell, the Gandaks lost their significance. Now they run Twelve Rhinos, an inn in Amravati."

"You mean the mythological city?"

Anku nodded.

"Ruled by Indra?"

"Yup!"

"The lord of thunder?"

"Yes, and Wantra is connected to Amravati through ladders. Haven't I told you already?" Anku snapped to put a stop to my questions. "I had forgotten all about the ARAC, the Aravali Rahu Amavasya Carnival that takes place every blue blood moon. Who knows what kind of filth will stream down this ladder throughout the week? We better be wary."

The idea that even the celestials, the divine beings, could be filthy was unsettling. She moved the curtains to the

Underbridge aside and stepped in. I regarded the ladder for a few seconds then followed her.

The Underbridge looked neater, with the furniture arranged perfectly, dressed in crisp fresh linen, a sandalwood essence stick wedged into a crack in the wall.

"Why do Maruts keep on living in Wantra? This place is dead, dreary, and dangerous," I said.

Anku's eyes widened in disbelief upon hearing my observation. "Would you rather live in a place where you are the hero, or the place where you are mocked for being a coward?"

This wasn't a difficult choice to make for me, but I had a hunch that Anku would not have liked my answer, so I remained quiet.

"Maruts were created for defending Samsara," she continued. "But we lost Wantra to Boors. As a result, Amravati and other places grew unfriendly toward us. We are failures in their eyes."

Anku stepped around the wooden cupboard in the center of the Underbridge toward the armchair where we'd left Surp. A loud gasp brought me running to stand next to her. The armchair was empty, and a quivering Chinni sat on the floor next to the armchair. She was shivering despite the layers of sweater, shawl, thick woolen socks, and leather sandals, but she was otherwise unharmed.

"I asked her not to leave, but she wouldn't listen," Chinni said, teary-eyed.

"What happened?" Anku asked, running her hand comfortingly over Chinni's arm.

"She used her silhouette's strength," Chinni said. With

considerable effort, she removed her shawl and shuffled toward the far end of the alley. She carried back a cushion on which lay the unmoving body of Surp's koel.

Anku smashed her right fist in her left palm. She would have broken into a full-blown rage had Chinni not started sobbing loudly.

She enveloped Chinni in a hug and said, "At least she's alive." The koel's eyes were unblinking and her legs were stiff, but the faintest dip in her chest was proof of life.

With a loud sniff, Chinni wiped the tears off her face and produced a note from under her shawl. "I heard yelling outside the Underbridge. They must have been waiting for her. By the time I got there, all I found was this stuck on the lamppost."

"You said the Underbridge is hidden from Yechs," I said, looking up at Anku, who read the note aloud.

"Return what is ours to get back what is yours… DM." She looked up. "Dakini Malini!"

"Without the help of a celestial, they couldn't have breached the glow of the lamppost," Chinni said, her eyes large with worry, her squirrel nose wet with tears.

"How can you save someone from burning when they insist on walking into the fire again and again?" Anku said. This was the first time I had seen her defeated.

I still couldn't figure out how Surp had left the shelter by herself. "She couldn't even open her eyes," I said.

"Her silhouette was unhurt. She used up its strength."

"But why would she do that?" I said, more to myself, knowing well enough that this was why I could never be a hero. Heroes were not bothered by the fear of looking or sounding stupid when they took risks. They didn't have the ever-present voice of Naani in their heads.

"To save Rudra," Anku said without attempting to hide her rage as she clenched and unclenched her tiny fists. I took a step away from her.

"Rudra?" I asked with an inexplicable gnawing in the pit of my tummy. The sensation was new. Before I met Surp, I had never felt this attracted to anyone.

My question seemed to bring Anku back to her senses. "Mmm, aah…" she muttered, narrowing her eyes and thinking hard, glancing at me from time to time. Finally, she said in a low voice, "Rudra is Surp's boyfriend."

Everything was making sense now. Surp was trying to save her boyfriend, who had been abducted by the Yechs.

I felt Anku's eyes on me. She had made no bones about her poor opinion of my Marut skills, but I wasn't about to let her see me distraught from the news.

CHAPTER 10

It was horrible knowing that Surp had a boyfriend. I felt a wave of despair wash all over me. That Anku had a hunch about my crush on Surp was even more embarrassing. Just like that, I was back to feeling like a loser.

It was at these moments when I missed my silhouette. In silhouette, I didn't have to feel any emotion other than the fight or flight response. Survival and escape overruled every other instinct.

Anku had dangled the possibility of Surp going out with me to get me to stay back in Wantra. I made a mental note not to blindly trust Anku again, but first, she owed me some answers, truthful ones. I clenched my jaw and tightened my fist.

"Why did you lie to me? What are you and Surp really doing in Wantra?"

"I lied to you because you had a celestial dagger which can be of great help to us," Anku said, unrepentant. She glanced at the worried face of Chinni. "Children, both human and Marut, have been disappearing from the streets of Delhi. We feel

Dakini Malini has something to do with it."

I had seen pictures of Dakinis in comic books. Dakinis were said to be the vilest among supernatural creatures. A typical Dakini had red eyes, fangs dripping with blood, and hair that fell in a jagged mess around her shoulders. It was said that Dakinis wore white saris and accosted innocent travelers on highways or stray visitors in abandoned buildings. They were spirits that refused to leave the material world and stayed back for vendettas. Hotspots haunted by Dakinis in Delhi and around the world were generally well-known and avoided by everyone.

"How about informing a grown-up?" I suggested. She had talked about someone called Mothy Maddy a few times. Although it was clear from recent events that she and Surp had entered Wantra without Mothy Maddy's knowledge.

"Really?" Anku said as if I'd suggested the unthinkable. "When has a grown-up ever helped you?"

She was right, grown-ups did not help. They sermonized. The only grown-up in my life had been Naani, and she had never helped me without making me feel like scum.

"There's no shame in seeking help," I said.

"If your mistake is grave but fixable, then involving grown-ups is foolish."

"Perhaps a tantrik?" I suggested. Tantriks were men who practiced dark magic and voodoo. It was easy to spot a tantrik on city roads: their braided hair held in a bun, their faces and bodies smeared with ash, a string of rudraksha beads hanging over their bare chests.

"Tantriks are on Rahu's team. They're in cahoots with Dakinis. Don't you know anything about our world?"

"No, I don't, and I don't *want* to know anything. Especially from someone who lies like she was born to," I retorted.

Anku snorted, but I could see that I'd caught her on the back foot.

"I can't trust you now," I continued. "You made me miss my exit window from Wantra. I doubt you even know where to find Patches."

"There's a bigger picture here, Adi," Anku said.

"I am not interested in the bigger picture," I said. "I was to meet my aunt and start my life afresh."

"You know what?" Anku said, squaring her shoulders and squinting her eyes. "You only think about yourself. You can never be a Marut."

Blood rushed to my face. "I don't want to be a Marut!" I shouted at the top of my voice. My voice rang in my ears, and blood rushed to my head.

You're not ready, Naani's voice rang in my ears.

Suddenly, I saw Anku's monogrammed shoes at eye level. *Drat!* I had silhouetted. Naani warned me never to let anger get the better of me. My snake body lay buried under my clothes.

Anku's shoes got closer. She and Chinni dropped down to their knees and brought their faces close to mine. It was a brave move because I was still seething with anger, and in silhouette, I could have bitten Anku without regret.

"Naga Marut Adi. Let's just say we're both good at telling lies. At least I do it to help others," Anku said and left, a smirk on her face.

I got into my clothes after I silhouetted back. There was no need for me to give in to Anku and her guilt trips. But Naani's voice kept taunting me: *You're not ready, Adi.*

I tied Kaleeni on my back with a scarf, snatched up my satchel, and walked out of the Underbridge. I would show Anku and Naani that I didn't shrink from helping anyone.

My flight to Goa to live with my aunt would not be an escape but rather a choice. As for Rudra, I doubted he would last long as Surp's boyfriend. After all, he had been captured and also put Surp's life in peril. Moreover, she had just met me. I was sure we both felt a spark between us. I felt my cheeks grow warm at the thought.

I emerged from the alley to find Anku arguing with someone. There was no end to the trouble this girl could get into.

When that man saw me, he did a double take. "A new recruit," he said. His eyes lingered first on my bag and then on Kaleeni. "I knew you were hiding something."

"Leave us alone, Thauma," Anku said.

"Indra has already been alerted to your presence in Wantra," Thauma said. "The Apsara sleuths will be on your tail in no time. What do you think will happen when the gatekeeper figures out that you kids have trespassed into Wantra?" He removed his cap and ran his hand through his greasy, uneven hair.

"The gatekeeper has bigger worries with Gandaks and Yechs roaming the streets."

"You clearly don't know what Ugra can do," Thauma whispered. "The last Marut he caught trespassing was fed to the Panish."

I had read enough mythology to know that Ugra was the bull that Yama, the deity of death, rode. I guessed Ugra moonlighted as the gatekeeper, too.

"Who made you the police?" Anku snapped.

"I smell foul play. Where there's foul play, there are spoils. You know I am a collector." Thauma's eyes glinted.

He folded back the sleeve of his overcoat to reveal the strangest watch on his wrist. It had an open dial made up of cogs, wheels, and chains. There were three needles that each ended in a metallic symbol—a heart, a weapon that looked a lot like Gargouille's death pike and a moon. The rim of the watch was etched with ancient runes. All three needles were pointing toward me.

"My Vilupta Catcher brought me here. It doesn't lie," he said before adding, "mostly never."

"I'm telling you," Anku said. "We are just here for a tincture from Tara's Attars."

"Really? So if I went to Madhav with the news that you are here without Surp, with a strange boy," he said, jerking his thumb toward me.

"What do you want?" Anku said, exasperated. She had collected her hair in a bun that made her look grown-up.

"Nagas like to fly in comfort," Thauma said. I caught a maniacal glint in his eye as his face wrinkled into a smile.

Anku glared at him. "Spill it."

"Kaleeni!" Thauma whispered.

"This is unbelievable. You're trying to take advantage of children," Anku exclaimed. I noted she had a gift for dramatics, another tool in her arsenal of deception.

"I am Thaumaturge, a magician of the Narada clan," Thauma said. "I trade information for rare objects. It's a business, and it serves as a hobby. It is not exploitation."

In his frayed coat and shabby bearings, he came across as a ragpicker or a homeless hippie rather than an antique collector. Thauma's nose looked like a beak. Slanting eyes and eyebrows brought to mind a vulture. Droopy fingers and overgrown nails added to that effect. His long and uneven hair was unable to hide the tiny metallic loops that pierced various parts of his ears like lovelocks on a grill. His old, faded overcoat was just enough of a layer for a chilly February Delhi morning.

I peered at his Vilupta Catcher again. Even if it were possible for a gadget to track down magical objects, how had Thauma known it was Kaleeni that the Vilupta Catcher had found? Then I remembered the curious expression on his face when he saw my bag with the embossed Naga symbol. Perhaps in Wantra, it was common knowledge that Nagas owned flying carpets.

"What makes you think we'd be interested in your information?" Anku said.

Thauma's shoulders relaxed. His teeth, lined with gold and silver fillings, flashed in a wide but insincere grin like a salesman who knew a customer had walked into his snare. "It was Dakini Malini," he said in a conspiratorial tone.

"You saw what happened here? When they took Surp?" Anku exclaimed. "Why didn't you help?"

Thauma moved back, as if fearful of being smacked by Anku. "You know it's not in my nature to meddle," he said.

I shifted on my feet. Except for his shabby appearance, Thauma sounded a bit like me.

"But I can tell you where they took her," he offered.

"Everyone knows Kalpavriksha is Dakini Malini's haunt," Anku said and started walking toward the main bazaar.

"Okay, alright," Thauma said, running up and barring her way with his arm. "The boy will need a weapon. I can get him one."

"In exchange for?" Anku demanded.

"In exchange for Kaleeni," he said.

I looked at Anku in alarm. She put up her hand to me in a gesture that meant "hold your horses" and then said, "And you secure our entry to Kalpavriksha through a hidden pathway."

"What?" I cried. "There is no Kaleeni. I am not giving up anything. I must get back home with the carpet or Naani will kill me."

"Naani? You mean Manasa?" Thauma said, sidling up to me. "Is she alive? Of course she is." He squinted his left eye as he studied me.

I turned to Anku. "Could I remind you that I already have a weapon? I don't need another one."

Anku rolled her eyes, pulled me aside, and whispered in my ear, "At some point, you will have to part with the dagger. Don't you keep saying it doesn't belong to you? You need a challastra," she said, tugging at the key ring that swung from a loop around her waist. "Every Marut carries one. Ideally, you should have received one when you silhouetted."

"But is it worth giving up Kaleeni?"

"Thauma knows the hidden paths into Kalpavriksha. If we take his help, we could rescue Surp and Rudra and get you home in time for your rendezvous with your aunt."

I glared at her. She must have read Aunt Padma's letter

while I was in silhouette. "Or I keep the dagger, and Kaleeni and I can leave right away," I said to Anku in the same hoity-toity tone she had used.

"Surp put her life on the line for you," Anku said, her eyes flashing.

"Yeah? I never asked her to." We glared at each other for a few seconds until finally, I relented. "I will come with you on one condition."

Anku raised an eyebrow.

"I want a say in the plan. You must consult me when you make decisions and not treat me like a kid," I said.

"You are an ungrateful brat. All the best looking for Patches by yourself," Anku said and flounced off. She was not willing to relinquish control of anything!

"I could help you find Patches if you let me ride Kaleeni once," Thauma said, sidling up to me again. "What do you say to our own pact on the side?"

Despite his fixation on Kaleeni, it was tough to dislike Thauma. He had an eager, open face and twinkling eyes. His vagabond getup was either a disguise or proof that he was not ambitious.

People like him made no claims of heroism. A curtain of greed blinded them. Cunning schemes were their second nature. They would never harm anyone intentionally, but they would also not stop anyone from misdeeds.

"Since Kaleeni belongs to me," I said to Thauma, "you will need to do something for me."

Thauma nodded eagerly. "Anything. But remember, I provide only information." He paused and added, "I deliver messages, too."

"After we've rescued Surp," I said, "I need to know everything about Shesh Nagaraj."

"Of course," Thauma said as if surprised by the simple request.

"You can't lie or make up anything," I warned.

"Guaranteed," Thauma said, nodding, and caught my hand, shaking it vigorously. "You don't have to go with her, you know. The Kalpavriksha is infested with anacondas." He shivered.

"Anacondas?" I cried.

"Yes, and the Yechs that ride them. Together known as Rocuja," Thauma said. Worried eyes on a sly face made him look shiftier.

Anku had disappeared around the corner. While I wasn't sure what Anku had in mind to fight the Dakini, the Yechs, and the Rocuja, I was quite sure that Thauma would abandon anyone in need without qualms. He was no substitute for Anku, who though prone to lying was loyal to a fault.

"I have to go with Anku," I said.

Thauma frowned but fell in step with me as I hurried after Anku. She said nothing; I offered no explanation. She asked Thauma to lead us to the arms dealer.

"I didn't know you could get weapons in Chandni Chowk," I remarked.

"This is Wantra's main bazaar. Hasn't Madhav brought you here yet?" Thauma asked, getting suspicious.

"Mothy Maddy's been extremely busy," Anku said.

"I heard he works for that painter turned politician, Vinay

Chaubey?"

Anku shrugged. "Even paladins need to work to earn food."

"But a paladin would never leave a Naga Marut alone. You know, because of the prophecy," Thauma said. As if struck by a thought, he turned to me. "Are you a wastrel?"

"A what?" I cried. I had been called many names by my teachers and classmates, but this one was particularly nasty.

"Relax, Adi," Anku said, trying to pacify me before I silhouetted in anger again. "A wastrel is a child who hails from a Marut clan but is unable to silhouette or has an incomplete silhouette, like a missing body part or something." She glared at Thauma. "He's a Naga, and he is safe with me."

Thauma rolled his eyes at her and loped ahead of us. "What does the prophecy say?" I asked Thauma.

"They say that a Naga Marut will one day reclaim the ring of Kundalini from Rahu and save the world," Thauma said over his shoulder.

Save the world? Goosebumps crept all over my body. The prophecy could *not* have meant me.

Anku nodded at me. "Sounds rather grand for you, doesn't it?"

The cheek of her!

A few streets later, Thauma suddenly held up his fist to signal us to stop.

Against a wall to the right, a cobbler had set up his makeshift atelier under a tarp. The aged cobbler was hunched over an anvil, intent on fixing a boot.

A few paces away from the cobbler, some men had gathered

around a juice kiosk like bees crowding a hive. In addition to juice, the shop was selling mini-sized snack packs and quick reads, like racy magazines, counterfeit novels, and newspapers.

"Takka!" the juice kiosk operator, a flashy guy with cheap sunglasses, cried to the cobbler. "Going without lunch again? You will die if you don't eat, old man!"

The juice seller had a hint of red spittle on the corners of his mouth from chewing betel. Incredibly brawny, he belonged in a gym rather than behind a juice cart. He certainly looked like a goon who would have illegal weapons on him.

The cobbler didn't respond. He was either deaf or pretending not to have heard the juice seller, who moved from behind the counter, a glass of juice in his hand.

"Here, Takka!" he said and handed the cobbler a glass of juice.

The cobbler lifted his head, his wispy white mustache and long eyebrows looking foreign. He had collected his thin silky hair in a ponytail. His wrinkled face was wizened, but his manner was sharp. He grabbed the glass of juice and downed it in one go.

The juice man patted the cobbler's back and said, "I've bet the grocer that you won't cop it for another ten years. I've got to keep you alive."

So the juice seller is a kind-hearted underworld don, I thought. My eyes followed the juice seller as he served his customers back at his kiosk.

Thauma led us to the cobbler's shack and sat us down on a wooden bench. Perhaps he planned to wait for the crowd to thin around the kiosk. You can imagine my surprise when the cobbler said, "What news, Thauma?" The strong fumes of cobbler's glues and adhesives assailed my nose, instantly producing tears.

"Takka," Thauma said, bowing slightly. "I need a weapon for this boy." He jerked his thumb toward me.

I wiped my eyes with my sleeves. This old man was an arms dealer?

Takka, the cobbler, was grumpy and old. He wore scratched, black-rimmed spectacles and a dark-gray field jacket with four bulging pockets. His military cargo pants glistened with dirt, and his Velcro sandals looked over-mended. His graying hair was limp and silky, and his sparse goatee and thin mustache moved in the breeze.

A slight frame and controlled movement suggested erudition over physical strength. He reminded me of wise and hardy Sherpas who accompanied hikers on Himalayan treks. He seemed to belong to another age, like Naani.

"What do you have for me?" Takka said without looking up, punching the sole of a shoe steadily with a sewing awl.

"This blood moon, he will be there," Thauma said. Takka's hands paused, but he didn't look up.

"Which one?" he said.

"Before I tell you, I need to get this boy a weapon," Thauma said.

Takka looked up for the first time. I could swear I saw a transparent film under his eyelid move back and forth, but it happened so fast that I was sure it was a product of my overwhelmed imagination.

Takka grunted as he got up and shuffled to the padlocked

cupboard. I was a little disappointed that Takka had turned out to be the arms dealer. The juice seller seemed more resourceful. At Takka's touch, the padlock fell open.

The cupboard that he reached into was so small that it could only contain cobbler's tools. He withdrew a wooden toolbox, set it before Thauma, and flipped the lid. Under the lid, a dozen keychains, similar to Anku and Surp's, hung on hooks. They had tiny metallic models of weapons like knives, bows and arrows, swords, and the like.

"My information is definitely worth more than these trinkets, Takka. How many centuries have you waited for this, my friend?" Thauma said like a seasoned negotiator.

Anku and I glanced at each other. Thauma knew how to sell information for the best price.

Takka grunted again, pursed his lips, and put the box back into the wardrobe before withdrawing a chipped wooden box carved with a tree. Inside the lid were three keychains.

"Parashu, or Parshuram's axe. Kuber's Shibika, or what we call a club. And Satya Pasha, or the noose of truth," Takka said. Anku gasped.

"Akashi Challastras, once wielded by devas. Now we're talking," Thauma said.

I had a faint idea about the people Takka mentioned. I knew Parshurama had been a powerful sage and Kuber was the god of wealth, still, these were mythological characters.

An awestruck Anku reached her hand to touch a key ring when Takka slapped her hand away. "If you touch another's weapon, it may turn on you. Hasn't Madhav taught you anything?" Then he turned to me and asked me to touch each key ring, one by one. "While challastras are synced with Marut clan DNA, Akashi challastras are celestial property. They must deem you worthy of wielding them."

Of course, if a carpet could have feelings, a weapon may as well flaunt an attitude.

With a thudding heart, I reached for the axe.

"Parashu is said to have supernatural powers. This axe is double-edged with spears on both ends. The most lethal close-combat weapon of its time," Takka said.

If I swung Parashu around me, it would slice any number of monsters surrounding me. It felt like a deadly and efficient weapon. I tried to unhook the key ring, but it wouldn't budge.

"It's stubborn, as was its master. It doesn't want to go with you," Takka said in a monotone.

I touched the second key ring.

"Crafted to grant justice," Takka said, "Shibika can sense evil. It orients itself and the warrior toward the enemy, thus providing an edge in combat."

A club with spokes all along its body, like a bulbous cactus, would be heavy in my hand but would clobber anyone or anything that got in its way. I pulled at the key ring this time, but it remained glued to the hook as well.

My heart fell when I saw the third key ring, a mere rope with a noose at its end. It was a joke of a weapon. And as is my luck, it came off easily in my hand. A loser weapon for a loser.

"The noose that forces the opponent to tell the truth. It's interesting that it chose you, for it belonged to the famed enemy clan of Nagas, the Nevala," Takka said, eyeing the symbol on my satchel.

Mongooses were known as Nevala in this part of the country, and fights between snakes and mongooses were considered epic.

"What use is a noose as a weapon?" I said, dismayed.

"In a world filled with treachery and betrayal, this noose will help you avert the very battles that the other weapons are used to fight."

"What if the battle is already on?" I said.

All of a sudden, Takka looked into my eyes and said, "These astras belonged to celestial beings. They are not for the fainthearted. If these astras detect cowardice in the bearer, they will return to me."

He shut the box and placed it back in his wooden cupboard, locking it with a heavy chain. Thauma leaned forward to whisper something in Takka's ear, unaware that my acute hearing, like a curse, would bring all unwanted and unwelcome sounds to my ears.

"It's arranged. On the eve of ARAC, the headless exit of the kings," Thauma whispered. Takka nodded and ushered us away.

We got up and stepped out from under the tarp kiosk. I hooked my sad key ring weapon in the loop of my jeans. I would have to depend on the dagger, the Dusht Uchchaihshravas, to protect myself.

From the street corner, I looked back to find that the cobbler's shack had been shut down, and Takka was nowhere to be seen.

Thauma was grinning from ear to ear as he looked from Anku to me. "Now to get you into Kalpavriksha, the wish-fulfilling tree," he said to us, making a check sign in the air as if he were ticking off tasks on a to-do list.

CHAPTER 11

It was late afternoon already. Thauma dropped us back at the shivir and left with a promise to return soon. "Once you're in Kalpavriksha, Kaleeni is mine," he said, holding up his forefinger in a warning. "In the meantime, stay put at the shivir and stay on your guard while I make arrangements."

That night, we lit a fire outside the alley to keep ourselves warm and took turns watching the lamplight for intruders.

As we sat around the crackling fire, strange creatures went about their business in Wantra, their bodies contorted further by the glow of the lamplight. Winged Yechs with ungainly gaits moved in gangs, rapping unsuspecting roadside dwellers, causing them to writhe in sleep or wake up startled. A few Yechs like Kabeela, with triquetra pendants hanging around their necks, snatched human identities, turning these people into street rowdies who knocked over trash bins and broke streetlights. Silent shapes floated past us; noisy beasts slithered and slurped close to us, causing me to jump a few times.

"No one can penetrate the layers of Akashi magic that

protects the Underbridge," an unperturbed Anku said.

"But the lamplight was breached last night. There has to be a glitch somewhere," I said.

My words produced the strangest reaction in Chinni, who got up in a huff and said, "Oh really!"

Anku had been hugging her knees to her chest. She pursed her lips and said, "We don't mention the word 'glitch' at the shivir." She gave no more explanation and settled in for a nap.

I wondered why someone would react to a word like "glitch."

The next morning, as promised, Thauma arrived at the shivir looking unnaturally chipper given the nature of the journey that lay ahead of us.

"If you get in and out of Dakini's den before evening, you could avoid the beasts of Kalpavriksha," he said. "You have time. She won't kill Surp straightaway, you know, given Surp's connections."

I looked at Anku in alarm. *Surp had connections in Kalpavriksha?* She blinked her eyes at me in reassurance.

"I have found a deity willing to help you," Thauma said. "So we could either climb the ladder to transit through Amravati to Kalpavriksha or take the wilder, more dangerous path."

"Ladder sounds good," Anku said.

"Wait, what do you mean by the wilder path?" I asked. Ulupi had warned me against trusting any deity. At this point, my trust in Anku was shaky too. What if the deity we met was the one after my blood?

"We find an ancient banyan tree. That way, we could stay

hidden from both the Yechs and the deities," Thauma said. "But there may be run-ins with the beasts of Kalpavriksha."

I considered the options. "We go through the banyan."

"But—" Anku started to say.

I held up my hand. "I get a say in the matter."

She scowled. I caught Thauma suppressing a smile.

I was surprised when Thauma led us back to the banyan tree in the village next to my home, the spot where I had met Gargouille.

"What are you playing at?" Anku said, spinning around to face Thauma.

"I saw Yechs peel themselves from that tree bark," I said, waving toward the tree.

Thauma held up both his hands. "That is why I said you should be back before nightfall. Dark spirits love hanging about banyan trees. I thought it was common knowledge."

"Fine, let's go," I said before Anku changed her mind.

It was already noon, and the place was teeming with people. Did these people know that in the deep night, chilling events took place around this very tree?

How can a tree grant wishes? I thought to myself, studying the banyan tree, an aged tree with dry, weathered branches and dark-green leaves. Even though most parts of the tree were dusty, its tired branches bent, and young leaves were beginning to grow in places. It was a grand old tree with a fighting spirit.

Thauma sprang up onto the cement platform around the tree. I followed and turned around to help Anku, but she ignored my hand. As Thauma started to climb the tree, someone asked him if he had lost his mind. While Anku and I were invisible to people, Thauma was not. I figured a lone ragged man climbing a tree must seem weird. Thauma's peculiar getup served the purpose of making his actions seem eccentric. He aroused curiosity, not suspicion in those around him.

It struck me that if celestials like Thauma, Rahu, Dakinis, and the Fallen Ones lived in the real world, they could be anyone around us.

Thauma's feet disappeared into the thicket of branches and leaves. Anku followed by lodging her feet in the nook of the tree and swung up. As I waited for Anku to climb up after Thauma, I wondered what Naani and Mohan were doing across the wall. Had Naani reported me missing to the police? Was she secretly happy I had disappeared? Had she bolted from the flat for fear of Mohan being hurt? After all, that was all she cared about: Mohan's safety.

I was about to follow Anku when I spotted a little boy standing on the other side of the tree, looking at it without blinking. It was Mohan. What was he doing here? I had never talked about the delivery with him. Nor had we ever discussed this particular tree on the numerous occasions we'd visited the village.

But Mohan was staring at the tree as if he expected someone to walk down any moment; as if he could sense my presence. He looked anguished. A child with dark circles around his eyes and a long face stands out. I felt my heart squeeze. It was hard to see my brother in this state. Why wasn't he at school?

Before I could figure out the answer, I saw Mohan's body jerk and fall forward on the ground. Someone had deliberately pushed him. The boy who had pushed him stepped forward to tower over Mohan. It was the confectioner's son with his three cronies.

I called out to Anku, but both she and Thauma had disappeared into the foliage of the tree. The four boys surrounded Mohan. I looked around wildly. I knew I couldn't save Mohan. My punches wouldn't land on these kids, and I could not call any adult's attention to the situation. But I couldn't leave my brother with these brutes.

An unattended cart laden with plums caught my attention. I jumped toward it. Using the dagger, I picked a plum and aimed it at the bully with full force. The plum splattered on the boy's cheek, and he shrieked in pain. The divinity of the dagger must be impervious to the boundaries between Wantra and Samsara. It meant I could use the dagger on someone in Samsara while I was invisible.

Unable to spot the thrower, the boy started slapping Mohan.

I picked the plums one by one and hurled them. The boy ran, his arms wrapped around his head and face, his friends in tow. I saw Mohan get up and scramble toward the gate to our condo.

Having made sure that he'd escaped, I bounded up on the parapet and pulled myself up the tree. The cart owner had returned. Someone directed his attention toward the fleeing boys. It was time for just deserts.

My mind was still in a muddle about what Mohan was doing near the tree. I climbed up fast, scrambling over the branches like a monkey. It was when my hands touched a wet branch that I realized I couldn't see daylight through the branches above. I looked down and found the leaves closing in, growing dense under my feet until it grew oppressively dark around me. The air was dank, and the branch I was holding was slippery.

As I grappled to find firm and dry wood, my foot slipped, and I landed on bark that was wet, smooth, and velvety to the touch. I tried to anchor my body, but before I could orient myself, I zipped down the surface.

In desperation, I caught whatever brushed against my hands—small stems and tufts of leaves—but they broke off from my weight and speed. Wet soil caught under my nails, and needle-thin threads of the wooden branches cut through my skin.

I gave in to gravity and the twists and turns of the slide. It felt like I was being yanked in every direction possible, like riding a roller coaster in darkness. Though my back was cushioned by Kaleeni, the rest of my body grated against the tree bark. My face burned as if being stung by countless bees.

So huge was my fear of the monsters in Kalpavriksha that I smothered my screams. Just as I'd given up on trying to find a handle in this chaos, I landed hard on my bum with a thud. Kaleeni bounced, unfurled, and landed on my head. The carpet was more nuisance than convenience, but I could not afford to lose it for fear of Naani.

I spat out the leafage that had collected in my mouth during the fall and checked for my dagger and key ring. Both had survived the upheaval. Also, daylight had reappeared. But there was no sign of Thauma or Anku.

I got up and studied the surface under my feet. A path made of bumpy bark lay before me. Patches of smooth surface suggested this was a thoroughfare.

It wasn't clear if I was still among the branches of the banyan tree. Also, I had expected the tree to be crawling with beasts. The spot where I landed was surprisingly homey. It felt safe. A cool breeze made the leaves rustle around me.

Kaleeni safely secured on my back as I inched forward on the path, I noticed a guava fruit hanging close by. *A guava on a banyan tree?* I reached for the guava when a memory flashed through my head.

I was climbing a guava tree with my father holding my hand. With his other hand, he kept the branch steady. Tall and lean, Father helped me balance as I stretched to pluck the guava.

My mother said, "You can do it, Adi. Just a little further. Your father's got you."

Suddenly, Naani's voice cut in. "Let him do it himself. He does not need help."

But Father did not let go of me or the branch, as if he hadn't heard Naani's voice. I stretched farther to pluck the guava. The soft yellowing fruit with evenly scattered freckles was close when a scream pierced the air. "No!"

I blinked and found the guava had disappeared. The branch was just as before, slender and bare.

I looked for the source of the warning and found a pixie-like creature with pointed ears and a dainty frame peering around a branch stub. He was wearing a straw hat with a pointed top. There were flowers and leaves on the hat, but they weren't just stuck to it—they were growing from it. Multicolored sweet-pea flowers and tendrils swayed on the hat as if he were carrying a garden on his head. The pixie's body was covered with soft down, and his feet were bound in snug straw sandals.

"This is a whimsical tree. It punishes trespassers by luring them into illusions," the pixie said.

"Thanks," I said. Even though Naani's voice screamed, *Stranger danger! Be wary of unsolicited advice!* I disregarded it. The kid was all feathers and flowers! How could he possibly harm me? "Who are you?"

I couldn't pin the expression on the pixie's face as he stared at me. Was it curiosity or concern?

"You won't survive here," he said. These were big words for his size. He reminded me of Mohan. I didn't like being preached to by kids. Mohan had followed me like a puppy much too often.

"Could you help me? I need directions to Dakini's, er, office," I said. Maybe the kid had reacted to being asked his name; perhaps it was a rude and presumptuous act in his culture. Anyway, I wasn't here to make friends.

"Are you a Marut?" the child said in a soft but mature voice.

I nodded. The kid looked harmless and nothing like the beasts that Anku and Thauma had talked about. It felt safe to admit to him that I was a Marut. In fact, this was the first time I had acknowledged to anyone that I was a Marut.

I still had no idea what that meant for me. If Naani was a Marut and had known all along that I was too, then why had she hidden it from me? And why was Mohan different? Why couldn't he silhouette like me? Was that a secret too?

"You must be very brave," the child said.

Or stupid, I thought. "I am here to rescue my friend from Dakini," I said.

"Which Dakini are you looking for?" There was more than one? I had never thought of the possibility. He must have sensed my confusion, for he added, "Some of them are nice. "

"The wicked one, I guess. Dakini Malini."

The boy nodded. "Do you have a weapon to defend yourself?"

I fished out the dagger from my satchel. I had still not wrapped my head around the Satya Pasha, the "weapon" that had been thrust on me by Takka. You can't win wars with lassos.

"Dusht Uchchaihshravas!" the child said with a barely audible gasp. He took a step toward me. His wings spread out behind him, membranous, like a dragonfly's wings, glinting with joyful shades of the rainbow. He reached out to touch the dagger. "They belong in the skies," he said, his eyes worried. "They can fulfill their true purpose only when they're together. Two sides of a coin."

I turned the dagger every way for a clue as to what the child was talking about. The dagger had worked quite well against Gargouille and Aunty Tara. I certainly didn't want it to fly away.

In a sudden movement that startled me, the child plucked a feather from his head without wincing. I noticed a mass of light and long feathers instead of hair on his head nicely camouflaged under the garden hat.

"A single wave of this feather erases illusions. Keep it close," he said and then pointed to the path behind me. "Go that way without taking any other crossway until you reach Dakini Malini's den. Also, I wouldn't use Kaleeni unless completely necessary." Without waiting for me to ask why, he continued. "Kalpavriksha is rife with illusions that Kaleeni may not be able to skirt." Having said that, he flapped his wings and rose into the air.

"My name is Pavan," he said, resting his body effortlessly on the breeze, and added, "stay away from Panish Grove" as the breeze carried him gently away like a dry leaf.

I looked at the feather. The gold and brown plume, much like a pheasant's tail feather, was a flimsy defense against the terrifying chimeras that Kalpavriksha must hold. First the lasso and now the feather. Despite the inexplicable situation I had landed in, I couldn't help but marvel at the ineffective fighting tools I'd collected in Wantra. On a whim, I slipped the feather into my socks.

I brushed my clothes and studied the path that lay before me. The branch curved up and flattened into a gentler slope. Farther up, it brought me to a crossing with another tree branch to the right, going through a wooden-fence gate with a signboard that read Zephyr Rovers Valley.

"Zephyr Rover" meant rider of the winds. This literally described Pavan. The thought of an entire valley inhabited by Zephyr Rovers filled me with optimism. The last thing I'd expected of Kalpavriksha was warmth and cheer.

No sooner had the happy thought crossed my mind than a darkness moved over the signpost. A foul odor, reminiscent of the rotting body of an animal, reached my nostrils. It was accompanied by a deathly chill. I looked up to find the sky had disappeared, and in place of dark clouds were slithering black scales. *Anacondas!*

Given my silhouette, I was quite comfortable in the presence of snakes, but the size of the snake moving above my head was mind-boggling, even for me. Though anacondas were not poisonous and used constriction to kill their prey, this snake carried a single row of scales on its tail, which meant it was poisonous.

Could this be an illusion? I retrieved the feather and gave it a swish, but nothing changed. I lowered myself, huddled into a tree cranny, and held my breath as I waited for the beast to pass.

Once the sunlight reappeared, I stole up the path with my back leveled against the tree trunk, my palms pressed against the bark.

A dull repeated thud sounded ahead of me, mixed with shuffling noises, made me stop in my tracks. It was amazing how silence amplified the slightest of sounds. I wondered if it was Anku and Thauma, but neither of them was heavy enough to produce such loud thuds.

I unsheathed my dagger and stood at the ready just as a heinous shadow took shape on the branch before me. Long, thick tusks emerged first, followed by a lion's head! Something dangled from the creature's mouth.

Like in a dream, I had grown numb to strange sights in Wantra. Still, I wasn't prepared for what came next. This bone-chilling creature was shuffling on flippers! It had a seal's body, a head that resembled a lion, and a boar's tusks. It looked like an impossible cross between a walrus and a jungle cat!

In its mouth, it held the limp form of a Yech, and it looked intent on finding a comfortable spot to devour it in peace. I half expected it to smell me, but it didn't seem to register my presence at all.

Suddenly, it moved left to the branch that jutted away from the trunk. Its tail brushed my legs. I pressed my hands over my mouth to suppress a scream of terror as the creature disappeared behind a clump of leaves and branches.

Unable to quieten my thumping heart, I hurriedly climbed farther up the tree. I must have climbed some distance because it felt like an eternity, and when I stopped to catch my breath, I spotted the tusked lion-seal creature far below. It was napping in its nest. In condo height, it was at least five stories below me. The contents of its nest included dried stems, foliage, and bones. I hoped the bones were all Yechs.

My relief at having left the creature behind was short-lived, for a sudden chill and a familiar putrid stench returned. It was the snake, the anaconda. It half-slithered, half-flew over my head, skimming the strong branches of the Kalpavriksha. I backed into the charcoal-dark shadows of the tree trunk and tumbled over someone crouching there.

I felt a hand tighten around my mouth to muffle my cry. "It's me, Thauma," a whisper brushed my ears. Once the air had cleared, Thauma let go of my mouth. "The Rocuja never miss the smell of a foreign body."

He noticed the feather that Pavan had given me in my hand. I had taken to waving it at anything that seemed like an illusion—not that it had worked even once.

"Zephyr's pankh!" he exclaimed. "Do you know what that feather does?"

"It breaks illusions," I said.

"True," Thauma nodded enthusiastically. "But every feather has a unique quality hidden within it. It could make you fly, or turn you invisible." He reached out to touch the feather. "This is the first time I've seen a pheasant feather. Wonder what it can do for us?"

"Us?" I tucked the feather back into my sock. "You and Anku didn't even wait for me to climb the tree," I said, looking around for Anku.

"Once the tree embraces you, you can't turn back," Thauma said. "I asked you to stay close."

He was right. I'd been waylaid by Mohan's presence.

"So, where's the boss?" I asked, referring to Anku with a title that fit.

"She's gone," Thauma said. The glee that the feather had produced on his face vanished like an extinguished flame on a candle. He averted his gaze.

"What do you mean?"

"She followed the Yechs. Don't worry. She'll have Surp out in no time." He stood and stretched. "I think I should head back to Chandni Chowk. Time to complete our transaction now." He reached to touch Kaleeni.

I stepped away. "The deal was for you to lead us to Dakini," I said.

"I was asked to get you into Kalpavriksha," Thauma said, "and I kept my side of the bargain."

"In that case, I still can't give you Kaleeni. You said you would tell me everything you know about Shesh Nagaraj. And I signed no papers." I turned and started walking. When I didn't hear Thauma move, I looked over my shoulder.

Thauma stood frowning, his jaw clenched. "When you enter into an agreement with a celestial, it needs no paper formalities."

I tapped Kaleeni. "You're almost there, Thauma."

He relented. "Battle is not my strong suit, boy. I might cause more harm than help."

"I'm not asking you to battle," I said.

Thauma hesitated and then started walking. "I will only walk and talk as far as Dakini Malini's den."

From the beginning, I'd known Thauma could not be trusted, so I took what I could get.

"You are a magician. A celestial one, too," I remarked as I fell into step with Thauma. "Why are you so scared of Yechs and other creatures of Kalpavriksha?"

"My ancestors were news bearers. We delivered messages between deities, influential devas, and even Boors. With time, we gained a reputation as rabble-rousers. You've heard the phrase 'Don't shoot the messenger'?"

I nodded.

"That's exactly what happened to us. As messengers, we couldn't take sides. We would visit Boorlok, the Rakshasas, and the Daityas as frequently as the celestials in Swahalok. Until one day, Rahu's head Yech, Kabeela, captured me and blamed me for tipping off Shesh Nagaraj about the attack on Haveli." Thauma stopped with a far-off look on his face. "They obtained the ring of Kundalini from Shesh. Still, they blamed me for Manasa's escape. They tortured me. Dakini Malini even conducted experiments on me and then left me in the Maw to die."

Even though Thauma was talking about his own experiences, a tremor coursed through my body. I didn't know anything about the Maw, but it sounded terrifying. "You were present at the Haveli when the attack happened?" I asked.

"I managed to escape just before Gargouille landed."

"So you knew about the attack? Why didn't you help the Nagas?" Perhaps Ulupi had been wrong in blaming everything on Shesh Nagaraj.

"I *did* help them. I was the one who tipped Shesh off about the attack before I left. Even though I was at Haveli that night as a guest and not in the capacity of a messenger."

Earlier that day, Ulupi mentioned that Shesh Nagaraj had betrayed the divine trust by revealing to the enemy the incantation that protected the ring of Kundalini. "After my harrowing experience, I charted a new path for the Narada clan," Thauma said, reading my face. "Contraband. This way, I only deal in objects that are in demand, and the entire operation is undercover. I love antiques and the stories they tell."

We walked in silence.

"How do you know about Kaleeni?" I asked.

"It's a Naga heirloom. I came looking for it after the attack, but I learned that Manasa flew away with Kaleeni that evening. Had she stayed back, Gargouille would never have known that Shesh was alerted. My job and credibility would have stayed intact."

"Had she stayed back, she would have been killed. I wouldn't be here talking to you."

"Oh, well," Thauma said, nodding sagely to himself. "We both survived, but only time will tell if the world can survive us." I had no desire to know what he meant, so I remained silent. Thauma deftly changed the tenor of the conversation by saying, "Manasa was one unpredictable Marut, even then. And gusty enough to have kept herself hidden all these years."

Strangers seemed to know Naani better than I did.

"You knew her, as in actually met her, back then?"

He nodded. "Anku told me she still lives with you and treats you rather shabbily."

I lowered my eyes. Why had Naani treated me this way? "I still can't believe she's more than a hundred and fifty years old."

"Actually, a hundred and eighty-four years old, to be precise," he said. "I attended her naming ceremony. She came from a well-connected clan."

I asked Thauma how old he was, and he pointed to the earrings in his ears. "Each one represents one century of my life."

I tried to count the earrings in each ear but found it impossible, owing to the crowding. The skin on Thauma's face was leathery and wrinkled. But the spring in his step was still young.

We stopped at a branch that had a lookout point, a naturally formed deck with an unforgettable scene before our eyes. As far as I could see, the Kalpavriksha was connected by countless trees.

"This was a hot spot for celestial visitors in the past before Rahu took over," Thauma said. He gazed at the expanse of rising and dipping waves of canopies around us. He gave me some water and a protein bar. We sat on a wooden bench and stared at the view.

Like a crevasse on a cliffside, the lookout point seemed to be located somewhere on the midpoint of Kalpavriksha. The tree cover was thickest where we sat. It decreased in a gradual slope, ending in tree canopies on the horizon. Thick stems ran like arterial roads through the Kalpavriksha. I couldn't tell if the inhabitants of Kalpavriksha were missing. Even though these pathways seemed deserted, I caught flickers of movement. Perhaps the tree protected the identities of its residents. Perhaps it was my imagination after all.

The expanse wasn't all green. Vibrant flowers of red, yellow, and purple, plus fruits and leaves, made the landscape look like a patchwork blanket lit up by soft, mellow sunlight. A cool breeze touched my sweaty face. I sighed deeply. This adventure was hardly what I would call a holiday, but this sight did make up for all the missed vacations. Then it struck me. If all the talk about the prophecy were true, this was all the holidaying I would ever get.

"Thauma," I said. "Do you know where Rahu may have hidden the ring of Kundalini?" Given his dealings in celestial artifacts, perhaps he knew how I could get to the ring. The seed of the idea that the ring could be stolen was sown by Ulupi, and without my knowledge, it had taken root in my mind.

Thauma shifted uncomfortably on the wooden seat hewn out of the tree's wood. "Has Manasa told you anything?"

I shook my head. He seemed to relax.

"The ring of Kundalini was placed by the Big Three in the

care of the Naga clan," he said.

"The Big Three?"

Thauma looked up in surprise. "The creator, the protector, and the destroyer. Brahma, Shiva, and Vishnu."

"Oh, yeah, I knew that," I said, sticking out my chin to cover up my ignorance.

"Back then," Thauma continued, "Nagas were considered vicious warriors." He glanced at me from head to toe, leaving a lot unsaid.

"Where is the ring now?" I asked, ignoring his innuendo.

Thauma gazed at the horizon, deep in thought. "It's the most beautiful piece of jewelry I've ever seen." There was a faraway look on his face. "And I have seen countless celestial jewels." I didn't doubt his words. Thauma looked at me and shook his head. "The ring of Kundalini is not something you can entrust to a bank, a person, or a safe. I'm sure he has it on himself at all times."

"And why hasn't he used the ring already?" I asked haltingly. A part of me wanted this entire charade to be over. Also, who was to say the bit about Rahu waiting for my blood to awaken the spirit of Vasuki wasn't merely celestial yellow press or folklore gone morbid with time? Perhaps Rahu would be kind enough to prick my finger for the few drops of blood and let me go.

You're not ready, Adi, Naani's voice rang in my mind.

You know what, Naani? Perhaps I'm not ready, and I am not ashamed to admit it.

"The word on the streets of Wantra is that Rahu plans to wreak havoc on the planet come blue blood moon, which happens every hundred and fifty years or so. Now that you have surfaced, he must be scared witless."

"Why? I'm just a boy and he's a deity."

"The ring of Kundalini belongs to the Nagas. Vasuki answers to Nagas," Thauma said, pausing mid-sentence. "Though you are unlike a Naga Marut, I wonder if you could use that to your advantage."

I remained quiet and gulped down my anger. I knew I was not much of a Marut, but I still had feelings.

Thauma seemed to realize his mistake. "Don't take it personally. Manasa was very ambitious, and nothing was good enough for her. She would never let a Naga Marut surface unless she was sure of him or her. I wonder how you got into Wantra just five nights away from the blue blood moon!"

I wanted to tell him that it was hard not to take constant belittling personally and that Naani had not allowed me to surface. She'd tried everything to keep me buried.

But the night of the delivery when I met Gargouille at the banyan tree, I got a feeling that the real package being delivered that night was me. Still, I couldn't bring myself to link Batty with this turn of events. Thauma said he had never heard of Batty or Batra in Wantra circles. Whether Batty meant to set me up not, it was abundantly clear that for defeating Rahu, I wasn't up to snuff as a Naga.

Rescue Surp, get back Patches, head back home, and forget Wantra, I reminded myself.

We started our trudge toward Dakini and soon reached the entrance to a dark tunnel formed by a thick arch of leaves that seemed to continue endlessly. As we stepped into the tunnel, red eyes peered at us from the dense, verdant walls.

"Red-eyed tree frogs. If the Yechs look at these frogs, they go blind. It's one of the safest spots on Kalpavriksha."

I couldn't pay any attention to what Thauma was saying, as my mind became occupied with thoughts about the prophecy.

"Thauma, what do you think Rahu will do when he catches me?" I asked.

Thauma took a deep breath and turned to me. "The prophecy says that a Naga heir will clash with Rahu on the eve of the blue blood moon and reclaim the ring of Kundalini. What do you think he will do?"

So it would not be a pin-prick for a few drops of my blood. Rahu would kill me to eliminate a threat to himself.

"Tell me honestly, Thauma. Do you think it's me?" I asked.

"That you are the Naga heir is almost certain. That you will defeat Rahu in battle is almost impossible." We emerged from the tunnel and found ourselves at the cross section of three paths. "Unless you have a brother or a sister," Thauma added as if shaking an unnecessary thought from his mind.

"Even someone who can't silhouette?" I thought out aloud.

Thauma stopped in his tracks to look at me. "There's another Naga?"

I nodded. "My brother. But he can't silhouette."

"How old is he?" Thauma said, catching me by my collar and shaking me as if that would somehow make the information spill from me.

"He is ten," I said, pushing Thauma away with all my strength.

I was surprised by the change in Thauma. He'd been

dragging his feet until now. All of a sudden, he seemed to be in the grip of excitement.

I'm not sure why I told Thauma about Mohan despite Naani's repeated warnings against sharing any information concerning our family. Did I secretly hope Mohan was the real heir? Deep inside, did I wish for Rahu to take Mohan and leave me? Would a life without Mohan, knowing I was responsible for his death, be worth living?

You're not ready, Adi.

CHAPTER 12

"Hmmm," Thauma said, scratching his stubbly chin. "Two Naga boys. Who would have thought?" He removed his cap and once again ran his hand through his greasy hair. I made a mental note never to shake Thauma's hand.

"The older son is generally the heir," I said. Even I could tell it was a feeble attempt to correct my mistake of letting Mohan's identity be known. It was bound to pull me lower in Naani's eyes.

"Sure, sure," Thauma said, a tad startled. He seemed to realize he'd let on more than he wanted. He wore back his hat and pointed toward one of the signboards.

"Hell's Retreat," I said, reading the board. The other two signboards marked the entrances to Watering Hole and Panish Grove. For a chimerical tree, the signage was surprisingly impressive in Kalpavriksha, like in a town or a city.

"Home to water demons that can swallow an entire Marut. That's Panish Grove for you," Thauma said, nodding toward the board closest to the tunnel with tree frogs. "Panish or the water demons live in a lake next to the weeping bough. But we need her." He pointed toward the third board marked Hell's Retreat. "Den of the head Dakini."

"Someone said that the Panish are the most dangerous creatures on Kalpavriksha," I said as I followed Thauma's steps.

"I wouldn't say that. The Panish were created for a reason. Kalpavriksha bears a single fruit at one time. The fruit is the source of its name. Anyone who consumes the fruit could wish for anything to come true. But the fruit grows on the weeping bough. The moment someone plucks the fruit, like an alarm, the bough starts wailing. The Panish hate that sound, so they guard the fruit. It's quite a sophisticated system. In my book, creatures who choose to be savage are more dangerous."

This was an insightful comment, almost ill-fitting on Thauma, who was materialistic and proud of it.

Rowdy laughter reached our ears from the direction of the Watering Hole. Thauma hurried me on toward Dakini's den. The second I stepped on the path to Hell's Retreat, the amulet around my arm tightened a smidge, like it had the night I stepped through the back gate of the condo. I shrugged off the creepy déjà vu and said, "Watering Hole sounds like a cool name for a bar or a pub."

"Oh, it's a bar alright. That's where the animal rides of the celestials meet during the bestial hour. Fearsome savage animals!"

"If the celestials ride them, they can't be all that bad," I said. The only value I respected Naani for imparting to us was to respect animals.

"Gargouille is Rahu's panther. Did you find him pleasant company?" Thauma asked.

Anku had spilled everything about me to Thauma, including our run-in with Gargouille. I considered Thauma's words. Naani had once told me how various deities and devas rode animals to move around. I thought it was a cool form of transportation, but Naani had said that the deities could ride the beasts only by exerting immense control over their own impulses. The animals that the deities ride represent their own strengths and weaknesses harnessed for a higher purpose.

"Shani's crow, Shukra's crocodile, Brahma's swan! They're most savage during the bestial hour," Thauma said. "They could eat a village at one go."

A sharp scream somewhere up ahead brought me back to the present. "Anku!" I said and bounded up.

The smooth track was followed by wooden steps. I climbed these to arrive before a giant hollow, a large cavity where a bear could live. A gaudy silver and gold nameplate greeted me: Hell's Retreat.

I looked over my shoulder to find that Thauma had still not reached me. Or had he decided to flee? I wondered if he would notify anyone for help like Naani or Mothy Maddy. My gut asked me not to have any expectations from Thauma. At least he had left without exacting Kaleeni from me.

Soft chinking reminiscent of beaded curtains drew my attention to a hollow that could well be a window just above the entrance of the den. Had someone been watching my approach to the den? I stepped inside the cavity to have a spiral staircase greet me. The pressure of the amulet on my arm grew with every step I took up the staircase.

At the top of the staircase, I hesitated. A rolled-up carpet tied to my back was bound to invite questions. Even someone who didn't know anything about the flying carpet would want to know what was so special about it that I carried it on my back. Also, if I needed Kaleeni, it wouldn't help to keep it tied up. So I removed Kaleeni and kept it on the floor against the wall adjoining the window.

I advanced to stand before a curtain of pink and black beads moving in a light breeze. The beads tinkled as if warning me against taking another step. I shuddered to imagine what a Dakini's den might contain. I considered turning back and calling for help. Anku's shrill scream rang out again, closer this time.

I steeled myself and shoved aside the beaded strings to barge through. I was surprised to find myself in a fancy cove done up in pink and black. It was a den, alright, but not what I would expect of a witch's lair. There were no voodoo dolls, tantric symbols, dried-up lizards or bats, powdered animal bones, or skulls of any kind. There was no sign of Anku, either.

The sofa to the left had black fur with pink trimmings. The pink floor carpet contained a random pattern of black bubbles, and toward the right was a high-back chair upholstered in pink fluff, a worktable placed before it. There was a touch of glitter and sparkle to everything. The garish interiors reeked of uncontrolled ambition. I wondered why the walls were actual tree bark and not glossy or wallpapered.

Blue sky at the far end of the den was a welcome sight, as it meant there was a possibility of escape. I wasn't caught in a claustrophobic cave. But what if the far open side ended in an overhang? Like a sailor's plank, perhaps used to push prisoners off the tree. I shook off the thought. There was no point worrying about it at the moment.

"My! Aren't we in a hurry?" someone said.

Dakini Malini sat camouflaged against the chair and emerged from it like an apparition materializing into a physical form.

There was nothing about her that suggested she was a Dakini. Pleasant to look at, she was tall and had intelligent eyes. Still, her presence was dark and menacing, as if her wickedness had cast an evil aura around her.

"You managed to dodge us all last night," she said.

"Where are my friends?" I asked. My heart was beating loudly, but I feigned a bold stance.

Dakini snapped her fingers, and a Yech holding a struggling and gagged Anku appeared out of thin air like an illusion. This must be what Pavan, the Zephyr Rover, was talking about. Not that waving a feather would do me any good in this situation.

"You mean this one?" Dakini said, swiveling from side to side in a revolving chair. "This girl had the gall to use cheap doodads to try and get past me." Dakini Malini picked up the guptikr that was kept folded on her table.

"Let her go," I said. "I have the dagger you wanted." Anku made warning noises that I ignored. "You can take it and let my friends go."

I reached into my satchel for the dagger, but my hand was met by its grainy leather interior. It was empty! I tried not to let the surprise show on my face as I frantically searched for the dagger. Even Aunty Padma's letter was gone. *Thauma!*

"Well?" Dakini said. She walked over to stand before me and held out her hand to receive the dagger.

"I, er, seem to have dropped it somewhere, but I can go back and look for it. Give me time," I said, a note of pleading creeping into my voice.

"You have *what?*" Dakini cried while Anku gave a loud, painful moan. "You dropped the Dusht Uchchaihshravas?" Dakini squinted her eyes and bared her teeth. I'd never seen a creepier smile on a face. It extended in a diagonal line toward her right cheek. "I didn't expect this from a boy rumored to be the Naga heir."

Heirs are people too, I thought bitterly. How could I have known that Thauma had a knack for sleight of hand, too? You don't expect such behavior from celestials.

"You said yourself," I said. "It's just a rumor. I am no heir. I'm here for my friends." I found that sticking to one story was the easiest way of lying. The moment one starts adding layers, the lie pops like a balloon from too much pressure.

"Before we debate that further, I will get my boys to find the Dusht Uchchaihshravas first," she said and snapped her fingers.

In a terrible repeat of the scene with Gargouille at the banyan tree, Yechs emerged from the walls of Dakini Malini's den. Their bodies created craters that suggested these were permanent parking spots for them. Two Yechs left the den without waiting for instructions. One of them stayed back and caught my arms behind me.

"Gently!" Dakini Malini screamed at the Yech. "Make sure you don't harm him. I'll tie a ribbon around his head and gift him to Rahu."

"In your note, you asked for the dagger to be returned. That was the deal," I repeated. I avoided looking at Anku. I was sure she was still glaring at me for having lost the dagger.

"You don't have the dagger, now, do you, dahling?" Dakini Malini said in a patronizing tone.

"Let me go. I'll find it."

"Do I look like someone who keeps her promises?" Dakini Malini asked me, her voice dripping with fake sweetness.

"You'll regret hurting us, Dakini," I said. I'd seen heroes use this dialog in movies. I was quite sure it would not work with Dakini Malini, but it was worth a try at least.

"Who told you I was a Dakini?" she rasped, throwing a scathing look Anku's way. "I am *Doctor* Malini. Dakini is just a professional label in these parts. This was not a profession of my choosing." She held up an ivory cigarette holder. "Just because I was mean, cruel, and spiteful to my subordinates didn't mean I should be called Dakini! A girl's got to try hard to stay ahead of the rest."

Anku made an angry hissing sound. Dakini Malini chuckled as she walked to Anku and removed the gag from her mouth.

"Oh, what a pack of lies!" Anku burst out with a snarl the moment she could speak. "Everyone knows your story. You were a human. You sold your soul to Rahu in exchange for immortality. You conduct experiments on Marut kids for Rahu."

"My, my, we have a little know-it-all here," Dakini Malini said, patting Anku's face.

Anku tried to shake off her hand. I am generally not a

critical person, but I had to admit that this was not the moment to rile Dakini.

"Maddy knows about us," Anku said. "You will be dead by tomorrow." Her penchant for lying was faultless.

"Silly girl, Madhav has his own interests to protect. Though I wonder why you weren't dumped on a foster family like other silhouettes," Dakini Malini said.

"Maddy does not dump Maruts," Anku retorted.

"So you won't tell me your parents' names. Then I will just have to feed you my drug without knowing your ancestry." Dakini Malini threw up her hands. "This boy, on the other hand," she said, looking at me, "will go down in the history of the three worlds as the harbinger of a Boor revolution. You may even be worshipped in Boorlok."

Her stilettos clacked sharply as she walked toward the edge of the cabin and turned around suddenly, holding her hands up to the wall as if my poster were destined to hang there.

"After Rahu has used your blood to wake up the spirit of Vasuki, he will hand you to me for my research. The circle of life will be transferred to Boors, and Boors will emerge stronger than Maruts ever were."

Anku threw an alarmed look my way. I guess she hadn't known that Naga blood was needed to get the ring of Kundalini working for Boors.

"I am not a Naga," I said. In comparison to Anku's confidence, my voice sounded unconvincing even to me. I blamed Naani for this flaw in my personality, a glaring lack of confidence.

Dakini moved closer to me. The amulet on my arm

tightened, threatening to cut off the blood supply in my arm. "Didn't Manasa teach you that Nagas are not good at lying?" she said and lifted her long and curled fingernail, tearing my sleeve and revealing the amulet.

Anku drew in a sharp breath.

Dakini Malini eyed the amulet and whispered, "No wonder you've escaped us all these years. Well done, Manasa."

She snatched the amulet from my arm. Immediately, I felt like a burden, a heaviness that I carried everywhere with me, had been lifted. I'd never felt lighter in my life.

Dakini Malini held the amulet before my eyes. "What's your silhouette? Is it a magnificent cobra like Shesh, or a fire dragon like Manasa?"

It came to me that my mother wore an amulet just like mine for as long as I could remember. I wondered about her silhouette.

"Did you know that Manasa has been holding you back with this?" Dakini Malini asked. "This amulet contains Naga Vibhuti, or ancient snakeskin ash. It was keeping your animal spirit in check. It kept you hidden from Boors and Maruts. It also fooled my Rocuja, who have been searching the Kalpavriksha for you."

She walked toward a brazier and dropped the amulet into the red-hot burning coals. The thread that ran through the amulet immediately caught fire.

"She had no idea you would seek us out. Did she?" Dakini Malini said, grinning, her face very close to mine. I could smell the jasmine talc on her body. "Manasa should have known it wouldn't last. You don't expect someone as grand and humble as her to tempt destiny."

I was sure Naani never imagined I would enter Wantra. But what if she had? Would she have caged me until the day I died?

I could understand that she had been dead set on keeping me hidden for the sake of mankind. Still, it was hard to accept that she had no affection for me, her own grandson.

"Ever wonder why she thought so little of you and your parents? What if she had kept her faith in you?" Dakini said softly, stoking the fire of my anger and hatred. She joined her fingertips next to her chin and watched me closely.

"Don't listen to her, Adi," Anku warned me.

Thanks to Naani, I had enough practice in hiding my feelings from others. My face was expressionless, but my mind was in turmoil. Why had Naani been so negative?

Instead of running from the future, I could have trained in the ways of Wantra, in combat and stealth. If she really feared the prophecy, she should have abandoned me or squashed me as a snakelet and been done with it. Instead, she tied me up with the amulet and kept me from expressing myself.

Under my blank expression, anger and rage surged for all the times Naani had subjected me to self-doubt and humiliation because of my silhouette.

"Even if Naani believed in me, I would never have done what she wanted of me," I said softly. It was not true. Had Naani taken me into confidence and shown me kindness, I would have been an ideal grandson and perhaps a Marut.

"Anyone would resist being set up as a martyr," Dakini said and paused. "But you're a Naga, after all. Nagas are greedy and violent. Just a nudge is all it would have taken."

Gargouille had made a similar derogatory remark about Nagas at the Qutb Complex. What could Nagas have possibly done to earn such an awful reputation?

"You will go far," Dakini said, patting my cheek.

Perhaps it would help to let her think she had me figured out. But I couldn't help cringing at her cold, clammy touch.

"Look at me," she continued. "I convince people to join Rahu's army. My seduction methods are accepted here; my talent is recognized and rewarded." She dangled her diamond bracelet in my face as proof. "If you offer your services to Rahu, he might let you go free still."

"I don't have any talents to offer. You're wasting your time on me," I said in all earnestness.

"Really? Manasa might think you're a wimp, but not only did you manage to escape Gargouille, you also reached yours truly." She went to her chair, sat down, leaned back, and placed her knee-high fur boots on the table. "You have potential. Think about it. In the meanwhile, let's get started with you." She pointed a finger at a struggling Anku.

Just then, a Yech shuffled up to Dakini and whispered in her ear. She simpered in delight and walked over to stand before Anku. "So you are Durga's daughter. Does she know you're gallivanting with a boy?"

"Leave my mother out of it!" Anku snapped.

Anku had a mother? She'd led me to believe she had no family. Another one of her lies. And what did Dakini Malini mean by gallivanting?

Anku and I had been forced together on this escapade. Every moment, I wished it had been Surp instead.

"I wonder if I should send you straight to my lab in Amravati or torture you to get back at your mother. That would tickle her tail," Dakini said to Anku with a giggle.

Tickle her tail could only mean that Anku's mother was Marut with a cat silhouette like Anku.

"Isn't it funny? Both of you have powerful women on your side, but these women are forcing you to stay hidden, subjecting you to ordinary lives."

Anku struggled to free herself in vain.

"I am told you are quite the pet of Madhav," Dakini Malini said, addressing Anku.

As Anku and I tried to throw off the Yechs that held us, Malini looked up toward the ceiling and emitted a mirthful laugh.

"All the cards seem to have fallen in my hands." She turned to Anku. "Both Durga and Madhav will dance to my tunes to save your life." Then she turned to me and said, "And with you, I will teach Manasa a lesson in humility." She shook her head in disbelief. "I can't believe my luck. It's like Shani, the deity of bad luck, has finally quit Kalpavriksha."

Everything said and done, I felt Naani did deserve a lesson in humility.

"Shani would never favor beasts like you," Anku said, spitting in Dakini's direction. I recalled Anku's fascination with Shani.

"My dear girl, deities are paradoxes themselves. Brahma, the creator, can destroy to protect his creation. Lord Indra, the god of thunder, can bring about drought and famine to garner devotees. You'd be surprised to what depths Shani can stoop to stay relevant."

Shani, who also represented planet Saturn, brought bad luck to people he disliked. Naani said that silhouetting on the same day as the death of my parents was a sign of bad luck, of Shani's wrath.

"Hmmm…why don't we just let Rahu decide what's to be done with you both?" Dakini said. She snapped her fingers, and the Yechs started tying our hands with rope.

"Let me in!" a voice came from the entrance of the den just as a jerking, smoking head of a Yech rolled on the den floor to stop before us.

A tall and graceful woman in a black body suit and a silk cape walked in. She bore a striking resemblance to Surp, except she had a savage sneer on her face that I could never imagine on Surp. Her hands were hidden under the cape.

"Dakini Surpanekha!" Malini said and sprang from her chair.

"Who have you caught now, you backbiting vixen?" Surpanekha said.

Dakini Malini quickly regained her balance. "You would have known already if your daughter had not deserted the Boor cause."

"My daughter deserted no one. She was never a Boor," Dakini Surpanekha said.

"Then why don't you ask Rahu yourself? Oh, wait a second, you're not on the team for Project Blue Blood Moon!" Dakini Malini said dramatically.

"I am as much of a Boor as you," Surpanekha snarled without glancing at us. Her lips and chin trembled as she spoke. It was, however, her nose that presented the strangest sight I had ever seen. It was stuck on her face with Scotch tape!

Everyone knew Surpanekha's story. The demon princess was shunned and mocked for her looks and had her nose sliced off by Laxman, a celestial prince. A horrifying tale of social callousness.

"You are a defector's mother," Malini said. "But don't worry, we have a plan to bring your daughter back into the Boor fold."

I expected Surpanekha to react, but it was becoming quite apparent to me that the parents and grandparents of Maruts were a cold-hearted lot.

Surpanekha ignored Malini's threats regarding Surp and instead withdrew her right hand from under her cape. In her hand, she held a cardboard file of papers, the kind you find piled up in government offices.

"My spies stole this from the paladin," she said, holding up the file. "He is on to you. He has the coordinates of your factory, and he's getting closer to Ketu. The police are on his side and all thanks to the rampant kidnapping of children for your experiments."

Surpanekha threw the file at Malini. Papers slipped out of the folder and flew all over the den.

"But have you seen the stats on crimes committed by children?" Malini said. She picked up a remote from her table and switched on a TV, which suddenly appeared on the bark wall. I wondered what else lay hidden on the walls of this den.

The newscast was reporting a crime committed by three underaged boys. "More and more children are turning toward darkness, all thanks to my drugs," Malini said with a chuckle. "And you are afraid of the police!"

I could see how she had earned her position as the head Dakini. The animal inside her had consumed her.

"What about the children who never return home?" Surpanekha said.

"They serve a worthy cause. I must pay my bounty hunter after all," Malini replied, examining her nails.

"Your actions will endanger us all. Outside Wantra, you and I are as weak as the humans. We don't have the divine immunity that Rahu or Ketu enjoy. They're deities. They can't be harmed physically. *We* can die out there."

"Now you grudge the gods for their divine immunity. Interesting." Malini switched off the TV and jotted down something in her notepad. "Wouldn't Rahu like to know that."

"You are a fool to think Rahu will ever favor you. He loves Chayya," Surpanekha said.

Two Dakinis were fighting for Rahu's affection? I wondered what was so special about him. After all, he was the god of disease!

Malini withdrew into stung silence following Surpanekha's remark. "Once he sees what I've managed to achieve in my lab, he will forget Chayya. I have created a drug that turns humans into Boors. In the future, there will be no need for Gargouille to lure dead souls into the Yech fold. A few drops of my serum will do it."

"Managed to snag more magical feathers from the Zephyr Rovers?"

"Not feathers, dahling." Malini opened her table drawer.

She fished out something that she placed lightly on the table and beamed like a kid as everyone stared at a corked vial secured with a black ribbon with pink polka dots. "Marut silhouette essence mixed with Daitya bile. The pathetic wishy-washy feathers of Zephyr Rovers don't work half of the time. This serum takes effect immediately. I would have tried it on these bozos," she said, nodding at Anku and me, "but it still needs a lion Marut's essence."

"No, no, no," Anku whispered. "Not Rudra."

"The paladin will butcher you if you harm his students," Surpanekha said, the hollows of her cheeks growing deeper, her cheekbones sharper.

"Don't feel bad for the lion silhouette," Malini said. "It's one sacrifice for the benefit of many. Though it's all the same to me." Glee seemed to pour from every cell of her being. "The best part is that in the zoo, the boy was a sitting duck for my agent."

If she could force a Marut with a lion silhouette to submit to her, what chance did we have against her?

"How do you get past the gatekeeper?" Surpanekha continued to grill her.

"I have friends in the Marut clans. You should step out of Kalpavriksha sometime," Malini said, trembling with excitement now. "With my new drug, Zephyr Land will be ours. The Maw will submit to us. And once Rahu obtains the powers of the ring, we will be one large, united, and ever-growing Wantra. Our next stop will be Swahalok."

Surpanekha had still not registered our presence. Was she pretending to ignore us?

"If Rahu asks me, I warned you," Surpanekha said and made to glide out of the den when she saw Anku and stiffened. Her glance shifted to me, but without a word, she moved toward the exit.

A miffed Malini called after her. "Don't you want to know how I plan to bring Surp to our side?"

Surp was Surpanekha's daughter. How could I have missed it? Surpanekha stopped short and said over her shoulder, "Surp is an adult. Her life is her choice."

"So you won't mind seeing her vampire fangs grow, her hair bristle, and," Malini paused maliciously as if savoring every word, "her nose fall off?"

Just as Malini finished speaking, Surpanekha turned around, and her nose dropped off her face, revealing two bony cavities instead of nostrils. It triggered a torrent of laughter in Malini.

Suddenly, I connected Rinca and Gilli's nose-related jabs at Surp. It had something to do with the multiple scars on Surp's petite nose, which I had found unique and endearing. I'd never heard of scars being inherited, but clearly, there was a connection here.

"Dakinis are not supposed to go looking for romance among Maruts or humans. You should have known you would get judged and banished," Malini said amid gasps of delirious laughter.

Surpanekha cursed the tape. She stuck her nose back on and turned toward Malini, her hands held out like claws. "I will scratch your eyes out," she said, rushing toward Malini, in the process bumping into the Yech who was holding me and pushing me toward the overhang.

As I rolled over, flailing to get hold of the edge, I saw the Dakinis land on each other in a freewheeling brawl. Anku kicked the Yech holding her and swung her club hard into its head. She sprang forward to catch my slipping hand.

I caught a gnarly knot in the branch with my other hand. As I struggled to find purchase, I saw the Yech who had got knocked down by Surpanekha rise up. He spotted us. Would he push Anku, thus sending both of us to our deaths? Or would he haul us up and send us to Rahu, a different kind of slow and agonizing death?

I lifted a leg and hooked it over the ledge. The Yech was standing over Anku now with a death pike in his hand.

"Vasuki Upakritam," I whispered.

Just as the Yech lifted his death pike to strike Anku, I caught her hand and heaved myself off the edge. We landed on the silken lap of Kaleeni. The Yech's death pike crashed into the edge of the overhang, causing shards of wood to fly out. I pulled the golden tassel to sink into the blessed anonymity of Kaleeni's invisibility.

"Quick, Adi. Take us back into her den," Anku said.

"No," I said firmly.

"Trust me," Anku said.

Against my gut instinct, I directed Kaleeni back toward the den. I was a tad curious to know how the battle between the Dakinis had ended. I was rooting for Surpanekha.

"Toward the table," Anku whispered as we entered the den. Then I saw why she wanted to return. Dakini Malini had Anku's guptikr, and Anku was not someone who would let anyone get away with her possessions.

While Anku swiped the guptikr off Dakini Malini's table, I watched the Dakinis still engaged in a vindictive catfight complete with wild punches, hair-pulling, and screams.

Malini was using scissor kicks and chops while Surpanekha ducked her blows by gliding out of the way and attacking as soon as Malini's back was turned.

Anku joined me to watch. "Surp is a Dakini's daughter," I said.

Anku nodded. "But Mothy Maddy is closest to being Surp's real mother."

I glanced at Anku. Dakini Malini had mentioned Anku's mother, Durga, but Anku did not offer any information about her. I had my secrets, too. It was best for both of us to keep quiet. It was easier to respect each other's boundaries this way.

I directed Kaleeni away from the den. The screaming, shrieking, and shouting of the Dakinis grew fainter as we alighted Kaleeni at a hideout, which had a clear view of the den.

CHAPTER 13

Once we were safe and unobserved, Anku spun around to face me. She poked my chest with her forefinger accusingly. "What took you so long?"

I was sure she would next bring up the lost Dusht Uchchaihshravas. So I decided to fight fire with fire. "Just stop," I said, waving my hand. "Why didn't you tell me Surp's mother was a Dakini?"

"It was not relevant," she snapped.

"Okay, why are you and Surp really here? It's not for Rudra. Dakini is holding him in her lab in the city, not in Kalpavriksha. She said so herself."

Anku's eyes darted around. I could sense her mind trying to cook up an excuse. Finally, she sat down cross-legged with a sigh. "Rudra, Surp, Bala, Angad, and I live at the Underbridge with Mothy Maddy. We help vulnerable children on the streets, in orphanages, and in schools whenever we can. As you saw yourself on the TV in Dakini's den, our efforts are a drop in the ocean."

She leaned back against the tree and stared vacantly at the branches above us.

"When a Marut silhouettes for the first time, the mirror, Ichcha Darpan, captures the celestial activity. Mothy Maddy visits the parents and provides them with tips and support to bring up a Marut kid. Where he feels parents might harm the child, he places them in foster homes or safe animal shelters."

It was fascinating to think there might be other kids like me who could silhouette into animals. "How often does a Marut silhouette?" I asked.

"Two to three Maruts in a year, but not all of them are saved. Last year, four children went missing before Mothy Maddy could reach them. The parents said that a doctor appeared at their doorstep saying she could cure them."

"You think it's Dakini Malini?" I asked.

"You heard her. If she gets to the Marut first, that child is never heard of again." Anku took a deep breath. "Two days back, Rudra took new Maruts to the zoo. Generally, first-time silhouettes get very skittish in the presence of other animals. The zoo is good practice in learning to control one's instincts and communicating while in silhouette."

"That was where she trapped Rudra?" I asked, piecing together the story in my head.

Anku nodded. "Mothy Maddy and Surp have taken up ordinary jobs to uncover the human identities of Rahu, Ketu, and Dakini. Rudra asked me to accompany him to the zoo, but I wanted a break from whiny kids." Anku stopped speaking and lowered her gaze. "Angad and Bala offered to accompany

Rudra instead. The three of them and the new Maruts never returned."

"Angad and Bala…" I had never heard them mentioned before.

"Angad and Bala are both fifteen, like me, but they have supportive Marut families, unlike mine. They visit from time to time. I couldn't bear the thought of facing their parents."

"You feel responsible for Rudra and others getting captured?"

"I know I couldn't have prevented it from happening," Anku said in a low voice. "But I can't help thinking that if I had been there with them, just one more Marut might have made a difference." She shut her eyes tight. "Surp said she didn't blame me, but she wouldn't talk to me. She's my best friend."

"Why didn't you inform Mothy Maddy?" I asked.

"It was Surp. She said we shouldn't disturb him. I was too scared to face him. That night when we picked up Boor activity in Ichcha Darpan, we dropped in to investigate near the banyan tree."

"But I was in Wantra. How did you enter without paying the gatekeeper?"

"Like all animals, silhouettes are present in both worlds at all times. As soon as you silhouette back into your human form, you are in Samsara. When you entered Wantra without meeting the gatekeeper that night, you brought us in with you. It was an accident." She pursed her lips in resignation.

"Do you think Surp left to meet her mother?"

Anku shook her head. "I don't think so. From what I know, Surp can't stand her mother. The only silver lining is that the Dakinis are not on the same page about abducting Maruts. There's dissension among them."

My hands rested on the jagged, dry, and rough bark of Kalpavriksha. I noticed a lack of tree insects around us. "What do you think Dakini Malini does with the kids?" I asked, scraping the bark under my hand to see if the insects were hiding underneath it.

"Mothy Maddy believes she steals their silhouette identities and feeds them a drug that turns them dark."

"Daitya bile," I reminded.

Anku looked up at me. "Did you know that a few parents have contacted her themselves to get their kids treated?" she said, using air quotes for "treated."

I understood the parents wanting to rid their kids of their silhouettes. It can't be easy to watch your child turn into an animal when in the grip of intense emotion. Still, I had grown to accept my silhouette like my shadow. It was true; it scared me sometimes. At other times, it provided me with company. I guess I had to be thankful to Naani for not trying to change me through "treatment."

"Who are the Boors everyone keeps talking about?" I asked.

"Asuras, Daityas, and Rakshasas are all related clans and constitute Boorlok," she said.

"And Rahu is…" I whispered.

"…an Asura," she completed my sentence.

"And they're all wicked and savage?"

"Can't say. They're loved by their own kind. Deities have

always treated Boors with disdain and condescension."

I wondered if fairness was a thing at all since it lay in the eyes and mind of the one judging a situation. I was beginning to learn that survival trumped every namby-pamby emotion that popular culture had romanticized.

My thoughts were interrupted by a noise from Dakini's den. We peeked through the dense branches to find Surpanekha emerging from the den in a huff. I caught my breath when her gaze swept past our hiding spot. But she seemed to have not noticed us. She bent down to pick something up and then moved away to a path that led higher up the tree.

Our eyes followed her.

"She doesn't seem to care much for her daughter," I whispered.

Anku nodded. "She disowned Surp when Surp refused to follow her to Kalpavriksha and instead chose to live the life of a Marut like her father."

"I doubt Surpanekha will want to be seen as a traitor by the Boors," I said.

Anku bit her lip and knitted her brows as if engaged in a conflict. I could tell that her decision not to accompany Rudra weighed on her. For one act of cowardice, she felt compelled to choose one brave act after the other.

Finally, her chin resumed its determined stubborn rigidness. She asked me to keep an eye on Dakini Malini. "She'll be in no shape to go anywhere after her brawl with Surpanekha. If she does leave her den, follow her. I'll find you. And try not to lose Kaleeni like you've lost the dagger," she said as she crouch-walked to the path Dakini had taken.

I wished I had the quick wit to respond with something equally snarky, but just as with Ayesha Saini, I was simply left seething. Anku had a flair for ruining all sense of camaraderie with her high-and-mighty ways.

Before I could ask her how she would find me, she disappeared under the guptikr.

CHAPTER 14

Under my feet, Kaleeni lay spread out on the tree branch like a happy picnic rug. It was sure to attract attention, so I rolled it up and tucked it along the edge of the branch. I settled next to it, my eyes fixed on the entrance of Hell's Retreat. A light and cool breeze touched my forehead. I caught a whiff of jasmine and rose. Perhaps they grew nearby. Perhaps it was an illusion. Either way, it felt calm and soothing. My eyelids grew heavy, and despite the dangers surrounding me, with my fatigued body resting against Kaleeni, ensconced within the mighty Kalpavriksha's arms, I was unable to resist sleep.

I was standing outside a door with a symbol that I couldn't place. I was sure I'd seen it before. Three white lines intersected by a vertically placed eye. The eye blinked and moved over me. I heard the door click. I nudged the door open and slipped inside to find an odd company in deep conversation.

A muscular middle-aged man in jeans and a t-shirt sat on the arm of a sofa facing the window. Even though he was swinging his leg playfully, he appeared far from relaxed. His body was tense, and his forehead was furrowed. "Without training, it's not possible before this blue blood moon. The Naga child is not Shesh," he said.

Next to the man, leaning against the sofa, was a double-bladed scepter, the famous thunderbolt that belonged to Indra, the god of thunder and one of the fallen deities, according to Anku.

Across from him, a similarly aged man sat cross-legged. His manicured hands, beige pants with an immaculate crease, and white linen shirt imparted a surprising level of sophistication to this seemingly rushed meeting of ordinary people, if one disregarded the thunderbolt.

"If Swahalok got to know that there's an heir, we may have a war on our hands. All the waterpower of my seas put together will not be able to put out Agni's wrath. The deity of fire will blaze." He spoke gravely while casually flipping through a men's fashion magazine. Only Varun, the deity of the seas, could have waters of seas under his command. Okay, so these weren't ordinary folk. From the looks of it, I was in the presence of the Fallen Ones. Apart from Indra, the god of thunder, and Varun, the god of seas, I was not familiar with the other two deities present.

A lady wearing a light-blue sari was slowly pacing from one end of the room to the other. She wore a tiara made of white flowers and bangles woven with leaves. She had soft features, and even though her pacing conveyed restlessness, she was more poised compared to Indra, who seemed to be bristling with anger, and Varuna, who was disturbingly nonchalant.

The fourth occupant in the room stood against the sole window in the room. His face was in shadows as his rather large head blocked the light from the window. Was this Agni, the deity of fire? Or perhaps Vayu, the deity of winds? Both were fallen deities.

"We are decided, then. We must help the child," he said and stepped away from the window. I was struck by the ordinariness of this deity. In

contrast to the celestial glow the other three occupants of the room carried, this man had a washed-out look about him. The smile on his face belied the anxiety apparent in the dark circles around his eyes and prematurely white stubble.

"You seem to be forgetting what the word prophecy means. It's his destiny," Indra said. "You may be the creator, but even you can't challenge the laws of the universe."

The creator? Could he be Brahma? Dressed in gray tweed, black pants, and a tie, he looked like a weary professor.

"A prophecy is still words. Nothing is set in stone unless it comes to pass," Brahma said. "And we wouldn't dream of harming a child."

Indra grunted.

"We don't have to. Just reveal his location, let it be public knowledge perhaps, and get a scribe to do a piece on him. If Boors don't get to him first, Agni will. And if Agni misses his mark, Shani will be waiting in the aisles to finish him off," Varun said, waving his hand elegantly to indicate a simple and efficient solution to my end."

I felt like an intruder, but I couldn't get myself to leave the scene, especially since a plan to murder me was being discussed.

"We must not forget that he is under Manasa's protection," Brahma said.

"Manasa is a mere human, for all purposes," Varun said. "She has no powers left."

"She managed to elude us for a hundred and fifty years," the lady in the blue sari stopped suddenly and said.

"Look, that's the rule," Varun said. "The child will pay for the misdeeds of his forefathers."

"What are your thoughts about it, Aranyamani?" Brahma said, turning eagerly to the lady. Perhaps he hoped to find an ally for his cause.

THE LEGEND OF TRIQUETRA

The lady called Aranyamani gazed at Brahma with sad fondness. "I'm afraid I agree with Indra and Varun. The clash between the heirs on the blue blood moon will decide the fate of mankind. I have no love for humans. They have squandered the wealth of forests and nature. All I am interested in is making sure the ring of Kundalini remains unharmed. The renewal and regeneration of nature depends on it."

I had never heard of Aranyamani, but I guessed she was the deity in charge of nature.

Varun nodded. "Humans have polluted my waters too. They deserve what they are getting. Who knows? Perhaps Rahu and his Yechs may prove better for this planet than humans."

"The ring of Kundalini is a ticking time bomb," Indra said. "Even if Rahu wins the battle between the heirs and panders to our wishes, tomorrow the ring may fall into Daitya hands or some other creatures from Boorlok. If mankind is wiped out today, tomorrow it may be us. We must secure the ring and save the humans."

"But how do we get to the ring?" Aranyani asked.

"There's only one way," Brahma said, and I realized he hadn't moved his mouth to speak.

His three companions were waiting for him to continue. When he realized this, he said, "Apologies for the intrusion, but that was Buddhi, my left brain."

Then I noticed something. Something that hit me like a mental sucker punch. Brahma's head was like a single dice with a face each on four sides. A sad mop of messy hair on top of his head and his muscular neck kept his head from rolling off. I had read about the four faces of Brahma but figured it was a fictional prop in mythological stories, as it was as impractical an idea as it gets. How would someone with four faces sleep, for example? Wouldn't one of the faces get squished or suffocate to death?

I steeled myself to take a closer look and slowly circled Brahma. The front face was placed higher than the rest. While his left face was clean-shaven and wore a monocle, the right face had a goatee and plucked eyebrows. In contrast, the back face had bushy brows and an angry beard. Curiously, the four faces shared one set of ears.

Naani had told me how Brahma's four faces represented his wise, brainy, artistic, and passionate sides, and that he had modeled humans after himself. "The brain is not always wise. It can be cold-hearted," Naani had explained when I asked her why there were two separate faces for wisdom and intelligence.

Like a faulty remote control, flipping TV channels on its own, numerous thoughts crossed my mind. Had Brahma developed split personalities from the trauma of being forgotten by his own creation? Did his body contain multiple silhouettes? Could these faces lead independent lives and have their own romantic interests?

"If the Naga Marut's blood is needed to wake up Vasuki's spirit, then the child is the only one who will surely get to see the ring, perhaps even touch it," Buddhi, Brahma's left face, said. "All we need to do is help him along until he reaches the ring."

"And then what?" Indra snapped. "You can't expect a lily-livered Marut to steal the ring for us. I say let's kill the Naga Marut and avert the disaster."

Brahma's wise front face ignored Indra and went on. "Someone else can steal the ring for us. Someone who will travel with the Naga Marut all the way to the rendezvous with Rahu."

"You mean…" Aranyani said, sudden understanding dawning on her face.

Brahma nodded. "The Naga Marut has still not achieved Vibhaga. His silhouette does not have an identity. It can easily be controlled by another Naga silhouette, a more powerful one."

"You mean Manasa?" Aranyani whispered.

"We need Manasa on our team. We must poke her silhouette, force it to wake up," Brahma said.

"Hear, hear!" Brahma's faces spoke together.

"I wouldn't get too optimistic," Indra said. "The Nagas are a cunning lot."

"Nagas are warriors and have carried on the Marut tradition for thousands of years. We must see the glass as half full," Brahma said.

I thought it was a rather backhanded compliment, but my mind was in a tizzy over the dangers that lay ahead for me.

"We can't have the heir go on living," Indra demanded. It was an odd statement given the heir would save them.

"Nurture trumps nature. We should all know that by now," Brahma said. "It's how the child has been brought up that matters. The connection with those around him will determine his actions."

"I'm sorry, but I can't commit myself to the plan. My throne in Amravati is at stake," Indra said and looked at Varun for support.

Varun pursed his lips, his gaze fixed on his toe. He finally turned to Brahma and said, "Alright, do what you will, but if we get caught, I will deny any knowledge of the situation and stand by Indra and Agni."

Brahma nodded. A spurned Indra grunted and got up to leave. Varuna bowed to Aranyani and followed Indra out of the room.

Aranyani walked slowly to the door and then stopped to look back at Brahma. "I hope you know how important discretion is. If Swahalok finds out you're meddling with fate, you'll be banished to Naraka, the depths of Hell. And if Rahu succeeds in assuming the powers of the ring of Kundalini, you will fade away forever."

Brahma bowed to her. "Your concern is duly noted." For someone who was down and out just a few moments ago, he looked relieved and happy.

"I'll be in touch," she said and shut the door after her.

I wanted to wake up, but instead, I heard a door slamming shut somewhere in the building. A noisy bustle from the street began to permeate the stillness of the room. Bollywood music blared nearby as Brahma retook his position by the window.

I came to stand next to him. What did he mean by Naani controlling my silhouette? I wanted to speak, to ask Brahma questions, but I couldn't get myself to open my mouth, as if my mouth had been sewn shut. Along with Brahma, I watched Indra start his motorcycle, causing a loud rumble of the engine. He shifted the gears and took off.

I spotted a menu poking out from under the magazine on the table. The words Twelve Rhinos Café and Inn were printed in bold across the top. The clatter of the motorcycle grew fainter as a different sound, the loud clanging of metal, took over. It sounded like a hammer falling on a metal chain.

CHAPTER 15

I woke up with a start when something rattled close to me. It took me a while to remember where I was and how I got there. It felt like waking up from a dream within a dream. Night had fallen, but the tree was not doused in darkness. In fact, it was lit up by fire torches, and the Kalpavriksha resembled a twinkling mountain valley at night.

Something clunked again, causing a hollow sound on the wooden surface outside Dakini's den. I dared a quick peek to find a familiar figure waiting outside Dakini Malini's den. Gargouille was throwing and catching his death pike as if it were a yoyo. He was dressed in a suit and tie with cufflinks. In place of shoes, his panther paws jutted out from below his pants, the nails shining in the moonlight.

Dakini Malini bustled out wearing a figure-hugging pink dress with pink peep-toes. She tucked a loose strand of hair into her hair bun. In addition to a small bandage on her cheek and another couple on her arms, she had scratch marks all over her body.

Gargouille looked up from the spot where his death pike had gouged another crater. His panther eyes seemed to register the injuries on Dakini's body, but instead of getting upset about them, he grinned and said, "Catfights become you, my lady."

Dakini moved forward and hugged Gargouille. The sight was revolting and fascinating at the same time.

"It doesn't take a lot to keep you happy, my dear," she said. She withdrew and held him by his shoulders. "How could you let him get away?"

"You should know. I heard he gave you the slip too."

"How do you know?" Malini said, taken aback.

"Surpanekha has been tattling all over Kalpavriksha. That's two times he has managed to escape our clutches." He snarled and threw the death pike again, causing a crack in the branch where I was hiding. I ducked, frightened at the prospect of what another encounter with Gargouille or Dakini would bring.

"Surpanekha's daughter is driving the attack against us. I could get Rahu to believe that Surpanekha is spreading rumors about me," Malini said, shrugging. "In your case, four Yechs saw how you failed to notice the two Marut girls in silhouette at the banyan tree. Didn't those girls help the Naga Marut escape? By now, the entire colony of Yechs must know."

Gargouille harrumphed and glowered at Malini. "It was a fair omission. You don't expect to find any Marut silhouettes in Wantra anymore."

"Rahu may feel differently. Better get your story ready. Did you manage to talk to other deity rides about joining Rahu?"

Gargouille shook his head. "During the bestial hour, they all agree with me. But as soon as the divine spell comes into force and the bestial hour is over, they turn goody-goody and forget all about their promises."

"Rahu won't like that," Malini said.

"No, he won't, but I picked up a piece of important news at the Watering Hole. The paladin Madhav is on to us. He has grown suspicious of Chaubey."

"As long as my lab is safe, I'm not worried," Malini said. "Madhav has grown weak. Going against the paladin credo to remain unattached, he developed an affection for his students. It will be easy to hurt him." Her mouth twisted with pleasure. "If you ask me, Rahu will declare war on the three worlds this blue blood moon. He won't wait any longer."

"And if you keep appearing warworn, he might even dump Dakini Chayya to make you his queen," Gargouille said with a giggle. "After all, the queen's throne should go to someone who can fight tooth and nail for the Boor cause."

"I don't get what he sees in that raven-silhouetted Dakini," Malini said, holding up the train of her dress. She started walking toward the path Surpanekha had taken. Gargouille nodded indulgently and followed her like a smitten kitten.

Anku had asked me to follow Dakini Malini. But she hadn't told me what I should do with Kaleeni. Leaving it at the mercy of Kalpavriksha and its inhabitants was not a good idea in my mind. So I positioned it over my shoulder and stole after Malini and Gargouille.

My thoughts drifted to my dream. It got me wondering if

there was a pattern to my dreams. The one regarding the fire at Haveli was followed by my meeting with Ulupi. The dream about saving Mohan from the bullies landed me in a similar situation before I climbed into Kalpavriksha. What would this dream lead to? If I told others that I had met the Fallen Ones in my dream, who would believe me?

At school, I was used to falling into traps set by Ayesha Saini and other bullies. When Naani saw me hurt and heard my story, she would say, "Use your foresight. The third eye that your silhouette is blessed with." Then she would tap the center of my forehead.

Could my dreams be the metaphorical third eye?

I rubbed my forehead to rid myself of the image. Still, a cloud of doubt enveloped my head. How could I escape a destiny planned for me by the deities to serve their ends? They were betting on me securing the ring of Kundalini for them. If I failed, they would abandon me to Shani because, somehow, I had to pay for the misdeeds of my ancestors.

That also explained the random mishaps in my life, perhaps even the death of my parents. The thought brought a wave of remorse and guilt. According to Ulupi, it was Shesh Nagaraj who had betrayed the celestials by allowing Gargouille to take the ring, not me. Why should I have to suffer for the actions of Shesh Nagaraj?

If I'd refused to make the last delivery, I might never have learned of the horrific Naga past and my impending death. The blue blood moon would have been an uneventful affair.

The Fallen Ones believed that, like all Nagas, I could not be trusted. Brahma felt that the nurturing I had received would somehow change my basic nature. I disagreed with his observation that nurturing superseded nature.

To begin with, there was nothing wrong with my disposition, and it needed no modifications. And secondly, after my parents died, I had not received any nurturing in my life.

The globular moon, a few days shy of the full moon, seemed nearer than it ever did at home. I stuck to the shadows as I followed the evil couple of Gargouille and Dakini Malini.

The hike turned steep, and soon I started panting. These paths were not meant for people who couldn't glide, didn't have wings, or carried cargo. I looked around for a spot to park Kaleeni and found a cozy nook under a craggy branch. In doing that, I missed the moment when Malini and Gargouille slipped out of sight.

I hurried to catch up and came upon the most frightening sight a person could ever see.

The expanse of branches before me looked like a catacomb. But instead of being arranged in a tomb, the bones formed the walkways, walls, and roofs of cave-like dwellings. It was a settlement built of bones, and walking around were winged and wingless Yechs.

The caves were arranged like honeycomb cells, spread out vertically around one large cave built on top of a platform. This was also the only cave fitted with a door and a black onyx knocker. The depth of the cave was hidden by a thick cover of leaves. I spotted Malini and Gargouille as they stepped through the cave door.

The thought of navigating my way through the throng of grating and grunting Yechs gave me shivers. An invisible

Kaleeni could fly me to the cave.

"Vasuki Upakritam," I whispered. Nothing happened. Kaleeni did not appear.

My heart sank a little. Anku had asked me to keep Kaleeni close to me. I rushed back to the spot where I'd left Kaleeni. My hunch was right. It was gone. Someone had swiped it, and they could still be around, spying on me. Leaves glinted in the moonlight and murmured to a light breeze, casting a spooky vibe wherever I looked.

I waited for an attack, an ambush, but nothing moved. I stole back to the point connecting the foliaged path to the white bony steps that led to the main cave. I had been robbed so many times in Kalpavriksha that it was hard not to feel disheartened.

I brought out the Zephyr Rover feather and waved it before my eyes, but no help appeared—nothing that would make me invisible or help me reach the big cave on the platform.

If Anku was around me, she would roll her eyes and make sure I felt silly. I tucked the feather back into my sock.

I studied the Yechs. Though these creatures were terrifying to look at, their bodies were cumbersome. Most Yechs were three times my size, clumsy and purblind. If I covered my head with leaves and slipped into the throbbing mass of Yechs, their wings providing me cover, I'd have a chance of making it to the cave.

I executed my plan by fashioning an umbrella out of broken tree stems and leaves.

With a thumping heart, I entered the flow of Yech traffic.

Midway to my destination, a Yech suddenly stopped and

sniffed the air. I froze. Slowly, all Yechs stopped moving and started communicating in clicks and clacks. Their legs and wings crowded around me. In a matter of seconds, they would discover me, and my bones would become wallpaper for the Yech settlement.

I decided that cutting through the tangle of legs and wings was my best bet for survival. Hoping that their large bodies would be unable to react to my speed, I shot off, zigzagging through them, slapping into their leathery wings, causing them to jump and screech like a bunch of kids with a mouse loose among them.

As I bounded up after Malini and Gargouille, a Yech jerked in my direction. He had caught my scent. I hurried, pushing the black onyx door handle, but it was shut tight. I looked over my shoulder to find that the Yech had appeared over the platform.

Once on the platform, I was cut off from the sight of those plodding the paths below. I sucked in air, held my breath, and moved into the shadows next to the cave. The Yech started to sniff the air and inched toward the door. I moved farther along the wall of the cave, my eyes trained on him. He would follow the smell of my body.

Just as my lungs were about to explode, another Yech came rushing after the first one. He slipped on the last step and knocked over the first Yech, sending him flying over the edge of the machan-like platform.

When I heard plops of tiny pebbles and branches dropping into water, I looked down to find that the branch under the platform extended over a lake. The moon glinted eerily on the lake's surface.

The only reservoir in Kalpavriksha anyone had ever talked about was Panish Grove. A chill tickled the nape of my neck at the thought of the carnivorous Panish. I had expected Panish Grove to be crawling with water beasts, but this lake was soundless and its shores spotless. Its borders were clean and well-defined, as if the tree had decided to maintain a distance between the lake and itself.

The wingless Yech who had tumbled over the edge managed to hook his hand over the rim of the platform. The other Yech rushed to help, but his hand only managed to nudge the other farther out. The falling Yech let out a heartrending cry, which bordered between a wail and a desperate rasping as he plunged toward the calm lake waters.

The second Yech spread his wings and took to the air. But instead of diving to help his mate, he remained flapping his wings in the air, watching the waters curiously. More Yechs had now arrived on the platform to watch the drama. Thankfully, my scent was forgotten in the unfolding scene.

Before the first Yech's body could hit the waters, something sprang from the depths of the lake, caught the Yech, and dove back into the water. The surface of the lake smoothed immediately as if nothing had happened.

Whispering broke out among the Yechs on the platform. Would they remember they'd been chasing me? I was mulling this over when the door to the cave flew open and Gargouille strode out to survey the cliffside.

"What is this fracas? Don't you know there's a high-level meeting going on inside?" he barked at the gathered Yechs.

THE LEGEND OF TRIQUETRA

The Yech who had taken to the air was about to say something but appeared to change his mind and flew away, scratching his head. The crowded Yechs turned to leave, slipping over the edge and clambering to get away from Gargouille. I sneaked into the open door before Gargouille turned around.

I found myself in a corridor lit up by torches and lined with massive brass urns. I could hear voices up ahead. My back flattened against the wall, I advanced farther toward the voices when I heard the main door close.

Gargouille would be upon me in seconds. I jumped to reach the rim of a massive brass urn and slipped inside just in time as Gargouille strode past me.

After his heavy steps passed by, I tried to climb out, but my hands and feet found no purchase on the smooth insides of the jar. There was no other option but to silhouette.

With a quick prayer to the snake saints, I shut my eyes and snapped into my silhouette. Leaving my satchel and my clothes in the urn, I slithered up toward the voices and reached the room which could only be described as a large hollow space with cracks in its walls that served as windows.

I couldn't help but marvel at the girth of Kalpavriksha, which could afford such spacious living quarters for Rahu and his Yech. I heard an urgent knocking through the floor and realized with a start that the heels of Malini's pink peep-toe shoes were tapping in excitement, uncomfortably close to my head. She was sitting in a chair a hop away from me. It seemed like a cozy dining area. I counted four chairs placed around a table, but the occupants were hidden from my sight.

Dakini Malini cooed, "Let's uncover it already, dahlings!"

For a clearer view of the assembly, I searched the room for a vantage point. My sight landed on a bookshelf sunk in the shadows against the right wall. I slithered to the bookshelf without pausing to consider the folly of my actions. If I were discovered, it would mean the end of me and mankind.

What made me so bold?

Thanks to Naani's barbs, I had never before silhouetted without feeling like a victim. Today, silhouetting came to me like a spontaneous solution to a problem. It was a responsible decision and not one made on a whim to escape bullying or avoid socializing. My newfound confidence also had to do with the recent discovery of Anku's guilt, which lay buried under a cool and confident demeanor. I may not be as smart as her, but we weren't that different.

I lined myself just above the edge of the bookshelf and counted four people gawking at something covered with a red velvet cloth in the center of the table.

A man with no head sat on a chair opposite me. I waited for the head to pop out from within the shirt collars. Pretending to be headless by pulling up one's shirt was a trick that boys played on each other all the time at school.

But when the headless body spoke, I guessed that was all there was: a gaping cavity where the head and neck should have been attached to the body.

"Are we sure we want to do this, Rahu?" the headless man said. His voice came out like a blown speaker.

"It's time, Ketu," the man to the right of the headless body said. This man's head was bobbing up and down like a ball floating on water. He had thick curly hair and an ample mustache. His body was blocked from my view by Gargouille's massive form.

Naani had once narrated the story of the brothers Rahu and Ketu. I distinctly remembered it because Mohan had sat in Naani's lap as she told the story in great detail.

A demon once stole into the line of deities to receive a sip of amrit, the nectar of immortality. When Vishnu, the preserver, discovered the treachery, he used his chakra to slice off the demon's head but was unable to kill him because the effect of the nectar couldn't be reversed. It resulted in two separate entities. The body came to be called Ketu, the deity that brought sorrow and introspection. The head was called Rahu, the deity of disease and death.

"We've waited for hundreds of years for this moment," the bobbing head said. "I present to you the ring of Kundalini." He nodded at Ketu, who extended his hand to remove the red velvet kerchief.

In his hand, Ketu wore a black onyx ring. The piece of jewelry that Ketu uncovered glinted so brightly in the light of the fire torch that it momentarily blinded me.

When I recovered, I would have paused to study the reaction of the attendees were it not for the sheer beauty of the object on the table. A ring of breathtaking grace and unattainable perfection lay on the dirty wooden surface.

Dakini Malini exhaled. Rahu's head moved back from the light that the ring was casting on everything and everyone around it. I inched forward over the bookshelf to join in the scrutiny of the ring as the four participants, including the headless body, bent over the ornament.

Shaped like the Naga symbols on my amulet and my bag, this ring was only different in that it had seven serpent heads forming the crown of the ring. The bodies of the serpents merged into one band toward the lower shank. Crafted out of rose gold, it was set in diamonds with rubies as the eyes of the snake. The central snakehead was the largest.

So striking were the sculpted heads that it was easy to miss the tiny tail of the snake that ended well inside the central snake's mouth, held there tightly in place by fangs on either side.

"Our booty from the attack on the Naga clan years ago, delivered to me by my trusted servant, Gargouille," the bobbing head of Rahu said.

Gargouille preened while Malini flashed a conspiratorial smile at him.

"That fool Shesh could have saved the entire family by lending the ring for a day," Ketu spoke, startling everybody at the table.

Malini's elbows slid off the table. I couldn't blame her. The beauty of the ring created a trancelike state that was only broken by Ketu's blaring voice. It was weird to watch a headless body speak.

"Are you actually feeling bad for the Nagas?" Malini said, her voice laced with incredulity.

"It's all moot. Now that an heir has been found, the ring is ready to serve us," Rahu said.

I was the Naga heir, and I was presenting myself to them on a platter. I should have fled then and looked for Anku and Surp. But I couldn't tear my eyes from the ring.

A hypnotized Malini extended her hand to touch the ring just as a hammer landed on it, shattering it to smithereens. It was Ketu who had struck the ring with all his force.

I'm sure my snakehead jerked. But that was nothing compared to Dakini Malini's reaction.

"What have you done? Is this a joke? You've gone mad!" Malini screamed.

Her sharp canines glistened, and everything about her grew pointy, including her nails, teeth, and hair. Dark shadows appeared under her eyes, bat-like ears erupted on her temple, and her cheeks sank, leaving razor-sharp cheekbones over deep hollows.

"Are you out of your mind?" she hissed at Ketu, who still held the hammer in his hand. Gargouille jumped to catch hold of Malini's arms in case she launched an attack on Ketu.

I saw now what was making Rahu's head bob. A gush of dark smoke was keeping Rahu's head afloat. The smoke seemed to be emerging from his neck, but instead of spreading out, it stayed on as a thick column.

This was the man who had two Dakinis fighting for his affection? He didn't even have a body!

It's wrong to judge others without a look at oneself first, Naani's words rang in my head. Still, this was beyond weird.

"Stay calm, Malini. This was a mandatory test," Rahu said, his voice betraying a hint of rage.

"What do you mean?" Malini asked, starting to collect the shattered parts of the ring.

"As long as the spirit of Vasuki lives in it, the ring can't be destroyed. It took one blow to reduce it to this," Rahu said.

"We have been swindled."

"But Fangless confirmed this was the real ring," Malini said. Her optimism from a few moments ago had gone up in smoke. She was back to her sickening artificial self.

Rahu nodded. "Either he didn't know any better, or we underestimated his shrewdness." He turned to look at Ketu. "You didn't think of checking before letting Fangless go free?"

Ketu's headless form cowered. "Fangless is a wastrel, a milk snake without fangs or venom, an outcast in his own clan. He gains nothing from lying."

I wondered if Fangless had been born that way or if the fangs had been extracted.

"We should have crushed him when we had the chance," Malini hissed at Ketu, causing him to sink farther into his seat. "There's a reason anomalous silhouettes are squished as babies."

Dang, that was harsh. If that was indeed the way of Wantra, then by keeping us hidden, perhaps Naani had saved Mohan, who couldn't silhouette at all.

CHAPTER 16

As a twig snake, I was used to feeling inadequate and inferior. I often wondered if I'd be more confident had my silhouette been a cobra, a viper, or even a lazy python. But right now, I was just thankful that I had been born complete. It was hard to imagine the pitiful existence of a snake without its fangs.

Ketu's cowering form surfaced back into the circle of Boors as he readied to counter the collective badgering. "Fangless sent the boy to us. Why would he hide the truth about the ring?"

Batty had sent me for the delivery to Gargouille. Was Batty really Fangless, or did he work for Fangless?

"He wants us to kill the Naga boy so he can restore himself as the head of the Naga clan, you buffoon!" Malini screeched. "What use is the boy to us without the ring?"

"We will never know, will we? Since Gargouille let the boy escape," Ketu said, pointing at Gargouille.

"I would have caught him had you managed to keep that

nosey paladin, Madhav, and his mongrels out of my way," Gargouille said, standing up and leaning across the table toward Ketu. "You had to go and get chummy with the enemy."

"That's called spy work, and it requires diplomacy, of which you would know nothing," Ketu said, standing up abruptly and knocking over the stool on which he'd been sitting.

"Siiiiit dooooown!" Rahu roared. I caught a glimpse of curved canines and a vast expanse of tomato-red inside his mouth. "It doesn't matter who did what! Ketu is right. Why would Fangless send the only Naga heir to us? Fangless is a wastrel, and a wastrel can never be clan head. Even if he proclaims himself the Naga clan head, Swahalok will not accept him."

A knock sounded on the door. The company fell silent as a Yech shuffled in. His wings were crossed at the neck and covered his body like a shield. I froze when I saw the Yech's face. It had an uncanny likeness to the man whose mustache I had touched in the street of Chandni Chowk—the Yech that Anku had called Kabeela. Unlike the dumb zombie-like Yechs I had seen until now, Kabeela had intelligent amber eyes and an assured air about him.

"What was so important that it couldn't wait till after the meeting, Kabeela?" Rahu snapped.

"We apprehended someone near Hell's Retreat," Kabeela said, bowing slightly. He opened his wings, and the limp body of Thauma fell forward with a loud thud.

"Thauma!" Dakini cried.

"The Rocuja reported they saw him with the Naga Marut," Kabeela said, his eyes darting toward Dakini Malini.

"Never trust a magician!" Malini said, rolling her eyes.

"Thauma," Rahu said, addressing the magician. "Long time, no see. We believed you'd died in the attack on Haveli."

Thauma shook his head vigorously. "My lord, I was afraid I had failed you. But in truth, Shesh crossed me." He wheezed heavily from being cramped under Kabeela's wings. He knelt before Rahu and placed his forehead on the floor. "You know what deceit Nagas are capable of."

"What made you think it would be safe now to prowl around my territory?" Rahu asked. There was a hint of amusement in his voice. "You better have a good reason. Magicians are a rare meal for Yechs nowadays."

Thauma squirmed, his eyes darting here and there from the effort of concocting a reason. Unless Rahu was looking for a smuggled celestial artifact, Thauma was done for.

Slowly, Thauma's self-assurance returned, and he lifted his head, moving his hair away from his forehead. "I, er, I was on my way to meet you, actually. It's true that I met the Naga Marut on my way."

"I told you," Malini screamed. She rose with her hands stretched toward Thauma's throat. Gargouille and Ketu held her back and made her sit down.

"I followed the Naga Marut, as I was curious to know what he was doing here," Thauma said. "How could Manasa have been so careless as to let the sole Naga heir out of her sight?" Thauma shrugged Kabeela's hands off his shoulder and got up to stand. He stepped closer to the table. "The reason Manasa has sent him, my lord, is because there's another boy."

A loud collective gasp from Gargouille, Malini, and Ketu caused Thauma to smile. "This boy is not the sole heir, my lord. He has a younger brother. And if I know Manasa well, she is protecting that child."

After a heavy silence, Rahu said, "Is this true? Is there another child?"

A flustered Gargouille mumbled inaudibly.

"Are you saying no one cared to check where the Naga Marut lives, whether he has any siblings?" Rahu said, his voice snippy.

"The boy goes by a different surname than his forefathers in Samsara," Gargouille squeaked defensively.

"Or were you scared of running into Manasa?" Ketu asked, jumping on the opportunity to score points with Rahu by putting Gargouille down.

No one said anything for a while. Finally, Rahu said, "Thauma will be our esteemed guest until the blue blood moon."

"Please, my lord," Thauma said, his tone changing from a self-assured purr to a bleat in a second.

"What about the boy, sir? Should we keep searching for him?" Kabeela asked.

"If Manasa sent the boy by mistake, she would have torn Kalpavriksha down by now. The fact that she hasn't come looking for him shows Thauma may be right in assuming this boy is a decoy and of no use to us, perhaps even a wastrel. If you come across him, kill him. There will be other Nagas in the future. Don't waste precious time looking for him."

I retreated from the edge of the bookshelf. This was heavy stuff. I had always felt hurt by Naani's indifference toward me, but I secretly hoped it was tough love, that she truly cared for me. That sliver of hope went up in a poof. Even Rahu thought Naani had used me as bait.

What hurt more was that Naani was doing all of this to save Mohan over me. The only silver lining in the cloud of my gloom was that the Yechs would not be chasing me anymore. Over the years, I'd grown used to being overlooked, and it corroded my self-esteem. But this was the first time that being dismissed felt like a blessing.

I overheard a flurry of movement around the table. As soon as Kabeela left with a protesting Thauma, Rahu turned to Dakini Malini. "Is Surpanekha's daughter ready to talk?"

"She will be, once she's had a taste of this," Malini said.

For a better view of the table, I retook my position by the edge of the bookshelf so that my body merged into the beveling. Malini placed a small vial with a polka-dotted ribbon on the table. It was the same vial she had shown Surpanekha.

"It's ready, then?" Rahu said in an even tone. Malini could hardly contain her glee, and Rahu seemed incapable of expressing joy. When all you've got is death and disease to dish out, I guess being happy doesn't come easily.

"This is the silhouette essence shorn off the Maruts. Mixed with Daitya bile, when fed to humans and Maruts, it will turn them all into Boors," Malini said, gloating while Gargouille beamed at her with pride and Rahu nodded, satisfied.

"I have cylinders of this concoction ready in vapor form. Venomous Vapors or Venvap will be the most noxious substance ever created, the worst kind of disease humans have ever seen. More potent than anything Brahma ever created. All beings will be powerless in its grip," Malini said dramatically.

"Humans will get a taste of Boorlok, one way or the other."

Gargouille picked up the tiny vial and held it up to his amber eyes. "Maruts will help us in wiping out the human race. Who would have thought?"

"By tomorrow, Venvap will achieve its maximum potency when I add a lion silhouette's essence. Nabbed him and a couple of other Maruts two days ago," Malini said.

"You have Rudra in your captivity?" Ketu asked, a hint of alarm in his voice.

"Betrayed by his own kind," Malini said, exchanging a sly smile with Gargouille. Rahu nodded in appreciation. If Maruts had started helping the Boors, then Mothy Maddy and his band of Maruts were fighting a lost battle.

"And you are holding Rudra and Surp together?" Ketu said. "They have both attained the Vibhaga. Their warrior silhouettes are too powerful even for the celestials."

"I can vouch for that," Gargouille said. I recalled the night of delivery when Surp, in the form of a giant koel, had slashed at Gargouille with her razor-sharp wings. Gargouille realized he'd placed his foot in his mouth by drawing everybody's attention to his failed mission. "It's just as well," he added. "Surp will join Dakini ranks eventually, given her mother is a Dakini."

There was a general hum of agreement.

"But together, they can ruin our plan," Ketu said.

"They're not together," Malini said, putting up her hand to pacify Ketu.

Ketu waited for her to reveal where she was holding Surp and Rudra, but Malini studied her fingernails.

A gasp echoed from within Ketu's hollow neck. "You are

holding her in the Maw!" he bellowed. "It's against the rules. If she dies, Indra will get yet another excuse to evict us. First Swahalok, now Kalpavriksha—"

"Indra can't lay a finger on us," Rahu said, cutting his brother off mid-sentence. His statement was met with silence.

"Indra may be a fallen deity, but he can still garner an army of devas in Swahalok, brother," Ketu said.

"But he won't. Would you like to know why?"

His three lieutenants looked on, at a loss for words.

"It's true that this ring is not the ring of Kundalini. Shesh Nagaraj must have created a new home for the spirit of Vasuki. But the celestials don't know that. They still think we possess the ring."

A momentary silence was followed by Dakini Malini repeating, "They think we have the ring." Her face lit up as the truth dawned on her. Honestly, I was a bit surprised it took her so long to catch on, given her penchant for vileness.

Rahu nodded. "But we need to move fast," he said brusquely. "If we don't have the ring, it is still out there somewhere. The day they discover it, we lose our advantage."

The three attendees nodded.

"Gargouille, get Manasa's location," Rahu said. "Find the boy she's been hiding from us and bring him to the sacrificial altar this blue blood moon. Torture Fangless if you must."

Gargouille saluted in reply.

"Malini, Plan Venvap must be on standby. Warn Dakini Chayya to get her army of Dakinis ready to take on Swahalok's army of Apsara sleuths if it comes to that." Rahu turned slowly toward Ketu, his body half. "Send word to Madhav that we have his Marut girls and if he as much as steps near the altar, the girls will be fed to the Panish. I don't want the sacrificial altar hampered by the police."

"But it will blow my cover," Ketu protested. "It's taken me so long to gain Madhav's trust."

Rahu sighed. "It's time to let go of them, Ketu." The softness of his voice made my scaly skin crawl. "It's time to avenge the injustice done to our people, the Daityas, Rakshasas, and Asuras."

"Hear, hear!" Gargouille cried, and Dakini Malini thumped the table lightly with both hands.

After Gargouille and Malini left, Ketu got up to leave. I was petrified of being left alone with Rahu. I would have to plan my exit in such a way that when Ketu left, I would leave too, or at least get away from Rahu's sight.

I slithered down the rack, sure I wouldn't be able to make it in time without being spotted. Thankfully, Rahu called after Ketu. "Brother, you have changed."

Ketu stopped in his tracks and said, "Do we need to annihilate? I just wonder if there is any other way."

"We were one once. Together, my head and your heart decided that we deserved a drop of amrit. We worked so hard for it," Rahu said with a hint of desperation, like someone who is tired of reminding.

I reached the bottom of the bookcase. Ketu returned to sit down slowly on the chair Gargouille had vacated. If I moved now, they would see me. Even though Ketu's back was toward me, Rahu faced the entrance.

"Do you remember how they dumped us outside Swahalok

like garbage? We were not even given a funeral," Rahu said. He turned his back to Ketu. A cloud of smoke billowed under Rahu's head as it rose in the air. "Daityas, Rakshasas, and the Asuras were all abandoned after the devas received immortality. We were duped into believing we mattered."

He waited for Ketu to speak, but Ketu sat quietly, enveloped by the billowing smoke, which seemed to anger Rahu. His face twitched in indignation.

"You have lived with humans for too long," Rahu said. "Perhaps it's time to refresh your memory?" Even though his voice was contained, immense anger was palpable under the surface. "The Boors from Boorlok helped the devas from Swahalok to churn the ocean and attain amrit, the elixir of immortality. The devas never intended to share the elixir with us. And they punished the only Boor who demanded his share, by mercilessly chopping him into two."

This tale was common knowledge. The gods had fleeced the Boors. What surprised me was that the devas were naive enough to believe the Boors would forget the treatment meted out to them.

"Why must humans pay the price?" Ketu asked, his voice sounding like a faint echo in a well.

Rahu's head was floating so high now that I could easily move across the floor under the thick blanket of smoke. I made a dash for the first urn.

"Humans will not pay the price," Rahu said. He was towering over Ketu now. "Humans have moved closer to our ways. They are far from being Brahma's authentic creation. They are more Boor than Boors themselves. Greed and brutality run through their veins. They are ready to be led by an able leader. Someone who can harness their wickedness. We will release them from notions of right and wrong."

It was hard to imagine that the soppy Ketu and the cold, calculating Rahu had at one time been one person.

Rahu's eyes closed. His canines came to rest on both sides of his chin. "Our bodies will then be whole again. With Chayya beside us, we will rule the three worlds. The ring of Kundalini will reset the wheel of time. Darkness and disease will absorb all living forms. The gods will rue the day they deceived us." With these words, he seemed to enter a trance.

I couldn't tell if Ketu was heartened by Rahu's pep talk or frightened because he got up and marched outside with determination. Smoke was billowing up in waves in Rahu's chamber.

There was no time to get my clothes or my bag from the urn. I cursed Naani for not training me in silhouetting with clothes as I slithered out of the door in Ketu's wake.

Perhaps it would be easier to move through Kalpavriksha in my silhouette. Dakini Malini was holding Surp in a place called the Maw. It sounded ominous, but I couldn't think of a reason not to head straight there to rescue her.

The platform outside Rahu's den had turned into a stage for Gargouille. He stood facing the vast network of bony roads below and all around the machan, every inch occupied by Yechs. They had climbed onto one another's shoulders for the lack of space to stand. Some hung upside down from the tree branches like bats just for a better view of their leader.

Unaffected by the heaving collection of Yechs, Ketu cut through them, striding across the wet, slippery, bony floor. He bounded down the steps and disappeared into the darkness beyond. If I followed him in my silhouette, I would get trampled. I waited.

Buried within the din of rasping, there were ominous hisses. I glanced up. Like the concave walls of an auditorium, the Rocuja now covered the platform from all sides except the lake. The anacondas swayed restlessly as they waited for Gargouille to speak.

To the left of Gargouille, a huddle of women in black figure-hugging suits, high boots, and capes listened intently to what he had to say. They looked like a squad of commandos. I wondered why Gargouille hadn't brought these soldiers with him in place of the Yechs the night of the delivery.

Gargouille raised his hand. It was funny how his feet were still panther paws, but his hands, even with claws, looked human. "The time has come for us to take what is rightfully ours," he said. "My fellow Boors, you sold your soul to darkness to live forever, and Rahu promised you immortality. The day has come for the promise to be fulfilled."

The Yechs emitted a spine-chilling cheer.

"We are joined today by the special forces from Boorlok. The Dakinis, led by Dakini Chayya, will help us with our mission."

I heard panting, grunting, and even hooting from the Yechs.

"I invite Dakini Chayya to say a few words of encouragement," Gargouille said.

One of the women walked gracefully to the platform to

stand next to Gargouille. Dakini Chayya moved her fountain-like ponytail off her shoulder and raised her chin.

"They murdered our children," she said. "They will pay for their heartlessness."

This was new. I realized there was a complete absence of children in Kalpavriksha.

In response, the Yechs cackled and Gargouille roared, bringing more Yechs streaming out of their cubbies and shadows. Gargouille raised his hand, and the crowd fell silent. Wherever my eyes turned, I saw Yechs. Not a leaf stirred, as if nature itself had grown wary of this foul assembly.

A Yech scrambled up to the platform. He was holding something in his hand. Gargouille snatched it from the Yech's hand and held it up. It was a chameleon that looked uncannily like Patches. My heart skipped a beat.

I'd stayed back in Wantra to find Patches and bring him home. Perhaps this was some other chameleon, but my inner alarm bells rang ever so loudly with Gargouille's next words.

"Finally, the Naga clan will be wiped out this blood moon. We celebrate with a traditional offering to the Panish." Gargouille raised his hand and hovered it out over the lake. "All Marut clans will bear our wrath," he said, punching the hand that held the chameleon in the air.

I couldn't bear to witness the scene. I was tempted to slither closer to Gargouille's foot and break my silhouette right there. I could then call for Vasuki, and if Kaleeni didn't appear, I would push Gargouille into the Panish to end it all. Even if they caught me, I would save Patches. But then I remembered Rahu's interest in Mohan, the real Naga heir, my brother. If I had any chance of warning Mohan, it was by keeping a lid on my emotions and remaining in my silhouette. I reared into the mulch that lined Rahu's cave.

"Rahu Amavasya, Rahu Amavasya," Kabeela started chanting, and the audience joined in. The Panish, the terrifying mermaid-like creatures from the lake, began a frightening dance, leaping up, plucking Yechs off the branches, and landing back in the lake like trained dolphins at a theme park. When a Yech slipped, no effort was made to save it from these monsters.

"Let Panish and Boor unite," Gargouille cried and flung Patches into the air.

Two Panish leaped up and snapped Patches in two as I watched helplessly. It felt like someone had gripped my heart and squeezed it dry.

A huge cheer went through the Yechs.

I know snakes are incapable of crying, but being in silhouette didn't stop me from feeling immense sadness, like a boulder had landed on my heart. I stood frozen, staring at the spot where Patches had been snipped into pieces.

By and by, I came to my senses. I had to save Mohan, or I would never be able to forgive myself for allowing Patches to be murdered.

Rahu's lieutenants would soon get busy with their duties. Thankfully, Batty had not yet shared my address with Gargouille. Unless they dug out our address from the records kept at school, they'd have to first find Batty, or the guy they referred to as Fangless, if they wanted to get to Mohan.

I realized I was stuck between Rahu's den behind me and Gargouille's audience all around me. There was no exit out of the place unless I waited for everyone to leave. The dull brown and gray skin of my silhouette would keep me safe from being discovered. A saving grace for twig snakes. A cobra would have failed in this feat.

As I coiled up to wait under the weight of intense grief, suddenly everything went dark around me. Even though I was startled, I could still breathe, and I smelled damp wicker. The feeling was familiar. This was what being trapped in a wicker basket felt like.

The world grew topsy-turvy as my body was scooped up and placed in soft folds of silk in a wicker basket. Someone had captured me! Rahu's instructions were to kill me, and I went on to play hide and seek with his Yech. It was a matter of time before I got trapped by one of them. Though one would hardly expect a Yech to carry around a silk-lined basket, let alone have the sensitivity to hold a snake in it, I thrashed around in an effort to break free, enough to shake the basket.

"Hold on, Adi," I heard Anku's sharp voice say.

I ceased the struggle in relief. Of course, it had to be her. Only Anku would be bold enough to trap a silhouette with such impunity.

CHAPTER 17

My body jostled as Anku started to walk. Getting cooped up in the tokri had cut off the deafening screeches and squawks of the Yechs and the loud splashes of the Panish. I felt safe.

I was glad Anku had found me, from the bottom of my heart I was. But my mind was busy weighing the possible outcomes of staying in silhouette for the rest of my visit to Kalpavriksha. I had left my clothes in Rahu's cave, and there was no way I would silhouette back without my clothes around.

"Behind that wall," I heard a familiar voice say, which was not Anku.

I felt the basket being let down gently, and the lid was lifted. Anku's eyes looked even larger as they stared down at me. "You are a cute little twig snake," she said.

Cute? She knew that would irk me. I cursed my silhouette. I would have preferred if Anku were a little frightened by it. Generally, if humans saw me in silhouette, they would scream and run away. That felt far better for my self-esteem than being called "cute" by Anku.

She extended her hands toward me. I froze. Except for Naani, no one had ever handled me while I was in silhouette form. I felt vulnerable and naked. If a twig snake were capable of blushing, I would have turned dark purple when Anku's hands touched me. Thankfully, I remained the dull gray-and-brown color of stone and earth.

Anku placed me on a pile of clothes and stepped out of sight. I sniffed and flicked my tongue to catch the scent. These were my clothes. How had she managed to find them? I quickly popped out of my silhouette and got dressed.

Only after did I look around to get my bearings. I was in a den similar to Hell's Retreat, lit by a sole lantern. I was standing next to a dining table. Laying on the table was my satchel. I flung it across my body. That I had got my clothes and satchel back was nothing short of miraculous.

I heard voices beyond a makeshift wall fashioned from a sharp projection in the tree's bark.

"He's different," Anku said as if trying to reassure someone.

I stepped around the wall to find Anku and Dakini Surpanekha seated on stools around a low table. They looked up at me.

Before Anku could say anything, I said, "Patches is dead. The deal is off. I must return home."

I didn't tell her about Mohan being in danger. I had already risked his safety by talking to Thauma about him. I decided to keep mum about my younger brother, just like Naani had instructed me ten years ago. It was bad enough that Patches, my companion of ten years, had paid with his life for my oversight.

I could hardly contain the tears threatening to burst from my eyes, but I bit them back. I had never cried in front of anyone. And I would never give Anku the satisfaction of watching me howl.

"Your chameleon is not dead," Surpanekha said, bringing her arm forward. There, clinging to her arm, was Patches, looking leaner but otherwise healthy. His tail was wound around Surpanekha's wrist.

"This is not possible. I saw with my own eyes when Gargouille—" I began.

"That was not your chameleon," Surpanekha said with a sigh. "This guy must have been following you around, for I found him just outside Dakini Malini's den."

I placed my palm next to Surpanekha's arm for Patches to scurry on. I counted the reddish spots on his throat to check if it really was him. His eyeballs rotated independently of each other, a sign of his happiness at seeing me. For one of the most unsocial species, Patches was a rather affectionate chameleon.

His cold body moving on my skin was the most comforting feeling I'd experienced that day. Unbidden tears rolled down my cheeks as I touched the tip of my forefinger to Patches' forehead.

I was surprised when my stomach growled. Released from tension and despair, it suddenly discovered how starved it was.

"So did you find out anything about Surp?" Anku asked, extending her hand for Patches to hop on.

I reluctantly let him climb onto her hand and kept a watchful eye as Anku softly rubbed Patches' forehead with the tip of her finger. With Anku's cat silhouette, I had to be careful about letting Patches loose around her.

Once I was sure Anku had no plans to eat Patches, I turned to look at Surpanekha. "Malini is holding her in the Maw."

Surpanekha let out a moan.

Anku stopped stroking Patches, and a look of horror and fear moved across her face. "The forest of vampire trees?" she said, turning toward Surpanekha.

"Yes. It's the rotting limb of Kalpavriksha," a stunned Surpanekha whispered. "The part of nature itself that has turned Boor. Swahalok managed to contain the damage, and Indra decreed that the Maw be left alone. He forbade the residents of Kalpavriksha from feeding the Maw. He said that if we broke the agreement, we would be banished from Kalpavriksha."

"Dakini Malini didn't seem to care much for the agreement," I said.

"Of course she doesn't. She'd rather have the Maw spread on Kalpavriksha like a blight. It will become Boor territory then."

"But if the Maw is not being fed," I said, using Surpanekha's own words because I still couldn't picture trees butchering and eating people or animals, "it must be feeble or maybe dead?"

"Or hungrier and more savage than ever," Surpanekha said, her eyes large with worry for her daughter.

"Then we must leave for there immediately," Anku said. She put Patches back on the table, straightened her backpack, and brushed her clothes as if that was all the preparation required to fight a forest filled with flesh-eating trees.

I didn't move. I needed some time to consider my next steps. Surpanekha's manner changed as she smirked at me.

"Changed your mind about helping the girls, have you?" She turned meaningfully toward Anku as if to say, "I told you so."

I realized what was going on, why Anku had been talking me up to Surpanekha before. Surpanekha expected me to back out of the fight because I was a Naga.

I didn't answer. Perhaps Surpanekha was right. While I didn't care what a Naga would do in such a situation, I knew what *I* had to do. Rahu planned to capture Mohan, and I had to warn Mohan or Naani about it. Still, just the tiniest part of me wanted to let events unfold to see if Naani and Mohan got their comeuppance.

I felt a soft prickle of Patches' movement. He had crept close to me. His skin, generally a happy green in color, had turned many shades darker, which was a reflection of stress or anger. He had a knack for reading my moods and communicating his own opinion this way. I lowered my gaze in shame. How could I hope for my brother to be hurt? Then it came to me. My ill wishes weren't meant for my brother. It was Naani's heart I wanted broken, the same way she had broken mine. My resentment toward Mohan came from Naani's indulgence in him. He didn't deserve my hatred. And I would go back for him, not Naani.

I also figured that I hadn't seen any exit signs in Kalpavriksha. If I lost my way here, I would never be able to warn Mohan. The fastest way home would be to first rescue Surp. And it wouldn't hurt to have her see me as a hero.

I nodded to Anku, which got her beaming. But Surpanekha kept looking at me with an arched brow.

"I don't believe him," Surpanekha said. "You can't trust a

Naga. He will betray us at the first opportunity just like Shesh and Manasa did."

"I told you. He is nothing like them," Anku said in desperation. You might think Anku was being magnanimous or appreciative, but her suggestive tone was downright insulting. She may as well have said, "Oh, we thought we had chanced upon a Naga Marut too, but who knew he would turn out to be a wuss?"

"Give me one reason why I shouldn't hand you over to Rahu and ask for Surp's freedom in return?" Surpanekha asked me.

"Because I am of no use to Rahu anymore. The ring Rahu had was not the ring of Kundalini. It was a fake." My words drew a gasp from both Anku and Surpanekha.

I placed Patches carefully into my satchel. Outside his vivarium at home, my bag was the only place he would be most relaxed. Then I recounted what I saw and heard in Rahu's lair, leaving out parts that concerned Mohan.

I finished my story with, "They believe there's another heir, the real heir. Gargouille has left to look for Fangless to get to this boy. And Dakini Malini is making final preparations to get Venvap ready for deployment."

Anku tapped her chin with her forefinger. "Fangless always accompanies this Marut social worker, Mrs. M, who helps out Mothy Maddy with new recruits. Fangless could have told Dakini about Rudra's plan to visit the zoo."

Surpanekha narrowed her eyes. She walked toward the full-length open window behind the dining room, similar to Dakini Malini's den. The sky was studded with stars, and the moon was getting plumper.

I studied Surpanekha's den. Like Malini's den, it had an exit at the back. But unlike the fancy interiors of Malini's den, Surpanekha's den was bare. In addition to a traditional handwoven floor dhurrie rug, it had floor cushions, stools, and a low table. A spiral staircase led to another floor above. A picture of a child standing between her parents sat on a dresser. Surp and Surpanekha looked happy in the picture. Surpanekha's face shone from the joys of a loving family life, unlike the hangdog expression she wore at the moment.

Surpanekha walked back to where we sat. "If he doesn't have the ring anymore, then why does he still want a Naga heir at the altar? It doesn't make sense."

I hadn't thought of that. "Rahu seemed calm. When the ring shattered, he didn't react," I said. I took special note of that because I would have been hopping mad if I were Rahu.

"That is not normal. Something is not right," Surpanekha said and started pacing the branch. "I need to find out what he's up to."

"But Surp…" Anku said.

Surpanekha shook her head. "There's not much we can do right now to help Surp. The Maw will be crawling with Chamruks at night. It's best if you spend the night here. We will leave early morning."

After feeding us a dinner that consisted of hurriedly made wraps and hibiscus soda, Surpanekha led Anku to the floor above the den. She gave me a blanket and asked me to grab the dhurrie to sleep.

Later that night, Surpanekha called Anku and me to the

table and told us, "I have an important matter to attend to."

As we waited at the table for her, Surpanekha threw on a hooded cape and moved before a small mirror similar to the one back at the shivir. As I recalled, the mirror was called Ichcha Darpan, literally a wishing mirror, though the only wish it granted was the ability to spy on others with remote binoculars.

We sat still as Dakini Malini's terrifying face appeared in the Ichcha Darpan. She was standing before a bird cage with a raven inside. Malini was laughing loudly, and the raven was cawing plaintively.

"I'm afraid I might already be too late," Surpanekha said and wheeled around to face us. "If I don't return by the morning, you must head to the Maw yourself. Turn right when you exit my den. Follow the northwest path, past the Shani Nandana and Glitch Grotto. You will begin to smell the Maw."

"What kind of smell?" Anku asked.

Surpanekha drummed her fingers on her chin. "Imagine the foul odor of your neighborhood garbage dump. Add to that the stench of rotting carcasses, stink from the sewage pipes, a laundry basket full of smelly socks, and…"

"Alright, alright, we get it," I said, throwing an anxious look Anku's way. "We must be ready to smell the vilest odor ever."

Anku nervously tucked a strand of hair behind her ear.

"You must be alert," Surpanekha said. "The Maw may smell of death, but it's the land of the living dead."

"You mean the Chamruks?" Anku asked.

Surpanekha nodded. "Chamruks are the disgruntled, maimed nature spirits that take refuge in the Maw. Rampant massacre of trees, contaminated waters, and toxic soil have tampered with the very fabric of nature. It has turned on itself."

"What do you mean by 'turned on itself'?" I asked. Naani said that nature was regenerative. It was the only constant before and after death. How could it destroy itself?

"When you see a tree stump sucking the life out of a sapling, you'll know what I'm talking about," Surpanekha said. "Chamruks don't spare any living creature, whether it has sap or blood. Even Rahu thinks twice before sending Yechs down in the Maw."

A loud screech from the mirror made me nearly jump out of my skin. Dakini Malini was poking at the raven through the bars of the cage with a glinting sword.

Surpanekha swore under her breath and turned to us, speaking rapidly. "Every day, one element of nature is exempted from being devoured by the Chamruks. It could be stones, grass, branches… or pebbles. No one knows of this outside the Maw. You must discover this element once you are inside."

I tried to gulp down the tightness in my throat but couldn't. The saliva dried up before it reached the knot.

"Remember, the deader a tree looks, the more savage it will be. In the Maw, a tree never dies. It lives in pain and suffering." She tied a scabbard around her waist. "Leave early. It's at least a day's journey to the Maw on foot. You should get in and out of there before the mist settles."

"But where do we look for Surp?" I asked. My heart hammered at the very thought of entering the Maw.

"Once you reach the Maw, look for a huddle of dead trees.

The Chamruks would have crowded around a dungeon. That's where Malini will be holding Surp." Surpanekha walked toward the door-length gap at the far back side of the den.

Surp was surrounded by blood-sucking trees, in a dungeon, no less. "How do we know if she will survive the night?" I said to Surpanekha's back.

She sighed deeply. "Malini will be banished from the sisterhood of Dakinis if she harms as much as a hair on Surp's head." She paused to think and added, "But if she becomes Rahu's queen, we're all doomed. In absence of the ring of Kundalini, Malini's toxic creation is an invaluable weapon for Rahu in his plan to nab power in Samsara. Malini knows this and won't hesitate to eliminate competition. Rahu's motives have a backstory, but Malini's ambition is pure evil. She can't be allowed to prevail." With these words, she exited her den.

We followed her to the edge and peered over. It was a sheer drop, the bottom invisible from where we stood. Surpanekha had walked out effortlessly. My head reeled from the vertiginous precipice. Anku placed a hand on my shoulder and pulled me back.

"At least no one can easily climb in," I said with a grin. I was still dizzy, and Anku was aware of it. I didn't want her to think I was soft.

Anku nodded. We sat down on the dhurrie, our backs against the rough and poky wall.

Before long, I heard light snoring. She had fallen asleep, her arms around her bag. I extended my blanket to cover her from the cold night breeze.

I drifted to sleep, wondering what could be more important

for Surpanekha than saving her daughter. Was she aware that Surp had been fatally injured before she was captured by Dakini Malini?

I woke to the cooing of the koels. Anku and I had our heads together. Sunlight glinted off Anku's nose ring and glasses. I shook her gently to wake her.

Surpanekha had not returned yet. We washed up, ate a hurried breakfast, and left the den.

A few minutes into the walk up a steep path, I wished I still had Kaleeni. We could have simply flown to the Maw, but that was a sore topic both Anku and I avoided as we began our journey. I noticed that this part of the Kalpavriksha was pristine. The crisp morning air and a full belly cleared my head.

I had never been so sure of myself. Everything that my eyes fell on seemed brighter, as if touched by optimism, a sentiment I'd never felt before. Patches was curled up in my satchel, fast asleep.

I tried not thinking about Surp being surrounded by Chamruks, and I hoped Naani's layers of protection around Mohan were still in place. I hoped to rescue Surp and be back home by the evening.

Walking on branches was like hiking on a narrow trail in a mountain forest. The branches of Kalpavriksha crisscrossed all around us. Like on a mountain, life grew sparser as we climbed higher.

After trudging for an hour or so, we found ourselves before an arched gate. The arch was covered by pink rose bushes. A fence ran around both sides of the arch. Etched on the gate pillar was a sign that was so faint that if Anku hadn't drawn my attention to it, I might have missed it: Shani Nandana.

I detected an insignia under the name. Three petals held together by a loop. I traced the loop with my finger. I had seen the insignia in Anku's book, *The Wrath of Shani*, and again etched on a stone at Haveli. Anku's eyes followed my hand.

"The Srivatsa," she remarked. "It's closely linked to the Nagas."

"Never heard of it," I said. Up until yesterday, I didn't even know I was a Naga.

"The three corners of the triquetra," Anku said, tapping on the petals of the flower, "represent birth, death, and renewal. The loop running through the petals is the ancient snake spirit, Vasuki's body tying everything in a cyclical loop, the ring of Kundalini."

She ran her finger all along the circle till she reached the snake's head.

"They say Vasuki was one of the fire dragons of the east, and Nagas are his line. Clearly, these are just tales," she said cheekily, referring to my twig snake silhouette. Just above Vasuki's head, she dusted the etching to find a diamond-shaped dot. "The Nagamani stands for nirvana."

"But why does Shani's garden carry this mark?"

"Because of his brand of justice. Based on an individual's karma, he decides who gets to enjoy the circle of life and death."

"If Shani decides everything, why does Rahu want the ring of Kundalini?"

"The ring decides who gets to be reborn. It's like picking roses over chrysanthemums or cacti to grow in one's garden. But Shani decides each individual's fate within the circle."

I was set to suffer at Shani's hands for the deeds of my ancestor. Did she know his justice extended to innocent family members too?

"The Gandaks at the lamppost used the triquetra to snatch the identities of humans," I observed.

"Those are cheap lookalikes that you can buy in any store in Amravati. The identity theft is short-term and lasts for a few hours. The original triquetra erases the identity permanently. It's a powerful weapon. One loses any sense of purpose in life. I've heard that some pure Maruts feared the triquetra so much that they surrendered their silhouettes using a ritual called Chalvesha."

We peeked into the garden, which was nothing less than an advertisement for a resort. We saw charming koi ponds, snow-white swans, spotted deer with coats that shone in the sunlight, and a mind-numbing variety of flowers. A cobbled path through the ponds and the flowerbeds ran toward a grove of trees. It was like watching a dreamy landscape through a bioscope.

"Do you think Shani actually lives here?" I asked.

Anku nodded but pursed her lips glumly.

"Is anything the matter?" I asked.

Given that she adored Shani, one would expect her to be happy to see Shani's garden. But she remained as unpredictable as ever. "It's just…" She paused. "This place looks too fancy for him."

"He is the deity who brings misfortune to others. If he doesn't live in luxury, who will?" I posed.

An image of Rahu and his dank, bare den came to my mind. His head and body lived separate lives. That was no life for a god.

Suddenly, a crow flew out over the gate and perched on the wall's pillar.

"Kaga," Anku whispered.

Kaga was Shani's animal ride. I had seen Naani break into a sweat every time a crow sat on our balcony. Anku extended her hand to pet the crow. The crow cocked its head, its black beady eye seemingly fixed on me.

Shani has it in for you, Naani's voice resounded in my head.

I backed off and reminded Anku that Dakini Malini could be headed for the Maw that very second. She stepped away reluctantly.

"Do you think Shani is helping Rahu?" I asked once we had walked some distance from Shani Nandana. Knowing that Anku was an ardent admirer of Shani, I was ready for a sharp retort.

"Shani's justice is the touchstone of karma. He is highly misunderstood. He would never stoop to Rahu's level," Anku snapped.

If it were a question of karmic justice, then Rahu had a good reason to get back at the celestials. Not only had the celestials hogged the nectar of immortality, they had also beheaded the demon who got a sip of the nectar he'd rightfully earned with the rest of the Boors. Why didn't celestials answer to the rule of karma?

Thinking about Rahu and Ketu in this light rendered them less frightening. Naani believed that empathy should not be confused with weakness. "Ayesha Saini comes from a broken family. Her frustration takes the shape of bullying," she had said, hoping the information would humanize Ayesha in my eyes and make me less frightened of her. But it hadn't worked. Ayesha Saini was brazen in her attempts to belittle me. I hated her with vehemence and avoided any interaction with her.

"Isn't it strange that he chooses to live in Kalpavriksha, possibly the vilest neighborhood in the celestial world?" I asked, teetering dangerously close to a full-blown showdown with Anku.

"Rahu forced his way into Kalpavriksha. Shani did not choose Rahu to be his neighbor."

I held up my hands in a truce. "Why do you like Shani so much?"

"Unlike Yama, the god of death, who brings human souls to Hell for their actions, Shani provides learning opportunities to humans while they're alive. He is a Marut's friend."

He had been no friend to me. But there was no arguing with Anku, so I changed the subject to life with Mothy Maddy.

"Mothy Maddy teaches us ways to silhouette properly, wield the challastra, achieve Vibhaga, and fight human goons and the Yechs."

I realized that everything that Anku and Surp were learning was specific to their purpose in life. I wished I had been left under Mothy Maddy's care. I asked Anku about Surp and how the daughter of a Dakini had ended up under the bridge.

"Surp's father was a Marut who married Surpanekha against

his family's wishes. When he died, Surpanekha couldn't stand the social ridicule. She wanted to bring Surp to Boorlok, but Surp refused."

"Has Surpanekha ever gotten in touch with Surp?"

Anku shook her head. "I'm sure Mothy Maddy stays in touch with Surpanekha, though he denies it."

We stopped for lunch. Anku had packed some fruit, vegetable chips, and juice cartons.

"Why do you call Madhav 'Mothy Maddy'?" I asked, biting into a juicy peach.

Anku giggled, lifting her shoulders. "Maddy is a paladin. Mothballs mask the smell of paladins from the Yechs, so he keeps mothballs with him at all times."

"Paladin?" I'd heard the word before. "Are paladins Maruts?"

"In a way," Anku said. "No one knows where in the universe they came from."

"You mean he's an alien?"

Anku shrugged. "Does it matter? Mothy Maddy, Pilot Roy, and Red, who runs a restaurant, are the nicest, kindest paladins I've ever met."

Our path took a steep downturn. We seemed to be leaving tree terrain behind. Our next milestone, Glitch Grotto, was a valley made of grassy knolls that mushroomed all over the ground like some sort of skin disease on the earth's surface. At certain spots, three or four mounds huddled, but there was an equal number of solo ones in all sizes. The area had no gates or walls to keep out the intruders. Still, I got a feeling it was not as welcoming as it looked. There were small vents on either side of the mounds. Some of these vents were open, letting out ripples of smoke that carried yummy aromas.

"What kind of monsters do you suppose live here?" I asked Anku.

"Glitches are perfectionists, and some say they're prone to rage episodes. Though I've seen much angrier humans than Chinni. It took a few centuries for her to understand that she could fight her impulses."

Chinni was a Glitch! That was why she became upset with me for using the word.

"Anyway, Glitches use temper tantrums to attract attention. It's best to not engage with them."

Before I could tell her how outrageous the label "Glitch" sounded, we turned to a sharp voice behind us. "I can give you a tour if you like."

A smallish creature who looked a lot like Chinni stood peering at us. He was almost entirely squirrel with a twitchy nose, long-lashed eyes, and a bushy tail. His arms and legs were human, and he had long pointy ears like a rabbit's. He was different from Chinni only in that his skin had a tinge of green. He flashed a friendly smile. He didn't look dangerous in any way.

Dressed in a plaid shirt over a t-shirt and long shorts, he seemed about the same age as me. A tattoo of a bull, which looked like Shiva's Nandi, was etched on his arm, and he had an untidy mohawk.

"I am Ludo," the boy said.

I followed Anku's lead and kept mum.

"I am a Glitch," the boy said good-naturedly, unaffected by

what was clearly rudeness on our part.

"I've never heard of Glitches," Anku said, easily lying once again.

"There's a reason for that," another voice came from a larger knoll. The trapdoor on the knoll opened, and an old Glitch climbed out. He held a gnarled walking stick in his hand, and his skin was tinged with red.

"No one has heard of us because we are the applicants who did not make the cut for being chosen as Maruts. And do you know why?" Without waiting for our response, he continued. "Because we were thought to have a fatal flaw, a glitch, if you will. My red skin meant I was a rageaholic, and this boy's green skin means he knows only envy."

"That's not possible. Celestials have found a place in the universe for every creature," Anku declared, turning into an insufferable know-it-all.

"And yet, here we are," the old Glitch said, clutching his staff tighter so that it cracked.

I looked past him to find many angry Glitch faces popping up through trapdoors, their skins glowing with all shades of the rainbow.

"We are working on correcting the flaw," Ludo intervened in a squeaky voice.

"I would have made a perfect Marut," the red-skinned Glitch said, straightening his spine. Even then, he didn't reach our shoulder height.

"You would have made an excellent Marut," I said, picking up Ludo's placatory tone.

Anku harrumphed. But I ignored her. I could empathise

with Jarku. I knew what discrimination felt like.

"This is Jarku, the head of Glitch Grotto," Ludo announced.

I bowed. Anku ignored him and said, "We are Maruts."

"What brings you to our land?" Jarku asked, stiffening. "Does Swahalok want to take away our homes too?"

"We are on our way to the Maw," I said.

All of a sudden, Anku knelt to tie her shoelace, causing Jarku to duck behind Ludo. A loud collective gasp sounded from other mounds at the same time.

Anku smirked as if to say this was all the proof needed to show that Glitches were cowards. Knowing her, she'd made the sudden movement on purpose.

Ludo tensed and glanced over his shoulder. I couldn't tell what had produced the reaction in Jarku—Anku's sudden movement, or the news that we were traveling to the Maw.

"We're just looking for directions," I said and looked expectantly at Ludo. My intent was to divert Jarku's attention from Anku's insolent behavior, and I hoped Ludo might offer to show us the way.

Ludo's face perked up, his grin grew wider, and his tail waved happily in the air, but before he could give us an answer, Jarku said, "Ludo's expertise as a tour guide is limited to the Grotto."

The Grotto was the size of a football field. Clearly, Jarku was in no mood to help. I explained that Rahu was holding our friend hostage in the Maw.

"You should just let her die. Two alive is better than three dead," Jarku said and turned to leave.

"A Marut would never say that," Anku said.

Jarku stopped in his tracks and turned around.

"Now we know why you are not Maruts," Anku continued, like someone with a death wish.

"Just because you are brave doesn't mean you jump off cliffs!" Jarku grimaced. The folds on his olive-red cheeks deepened from anger. "Maruts also don't make stupid decisions like walking into the Maw just as the sun is about to set."

"Stupid is better than cowardly," Anku said.

Before Jarku's rage exploded, I intervened and asked for his leave. When Jarku's sight settled on me, it softened, and soon he returned to his normal grumpy self.

"It's just as well," he said. "Soon, Maruts will be extinct, and we will be available to fill your positions."

A fistfight between Jarku and Anku was threatening to break out. I hurried her away. She brushed away my hands, but I remained in her line of sight, preventing her from looking at Jarku.

"Do us a favor," Jarku called after us. "In case you manage to escape the Maw, do not return to Glitch Grotto. We are no doctors."

Anku tossed her head in disgust and flounced off, muttering something about the Glitch's nerve to think they could be Maruts.

I waved to Jarku and the other Glitches in apology and the hope we never got to meet again. I wasn't sure I would be able to save Jarku from Anku the second time around.

CHAPTER 18

The air turned dense and the silence grew heavy the farther we moved from Glitch Grotto. An occasional graze of the shoe sole against the tree root meant we would exit the tree soon. Already there were fewer branches around us, and the ground was laden with dry mulch. We moved cautiously when suddenly the air grew chilly and all foliage, dead and alive, ended abruptly, leaving a stretch of stones and boulders before our eyes. Through the sinister hush, we could hear the gurgling of a brook.

A shiver arose in my spine and traveled to the peripheries of my body at the thought of what lay ahead. For all the complaining by Jarku regarding the Glitches' station in life, Glitch Grotto was nestled in a valley surrounded by fruit-bearing branches and bathed in warm sunlight.

Anku pointed into the distance at a rock face. We picked our way toward it and reached a spout. Brick-red water, the grainy and earthy red of soil mixed with the rich and glossy red of blood, was gushing from the mouth of the spout.

A craggy outcrop stood guard over the area like a warning to travelers against entering. I heard a cry behind us.

"What now?" Anku said as we turned to find the hazy form of a Glitch with a mohawk running toward us.

"I can help you," Ludo said after he had taken a few seconds to stop panting.

Anku and I knelt to be at eye level with him. "Don't be offended," Anku said, "but the Chamruks will drink you like a cola."

"I'm not…" Ludo said and shut his eyes. Taking a deep breath, he started counting from one to ten. Anku and I looked at each other in amazement. Ludo opened his eyes and said, "…offended."

I was taken aback by the show of restraint to lash out in the little guy. Glitches could give humans lessons in anger management. Perhaps Jarku was right and it was easier to control one or two serious flaws in oneself rather than juggle a cornucopia of weaknesses like humans and Maruts did.

"It's been a dream of mine to go on a rescue mission with Maruts," Ludo implored as if he hadn't heard Anku's derogatory comment.

"We are not here to fulfill your childish wishes," Anku said, getting up abruptly.

"Actually, Glitches can be very useful in the Maw," Ludo said, grinning up at me. Anku snorted. "We have laser vision," Ludo continued, almost pleading. "We can see through the mist."

"Mist comes at night. We will be out long before then," Anku said, walking toward the rocks. She really meant it when she said that she didn't like whiny kids.

I looked at the sun, which was but an orange sliver over the horizon. Then I glanced toward the Maw. There was no sign of any mist. I shrugged. "Sorry, dude, boss says no."

I trotted after Anku, leaving Ludo looking dejected. Anku had already started climbing the rocks. Keeping my distance from the muddy, bloody waters of the stream, I followed. I hauled myself over the edge to have a revolting stench punch my senses.

It was true that Surpanekha had described it as a mix of rotting animal carcasses and a garbage dump. Still, I wasn't ready for the reaction the odor produced in me. I felt dizzy from the images of bloodshed and pain the odor carried with it.

Anku pinched her nose but seemed to carry on fine. I guess being a snake silhouette and extra sensitive to odors didn't help matters for me. I covered my nose with my sleeve and squeezed my eyes to stall the onslaught of the stench and gory glimpses of death.

By and by, I learned to take shallow breaths and studied the dreary landscape before my eyes. The first thing I noticed was gray, cloudless skies and the complete absence of daylight. As expected, there wasn't a speck of green. Dirty and splotched boulders, river stones, and pebbles hugged the ground, their grip over the land only broken by the talon-like roots of crooked, bone-dry trees. The branches of these trees were warped but smooth like skewers.

Some trees were mere stumps and appeared to be freshly sawn; others were diseased. Bloodlike sap had bubbled up and hardened on their bark so that the concentric rings in the trunks' cross section weren't visible. Like lilies scattered in an overcrowded pond, dry and haggard Venus flytraps lay waiting, their crisp and burnt petals fringed with piranha-like teeth.

Given the sparseness of the terrain, it wasn't hard to locate a thicker mass of tree trunks in the depth of the Maw. Parts of a cobbled path were visible in snatches through the dried-up forest. Streams of repulsive liquid flowed through the Maw like a network of arteries, giving out toxic fumes. Tiny pools of red mulch dotted the terrain. It was a somber reminder of how abuse and neglect could reduce a forest full of life into a wasteland.

"Where is all the blood coming from?" I whispered, aghast.

"So it's true," Anku whispered in disgust. "I've heard that since Kalpavriksha refuses to feed them, in overly polluted cities, trees have turned into vampires. They chomp up the birds and squirrels," Anku said. "Like Kalpavriksha is connected to nature in Samsara, the Maw is getting its fodder from the real world, too."

At least the Chamruks wouldn't be as starved and deprived as Surpanekha had suggested, not that it made this desolate place any less frightful and dangerous. In absence of sunlight, even the wind seemed to have abandoned the bleak surroundings of the Maw.

"I don't see any Chamruks," I whispered.

Anku pointed at the trees with sharp pointy branches.

"But they aren't moving," I said.

"Because there's nothing to eat here at the moment."

Anku began to descend the escarp. The inner slope of the

outcrop was steeper.

We climbed down toward the cobbled path that ran through the Maw. Anku was about to step off the rocks on the pebbly terrain when I asked her to stop.

"Hand me a packet of milk biscuits," I said.

"This is not the time to snack, Adi," she said, handing me a packet all the same. It must have sounded like a dying man's wish to her.

I broke the biscuit and tossed a piece on the ground. Immediately, a puddle of blood bubbled up at the spot. A loud glug and a few bubbles later, the biscuit was sucked in and the blood drained, leaving behind not stones but bones of all kinds: birds, animals, Yech, and human. Bloody liquid seeped up through the remnants to fill the puddle.

"Surpanekha said one element in the Maw is spared from evil," I said.

Anku wrinkled her nose, her upper lip pulled up in disgust, and took half of the biscuits from me. She started tossing broken bits around as if she were feeding ducks. Wherever the biscuit bits fell, a crack appeared, and the biscuits disappeared.

After we had chucked the entire packet of biscuits, we figured that the puddles, the patches of dead grass, gravel, and the cobbled path that cut across the Maw were unsafe. The Chamruks had still not moved.

It was getting late, and we still hadn't figured out the path to the dungeon.

"They're waiting for meat," Anku said, sounding worried for the first time since we left Glitch Grotto.

I pointed to the bit of biscuit that had landed on a Venus

flytrap. It remained inside the petals, and the plant didn't move to trap it.

"That can't be right. That's a carnivorous plant, for Brahma's sake!" Anku said.

We tried out other Venus flytraps. The biscuit piece would roll down their centers, and their mouths remained open.

"Try not to be eaten," Anku said and leaped to land on a flytrap on both feet. No sooner had she touched the plant than its petals started to close in.

Before the flytrap's teeth could sink into her leg, Anku jumped onto the next plant, but this time, she landed on one foot in the center. She balanced herself, her arms outstretched, her other leg folded back. The petals remained still this time.

I mimicked her, and soon we perfected our steps, but the movement was slow. My goal to get back home by day's end seemed far and uncertain. In the meantime, soft moonlight enveloped the sky, casting a ghostly pallor on the landscape.

About fifteen minutes into our foray, I heard Anku's voice. She was pointing to something up ahead. Through the roots of the gathered Chamruks, I made out the mouth of a cave.

"That must be the entrance into the dungeon!" Anku cried.

A glimpse of the entrance was enough to lift my spirits. Still, something troubled me. It was the ease with which we had reached the dungeon. Until now, the expedition had turned out to be a breeze. Now that we were on the last leg of the nightmare that began two nights earlier for me, I suddenly wondered how I could have made it this far. Life was never easy for me. I expected my path to be strewn with hindrances and misfortunes because, well, it was me!

We had only a few jumps left to reach Surp, treat her with shrapmukta tincture, and head back the way we came. Just when I thought that Shani, the deity of misfortune, had finally forgiven me, I caught sight of the mist rolling in behind the dungeon. Surpanekha had warned us about the mist, but she didn't tell us what to do if we got stranded in it.

"We need to hurry," Anku said and jumped to the next flower.

This was when I heard a light noise behind me like the scurrying of a mouse. I turned around to find Ludo sitting on his haunches inside the Venus flytrap. He was sitting cross-legged, while we comically stood balancing ourselves on one leg.

A wave of irritation passed over me. Ludo reminded me of Mohan, who insisted on following me wherever I went. Even at school, Mohan sought me out during lunch breaks. I would often hang out with Batty just to avoid Mohan.

As Batty's face appeared before my eyes, I lost my balance and fell back into the flytrap. The petals of the plant started moving with the slow surety of a machine. Before its teeth could hook into my legs, I bolted off and landed on pebbled ground.

Life flowed into our surroundings suddenly, like an electric switch turning on an amusement park's festive lighting and rides. The trees around us started shaking and twisting as if trying to release themselves from the ground. The gurgling sound of the streams got louder, hungrier. Having sensed danger, even Patches started to squirm in my bag.

As I backed away, my foot struck a tree stump as tall as my ankle. The decaying core of the trunk was filled with dead plants and insects. It looked like a witch's cauldron brewing soup for the damned. One part of the stump was distorted from decay—a tree that refused to die.

Ludo landed on a flytrap close to me, as did Anku. She extended her hand to pull me out of the danger zone, but my shoe was stuck as if someone had nailed it to the stump.

I gripped my leg and tried to pull my foot out of my shoe but it remained jammed, as if it was not my shoe but my foot that had landed on discarded and viscid chewing gum. I spotted a growing bloodstain on my shoe which was strange because I felt no pain. I was sure I had landed clear of the stump.

Then I saw it: the pointy tip of dry wood poking up through my shoe. It was a wispy thin dried-out stem connected to the tree stump. A loud scream, which was not mine, was followed by Anku's club whomping that part of the tree stump. Blood from the tree splashed onto my face and clothes as Anku battered the tree trunk non-stop until it was reduced to pulp.

The ground started to shudder. The Chamruks were rising all around us, their roots splitting with a sharp crack from the soil. The rocks started giving out fumes, and the bloody sludge grew thicker around our feet.

Everything that is supposed to be dead comes alive in the Maw, Surpanekha had said.

As the mist embraced us, the root that pierced my foot reappeared. The packet of biscuits fell from my hand.

"Wait here!" Ludo cried and disappeared into the mist.

Anku was teetering on the flytrap now. With enough space for one foot to wedge itself between the petals, she was hopping from foot to foot. "You shouldn't have encouraged the

Glitch!" she screamed at me.

Trust her to jump on any excuse to say, "I told you so!"

The pool of blood near my feet emptied with a loud gurgle, and Anku shouted, "Look out, Adi!"

She clubbed the root again, but as soon as she moved away to fend off other cannibalistic tendrils, the root grew back, pulling me toward the ground like a peg driven by a hammer. I kicked it with my other foot to try and leap to the safety of the flytrap, but I was truly pinned. The pain from the wound was becoming unbearable.

The Chamruks were closing in on us. The mist was so thick that we couldn't see the Chamruks' arms until they were close. Anku clubbed any approaching twig or stem, ripping it and spraying us with red, brown, and green sap.

No amount of fighting made the situation better, just like every effort to release myself from Naani's negativity and disapproval had failed. The chances of my survival kept getting bleaker. And this time, I would be responsible for Anku and Surp's death, too.

With a loud scream, Anku jumped off her flytrap when its petals started closing in, and she landed next to me.

That was when we heard the sound of thumping hooves growing louder and closer on the stony path. I hoped they were reinforcements sent by Surpanekha. Or perhaps Naani had suddenly woken up to her grandmotherly duties and come to our aid.

Through the mist, Ludo appeared on the cobbled path, sitting astride a strange creature with a rhino's body and a horse's head.

"A Rhino Yali!" Anku cried, her eyes growing large in disbelief.

Ludo's eyes were blazing blue like a laser beam. He bent and whispered something into the Yali's ear. It started wading through the slush of blood toward us. Everywhere it stepped, the habitation of the Maw retreated. When it reached me, the barb that had pierced my foot began to withdraw. I slowly sat up. The ground around us was clear of bloody muck now.

Ludo leaped off, safe in the bubble of the Yali's presence, while Anku dabbed jambukita tincture on my wound. I felt better immediately. I fist-bumped Ludo while Anku gave him a frosty glare.

"We told you not to follow us," she said.

"The mist would have misled you. It addles the brain and causes delusion," Ludo said.

Anku's body relaxed, but her eyes remained narrow and her brows furrowed. For someone as egoistic as her, admitting she'd been wrong would never come easy.

"Why isn't the Maw attacking the Yali?" I asked.

"No one messes with the Yali. They have an appetite for evil creatures, and their favorite foods are Yechs and Chamruks," Ludo said, grinning.

The Yali was grazing on the bloody twigs and tendrils, which were fast receding away from it.

Ludo stroked its mane. "Malini is on her way. I saw her Yech just outside the Maw," he said like a child eager to please the cool kids. "Both of you can ride to the dungeon." He patted the Yali's snout.

"What about you?" I said.

"Don't worry about me. I'll wait on the flytrap until someone finds me. You're safe from the mist with the Yali by your side."

"We can't leave him here," I said, looking at Anku.

"Oh, cut out the drama!" Anku said, addressing Ludo. She easily slid onto the Rhino Yali's back. "We can't reach the dungeon without your mist-piercing sight."

"You mean it?" Ludo said, perking up.

I hated to burst the bubble of newfound warmth, but there wasn't enough space on the Yali's back for the three of us. Right now, I alone could see the crucial flaw in the plan. Unless one of us caught the tail of the galloping Yali, it would be impossible for the three of us to ride it. If Anku managed to save Surp before Dakini reached us, there was still a chance of three lives being saved.

What I did next was a practical choice, on the face of it, but the feeling that no one really cared if I was alive did play a part. My biggest regret at this moment was that I wouldn't be able to warn Naani about Rahu's plans. But even if I did make it back home in time, who's to say Naani wouldn't find a reason to yell at me instead?

I picked Ludo and flung him onto the Yali's back. Then I patted the Yali hard on its back and yelled out to a confused Anku, "Warn my Naani to keep Mohan safe from Gargouille!" Naani might take the warning more seriously if it came from someone else.

The Yali bolted. Wherever its hooves landed, the earth cleared as if invisible wipers were polishing it. As soon as it was gone, the predator Chamruk moved in on me.

Anku's horrified screams over the gore that was about to take place drained in the mist. I felt a tug on my ankle. A stringy, dried-up vine dug its way up through the dirt, encircling my foot.

The only choices I had for a weapon were between a feather hidden in my sock and the Satya Pasha, the challastra hanging by the loop of my pants. My hand reached for the challastra. Another thorny stem of a bush penetrated my shoe and skin.

At the same moment that I swung the challastra on my finger, the vine wrapped around my leg sprouted white thorns, threatening to chomp my leg off.

Chamruks were snaking their way toward me like a bunch of drunk, violent hoodlums. I held the Satya Pasha in my hand, wondering for one last time how anyone could have imagined a lasso could serve as a weapon. I aimed the noose at the tree closest to me.

"It never misses its mark," Takka had said.

True enough, the noose landed cleanly around the tree. The tree was oozing a red sap from the cracks in its bark, but it was caught by my lasso.

I kicked the toothy vine on my leg to push it off, and I used the noose to pull myself away from the vine's grip. It was another matter that the tree I chose was close enough to sink its multiple branches into me at any time.

It took a few seconds to feel that the tree my lasso was holding on to had stopped moving. I looked up in alarm.

A miraculous transformation was underway in the tree. The cracks in its bark started to disappear. The red muck on it hardened into dark brown knots of wood, and tiny leaves appeared at the shoots. The roots of the tree sank into the soil and grew strong and stationary.

It had started to heal!

Satya Pasha, the noose of truth, had revealed the reality of the tree. It also meant that inside the Maw, nature was still hanging on.

With renewed hope, I pulled on the rope to get traction, but the vine around my ankle remained tightly wound. There was a pool of blood around my leg into which my foot had disappeared. No matter how much I pushed and kicked at the vine, it remained glued to my skin, eating through it, growing plumper and juicier.

I felt my grip on the challastra loosen. Energy was deserting me. A vine had climbed around my hand, as well.

I was about to let go of the Satya Pasha, my outstretched arm in danger of being pulled apart, when I felt a tug on my hand.

It was the tree. It was pulling me up. The grip of the vine grew stronger in response.

This tug-of-war would tear my body in two. I had to take my chances. With all the force I could muster, I dug my nails into the vine, spilling the blood it had sucked from my leg. For a moment, I felt the vine loosen, but my sight grew dim and my breathing became labored.

I staggered under the green umbrella of the grand Himalayan Deodar that the Satya Pasha had helped revive. The trunk of the tree grew thicker, and under its aura, the Maw and the mist receded.

I was free from the vine's clutches, but I'd lost so much

blood that I couldn't feel my leg. At some distance, the Chamruks crowded and swayed around me and the Deodar, listless and hungry.

I wondered how long the spell of the Satya Pasha would last; how long before greed and savagery would reign over the Maw once again.

I fell onto my back, my satchel clutched to my chest, my eyelids drooping from exhaustion and despair. The green of the baby leaves was the last thing I saw before I passed out.

*There was neither non-existence nor existence then,
Neither the realm of space, nor the sky which is beyond.
What stirred? Where? In whose protection?*

*There was neither death nor immortality then,
No distinguishing sign of night nor of day,
That One breathed, windless, by its own impulse;
Other than that, there was nothing beyond.*

—Nasadiya Sukta, Rigveda 10.129

CHAPTER 19

I squinted in an attempt to open one of my eyes but shut it again. The glare of the sunlight was unbearable.

The sound of a door being opened was followed by someone landing hard on my body. My immediate reaction was to dislodge the person. I tumbled to the other side of the bed from the force.

"Ouch!"

"You're back, Adi!" Mohan landed squarely on my chest again. "I knew you hadn't run away."

It was true, then. I was back in my room.

My hands strayed to my leg to check for the wound that the carnivorous vine in the Maw would have made, but the skin around my ankle was smooth. Somehow, I'd managed to escape the Maw's vampire trees and heal myself overnight.

I felt the back of my head where Gargouille had hit me with his baton the night of the delivery. Even though the wound on my head was already healed, it should have left a scar. There was nothing there. Nada.

"Where were you the last two days?" Mohan asked. He was hiding something in his hands behind him.

Unsure of what to tell him, I shrugged.

"Naani says you were misled by a bad person into running away from home," Mohan said.

Again, I shrugged. I was so relieved to see Mohan unharmed that I was willing to believe the events of the last two nights were a dream.

Mohan brought his hands forward with a "Ta-da!" He bounced on my tummy. "Quick, open your birthday gift!" There was a tiny box in his hand covered in shiny, crinkly purple gift wrap.

"I will, if you stop moving," I said.

Mohan stopped bouncing and suppressed a smile, quivering from having to control his impulses.

I took the box from him. At the same time, my eyes searched for my satchel and Patches. Patches was in his vivarium. Donning a relaxed pale-green hue, he sat unmoving on the branch, which meant he was sleeping.

My satchel lay on the chair next to my study table, as it had before I left for the delivery three nights ago. I felt the urge to check my bag for the dagger, but despite his light and lanky frame, Mohan had me grounded.

"Open it, open it!" he sang.

Instinctively, my hands reached for my glasses on the bedside table, and I put them on. I opened the box. It contained a pendant on a black leather cord. The pendant was wooden, the size of a coat button. It had the yin-yang symbol painted on it in black and white.

Yin-yang, or cosmic duality, was Naani's favorite topic. Sometimes, opposing forces rely on each other to exist. There can be no light without dark or good without evil. The paint on the medallion was uneven. It was clearly the work of a child.

"It's nice," I said. "Thanks."

It must have been Naani's idea that Mohan design this for me. To help me embrace the dark within me for the good of others.

I watched Mohan's face, shining from anticipation. He pulled out a thread and pendant from under his t-shirt. "I made one for myself too," he said with uncontrolled glee. "This is an unbreakable bond between us," he intoned solemnly. "You will never be able to leave me now."

I sighed.

"Wear it! Wear it!" he sang.

I clasped the cord around my neck.

"You look like a rock star," Mohan said, preening. "Promise me you'll never take it off."

One thing worse than being a social pariah among one's peers was the aspiration to dress cooler than them. Naani's birthday gifts to me, when she remembered my birthday at all, had included a pair of orthopedic shoes, glasses, and a new hearing aid. Her gifts wouldn't ruffle a single feather in the herd of bullies that tailed me, but a piece of jewelry would call out to them like a beacon.

I pulled Mohan's hands away from around my neck and promised to never take off the necklace, which earned me another hug. I decided to slip the pendant under my t-shirt when Mohan wasn't looking. I wanted him out of my room so I could figure out what had happened last night. How had I traveled from the Maw back to my room?

I could hear Naani humming as she cooked breakfast for us in the kitchen. Did she know anything about last night? It was obvious she had lied to Mohan.

I still didn't know the full extent of Marut powers, and I knew even less about pure Maruts like Naani. Did she have something to do with my return? But Thauma said she'd given up her silhouette. Did that mean she was not a Marut anymore? Before I could confront Naani, I had to first make sure the past two days weren't a dream.

After Mohan left to get ready for school, I reached for my satchel. If the last two days were a dream, then the dagger and Aunty Padma's letter would be there.

The bag was empty. Naani couldn't have emptied my bag. She rarely entered my room.

I tiptoed to the living room. Kaleeni was gone, and a different rug was spread out on the living room floor. I heard a sound behind me. I turned to find Naani.

"You're late for school," she said as if nothing out of the ordinary had happened. Even if she believed I'd run away, like she'd led Mohan to believe, shouldn't she at least inquire after my wellbeing?

"Where's Kaleeni?" I asked.

"What?" Naani snapped.

Would she ridicule me if I suggested we had a flying carpet?

"The carpet," I mumbled.

"I sent it for dry-cleaning last week. If you paid more attention to your surroundings, you would remember such things better and your grades would improve, too."

What did grades have to do with this? She didn't appear to be in the mood to chat, so I left the room to get ready for school.

"Adi, don't fill your brother's head with fanciful stories," Naani called to my back.

I didn't turn around. I slammed the door behind me. I had been away from home for two days, and she hadn't once asked me if I was hurt. Even now, Mohan was the only one who mattered.

CHAPTER 20

The school day began on a gloomy note. I got no time to settle down in the class or zone out the stares and murmurs of my classmates. As soon as I arrived, my teacher marched me to Principal Bahri's office, where I was lectured on the gratitude I owed Naani for looking after me.

"Is this how you thank someone for their love and care?" Principal Bahri asked me. "By running away from home?"

I remained silent. Wherever I went, children whispered behind my back. I kept my cool. Nothing the world said could hurt me more than Naani's indifference that morning. I felt tempted to call Aunty Padma again, drop everything, and leave with her.

My hand involuntarily traveled to the pendant under my shirt, the one Mohan made me promise never to take off. In my anger at Naani, I'd forgotten to remove it.

Whether the last three nights had happened or not, I knew Rahu wanted Mohan. Though the ring of Kundalini had been destroyed, for some reason, Rahu still wanted the Naga heir.

How could I leave with Aunt Padma, knowing that a band of monsters led by a vengeful deity was looking for Mohan? I had to make sure that either my story was a dream or that Mohan was in safe hands. Only one person could clear that up for me.

I searched for Batty at our usual meeting spots: the staircase to the terrace, the bathroom he used as a storage cabinet for his janitorial duties, the cafeteria, and the playgrounds near the bleachers. When I couldn't find him anywhere, I approached the school PE teacher, Mr. Stanley.

"Batty the janitor?" he asked quizzically. "Kanta has been in charge of cleaning ever since I remember." He pointed toward a stocky lady in a sari who had a string of jasmine in her hair and was holding a mop.

Mr. Stanley gave me a suspicious look but dropped the matter. My elementary school teacher, Mrs. Duggal, would have made a case for me to see a psychiatrist. Would she have been right? Was Batty an invisible friend that I invented out of loneliness?

I moved around the school in a cloud of confusion that morning. Mohan had badgered Naani to give me a packet of candies to distribute to my classmates for my birthday. The packet disappeared mysteriously during the first period. I didn't need to catch Ayesha Saini giggling to figure out what had happened to my candy. But that wasn't the sole cause of my gloom.

Though there were no Yechs, Dakini, or Gargouille chasing me, I was in agony because I was my usual self again. I'd met an awesome version of myself in Wantra three nights ago. Someone who didn't need prosthetic shoes or thick glasses. Someone who could wield a dagger called Dusht Uchchaihshravas. Someone with connections to a fire-breathing clan of Maruts. Someone who was the opposite of me.

I was sitting alone on the bleachers at lunch when a group of boys passed by. It was the gang of bullies who loved to pick on me.

Chetan, the leader of this gang, was a star student and played football at the national level. He thought he was a Greek god what with his mop of curly hair, chiseled face, and ripped body. The girls oohing and aahing over him fed his self-delusion and arrogance. Chetan's close friend Aarya was a top scholar. The other two boys were Mickey and Chintu, members of the school's rock band. Generally, bullies are shown to be maladjusted kids who are trying to hide their insecurities by picking on others. But these boys had nothing to be insecure about.

They never missed a chance to stare at me deliberately, eyeing my shoes or my hearing device. Their silent stares seemed to be screaming a message: *Adi Yoshi, you are a freak show.*

If they knew I'd fought a Chamruk, escaped the Yechs, or flown a flying carpet, would they still behave this way?

Somewhere in the pit of my stomach, I felt like a loser for having to depend on monsters and flying carpets to feel good about myself. I wished I had the natural self-assurance of Anku. From the far end of the bleachers, Chintu, forever eager to please Chetan, gave me a chin flick. To my surprise, I held up a clenched fist.

Before my escapade in Wantra, I would have drifted away, hoping these guys would leave me alone. But overnight, my reactions had evolved. If I fled now, I would feel like an impostor, which was worse than feeling like a loser.

Then it occurred to me: What if Wantra and Kalpavriksha had been a dream? At school, everyone knew Adi Yoshi, the loser. Every day, I came prepared for the challenges of school. How could I expect everyone to see me as cool and courageous Adi Yoshi based on a dream?

"Whoa! Dorky wants to fight," Chintu said, pointing at me. The gang rushed back to flock around me.

"I-I didn't m-mean to," I stammered.

They had me surrounded. "Heard you ran away from home on your birthday," Chetan said, turning to Aarya. "Do kids like Adi Yoshi deserve birthdays?"

Aarya shook his head. "Burden on our society."

Mickey snapped his fingers. "And taxes? Our taxes go into supporting people like him."

They all nodded.

"To support freaks, good-for-nothings like you," Chetan said, for the want of anything better to say

"Good-for-nothings. Nice touch," Mickey said.

Chetan nodded in thanks, as if every word out of his mouth deserved a standing ovation. "It's a gift."

I looked at them in bafflement. I didn't need to be the heroic Adi from my dream to be better than these galoots. I stood up shakily and said, "As if your fathers are the kind who pay their taxes."

Where did that come from?

My legs were trembling, but my mouth was set, and I wanted to punch someone really badly. Naani had warned me against letting these feelings get the better of me, but I had seen the other side of fear, even if it was in my dreams.

"He's saying our fathers are tax evaders," Mickey cried.

Chetan stepped closer to me while the other three huddled around him, shutting me off from the outer world.

"I wouldn't do that," I warned him as he lifted his hand.

"That's better, then," Chetan said, jerking his head and mimicking me, his eyes red from anger and his face flushed. He aimed a punch at me and delivered it clean on my left eye, shattering my glasses.

I felt a trickle of blood on my cheek. My eyesight blurred, not from blood but rage.

The next thing I knew, I was in my silhouette, and I'd bitten Chetan, Aarya, and Mickey as they searched around for me, flummoxed by my disappearance.

While the brouhaha ensued with screams and shouts, other kids surrounded us. I escaped into the grass under the bleachers. My clothes lay in a pile on the ground. Mr. Stanley reached the spot in a jiffy and started quizzing the kids about my clothes.

When Mickey told him I'd transformed into a snake and bitten them, even Mr. Stanley, usually a patient teacher, lost his cool and marched them to the principal's office. He sent one of the spectators to call the school nurse and forbade all other students from playing in the area.

I kept an extra uniform, an old but still in working condition hearing device, and a pair of glasses stashed in the abandoned bathroom for such an emergency. It had been Naani's idea. *If we're not careful, we'll have the whole world at our doorstep.*

I couldn't take the stairs in my silhouette without being spotted, so I slithered my way up on the side wall to the terrace.

Being discovered was a terrifying possibility for both Naani and me, for different reasons. She was worried about Mohan's safety, and I was terrified of being slotted as a freakshow. Being a snake was one thing. Being called "a snake," with all its insulting connotations, was another.

The problem was that neither of us had thought about shoes.

As I got dressed, I looked at my bare feet, racking my mind for a plausible story. I could say that the boys took my clothes from the locker and tried to frame me by releasing a snake on the school premises. Or I could deny any knowledge of the incident, which would get everybody off the hook. I rejected the latter option. Every bully deserved a lesson.

I heard a noise from the stairwell. Lunch was over, and a hush had fallen over the school premises. I hid behind the bathroom door and waited. I was surprised to see Mohan emerge from the stairwell.

"Adi, are you here?"

He was holding a used polythene bag in his hands.

"You'll get into trouble for leaving class without permission," I said, stepping out. I didn't want Naani ranting at me for something that wasn't my fault.

"I heard what happened. I brought shoes for you," Mohan said.

"But how did you know?"

"I've known for a while. You can silhouette into a snake. You are the coolest brother ever," Mohan said. His eyes were shining with pride and love for something that I hated in myself. "When Naani asked you to store an extra uniform, I realized she forgot shoes, so every day, I carry a spare for you."

Every day? Why did he have to be so loving, so nice? I would never have done something like this for him.

Without a word, I took the bag and pulled out the shoes. They were the shoes I had worn in the Maw. The black canvas had mixed with blood, turning it to a stiff, muddy red. The shoes even smelled of blood and were in no condition to be worn.

"Naani threw them in the chute for some reason," Mohan said, peering into the abandoned bathroom with curiosity.

"Is Naani aware that you know about my silhouette?" I asked.

Mohan shook his head and flashed a goofy, conspiratorial smile.

"We need to talk once we get back home," I said.

Naani couldn't know that Mohan was aware of my silhouetting. *He has a delicate constitution, your brother,* she said to me once.

Mohan nodded. "When I was looking for you outside the playfield, I met a girl who directed me to this place," he said. "She had all your candy."

He looked confused. It was the look of a true-blue fan who felt short-changed. He had no idea that the older brother he idolized was treated like a ninny by his peers.

"She begged me for candy," I lied, putting on my left shoe.

Ayesha Saini would have blabbed to Mr. Stanley and the other teachers by now. "Hurry, you must leave," I said.

It was bad enough that I had silhouetted. If Naani found out that I'd gotten Mohan in trouble too, I would rue my fifteenth birthday forever.

Mohan scurried down the stairs without any fear of getting caught. He was a bright kid. He was also quite tall for his age and could easily pass as a middle-school student. Moreover, with his big brown eyes and chubby baby face, he could get out of any situation. He was the lucky one. But would his luck hold when Gargouille came for him?

I put on the other shoe when something sharp poked my foot. It didn't feel like a pebble. I shook my shoe, and out floated a feather. It was the same feather Pavan the Zephyr Rover had given me. Its thick bottom shaft had poked me.

The feather was the one object that had excited and disappointed me the most in Kalpavriksha. But right now, it was also the only clue to the truth about Wantra and my visit to Kalpavriksha.

I waved it around, hoping for some magic to happen. Nothing. I heard voices instead. It was Principal Bahri and Mr. Stanley.

"He is generally a quiet boy. He was asking about someone called Batty this morning," I heard Mr. Stanley say.

"Come on, you silly feather, do something!" I said. I tapped the feather on the wall, hoping for some magic that could save me from being punished. Detention would mean Naani being called to the school, and I'd had enough confrontation for the day.

In desperation, I turned to other janitorial sundries stored in the bathroom. I tapped the feather on the bucket, the broom, and the mop. Now they had reached the landing at the top of the staircase. I grazed the feather all over my clothes, hoping it might make me invisible. Nothing.

When I looked up, Principal Bahri and Mr. Stanley were standing before me.

"Are you hurt?" Mr. Stanley asked, looking a little surprised to find me holding a feather. Perhaps he expected to find me beaten up and bruised.

Principal Bahri was a portly man who always wore a white linen shirt and gray trousers. In winter, he added a blue blazer to his attire. He was so consistent in his appearance that sometimes students simply missed noticing him when he did the rounds of the school. What struck me most about Principal Bahri was his round, jovial face. He had a thick mustache, and his cheeks sank into deep dimples every time he smiled. But thanks to the same facial features, when angry, he looked twice as menacing. At the moment, he was staring at the feather in my hand, his brows knitted and his arms crossed.

I kept mum. One advantage of being viewed as an oddball was that you could get away with strange behavior—an advantage I shared with Thauma.

"Did those boys take your clothes?" the principal said.

I remained quiet. I knew it was wrong to lie. I was also truthful to a fault, unlike Anku. And there was no doubt that I'd played a role in this mess. I'd called the boys' fathers tax evaders and then bit them. If I spoke, I would tell the truth. I opted for silence.

"In my office, Adi," the principal said.

I followed him to his office, bidding Mr. Stanley goodbye on the way. Stanley patted my back and said everything would be okay. I really wanted to believe him.

When I stepped into Principal Bahri's office, my spirits dipped further, for Naani sat waiting for us. Her shoulders were straight and her expression stern. The only clue to her anxiety was her tapping foot. Chetan, his leg bandaged, sat remorsefully in another chair.

Naani rushed to hug me. And this was the reason why I hated lying. In public, Naani put up a grand pretense of caring for me. Just to show others that she loved me. I stood still as she brushed my hair off my forehead and dusted my clothes.

"What did those brutes do to you?" she asked me, holding my face in her hands. I refused to look at her.

"Mrs. Yoshi, snakebites were found on the legs of the boys," the principal said.

"Snakebites? Are you saying Adi released a snake on those kids?"

The principal immediately backed off. "I'm just saying I would like to know from Adi if he knows anything about it. Everyone in school knows he has a pet reptile."

"Adi can't tell you anything. He can't even walk to school by himself every day. His ten-year-old brother escorts him!" Naani said, bringing false incredulity in her high-pitched voice. "Moreover, his pet reptile is a piddly chameleon. It's impossible to carry a chameleon to school unnoticed."

Patches would hate to be called piddly, and Naani just provided more fodder for the bully by saying that Mohan escorted me to school.

"The boys could be mistaken. Perhaps it was a chameleon," the principal said, lifting his shoulders.

"There you go. Chameleon bites are not poisonous," Naani said, dismissing Principal Bahri's words with a handwave.

"It was a snake," Chetan said emphatically.

"These boys are lying. Instead of punishing them for bullying Adi, you are grilling my grandson," Naani said. "I will write to the school board."

"There is no need to be dramatic, Mrs. Yoshi." Principal Bahri asked Chetan to leave and then said, "There's a reason why I thought it prudent to investigate. A gentleman visited our school the other day asking about the sightings of a twig snake. Said he was a herpetologist."

Naani and I looked at each other, alarmed.

The principal continued. "Also, in all fairness, I will have to award a penalty to Adi. He will have to stay back after school today. You can leave now, Mrs. Yoshi."

"Naani, don't let Mohan walk back alone," I whispered as she got up to leave.

She gave me a leveling look and turned to the principal. "No, thank you. I will wait for school to be over so I can bring both my grandsons back with me."

CHAPTER 21

That evening was no different for me than any kid whose parents are called to school.

Naani was livid. "Silhouetting at the merest provocation! That, too, with a herpetologist prowling around," she muttered in anger. Without a word of sympathy, she banished me to my room. She even forbade Mohan from entering my room.

I had half a mind to run away from home. Everyone expected that of me anyway. The thought of leaving Mohan behind with Naani was heart-wrenching. I wondered if he would come away with me to live with Aunty Padma. Who would he choose between Naani and me? I left it for later to tug on that thread. That night, after Mohan went to bed, I gathered up the courage to talk with Naani.

"Naani, do you know anything about the ring of Kundalini?" I asked her as she sat knitting next to an old wire heater.

"Been reading too many comics? Try focusing on your

schoolbooks," she snapped.

Scuffing sounds from her room reminded me that it was the same Naani who brought injured animals home to care for before shifting them to her pet shelter, Jantu House. Why was she so hard on me?

"Who is Shesh Nagraj? How are we related to him?" I persisted.

Without a pause in the clickety-clack of her knitting needles, she said, "Never heard of him. Go back to sleep."

It was hard not to take her refusal to talk personally. I knew she thought very little of me and my silhouette, but right now we had to come together for Mohan's sake.

"Naani," I said. "I'm sorry."

"For what? For embarrassing me with your misbehavior in school today?"

"That," I said, "and anything I may have done in the past to hurt you or Mohan."

Naani stopped knitting and stared at the heater. Slowly, her face mellowed, and her chin started to quiver. I realized she was crying. Her hand traveled to her cheek to wipe away a tear. Had I touched a raw nerve? Naani had allowed herself to look vulnerable in my presence for the first time.

"Being able to silhouette must make you feel powerful," she said, "but remember that power attracts attention and comes at a cost. Great cost. Living an ordinary life with extraordinary powers is not an easy feat."

My life was worse than ordinary. Couldn't she see that?

"Mohan's life is in danger," I said. "In Wantra—"

"Five generations lived happily before you came, Adi,"

Naani cut me off. Her eyes were still fixed on the red-hot glowing coil of the electric heater. "But you're not to blame. Sooner or later, our actions catch up with us. Shani spares no one."

If Anku were here, she would have given Naani a sharp retort, but I had no special feelings for or against Shani. As Naani sat with her eyes fixed on the heater, I wondered what was going on in her mind.

"We must do something to protect Mohan," I said desperately.

"As long as you two wear the Nag Vibhuti amulet outside our home, you will be safe," Naani said.

I gulped. I should have told Naani then that Dakini had burnt my amulet, but in light of the blunders on my part, I decided to put a pin in that confession.

"Don't you want to know what happened in Wantra?"

Naani put up her hand. "Wantra never happened. You were dreaming."

"But the prophecy," I said.

Naani put down her knitting in her lap and looked at me with raised eyebrows. "What about it?"

"It says the Naga heir and Rahu will meet in battle."

She considered my words for a few moments. "Tell me. Do you think you can defeat Rahu? Do you think anyone can defeat Rahu? He is an immortal deity with an immortal body half."

I looked at her, at a loss for words. Just because Rahu was invincible didn't mean that Mohan and I shouldn't defend ourselves. Living in fear and hiding was worse than death itself.

Naani turned back to her knitting. "Mohan will not attend

school until the blue blood moon is over," she announced, putting an end to the discussion. "As for you, Adi," she added sternly, "it's clear that my warnings mean nothing to you. But if you care for your brother, you will not attend school either."

I left Naani to her knitting. As soon as Batty spilled the beans about where I lived, Gargouille and his Yechs would land at our doorstep. Without the amulet, I was a beacon for the Yechs to find Mohan, but this was also the only way I could connect with other Maruts. I was the inevitable bait any which way.

It was my choice to attend school the next day. If my actions brought me bad luck, I promised myself, I would not blame Shani for it.

CHAPTER 22

At school the next day, I waited for someone—anyone—to show up. Either the Yechs would be drawn to my Marut scent or the Maruts would discover me on the Ichcha Darpan.

Meanwhile, I kept a lookout for Batty. According to the school, Batty had never existed. In my memory, I had never seen Batty interact with students or teachers. But I was sure he existed.

The day went by in a blink. To my dismay, fifteen minutes before school ended, I was summoned to the principal's office again.

Another day of detention suited my objective to stay away from home. When I stepped into the office, I received a peremptory nod from Mr. Bahri.

"Adi!" he said, giving me a fleeting look. He got back to his paperwork. "He's here."

"Who, sir?"

"The herpetologist I was talking about yesterday," he said

absentmindedly, focusing on a pile of papers before him. "Says he's studying twig snakes in the region. You could help him, I figured, since you have a pet reptile."

This was a surprising turn of events. I was glad that I wasn't being given any more detention and that I could investigate the whereabouts of Batty in school. As I headed for the school conference room, I mulled over excuses I could use to send the herpetologist away.

The conference rooms were circularly arranged around a waiting area. In the waiting area, the receptionist, busy talking on the phone, didn't see me approach.

It was when I heard voices from one of the rooms that it occurred to me that the herpetologist could be Gargouille or Kabeela in a snatched identity. A fierce battle of words was underway in one of the rooms. I was about to tiptoe out when I heard Naani's name.

"We should have reached out to Manasa," a voice said in a singsong.

"There's no telling how the old dragon would have reacted. The child will be more approachable," a calm and authoritative voice replied.

"You make decisions without consulting Kalakar or me," a gruff voice said.

"Krodha is right," the singsong voice said. "Buddhi can be harsh. If you listen to him, everything could be lost, and you won't get a second chance in case you're hoping for it."

These couldn't be the names of people. Kalakar, Buddhi, and Krodha were attributes that meant artistic, brainy, and angry.

The receptionist left her chair, still not noticing me. I stole closer to the slightly open door. A man dressed in a gray tweed coat with brown elbow patches, black pants, and a tie was sitting all alone in the room.

"Adi Yoshi is the Naga heir," the authoritative voice said. "Ergo, the heirloom belongs to him. Manasa gave up the right to that legacy the day she went underground. That is not the hero's way."

I wanted to tell the man that I was not the Naga heir. But I decided against divulging my identity. After all, he wanted to present me with a Naga heirloom, and I needed all the help I could get. Perhaps the heirloom was a powerful Yech-slaying challastra? Also, more importantly, it meant that he was not a Yech—although I wasn't so sure about the other people present in the room.

I tried but couldn't locate the source of the other voices. It was a small room with a white table and four chairs. There were no speakers or phones or video screens to suggest someone may have joined online.

I could have sworn the voices were all coming from the same man. But how was that possible?

"And you believe a boy who is ready to elope with his aunt is being heroic?" asked the disgruntled voice.

"Wanting to live a peaceful life is not a crime," the melodic voice replied.

This was wild. Clearly, the man was not here to discuss twig snakes. I knocked.

The man straightened in his chair and turned to look. On seeing me in the doorway, he got up. "Come in, come in, dear boy. So sorry to catch you in the middle of your lessons. My name is Dev Vidhata."

I had never heard the name Dev Vidhata before. Still, something about him struck me as familiar. "Mr. Bahri said you needed information about twig snakes?"

Dev Vidhata jerked into stillness. "Twig snakes?"

"Yes, twig snakes," a calm voice came from him, even though he hadn't opened his mouth to speak.

"That's right," Dev Vidhata said, slapping his forehead lightly.

I sat on the chair closest to the door. Dev Vidhata seemed to notice my unease. He retrieved a bundle of envelopes from the inner pocket of his coat.

"I believe these are yours," he said, handing me the packet.

I recognized the envelopes. These were all the letters I had written to Aunty Padma.

"Where is Aunty Padma? How did you get these?" I got up in a huff, knocking my chair over.

He waved his hand in the air. "Calm down, Adi. There is no Aunty Padma. Or…" He paused. "I am Aunty Padma, for now."

"What do you mean?"

"Check for eavesdroppers first," the sharp voice said, and Dev Vidhata nodded his head like an obedient kid. Having made sure that the waiting room was empty, he shut the door.

"All clear," he said to me with a grin.

His smile was infectious, but I had no reason to return it. What had he done with Aunty Padma? I sat down slowly.

"Your father did have a sister called Padma," he said, "but

she moved to live in the hills ten years back when your mother died."

"But I've been receiving letters from her," I said. Dev Vidhata smiled and waited as the truth dawned on me. "*You* have been writing back to me!"

Dev Vidhata had been posing as my aunt and getting all the information about Mohan, Naani, and me through my letters. I shuddered to think what Naani would do if she learned that I had shared details of our carefully concealed life with a stranger.

"It's clear that you know nothing about your parents, and your shrewd Naani has…" Dev Vidhata paused and moved back in his chair, grinding his teeth in thought. "…for her own reasons, not shared anything with you. I am not judging her."

"Of course we are!"

"Curses to Manasa!"

"She did what she had to do."

The voices erupted together in Dev Vidhata.

I moved back in my chair.

"Please don't be scared. The voices in my head are audible to others. It's an affliction I must live with," Dev Vidhata said.

"Voices?" came a growl.

"Actually, these are all respected identities that live within me."

"Damn right we are," the singsong voice chimed.

I figured Dev Vidhata must have one of the conditions mentioned on tincture bottles in Tara's Attars, perhaps Immortal's Dissonance, as there was absolutely no harmony among the voices in Dev Vidhata's head. If I believed in ghosts, I would have guessed he was possessed by three ghosts at the same time.

"But we can't get into introductions just now," Dev Vidhata said urgently. "When you didn't show up at the bus stop as decided, I knew something had happened. I had to make sure you were alright."

Even though Dev Vidhata had pulled a fiendish plan to fool me, his manner was sincere. Had my delivery to Gargouille been uninterrupted, I would have fled home to live with Aunt Padma, as suggested by her—or, as I now knew, by Dev Vidhata.

"Why did you ask me to move to Goa?" I said. "Do you have any idea how irresponsible that is?"

Dev Vidhata moved back in his chair. "I'm sorry if I made you feel unsafe."

"I feel unsafe now," I said indignantly. Tricking a kid to leave home without telling anyone was predatory and criminal.

Dev Vidhata nodded. "I can't apologize enough."

"You could try," a gruff voice resounded from him. Dev Vidhata frowned and rolled his eyes at himself.

"Bear with me, Adi. Many, many years ago, when Haveli of your forefathers was attacked, we tried to contact Manasa because the ring of Kundalini was untraceable," he said, holding his hands interlaced on the table.

I had a dirty feeling that more secrets from Naani's closet of lies and hypocrisy were about to spill out. Every person I met had added another shade of intrigue to Naani's persona. Who was she?

"We figured Manasa had something to do with it, but she

couldn't be traced either. For hundreds of years, I searched every corner of the world for her."

He paused for a deep breath as I squirmed in my seat, again reminded of how I had blown Naani's carefully planned cover, which she'd managed to safeguard for hundreds of years.

"Ten years ago, when your father was killed on the road, I read the news in the papers. The same articles mentioned your mother's death too. Leela Nagaraj Yoshi. I wonder how they got her middle name."

"Mother said she would never give up her maiden name," I whispered.

Dev Vidhata sighed. "That was how I tracked you down, but by the time I got to your house, Manasa had packed you and the baby out of Bangalore. I made inquiries and got your Aunt Padma's address. That was how I set up camp there."

It was not all my fault that Dev Vidhata had found me, and I was immediately assailed with guilt for pointing a finger at my dead mother. She'd had the courage to stand up for herself, for her roots. All I had ever done was crib about being a Naga.

"And tell him what everyone said to us," the singsong voice interrupted.

Dev Vidhata nodded, pleased, and pointed to his head. "That's Kalakar. He is very talented and creative."

"Tell him," Kalakar cooed this time.

"They said it wouldn't work. Manasa does not leave loopholes. But here I am, the first celestial to establish contact with the heir of the Naga clan." Dev Vidhata was grinning broadly, but his smile faded when he saw my face.

"You were making a fool of me all this time," I said. I

clenched my fists in my lap. The preparation for fleeing my cold and unfriendly home had got me through the day. There was nothing to look forward to now. It felt like someone had pulled the rug out from under my feet—as if my future had been stolen.

He shook his head. "I wanted to gain your trust. There is no one more dangerous than a reluctant silhouette. I wanted to prepare you for the blue blood moon," Dev Vidhata said, trying to placate me.

"But the blue blood moon is two nights away," I said. "Why now?"

"I have recently acquired a piece of the puzzle, an heirloom that could save the day," Dev Vidhata said after a deep breath.

"What puzzle?"

Did this have to do with the riddle that Aunty Tara had mentioned? *Is spirit the home or the circle it lives in?* I had solved that one in a jiffy while fully aware that celestial puzzles couldn't be that simple!

"It concerns a specific ritual that involves your grandmother and her silhouette."

"Why should I believe you?" I said, getting up to leave. I had no interest in knowing anything about Naani's silhouette. She had never cared for mine.

"Because that is the only way, Adi." He rested his chin on his hands, seemingly weary and overwhelmed by my distrust in him. "I was extremely sorry to know how unhappy your life has been." He tapped a finger on the bundle of letters. "Manasa gave up her silhouette and its perks for you. Her silhouette is repressed. Once she gets in touch with her Marut self, she will understand you better. She will help you find the ring of Kundalini and bring it back."

"Rahu doesn't have the ring of Kundalini," I said. "I saw it destroyed with my own eyes."

Dev Vidhata nodded repeatedly. From his perturbed expression, I could see that he hadn't known about this development. "Rest assured," he said finally, "he has something worse with him."

I waited for him to continue. "Discretion!" three voices echoed a warning to him.

"I can't divulge more than that. I can't get in the way of the universe," Dev Vidhata sighed and rubbed his stubble. "The blue blood moon takes place on Sunday morning. This is your only chance."

"I don't know." I shook my head. It wasn't hard to see Naani as my well-wisher; it was impossible. Also, I couldn't trust someone who'd woven a web of deception around me for so long. "I'm sorry," I said and got up to leave. My heart was heavy from learning that I had no aunt to turn to and that the heirloom was not for me but for Naani.

"You can still have a life with your aunt," Dev Vidhata said to my back. "But if Boors take over the world, nothing will matter anymore."

A knock sounded on the door like a jarring call to reality. It made me jump backward. Mr. Bahri peeked in. "Hope everything is in order? The school day is about to end," he said with a wide grin that reminded me of Santa Claus.

"We're just winding up," Dev Vidhata said, sliding in front of me and bowing deeply to Mr. Bahri.

"If Adi's grandmother allows it, Adi could stay back after school to help you out with further information," a pleased Mr. Bahri said.

Dev Vidhata waved away the offer. "There will be no need for that. Adi knows more about chameleons than snakes." Of course, he knew about Patches. Through my letters, he would know all about my embarrassing run-ins with Ayesha Saini, too. *The nerve!*

"That's good, then. We've combed the school premises. There's no sign of a snake anywhere."

"Great news! I will take your leave," Dev Vidhata said and turned to me.

While Mr. Bahri's attention was diverted by the receptionist who had returned, Dev Vidhata produced a brown paper bag from his inner coat pocket and placed it in my hand.

"Thanks for your help," he said. "I'm sure Patches will love to play with this." He pulled me into a friendly hug and whispered into my ear. "All you have to do is plant this in Manasa's hands when no one else is around, especially your brother. But be warned, it won't be easy."

"Perhaps Adi knows where to find the snake tongs you've been looking for," Mr. Bahri said behind my back.

Snake tongs! I looked at Dev Vidhata, alarmed, as I left the room. All snakes hated tongs. He should know that.

"I've heard you can get almost anything at the Hauz Khas night market in the capital," I heard Dev Vidhata say to the principal.

"You mean the thieves' market?" Mr. Bahri replied. They chatted as they walked toward the school gates.

I rushed across the waiting area and made a beeline for the nearest bathroom. Once there, I upturned Dev Vidhata's paper bag. A small metal symbol dropped into my palm. It had three overlapping petals of a flower. Unlike the flashy ones the Gandaks wore at the shivir in Chandni Chowk, this triquetra was a dull brown, the color of parched earth.

I remembered Anku mentioning that the real triquetra had many powers, most of which were still unknown. But this triquetra looked as ordinary as the man who had handed it to me, if you didn't take the voices in his head into account.

The clanging bell announced the end of the school day. I stashed the triquetra in the outer pocket of my school bag and was about to throw away the brown paper bag when I noticed the logo on it: Twelve Rhinos Café and Inn.

I realized now why Dev Vidhata had looked so familiar. He was none other than one of the fallen deities I had met in my dream. He was Brahma, the architect of the Universe, the creator.

My school was a kilometer's walk from home. On my way home, I spotted Mohan walking ahead with a couple of neighborhood boys, who were listening in rapt attention to what he was saying. He was supposed to have skipped school that day.

Fear and annoyance swelled in me like a tidal wave and left me drenched in goosebumps. Like an older brother would, I wanted to tell him off for being careless. Choice expletives bobbed in my mind to be plucked and flung at Mohan. But ever since I had tattled to Thauma about Mohan and seen the glee it had produced in Rahu and his coterie, I couldn't bring myself to be harsh with him.

"What are you doing?" I said urgently. "Naani asked you not to leave home."

"Naani isn't fair. She said, 'Adi can hurt you,'" Mohan said, grinning and mimicking Naani. "But we are brothers. How could you ever hurt me? Look." He lifted his arm to show me the mark left by the absent Vibhuti amulet. "Like you, I've removed it. That will show her."

"Mohan, this is dangerous," I said. My fingertips and toes were tingling from panic now

"Don't worry. Naani won't know. She left home early in the morning," Mohan replied, shrugging his shoulders.

We had to get back to the safety of home, and quickly. My stomach churned at the thought of Mohan stuck in one of Dakini Malini's labs.

"Just stay with me," I said.

We walked the path festooned with vibrant neon pennant flags in all colors carrying pictures of the local candidate, Vinay Chaubey, in a starched black turban and garlands of marigolds. I remembered Gargouille had mentioned Chaubey outside Dakini Malini's den.

Written across banners were words:
Vote for Chaubey!
Only Chaubey
Can save the day!

Election fever had gripped the city. Three-wheelers with megaphones attached to their sides had started patrolling the roads. It was an unexpectedly noisy and busy day.

The road outside our condo was barricaded. Some men in

white caps were handing out flyers to the schoolchildren. What would children do with election flyers?

A few steps ahead, a commotion started. One of Mohan's friends was shepherded to the side to be questioned. While some adults moved to rescue the boy, I hurried to steer Mohan through the barricade. But I should have known Mohan wouldn't abandon his friend.

"Let him go!" Mohan cried loudly, stepping toward his friend.

"No, Mohan!" I whispered urgently.

The man questioning the boy had his back to us. When he turned around and I saw his face, my feet suddenly went as heavy as lead. Dark-skinned and amber-eyed, even in human form, Kabeela struck a fearful figure in a black kurta pajama, turban, and embroidered leather shoes. He was the Yech I'd met in Chandni Chowk, the one who brought Thauma to Rahu in Kalpavriksha.

"Tell me your name, boy," Kabeela said, moving toward Mohan, still holding Mohan's friend by the collar.

Never answer that question, Naani had instructed us.

Mohan looked at me. I shook my head at him. Kabeela had only sensed my presence when I pulled at his mustache in Chandni Chowk. I wondered if he would recognize me now.

"My name is none of your business," Mohan said.

"Too afraid to share your name?" Kabeela taunted him. "This one squealed out his name in a second." He shook the boy, who whimpered.

Mohan squared his shoulders. "I am Mohan Yoshi."

While I gave in to rage easily if someone made a personal

attack on me, in a similar situation, Mohan generally kept his cool. But social injustice called out like a foghorn to his aggressive side. If you ask me, he loved sticking his nose into other people's business.

Upon hearing Mohan's name, Kabeela went still. A few people stopped to investigate what was happening. I looked around to find that the barricade had been removed and the crowd had started moving. Political workers for Vinay Chaubey's party moved to stand between Mohan and me. I tried to push my way through them, but by the time I got through, Kabeela had already snatched up Mohan and boarded a car.

As the car disappeared around the corner, leaving clouds of dust in its wake, my world crumbled. Mohan had been kidnapped in bright daylight.

I looked around wildly at the whispering crowd. Some people had recorded the incident on their phones. A couple of them called TV channels and newspapers. In a few seconds, the zealously protected anonymity of the Nagaraj clan had gone up in smoke.

How would Naani react? There was no way I could face her after what had happened. Mohan was her life. She had feared that I would one day prove dangerous to my brother. I had scoffed at her wild imagination then, but now I felt my legs go weak. I thought of Dakini Malini, Gargouille, and the Yechs gloating over their conquest. I forced myself not to think of what Rahu planned to do with Mohan.

"Are you related to that boy?" someone asked me.

I nodded.

"Will you talk to the journalist?" someone asked, holding a

phone to my face.

I moved away without answering.

"We have the car license plate on our cameras!" somebody cried.

I knew that would not help.

CHAPTER 23

I slipped into the narrow curving lanes of the adjoining village. Someone called my name, but I was in no shape to talk to the kids from school. Copious tears streamed down my face. The last time I wept that hard, I silhouetted—and right now, silhouetting seemed a tempting escape from the chaos and confusion in my life.

I started running, my heavy school bag bouncing on my back as I gave in to spurts of weeping and wiping my face. How had everything gone wrong overnight? Aunty Padma had turned out to be a hoax. Mohan had been kidnapped by Yechs, and Naani was either in denial or struck by amnesia.

I stopped running and bent over to catch my breath. I could call Naani and tell her everything at the risk of losing any shred of affection she had for me. But that was the only way I could save Mohan. She would have no choice but to use the triquetra to bring back her silhouette.

The emergency mobile phone I kept in the outer pocket of my bag had never served any purpose. Naani hadn't allowed me to download any apps or games on it. In fact, most days I forgot I even had a mobile phone.

My finger hovered over the call button. Something held me back from tapping it—a terrifying thought. Could I trust Naani to take action? I found Naani evasive and cowardly. She wasn't the fierce Manasa Yoshi everyone knew in Wantra. What if she succumbed to the grief of losing Mohan to the Boors?

Dev Vidhata believed Naani's repressed silhouette could be brought back with the triquetra, but I doubted that. She was too fond of Mohan, and only I had seen this vulnerable side to Naani. I put the phone back in the bag and wiped the tears off my face with my sleeve.

"Vasuki Upakritam," I whispered on a whim, but no Kaleeni flew to my rescue.

I took the triquetra from my school bag and placed it carefully in the pocket of my pants for safekeeping, picturing Anku shaking a cautionary finger at me for having lost the Dusht Uchchaihshravas and Kaleeni. *And Mohan, too,* Naani spoke in my head right on cue.

I shook my head to clear my thinking. I had to get to one of the paladins, and fast. Anku had mentioned Mothy Maddy, Pilot Roy, and Red, the restaurateur.

"Rickshaw, rickshaw," a rickshaw puller intoned as he braked next to me.

Every second was crucial. I jumped into the rickshaw. I calculated the fare to the metro station as the rickshaw puller labored on the uneven, baked mud lanes of the village, heedless of the discomfort caused to his passenger bouncing on the hard straw and Rexine seat.

The last known location of the shivir had been Chandni Chowk.

"Could you go faster?" I asked.

"It will cost you double," replied the rickshaw puller, his voice unclear for the muffler that was wrapped around his neck and mouth.

"But I only have twenty-five rupees," I said, allowing a hint of pleading in my voice. It generally worked.

"A piece of jewelry will do, too," the man said with a furtive glance over his shoulder.

The moment he said these words, my eyes fell upon his earlobes, where numerous hoops hung from the cartilage.

"Thauma!" I cried.

The rickshaw puller stopped pedaling and pulled off into the shade of a roadside tree. "How do you know me?" he asked.

"It's me, Adi," I said, removing my thick glasses. With my glasses and hearing aid, I must have cut a sorry figure compared to the Adi in Wantra.

"By Brahma's beard, you are!" Thauma said.

"So you remember me?"

"Of course I do," Thauma said. His jaw relaxed and his brows unfurrowed. "Tell me. Who was responsible for uthaan?"

"What's that?"

"Leaving Wantra without paying the gatekeeper. It's called uthaan. It takes you back to Samsara, bringing along anyone who entered Wantra at the same moment you did."

"I don't know." I shrugged. "We were in the Maw when I

passed out and woke up back home." I gave a brief account of our escapade in the Maw.

"You let Anku escape on the Yali?" Thauma asked me, astonished.

"I had no choice."

"I would have taken the Yali for myself, so I would say you did have a choice," he said without hesitation.

I wanted to lash out at him for letting Rahu know about Mohan, but in all fairness, I couldn't blame him for my own lack of discretion.

"Does this mean Surp and Anku would have returned too?" I asked, a drop of optimism falling on the parched and hopeless terrain of my morale.

He nodded, pouting thoughtfully. "Though I'm not sure how uthaan works in the Maw. Dakini Malini may have created a firewall around the dungeon… anyway, we owe a big one to whoever made it happen."

"Wait a second. What about Kaleeni?"

"Celestial objects are immune to uthaan," Thauma said, spreading his hands. "Kaleeni belongs to me for my services to the Maruts."

"The transaction was never completed," I pointed out.

Before I could bring up the matter of the stolen dagger, Thauma said, "Alright, you can have it back."

"I can have it back?" I repeated.

"If you have something to give to me in return, you can have Kaleeni back."

This was a start. At least he had considered parting with my flying carpet.

"But you already have something of mine that doesn't belong to you," I said.

Thauma cocked his head at me like a parrot. "What are you talking about?"

"The dagger, Dusht Uchchaihshravas," I said. "You stole it from my bag."

"I would never take anything unless a deal was struck," Thauma said, his nostrils flaring. "If that is how little you think of me, I'll leave you to your business." He struck a pose like a theater artist and flung his muffler around his neck once again, turning around to leave. "Contact me if you have anything to trade."

My hand traveled to my pocket, and I felt the relic that Dev Vidhata had given me. I could use it to snatch identities, but the whole idea sounded dodgy to me. I could hardly handle my own two identities of human and silhouette. But Thauma would go to any length to obtain it.

I held up the triquetra. "Would this work?"

Thauma gasped. He stared at it, speechless for several moments. "Kaleeni is yours," he said, snatching the triquetra from my hand, but before he could pocket it, I swiped it back.

"You will get it when I get Kaleeni."

He pursed his lips. "As obstinate as Manasa, aren't you."

"Thauma," I said at the mention of Naani. "Can a Marut get back the silhouette they gave up?"

"Once relinquished, a silhouette is lost forever. But through Chalvesha, silhouettes can also be made to fall asleep." He snapped his fingers. "Take Takka the cobbler, for example. He has revenge smoldering inside of him for when his family was wronged by prince Arjuna, a protégé of Indra. Indra performed Chalvesha on Takka, and now, on the outside, he is an old man who collects Marut weapons like a maniac. He knows he must avenge the murder of his family, but his animal side is gone. He is helpless."

"Why don't you tell him?"

"That's the beauty of Chalvesha. The identity lies dormant, as if in a bubble, in some part of the brain. It needs to be shocked into waking up."

I was sure Thauma would trade the triquetra with Takka for something more valuable, perhaps an invincible challastra.

"How did you get the triquetra?" Thauma asked, suddenly growing suspicious. "It was placed in the strongest safe-deposit box at the Bank of Karma after the attack on Haveli."

"I met a man who spoke in four voices," I replied carefully. I was reluctant to admit that I'd met the creator Brahma for the fear of sounding stupid. "Not languages, but different voices, as if different people lived inside him."

"You don't say!" Thauma squinted his eyes in amusement. "I dare say we'll have a merry gathering of has-been celestials in Hauz Khas thieves' market tomorrow." He patted me on the head. "Stay safe. Tomorrow evening at ten, come to Hauz Khas thieves' market to complete the transaction." He got into the driver's seat of the rickshaw. "You may yet get to witness a once-in-a-lifetime spectacle."

I couldn't wait that long. But if I confided in Thauma about Mohan's abduction, there was no guarantee he wouldn't double-cross me.

"So where were you headed?" Thauma asked as he started

to pedal the rickshaw again.

"The shivir," I said, a tremble in my voice.

Thauma braked again. "You don't need a ride in the rickshaw to get there." He removed a challastra from around his waist. "Though my rickshaw driving skills are legendary. Riding my rickshaw is an experience you would not forget."

I didn't doubt his claim.

Thauma swung the key ring in his finger. A giant key the size of a banana appeared in his hand. We heard someone gasp near us and turned to find an old and frail lady sitting on a rope mesh bed outside her single-room house. She had been tossing rice in an open plate to separate it from the chaff.

Thauma walked past her, tapped the door of her house with his key, and stood aside.

"What do you want?" the old lady cried, shaking her fist at him.

Thauma ignored her and beckoned to me. As I passed by the lady, I gave her an apologetic smile. She glared at us, her rice-filled plate frozen in her hand, her mouth agape. As I stood at the threshold, musty smells of cotton mattresses and poorly ventilated rooms ran riot in my nose.

Thauma placed a hand on my shoulder. "Paladins and magicians are allergic to one another's company. Best not to mention me to Madhav or Pilot Roy."

CHAPTER 24

I stepped over the raised threshold to find myself gasping for breath. Unable to open my eyes for the immense pressure all around, the sense of claustrophobia grew dire as the white noise from the village receded. It felt as if my ear and nose cavities had filled up with water.

Just as I thought I would pass out, I emerged on the pavement outside the bridge to find my way blocked by a white staff with gnarly bumps all over that looked suspiciously like bone joints.

I looked over my shoulder to see if I could turn around and run but found myself backed up against a wall. The smell of moth repellent invaded my nostrils as my gaze moved to the man holding the staff.

Broad-shouldered and muscled, the bearded man was as tall as Kabeela and Gargouille. He had gray eyes and salt-and-pepper dreadlocks held together with a rubber band. Like Anku and Surp, he wore jeans and a kurta. Next to him, a fox with red and brown fur growled at me. In his right hand, the bearded man wore a black onyx stone ring set in gold. I had seen the ring before but couldn't place it. He had grime on his face and clothes, and marks of a fight on his body.

"Mothy Maddy," I whispered, and he narrowed his eyes in response. "Who are you?" he asked in a gruff but not unkind voice.

"My name is Adi Nagaraj Yoshi," I said suddenly, unsure how I would explain what had happened in the Maw and why Anku and Surp hadn't returned.

He held me by my shoulders and searched my face till recognition dawned on him. "What are you doing here?" he said. "You should not have left home. Where's Manasa?"

So he knew Naani and me after all. A sob of relief escaped my mouth. "They've taken Mohan."

Mothy Maddy's jaw clenched. "Tell me everything."

He herded me toward the burlap curtains of the Underbridge. I looked around his massive form to find the lamppost and the ladder were back at the Lodhi Road Underbridge.

"For some reason, the shift was reversed," Mothy Maddy explained when he saw the confusion on my face.

"I know why," I said. Uthaan must have reversed events in the spaces shared between Wantra and Samsara.

Chinni, the Glitch housekeeper at the Underbridge, brought me some warm milk to calm me. As she rubbed my back softly, I recounted everything, leaving out the meeting with Dev Vidhata and the triquetra.

"Thauma says we got lucky that someone triggered uthaan," I said.

Mothy Maddy nodded. "But Thauma knows of only one

side: his own. At this moment, he may be on his way to inform Gargouille of your whereabouts. We must leave immediately."

I knew Thauma wouldn't double-cross me until our transaction was complete. "They have Mohan. What would Gargouille want with me now?"

"To finish the threat you pose forever."

Rahu didn't see me as a threat. He had said so himself. I remained silent in the hope that Mothy Maddy would keep me close to him.

"You are a brave Marut," Mothy Maddy said after a few moments of silence.

This was unexpected. He was the first grown-up I'd ever met who didn't try to point out my mistakes or tell me what I could have done instead. To someone already aware of their mistakes, nothing was worse than being called out. The biggest blunder on my part was agreeing to deliver the packages to Gargouille. Mothy Maddy would think less of me if he knew the entire story. I bowed my head, unable to receive any kind words at that moment.

"Not many kids would have risked their own lives in the Maw," Mothy Maddy persisted.

"I'm sorry I couldn't help Surp and Anku," I said in a whisper. The list of my failures was long and unending.

He shook his head. "Maruts are trained to keep the world safe. They're warriors. They don't get swayed by emotions." His face, haggard from worry, told a different story. "It so happens that I work for Vinay Chaubey."

"The local candidate in the election?" I asked. "Kabeela was dressed as a worker for Vinay Chaubey."

Mothy Maddy nodded. "He provides safe umbrellas to goons like Kabeela and Dakini Malini for their illegal works. There are rumors about a research program he funds, where drugs are tested on children."

When Rahu asked Ketu to ensure Mothy Maddy didn't reach the sacrificial altar on the blue blood moon, Ketu had been worried it might expose his real identity.

"Do you think Vinay Chaubey is Ketu?" I asked Mothy Maddy.

"It's possible," he said. "Though Vinay Chaubey has committed crimes that even Ketu would shudder to commit."

From what I had seen and heard of Ketu, he was not a bad sort. His reluctance to be Rahu's partner in crime had surprised me as much as it had shocked Dakini Malini.

"I've worked hard to get into Vinay Chaubey's inner circle," Mothy Maddy said. "He has come to believe we're best friends."

"But they know you're on to them. I heard them say so in Rahu's lair. Your life might be in danger."

"Today, there is an event at Vinay Chaubey's residence," Mothy Maddy said, ignoring the panic in my voice.

As I waited for him to elaborate, he walked toward the metal wall and disappeared behind it. Next to me sat Mothy Maddy's fox silhouette, Lomri. If I trained enough to attain Vibhaga, my silhouette could be my pet—just like Mothy Maddy's silhouette, Lomri, and Surp's koel.

The best part of Vibhaga, though, was that I'd be able to access my warrior silhouette. I couldn't help wondering what my warrior silhouette would look like. Surp's koel came with armor and razor-sharp wings. Perhaps I'd have a muscled human body and the deadly tail of a snake that could shoot poison darts.

My fragile and tiny bubble of joy was popped by Mothy Maddy's voice from behind the wall. "Today is a good opportunity to comb Vinay Chaubey's residence and attached warehouses for hostages," he said.

My folly had landed my brother in this pickle, I realized. Could I be trusted in my warrior silhouette? I could hardly stand myself when I was in my twig snake silhouette.

I made a mental note to never strive to achieve Vibhaga. What use was a warrior silhouette to me if I had no long-term plans for staying in the Marut fold? At the first instance possible, I would opt for renouncing my silhouette, or what they called Chalvesha. Moreover, I loved Patches dearly. I would never want another pet.

I felt a tug on my shirt and found Chinni holding a finger to her mouth. She gave me a roughly scrawled note.

Meet me at Jawahar Stadium Station, Anku.

The Jawahar Lal Nehru Stadium metro station was nearest to this Underbridge. I quickly stuffed the note in my pocket as Mothy Maddy walked out dressed in a freshly washed and ironed pair of jeans and a kurta.

Why didn't Anku contact Mothy Maddy if she had indeed returned from Wantra? I wondered. Seeing the note by Anku suddenly added a shot of possibility to the hopeless situation I found myself in. I tried to keep a straight face as Mothy Maddy talked.

"While his aides are in attendance at the celebrations, Lomri will check out the godowns," he said, picking up Lomri and placing her in his cloth jhola. Then, softly, he added, "I trained Surp, Rudra, and Anku for this moment."

"I can help," I said eagerly. I preferred fighting Kabeela over facing Naani.

"Listen to me very carefully, Adi. I want you to go home to your grandmother and tell her everything. I know she gives you a hard time, but she loves you." He led me to a ramshackle Royal Enfield parked next to the curb.

"You don't know her," I protested.

Mothy Maddy put on his helmet and retrieved another from the saddlebag of the motorbike. This helmet was pink and had Anku written all over it. It even smelled like her: oranges and caramel candy.

Mothy Maddy held up his hand. "I will drop you at the metro station and you will go back home. It's the safest place for you to be."

It hurt to know he thought I was lesser than Anku and Surp, but in his defense, he didn't see me in action in Kalpavriksha.

From the pavement next to the metro station, I watched Mothy Maddy leave. I had no intention of returning home. I needed to find a place to lie low for the night.

Tomorrow, I would get Kaleeni from Thauma. If Mothy Maddy failed to rescue Mohan, I might have to live in Kaleeni, with its invisibility booster on, forever. Luckily, Mothy Maddy dropped me off at the meeting point Anku had requested in her note.

"Yo, Adi!"

I spun around to find myself face-to-face with a fuming Anku. The first emotion I felt when I saw her was relief that she had survived.

"Take off my helmet," she said.

Standing alongside Anku was a boy with a mohawk and a squirrel's nose. He wore a cap to cover his ears. His tail, tucked under his pants, gave him a silly waddle. I wished he didn't have to hide himself.

"Ludo!" I cried. "But how…"

Before I could even finish the question, Anku said, "Could I have my helmet?"

"Do you even need it?" I asked, handing it to her.

Her clean new clothes contrasted with her grubby monogrammed shoes, which I noticed still had a few specks of blood from the battle with the Chamruks in the Maw.

"When uthaan happened," Anku said, "Ludo was pulled back into this world with me." She took the helmet and stuffed it into her backpack.

"What about Surp?"

Anku gave a despondent headshake. "We couldn't reach her."

I let the implication sink in. Surp had been in the Maw for four days now. Even if the Chamruks didn't get to her, starvation and thirst would.

I was about to ask Anku why she hadn't met Mothy Maddy yet when the answer came to me. It was for the same reason that I hadn't returned home to Naani. Anku feared Mothy Maddy's anger for defying his instructions just like I dreaded facing Naani for leading Boors to Mohan.

"How did you find me?" I asked.

"Ichcha Darpan." She unzipped her backpack to show me

the chipped magical mirror. "Chinni procured it for me."

"That was why Mothy Maddy didn't pick up my silhouette at school." I had expected Mothy Maddy to trace me in absence of my Naga Vibhuti amulet. "Why didn't you come to look for me?"

"We did," she said and paused. "We saw the kidnapping and followed you, but you disappeared so quickly, as if Apsara sleuths were on your tail. Finally, we found you just as Thauma opened the door with his Chaabi challastra."

"You could have intervened to stop them," I said ruefully, though I knew full well that even if she had jumped in with her challastra to fight the kidnappers, we'd have been no match for Kabeela.

"I've been investigating the whereabouts of Dakini," Anku said, to which Ludo gave a light cough. "We've found clues to where her lab might be. That's where Kabeela would have taken Mohan," Anku continued with an emphasis on "we" that got Ludo grinning.

Ludo had started drawing stares for his quirky appearance when a thought occurred to me. "Can you bring a message to someone in Kalpavriksha?" I asked Ludo, grasping at straws.

"Only if I must. I could be of invaluable help here," Ludo protested. He wanted to be in the thick of the action but didn't realize that his odd looks wouldn't be seen kindly in Samsara. He wasn't aware that the real world would be harder than Kalpavriksha on him. I had enough experience in that matter.

I tore a piece of paper from a notebook and scribbled a message down on it with Ludo and Anku peering over my shoulder.

"Hmmm," Anku said. "One Dakini against the other. This is risky. You really think it could work?"

No, I wasn't sure, but we were out of options. I folded the paper and wrote the name of the recipient on top: Dakini Surpanekha.

A disgruntled Ludo fished out a key ring similar to Thauma's. He used the key to open the door of a transformer box and disappeared inside.

"Dakinis are not known for helping," Anku said.

"For all we know, Dakinis themselves need rescuing from Dakini Malini. Surpanekha will only be helping herself," I said, unloading my school bag next to a streetlight. "We must get to Dakini Malini's lab."

Anku shook her head. "Not without reinforcements. She's powerful in Samsara, enough to overpower Rudra's lion silhouette. We're the last ones left to know the truth. We need a paladin. Someone who is immune to Dakini powers and won't be worried about breaking celestial rules. We need Pilot Roy." She raised her eyebrows and exhaled.

"But Mohan's life is in danger," I said, knowing full well that Anku was right. She didn't seem the least bit surprised by the fact that Mohan was the real Naga heir.

"Malini won't touch Mohan before the blue blood moon. Rahu needs him for the ritual."

"And the Maruts?" I asked. "Malini said she would extract their silhouette essences."

"She would have done that by now," Anku said softly. "But for the silhouette essences to work, the Maruts will have to be kept alive. If they die, the silhouette dies with them, and

Venvap will become ineffective." Her tone suggested her information was a hunch.

I glanced at my watch. Naani would soon find out what had happened. I had to keep her negative and critical voice out of my head. I hoped to find Mohan and trade the triquetra for Kaleeni before the blue blood moon.

"Do you know where to find Pilot Roy?" I asked Anku.

"Pilot Roy is a floater, but I have an idea about where he might be," she said. "If we can't find him tomorrow, we'll have to take Red's help. The eclipse doesn't take place till 2 a.m. tomorrow night."

"We could go to Red right now," I suggested. Why wait for Pilot Roy when another paladin could be reached easily? We didn't have the luxury of spending the entire night without doing something to help Mohan.

"Do you know what the special power of paladin Red is?" Anku asked me in the same all-knowing manner that irritated the bejesus out of me.

"No, I don't," I said.

"He owns a restaurant. His special power is celestial food."

CHAPTER 25

On the way to our hideout, I pondered over how someone who specialized in food could be a paladin. Before we started, Anku made me switch off my mobile phone, saying, "They could trace us."

Only Mohan and Naani ever messaged me. I checked my phone. There were no messages.

The moment we arrived at Chandni Chowk metro station, I realized the setting of Anku's hideout: the Haveli. Chandni Chowk felt like home to me, not just owing to the Haveli being located there but because of the anonymity provided by its crowded lanes.

On our way to the Haveli, Anku used yet another one of her talents, sleight of hand, to acquire some food and drinks for the evening. "They owe us," she said. By "they," she meant humans, and even though it was a little high-handed, I agreed with her.

She removed the bramble that was being used to cover a gap in the wall next to the thick wooden gates of the Haveli.

THE LEGEND OF TRIQUETRA

While she prattled on about why Maruts were absolved of petty theft, I stood back to look at the Haveli.

Over the years, I'd viewed the house in my dreams in brief snatches: horrifying screams here, a lick of fire there, a glimpse of the corridor, a view of the manicured lawns. I blamed the movies I watched for these dreams. Perhaps it had something to do with my lineage. Was it possible to grow up dreaming about the places one's ancestors inhabited?

The lawn of the Haveli was large. Thanks to the deluge of rubble, it had escaped encroachment. Some of the walls were still standing. I counted these and figured that the house must have contained at least six or seven bedrooms.

The house itself was proof of gruesome murder: the blown-up staircase leading to the upper floors, the butchered walls, the splintered unsupported doorjambs, and the collapsed roof all looked like mangled innards of a body. A turret on its right was the only structure that remained intact. Its entrance was probably hidden in one of the rooms. It wasn't difficult to imagine the splendor of the Haveli in its heyday.

Anku switched on the torch from her phone as the last few remnants of daylight gave way to darkness. We picked our way over the debris to the dark interiors of the Haveli ruins.

I recalled my meeting with the Naga princess, Ulupi, when I first stumbled upon Haveli. She had risen from a portrait buried in debris. Despite her claims of being a celestial, I had a strong suspicion that she was a ghost, waiting for her stolen piece of jewelry—the ring of Kundalini.

"Is she here?" I asked. "Ulupi. Have you met her?"

Anku shook her head. "I put her portrait in the room on

the first floor of the tower. If we survive the lunar eclipse, we can hand it to the authorities and have it placed in the museum."

We ducked under broken beams on the ground floor and wove our way through a maze of walls—some still standing high, others eroded. Anku moved aside a black makeshift curtain, which I realized was actually a sari. We stepped into a room with an arched window and an intact roof. Moonlight streamed through the window to reveal a hideout that looked like a setup for professional spies to run undercover operations.

The floor of this room, cleaned of rubble but nonetheless broken and bumpy, was strewn with books, a map of Delhi, building blueprints, battery-power packs, pens, papers, and a laptop.

"What do you think?" Anku said smugly when she noticed the awe on my face.

"Aren't you worried someone might steal all this?"

"This is the most haunted spot in Chandni Chowk. No one ventures close to it," she said, flinging her jacket on a chair and flopping down on an old mattress.

"What do you use the laptop for?"

"The celestials are hopeless when it comes to handling human technology. They leave clues all over the internet. That's how I managed to trace Dakini. Let me show you something."

She flipped open her laptop. I sat next to her, shoulder to shoulder, our backs against a crumbling brick wall. I realized how comfortable it felt sitting next to Anku. I would have been a bundle of nerves had I been sitting so close to Surp.

THE LEGEND OF TRIQUETRA

Anku clicked on the Facebook profile of a Dr. Mala Chaubey. And there she was: Dakini Malini, grinning from her profile picture. She was dressed in leather boots and a fur coat. Trees laden with cherry blossoms provided the background for her photo. The photo was captioned: *Living it up in Central Park, NYC*. She hadn't been joking about the perks of joining hands with Rahu. Despite her human appearance and a "say cheese" smile, there was something dark about her that caused goosebumps on my arms. All that was missing were her sharp pointy canines.

"Look who she's married to," Anku said, scrolling down.

A picture of Vinay Chaubey popped up with a demure Dakini Malini standing next to him. We scrolled down further to find more pictures of the lovey-dovey couple.

"Ugh," Anku said, closing the window and switching off the laptop in case our activity drew attention.

"She has political connections," I said.

"This is why we could never find her. The policemen contacted by the parents of Maruts who got abducted or 'treated' by Dakini Malini obviously had their orders. By the time we got there, she would clear out and disappear. If I hadn't met her in Kalpavriksha, I would have never known."

"At least one thing can be ruled out," I said. "Vinay Chaubey can't be Ketu. Dakini Malini and Ketu can't stand each other."

Anku nodded. "I also found a Gargo D'Souza on Facebook, a musician who lives in Goa."

I couldn't bring myself to picture Gargouille as a musician, not even a heavy-metal guitarist. He was just too gruff and uncouth. "Any sign of Rahu?"

Anku shook her head.

"So Vinay Chaubey could be Rahu?"

She raised her eyebrows. "Maybe."

The deity of death and disease had snatched the identity of a politician who'd promised to serve people! Was it irony or a sad, tired cliché? After all, no one trusted politicians anymore.

Anku handed me a blanket and snuggled into her own, pulling on an eye mask that read *Disturb at your own risk*. Subtlety was not her forte.

It had been *a tiring day for me, physically and emotionally. I watched the moon in the sky, white and stationary, oblivious to the darkness that would take hold of it on tomorrow night's eclipse.*

All of a sudden, a star appeared close to the moon, and then another one. This was odd, unless these were UFOs planning to attack the city. One by one, more stars appeared like sparkly fireflies filling up a garden.

This had to be a very vivid dream because Delhi skies weren't exactly known for their clarity or stargazing.

I heard a slight whimper. I turned to check on Anku, but instead of Anku, I found myself looking at a terrified Lomri. She stood next to a squatting Rajasthani shepherd who wore thick-soled leather juttis and loose-fitting dhoti pants with ample room around the knees, making them ideal for any kind of seating. A multicolored turban so large that one could camp under it lay coiled like a heap of ropes on the shepherd's head. He was wearing a jacket with overlapping front flaps tied with colorful strings. The man was young, brawny, and very familiar.

No way! Dreadlocks were peeking from under the turban. It was Mothy Maddy. This scene had "Naga third-eye vision" written all over it.

I stood up and looked around to find a landscape plucked straight out of a horror movie. We were in the living room of Haveli from a hundred and fifty years back. This had to be a few days after the much-talked-about attack on Haveli, as the blood splattered on the floor and the walls was dry and cakey.

A lopsided chandelier tinkled to a playful breeze. Torn fragments of canvas hung from the frames of oil paintings on the walls. Half burnt furniture lay upturned. Not a single object was unspoiled.

As if to make sense of what I saw, the dank, metallic stench of blood invaded my nostrils. I cursed my silhouette and covered my nose with my sleeve. Even in my dreams, my silhouette had an impeccable sense of smell!

I jumped out of my skin when I heard Mothy Maddy speak. "The Yechs didn't come today." I realized he was talking to Lomri. "I guess they're done searching the house." He drummed his fingers on the bony staff in his hand. "The question is, did they find it, or did they give up?"

I guessed he was talking about the ring of Kundalini that Ulupi was sure had been stolen in the attack.

Mothy Maddy scattered the silverware on the floor with his toes, using his staff to look under the cushions and upturned artwork as he rummaged through this sight of mayhem.

He halted when his eyes followed a bolt of lightning visible through the blown-up part of the house. The lightning blazed toward the ground far south of the city.

"Looks like we missed the ride back home, Lo," he said to Lomri with a shrug. Looking at Mothy Maddy, I wouldn't be surprised if he had surfboarded his way to Earth on lightning.

I followed him and Lomri to the other rooms to find the same story being repeated. The Yechs had even stabbed the smaller family portraits as if they were real people. They had dug out the floor in places. Round wicker baskets of different sizes lay broken or crushed. Every object, including the baskets, carried the same symbol that was also etched on the building stones of Haveli and my leather satchel: a coiled snake, its tail ending in its mouth, the symbol of infinity, the ring of Kundalini, the Naga stamp.

All the baskets lay open. The shriveled-up and decaying corpses of snakes were piled up in corners. Were these Maruts who had silhouetted only to find themselves cornered by the Yechs? A tremor racked my very spirit at the thought.

"And what is that?" Mothy Maddy muttered, drawing out an unopened wicker box that was lying on its side under the lower ledge of the massive fireplace.

It was a fancy little basket made of lacquered and embroidered wicker, but it was so tiny compared to other baskets that had been smashed that it had gone unnoticed.

"Could this be the fire-breathing dragon?" Mothy Maddy whispered. With trembling hands, he removed the lid to find an egg inside. It was wrapped in a piece of paper with frayed edges as if hurriedly torn from a book to pack the egg.

I studied the egg over his shoulder. Unlike snake eggs, which were mostly white or beige, oblong or peanut-shaped, this one was a speckled blue oval. How could such a tiny egg contain a dragon?

With the egg in his right hand, Mothy Maddy read a verse in red ink from the wrapping paper held in his left hand.

"When Rahu swallows the moon
And it turns blue,
mankind will tether on the brink of doom.

*Fate will bear witness to the clash
between the heirs,
One a Marut, the other born of ash.*

"Born of ash," he muttered. "Rahu has lethal smoke inside him, which carries the seeds for unthinkable diseases."

He seemed overwhelmed by the discovery as he carefully wrapped the egg in the basket and slipped it into his angarakha jacket.

All of a sudden, his head jerked when he heard a whistling sound that grew louder with every passing second.

It sounded like the loud, shrill whistle of a pressure cooker about to explode on our heads. I ducked instinctively, but Mothy Maddy jumped over me, and Lomri skittered right through me toward the explosion inside the house.

As I exited, I noticed a blank area on the wall—the kind of large clean patch that appears when a photo frame or artwork is removed from its original spot—a patch roughly the same size as Kaleeni.

I followed Mothy Maddy down the stairs. Something had crashed in the inner courtyard, causing clouds of dust. What I saw next blew my mind more than anything I'd come across in Wantra. As the dust settled, a man in pilot's gear stepped out from a wrecked propeller plane that had still not been invented, if this was indeed the 1850s.

Mothy Maddy was about to pounce on the pilot, but he stopped short when the pilot set his thumb on the nose of the crumpled airplane… and it began to repair itself!

First, the dents on the airplane's surface flattened. Broken bits flew in and fitted themselves seamlessly into the body of the plane. The pilot retrieved a piece of flannel from his pocket and dusted the plane down like a parent straightening out his child's outfit. Then stepped back to admire *his handiwork and clapped twice. The plane shuddered as its protruding parts began to sink into the body. The wings moved into the slits on the sides, and a few moments later, the plane folded itself into a metal trunk.*

Rattled by the whole scene, Mothy Maddy muttered, "Two bodies, one mind," and along with Lomri, he leaped into the air. Their bodies merged to form a ferocious, armored fox the size of a wolf. It landed on the pilot's chest, pushing him to the ground, its saliva dripping on the pilot's face.

Mothy Maddy's bony staff had transformed into a collar around the neck of the beastly fox. The collar had spokes so thin and pointy that they could have pierced the smallest of flies if they came too close.

Witnessing this transformation filled me with gratitude for all things Naga, including the third eye. It was the kind of scene one remembers all one's life, a memory that is bound to lift you up and force you to be thankful to be alive.

"Hold it!" the pilot said, snatching up a keychain in the form of a cleaver from his belt. The sight of the keychain seemed to calm Mothy Maddy. "I am a paladin. My name is Roy. They call me Pilot Roy. Though I am really a historian." He shrugged and nodded a head full of impossibly curly and bouncy hair. "See, I have the Vayu clan cleaver." He held up his challastra.

Not only did Pilot Roy look like an ordinary human, but he also had a clumsy, comical look about him.

"Pilot Roy?" the humongous fox growled. "Why are you here?"

"If the ring of Kundalini has indeed gone missing, I must trace the events that led to the robbery and note the consequences mankind may have to bear."

"Didn't they tell you it might involve getting your head bitten off by the Yech?"

"It's unfortunate that academicians are seen as cowardly," Pilot Roy

said, brushing his clothes and tucking his wild-child hair behind his ears. "I like to conduct my own investigations when I write history, or else there's no telling it apart from fantasy."

"The deity of war, the headmaster of Gurukul School for Paladins, Karthikeya, sent me to make inquiries, too," the fox said in a lofty manner that seemed uncharacteristic of the Mothy Maddy I had met.

"Don't mind me, paladin," Pilot Roy said. "I won't get in your way. In fact, I might even help you show Karthikeya his place."

The armored fox backed up and popped back into Mothy Maddy's human form and Lomri.

"What do you mean?" Mothy Maddy said with a hint of edginess.

"Paladins are not supposed to use their warrior silhouettes amongst humans. You pounced on me in your warrior silhouette, which means you don't care for Gurukul rules and therefore for Karthikeya."

Damn! Professors were shrewd.

"If you indeed are a Marut, what is your silhouette?" Mothy Maddy asked.

Even before he finished his question, an owl appeared sitting on the gleaming steel trunk that had managed to fit an entire airplane.

"How do I know you are not here to steal one of Shesh Nagaraj's celestial objects?"

The owl placed its talons around the trunk handle and flapped its wings hard. Mothy Maddy scratched his head through his turban, his face carrying a quizzical look that bordered on amusement. Having failed to carry his luggage in silhouette form, a sheepish Pilot Roy popped back.

"Everything Haveli had to offer has been looted," Mothy Maddy said, resting his chin on his staff.

"Yet the Yechs have been visiting the Haveli at night," Pilot Roy pointed out.

"I've scoured the site. There's nothing to show."

"Fair enough!" Pilot Roy said, picking up his suitcase. "Then let's see who gets to the bottom of this mystery first."

"What mystery?" Mothy Maddy growled, taking a threatening step toward Pilot Roy.

"The usual," Pilot Roy said cowering. "Looking for survivors, tracing them down if possible. Finding out if the Nagas left any snakelings behind."

"I used the spotting dust, nothing but human and snake bodies with a couple of bird bodies."

"What about eggs?"

Mothy Maddy looked up sharply. "Maruts never give birth in silhouette. This is something you learn in the first year at Gurukul."

"Some Maruts have that option," Pilot Roy said, holding up and shaking his finger.

"None except the fire-breathing dragons of the east," Mothy Maddy said.

"There you go," Pilot Roy said, adjusting his glasses, which were still smudged with dirt.

"The last time fire-breathing dragons were seen in these parts was during the battle of Mahabharata," Mothy Maddy said.

"If there are any eggs in there, the Fallen Ones will give anything for them, making you a class-one paladin in a second."

Mothy Maddy's hand travelled to his pocket. "Wait a minute! Why do the Fallen Ones want the egg?" he said, coming to his senses.

"To end the sway of Maruts of course! Indra blames Maruts for his fall."

"The Fallen Ones sent you to look for the egg?"

Pilot Roy shrugged.

"So they can destroy it?"

"That's right!" Pilot Roy said, tapping his nose with his index finger.

"And the same egg in possession of Rahu..." Mothy Maddy said, his voice trailing.

"Will make him invincible," Pilot Roy said. "The ring of Kundalini will make Rahu all-powerful, but a fire-breathing dragon will cinch the universe for him. There is nothing else in Haveli that Rahu would want more." Pilot Roy started to walk toward the door.

"How long will you stay?" Mothy Maddy called after him.

"The egg takes a hundred and fifty years to hatch," Pilot Roy replied over his shoulder.

Mothy Maddy shook his head as he watched Pilot Roy leave. "He is dead meat," he said to Lomri, leaning on his staff, a smile lingering on his face.

The verse talked of a clash between a Marut and Rahu, as he was the only deity that moved around on a jet of smoke and ash. This was nothing new. But nowhere did it mention a Naga heir or who would win the battle. It was a prophecy that announced an event, not the result. Just as Brahma had pointed out to the Fallen Ones.

It was heartening and painful at the same time because it left room for the Marut heir to win. The problem was there was no way Mohan could win the battle by himself.

I sensed someone watching me. I realized with a start that it was Lomri. She picked her way toward me and coiled her body around my leg. Wait a minute! I could feel her fur!

I opened my eyes in alarm to find myself back in Anku's makeshift camp in Haveli. Anku was fast asleep next to me, and lying close to my feet on the broken and bumpy ground was Lomri, Mothy Maddy's silhouette.

Lomri looked at me with intelligent eyes. She was holding something in her mouth. I extended my hand, and she dropped a black onyx ring into it. Mothy Maddy had been wearing this ring when I met him yesterday.

In a flash, it came to me where I'd seen the same ring before I met Mothy Maddy—on Ketu's hand in Rahu's lair. What was Mothy Maddy doing with Ketu's ring? Why had he been wearing it? A wild thought crossed my mind, but I brushed it away. There was no way that Mothy Maddy could be Ketu in disguise.

"What are you doing here?" I whispered to Lomri. "Where is Mothy Maddy?" I felt silly talking to a fox, but in my dream, I had seen Mothy Maddy talk to Lomri.

Lomri just stared at me fixedly. I was glad Anku was still sleeping and didn't see me talking to Lomri. I would hear no end of it from her hoity-toityness.

I checked the time. It was almost daybreak. The Naga third eye had kept me engrossed in the dream for the entire night. I felt tired, and I could still feel the nausea that the sights at Haveli had evoked in me.

I wondered what part of my dream was about to come true.

CHAPTER 26

I shook Anku awake. She started when she saw Lomri and said, "Where's Mothy Maddy?"

I shrugged. I'd scoured the Haveli with Lomri in tow, but it was in vain. I showed Anku the black onyx Lomri had dropped into my hand.

"That's Mothy Maddy's ring," Anku said.

"But black onyx is a Boor stone," I said. I told Anku how I'd seen the same ring on Ketu's finger.

"That's just a coincidence," she replied, trashing my observation and the underlying insinuation that Mothy Maddy was somehow connected with Ketu.

"Do you think he's batting for the enemy?" I stated the obvious anyway.

"It's impossible," Anku said, putting a stop to further discussion. She sprang up and grabbed her jacket. We'd both slept with our shoes on. It never even occurred to me to take them off.

"If Lomri is here," I said, "that means Mothy Maddy can't

silhouette into a warrior silhouette."

"Worse, if he sent Lomri away, he must have been worried for her safety," Anku said. "Though if something happens to Mothy Maddy, death would be a kinder fate for her." She refused to elaborate on her comment, saying, "It's best not to think about it."

We spent the morning and afternoon looking for Pilot Roy.

"Why don't you just call him on his phone?" I asked.

"You should know by now that Maruts, especially the old-schoolers, are extremely paranoid. Pilot Roy feels that smart phones are part of a conspiracy by humans to uproot celestials."

It sounded like something Naani would say.

We went to the scrapyard in Chandni Chowk that Pilot Roy liked to visit to collect machine parts. "He's obsessed with machines," Anku told me. "He can mend any broken transistor, TV, toaster, anything. You name the gadget or vehicle, he'll fix it."

"Airplanes?" I asked.

Anku looked at me, startled. "How did you know?"

"The Underbridge has a wall made entirely of parts from an airplane?" I said sarcastically with an "isn't it obvious" tone that was Anku's trademark.

I couldn't tell if she was surprised or impressed by my observation skills. "Pilot Roy's plane got destroyed in a crash. It's tragic that he's holding onto its remains. Makes him erratic and antisocial," she said, as if she were delivering a lecture on mental health.

From my dream, I recalled how Pilot Roy's airplane had

folded itself into a shiny suitcase. But now was not the time to challenge Anku.

We headed to Paharganj, where Pilot Roy liked to hang out with his cronies and play cards for petty cash. For a celestial paladin, he certainly hung out with questionable company.

All the while, it niggled at my mind that Mothy Maddy wore the same ring as Ketu. Could Mothy Maddy be trusted? What if Mothy Maddy were Ketu or Rahu in disguise? Perhaps Mothy Maddy's identity had been snatched!

"Have you heard of the Naga third eye?" I asked Anku.

"Never," she said. "Only Shiva, the destroyer, has a third eye. The day it opens will be the day of apocalypse."

It was bad enough that the Naga clan had been saddled with fighting Rahu thanks to a prophecy. I didn't want the apocalypse placed on our heads too. So I didn't press on about the third eye and my dreams.

"Can a paladin's identity be snatched?" I asked instead.

Anku paused to consider my question. "I would like to see someone try that. Paladins are trained by Karthikeya, the deity of war himself."

We couldn't find Pilot Roy in Paharganj, either. We visited the empty lots next to the airstrip of the Delhi Flying Club and his favorite roadside eateries. Meanwhile, Lomri tailed along faithfully.

Finally, in the late evening, Anku said, "I guess we have to go with the only paladin left to bring us to Dakini's lab."

"You mean Red the restaurant owner?"

She nodded. "Though we may end up protecting him," she

mumbled to herself. I figured that Anku's insistence on bringing along a paladin had something to do with her shaken confidence. She and Surp had entered Wantra without Mothy Maddy's knowledge, and matters had gone from bad to worse. Anku wasn't someone who changed her mind. But I had to make sure that if the need arose for *me* to go solo, I had all the tools.

I hadn't told her about the deal with Thauma. Unlike me, she had no qualms about imposing her opinion on others. But it couldn't wait any longer.

With as much authority as I could muster, I said, "We must first make a short stop at the night market. Thauma is waiting to make a trade." I brought out the triquetra from my pocket to drive home the urgency.

Anku gasped, and as was her habit, she swiped the triquetra from my hand. For someone so possessive about her own things, she was quite comfortable grabbing others' property willy-nilly. I was still sore about Ulupi's guptikr, which she constantly wore around her neck. Technically, it belonged to Nagas.

Thankfully, she didn't try to dissuade me, but all along the way to the night market, she scrutinized the triquetra. "Triquetras were used for identity theft. Why would anyone want to give it your Naani?"

"I think Dev Vidhata wanted me to use it to get Naani's silhouette back or something."

"There's nothing written about that anywhere." She inspected the relic from all sides. "Do you think Dev Vidhata was actually Indra? But he would have handed it to your Naani himself. Why you?"

I envied Anku for her ability to converse with herself. She must never have wanted for company.

"Perhaps." I shrugged. I'd omitted telling Anku about the numerous voices Dev had used to communicate with me. I was worried she'd laugh at me for thinking I had actually met Brahma, the creator of the universe.

By the time we reached the night market, darkness had set in. Even though there were battery-operated lights all around, the air was thick with the smell of burning oil lamps. The main path into the market was lined on both sides with tarpaulins or carts exhibiting their wares.

Sweaty and shifty-eyed con men offered us "special prices" as we crossed their stalls. A noisy wedding celebration was underway somewhere close by.

Unlike most night markets where lights, colors, and music drew the shoppers, here the sellers remained in the shadows and only emerged if someone showed interest in an article. Of the shoppers who trickled in, most wore some sort of camouflage like a cap, a muffler pulled up high to cover the chin and nose, or thick-framed glasses. The idea was to not draw attention to oneself but focus on finding what one came looking for.

"Everyone loves a bargain," Anku said when I asked her why a thieves' market was located in an affluent part of the city. Then she pointed toward a tarp that spilled onto the walking path. "Isn't that Kaleeni?"

I looked carefully. *Thauma would never be careless enough to spread Kaleeni out for the public to walk on,* I thought. We hurried to the spot. Sure enough, as we rounded a wall of faux "designer" bags, we found Thauma and Takka noisily slurping tea. Spread under Takka's anvil, wooden cupboard, and stone stools was Naani's precious carpet, Kaleeni!

I gritted my teeth. *What's done is done,* I said to myself as Anku and I lowered our heads to enter Takka's cobbling kiosk.

"About time," Thauma said when he saw me.

"How dare you!" I said through clenched teeth, unable to control my rage.

"I was making the best use of it," Thauma cried, spreading out his hands like a child. He did a double take when he saw Lomri standing next to me. "Madhav lent you his better half for protection?"

Before I could say anything, Takka spoke up. "Hey! Ask your girlfriend not to wipe her shoes on my carpet."

"*Your* carpet?" Anku cried at the same time I said, "She's not my girlfriend!" We both stopped and looked at each other. I felt heat creep up my neck and cheeks as Anku glared at me.

"Looks like you've touched a raw nerve," Thauma said to Takka. An impish smile played on his lips.

"You!" Anku said to Thauma, her hand on her challastra. "Quickly roll up Kaleeni for us."

Thauma and Takka exchanged a glance and quickly rolled up Kaleeni. I wished I could be as assertive as Anku.

"It helped me attract customers. Made them feel like royalty," Takka said glumly, handing the rolled carpet to Thauma.

"I thought you wanted to fly on it," I said to Thauma.

"You haven't told him?" Takka said, chortling. His

hunched-up shoulders shook with a burst of dry, grating laughter.

"Told me what?" I shot at Thauma.

"Could I have the triquetra first?" Thauma asked, his face blank. He extended his arm, and I put the triquetra in his hand. Without wasting another second, he handed the triquetra to Takka, who by now had stopped laughing and received the triquetra in shocked silence.

Thauma dropped Kaleeni in my arms. I cringed as my hands touched its grimy base. It was as if I were *collecting* reasons for Naani to hate me more.

With a deep, satisfied sigh, Thauma turned to me. "When uthaan occurred, it reversed the ownership of Kaleeni. I would have had to give it back and then trade it again if I wanted to use it." He waved his hand as if to say it was just not worth the effort.

"So it was not answering your commands?" I asked.

"Nope," Thauma said.

"But it didn't answer when I called either," I said.

"Did you use the correct chant?" Anku interjected.

I raised my eyes to the heavens in reply.

"Whoever wove Kaleeni didn't think about uthaan," Thauma said. "Someone from your clan had to reclaim it," Thauma said.

"So, if I hadn't asked for it…"

"It would have aged and grown threadbare like any normal carpet," Thauma replied without flinching.

My irritation with Thauma was turning into full-blown anger. Before I could say something biting, Anku placed her hand on my arm and signaled toward Takka. "Look."

Takka's eyes were shining yellow-green like a cat's eyes in the dark.

"What's the matter with him?" I asked.

"He's waking from a long sleep," Thauma said with a triumphant smile. He shooed us out of the kiosk and pulled down the tarp flap.

"He did promise a spectacle," I said.

"He's about to bring back Takka's silhouette," Anku said.

My phone vibrated through my pants pockets. I had turned it on the moment we stepped out of the Haveli in case Mohan reached out. I looked at the caller. "Naani." I'd been dreading this moment.

"You should answer," Anku said. "At least she'll know one of you is safe. She won't have to worry about both you and Mohan."

I pressed the accept button, but an eerie static noise greeted me. I placed my hand on the speaker and mouthed "pocket dial" to Anku. I should have known Naani wouldn't be worried about me.

I was about to hang up when I heard a loud Bollywood song through the phone speaker. I pressed the phone against my shirt to muffle the sound. It was the same music, note for note, that was playing at the wedding party right next door.

Either Naani was at the wedding party, which was next to impossible since she'd never in my living memory accepted an invitation to any kind of celebration… or she was here at the night market.

"I don't know what you're talking about," Naani's voice

came from somewhere nearby. I disconnected the call. Anku placed a finger on her lips and pointed to a huddle of scooters and motorcycles under a tree. We crouched amongst the vehicles, the tree casting a dense shadow in the full moonlight.

Anku pulled Ulupi's guptikr from around her neck, and we slipped under it. I almost fell over the bicycles when I saw Naani step out from behind one of the stalls selling woolen shawls. As usual, her olive-green salwar kameez was impeccable, and her hair was prudishly collected in a tight bun. She carried her bag on her forearm and held it across her belly like royalty, like a queen holding one end of her shawl. She was shaking her head crossly and muttering, "What a waste of time."

"Give me another chance," a man called after her.

Anku dipped her head and looked questioningly at me over the rim of her glasses. "That lady is the social worker who visits the shivir from time to time. She's the one who brings us news of recently discovered Maruts."

Naani, a social worker? The woman was all about herself and Mohan. "That's my Naani. You've got to be mistaken. She just looks… official," I said for lack of a better word.

Anku peered at Naani. "No. That's Mrs. M, alright."

"Mrs. M?" I repeated.

"We always assumed she was Mothy Maddy's girlfriend and so called her Mrs. M."

"She is Manasa Nagaraj," I said.

Anku gave a low whistle. "I did think Mothy Maddy could do better. Did you know she was seeing someone?"

"She's not *seeing* anyone," I snapped.

I wasn't prepared for what I saw next as Batty shuffled out from behind the stall.

"Fangless," Anku whispered. "He accompanies her on every visit."

Batty was Fangless? It was beginning to make sense. The Boors thought that Batty, or Fangless, had willingly sent the Naga heir to them, but Batty had double-crossed them by sending a decoy: me! What was even more surprising was that Naani seemed to know him well.

"He's her man Friday. There's a joke about them that he would polish the Qutb Minar, stone to stone, if she asked him to."

Before I could respond, Naani's voice carried to me. "You are a disgrace to the Naga clan!" she said to Batty with a sudden and vicious turn of her body. She poked her finger at his lean chest. "You were not supposed to send him for that delivery. He was not ready."

My jaw dropped. Batty had been sending me for deliveries, and Naani knew about them? Rahu was correct in assuming she'd used me as a decoy.

"You should talk to her now," Anku urged me. "We could use her help."

I shook my head. "She has no Marut powers. Everyone knows she gave up her silhouette."

Batty's urgent whisper reached us. "From what I've heard, Rahu will use the ring of Kundalini tonight."

That didn't seem to faze Naani. She raised a clenched fist at him and said, "Well, you have made it really easy for Rahu then, haven't you? My grandson's life is in peril."

She couldn't have been talking about me. She must have meant that Batty had imperiled Mohan.

"I'm not willing to pay that cost. You should not have put Adi up to it. He was not ready," Naani repeated.

I'd heard Naani say this numerous times, but it sounded even more insulting in the presence of Anku.

"I didn't have a choice. The triquetra was stolen from the Bank of Karma in Amravati. They say Rahu got it done. He plans to unleash a beast on the city—" Batty gulped loudly "—the Ihamriga."

Naani whirled around. "Your information is half-baked. You could have checked with me first."

"But you forbade me from calling you or visiting you! I had to wait to meet you here," Batty said in his typical whiny and nasal voice. "The theft of triquetra has shaken up the establishment. They've assigned a special force of Apsara sleuths to round up all celestial artifacts. Rahu knows the ring in his possession was fake all along. Gargouille is on the lookout for me."

"They have Mohan now. You are useless to them," Naani said. She could be heartless toward everyone except for Mohan. "We would have sent Adi tonight. The transfer of powers from the ring of Kundalini to Rahu would have failed. It would have bought us another hundred and fifty years!" She threw up her hands.

The color drained from Anku's cheeks. She looked at me, her lips pouting in worry and pity. I was touched by her concern, but it was of no use to me. My own grandmother had planned to send me to my death!

According to their original plan, I was to be the bait on the eve of the blue blood moon. By the time Rahu realized I was not the real Naga heir and his ring was not Kundalini, the eclipse would have passed, and Mohan would have been saved.

"What about the sleuths from Swahalok?" Batty said. "You have a quarter of the celestial treasury with you, including the Uchchaihshravas twins."

"Oh, get on with it," Naani said. "I would have handled Apsara sleuths. I've stayed hidden for hundreds of years!"

"But they would have found me and squashed me," Batty sniveled, his voice low and frightened. Ever since I'd learned that his silhouette was a milk snake without fangs, I understood that his decisions came from insecurity.

Naani softened as she looked at Batty. "We had a plan, Fangless." She sounded tired. "You decided without my permission."

Permission? She could have just said "consultation." This was the attitude that drove people away from her. She had to be so controlling.

"Now," Naani said, "where is the triquetra?"

"I heard that Thauma's Vilupta Catcher picked it up," Batty said.

"That's terrible news. Thauma will hand the triquetra to Rahu without a whimper," Naani hissed. "We can't allow it to reach Rahu."

I realized I was biting my fingernails when Anku gently patted my arm. Dev Vidhata had asked me to give the triquetra to Naani, and I had squandered the opportunity. Right then, my life felt hopeless beyond repair. The only small ray of light in my life had been the possibility of joining Aunty Padma in Goa.

That had vanished with the appearance of Dev Vidhata. Then Mohan had been abducted, and now I'd given away the triquetra to a flakey magician. That oversight would cost me dearly.

My heart ached at the thought that Naani had planned with Batty for me to die on the eve of the lunar eclipse. When she used to say, "You are not ready," she meant I was not yet plump enough to be a sacrificial lamb. I felt like the most unwanted child in the world.

Anku removed my hand from my mouth. "If you don't talk to her now, then I will," she said and squared her petite shoulders. "I just hope she remembers me."

Naani and Batty were still bickering in the background when Anku moved her hand to remove the guptikr off our heads. Suddenly, Lomri grunted and bared her fangs. Anku's hand and expression froze. I followed her gaze to Takka's closed-up tent, where streaks of unnatural light were tearing through the slashes and crevices of the patched-up tarp.

"Look out!" I heard Batty cry out behind us.

Anku and I were closer to Takka's stand when an explosion sliced the low hum of the night market. Shrapnel tore through Takka's tent in every direction, accompanied by burning contents from the tent including bits and pieces of shoes and sandals. From the shadows, people emerged, running around, the loud noise from the wedding reception in the vicinity drowning their frightened screams. I watched Batty lead Naani away.

The tree trunk had saved Anku and me from the force of the explosion, but the vehicles parked around had all toppled in a jumble. Anku tugged at my shirt to get my attention. She pointed toward Takka's tent, which was on fire.

Thauma slinked through the fire unscathed, followed by a tall man in a black robe with gold trimmings and a golden belt around his waist. The only resemblance between this man and Takka was the wispy ponytail and the wavy beard.

As the strange man followed Thauma, his chameleon eyes darted here and there. I saw what Anku had been staring at. From under a long robe, trailing behind Takka, was a scorpion's tail. The triquetra was clutched in his hand.

We heard a loud flapping sound that only massive wings could make.

"Yechs!" Anku mouthed.

CHAPTER 27

Screams of "help!" from the fire suddenly turned into hopeless shrieks of terror.

"I thought Yechs couldn't enter Samsara," I whispered urgently.

"Gargouille must have bribed or killed the gatekeeper," Anku said, crouching lower.

One Yech caught a fleeing man and picked him up by the collar. I saw the outline of the Yech in the light from Takka's tent. It was Gargouille. He grinned into the man's face, causing him to faint.

I read Gargouille's lips as he said, "Not fit to be a Yech," and tossed the man's limp body aside.

The Yechs had surrounded the tent like moths drawn to light. They landed above us on the tree and around us on the scooters and motorcycles. How long would it take for them to find us? For one moment, I considered surrendering to Gargouille. He could take us where they were holding Mohan. Then I remembered Rahu's instructions to the Yechs to kill me on sight since I was of no use to them.

I heard someone whistle nearby. Who would be silly enough to whistle in the middle of a fire and demon attack? It was hard to imagine a Yech whistling.

Anku and I crouched under the guptikr back-to-back. She withdrew her club, and I got ready to land my fists on whoever or whatever it was. In the light cast by the fire, I saw the shadow of a man arise from behind a fallen scooter. He was not a Yech, but he didn't seem afraid of them. The shadow grew larger, bobbing as it drew closer. He reached for the base of the guptikr.

"Here he comes!" I said and aimed my fist at the face that poked in. It landed on the man's nose and broke it with a loud *crack*. The man cupped his gloved hands over his nose and mouth, smothering a scream. He was not a Yech. But all I could see of him was the mop of hair on his head, so curly that it was almost an afro.

"Adi, stop!" Anku whispered as the man crawled into the safety of the guptikr, still holding his broken nose, blood streaming over his chin. "That's Pilot Roy. We can trust him," she said.

Pilot Roy saw Lomri and stopped short. "What is she doing here? Where is Madhav?"

"He left for Vinay Chaubey's house last evening," I whispered.

Pilot Roy seemed taken aback to see me. "Who are you?" he asked me, glancing at Anku.

"He is Adi Nagaraj Yoshi," Anku said, "the Naga heir."

Pilot Roy dismissed me with a nod, as if I were yesterday's

news, and said, "Follow me," his voice nasally from the broken nose. I felt no regrets for having punched him. He could easily fix his broken nose as he was a paladin, even if a clumsy and untidy one. He looked shaken from the blow to his nose; I was mighty impressed with it myself. Ever since I'd overheard Naani and Batty talk, the punch had been bouncing inside of me.

I looked around for Naani and Batty, but they were nowhere to be seen. Had the Yechs got them?

Still crouching, we shimmied between the cycles, scooters, and motorcycles behind Pilot Roy. The challenge was to keep our feet from being revealed, but a bigger challenge was to not disturb the bicycles that lay haphazardly on the ground around us. The slightest movement of a bicycle wheel would give us away.

Earlier, I had seen a few people clicking pictures of the Yechs. Was it possible to take pictures of these brutes? Would the world believe they existed?

The night market was bereft of human presence now. Pilot Roy brought us to the edge of the ground that hosted the night market. I lifted one edge of the guptikr and gently unrolled Kaleeni. On seeing the carpet, Pilot Roy straightened like an eager and curious child, unaware that he had blown our cover. Only the top halves of our bodies remained covered by the guptikr now.

"Vasuki Upakritam," I recited just as a Yech spotted us and started twirling his death pike like a competitor in a hammer-throwing competition.

I pulled on the invisibility tassel as soon as Kaleeni began to rise. It swerved, missing the death pike by a hair's breadth.

Pilot Roy's nose was still bleeding from my punch. Anku patted his arm and asked me to bring Kaleeni to Malini's research institute in the suburbs of Delhi.

"No!" Pilot Roy whisper-cried. "I must look for Madhav. I will take Lomri with me." He patted her head. That the fox allowed itself to be petted by someone other than its owner was a sign of closeness that the residents of the Underbridge shared with one another.

"But I know where Dakini Malini is holding Surp, Rudra, and others captive," Anku said.

"Anku," Pilot Roy said urgently, "you can't do anything for them. If Madhav fails, we're all as good as gone. Without him, Maruts are powerless."

"Dakini has my brother," I said fiercely.

"I can't leave Madhav in the lurch," Pilot Roy said to Anku, ignoring me. "If you must go chasing Dakini Malini, it's best you take Red with you. He has training in handling Dakinis." He hesitated. "You know I don't like Red. That mongoose silhouette is an imbecile and a show-off, but Madhav's standing orders are to take shelter at the Hungry Mongoose in case of emergency."

Anku nodded, and I asked Kaleeni to fly to the Hungry Mongoose. It was ten p.m. already. Four hours to the eclipse.

The tingling in my peripheries refused to fade away, and I knew it would get worse until I secured Mohan.

I studied Pilot Roy as Kaleeni rose higher and accelerated. Compared to the Pilot Roy I'd met in my dream, this man was plumper. His mop of hair, lush salt-and-pepper eyebrows, and handlebar mustache were the same. He wore thick, round, rimless glasses, blue jeans, and a black t-shirt with an airplane on the front and the words "Born to Fly" printed in white. His leather sandals screamed for repairs, and his leather gloves were torn so that his fingers poked out.

"Where were you the whole day?" Anku said suddenly to Pilot Roy. "We looked everywhere for you."

Pilot Roy pointed his bloody finger at Anku. "You've got the nerve to ask me about my whereabouts. After the way you and Surp have behaved."

Anku glared at him and then relented, removing her backpack. She produced jambukita tincture and dabbed some on a tissue. Then she handed it to Pilot Roy, who was now muttering curses under his breath. He took the tissue in his gloved hand and pressed it against his nose. The muscles on his face relaxed.

"After I get Madhav, we will meet you at the Hungry Mongoose," he said to Anku. "I doubt you will find anything at the lab. Malini would have cleared it out by now."

I protested, but Anku put up her hand to me. "There are no shortcuts, Adi," she said with a conspiratorial look.

I glared back at her. We had wasted the entire day looking for Pilot Roy.

A relieved Pilot Roy plonked on a cushioned seat. "What were you doing in the thieves' market, anyway?"

"Rescuing someone's carpet," Anku said, jerking her head toward me.

Pilot Roy gave me a once-over and dismissed me. It was nothing new for me.

"Pilot," Anku said as Kaleeni began its descent. "Do you know anything about the triquetra?"

Pilot Roy's body tensed when he heard Anku's question. "Where did you hear about it?"

We fell forward from momentum as Kaleeni suddenly stopped and hovered outside a gate. Hanging at the entrance was a wrought iron plate in the shape of a chubby mongoose in a chef's hat stirring a large pot. The glittery iron plate looked foreign and out of place in the neighborhood crowded with large etched stones for nameplates.

"Thauma has the triquetra," Anku said.

"Fake celestial relics have become commonplace. The triquetra was placed under heavy security at the Bank of Karma in Amravati," Pilot Roy said, but his manner had grown tense.

I wondered if he knew that Mothy Maddy had pocketed the egg for which Pilot Roy had flown into nineteenth-century Delhi. Pilot Roy looked like the gullible kind, not the brightest star in the paladin sky.

"Thauma gave the triquetra to Takka, and the triquetra made Takka change. He grew younger, if it were possible. In fact, his silhouette," Anku said, glancing at me for affirmation, "was a scorpion, a shrapit silhouette. You told us that shrapit silhouettes had vanished."

Shrapit meant cursed. This was the first time I'd heard shrapit silhouettes mentioned, and I did not like the sound of bedeviled animals walking around unchecked.

Kaleeni slid over the gates of the Hungry Mongoose and skirted the main entrance lined with BMWs, Audis, and Mercedes-Benzes. The lawns of the restaurant were alive with fairy lights and lounge music. A few people were waiting outside, and every table was taken. Compared to Mothy Maddy, who lived under bridges for a cause, Red certainly had a fancy lifestyle for a paladin.

The Hungry Mongoose was doing brisk business, and the mouth-watering aromas enveloped our senses. Naani had never brought us to restaurants. She preferred sweating in the kitchen rather than taking a single day off from cooking. Everything she'd done for us in life now pointed to one end: Save Mohan. I had resented Naani all these years for her treatment, but knowing that she planned to send me to Rahu was most devastating.

"Nothing vanishes in the true sense," Pilot Roy told Anku. "Just because a silhouette is cursed doesn't mean it won't reappear. Kundalini, or the circle of life and death, protects all." His eyes blazed with a maniacal glint. "Takka is the last of our worries. If the triquetra falls into the wrong hands, many other evils might wake up."

Anku's eyes grew bigger with astonishment. "You mean shrapit silhouettes?"

"The worst of them all," Pilot Roy said.

Anku gasped. "The Ihamriga?"

Pilot Roy stared into the night in reply as the grim reality of times to come settled over us. I wanted to ask what was so terrible about the Ihamriga, but I didn't have the gumption. I couldn't take any more doomsaying.

Kaleeni glided through the side lane of the restaurant toward a brick-laid backyard with a garage on one side. It gently settled on the ground, its three occupants shocked into silence.

CHAPTER 28

The back door of the restaurant flew open, and a slender bald man rushed out.

"Red!" Anku cried.

"You're safe!" Red said, pulling Anku into a hug.

I now understood why Anku had been of two minds about bringing Red on the mission. Red wasn't someone you'd peg as a fighter. He was skinny and delicate. Both attributes lent themselves well to his profession as a restaurant owner and his status as a socialite. He wore tight pants and a silk scarf around his neck. His balding crown was rimmed by a scant outer ring of hair that fell onto his forehead like a long fringe.

"You won't believe who's here," Red said, barely able to contain his glee.

"Are you sure?" Anku said as if she'd read his mind.

Red nodded and turned back around without glancing at me. Pilot Roy and Red didn't exchange a word. I waited for Anku to bark orders at me, but she rushed into the house with Red. I stared after her.

I couldn't bring myself to follow her, to share her excitement to meet anyone. This was no time to socialize. Then it occurred to me. How could I expect her to be worried about Mohan? He was my brother, not hers. Saving Mohan was my journey.

I whirled around to face Pilot Roy. "Take me with you to Chaubey's house," I said. I couldn't bear the thought of waiting. My mind would paint gory images of what Malini and Rahu were doing to Mohan.

Pilot Roy considered my offer. "It's not a place for kids," he said finally, holding up a hand. His nose was still swollen, but the bleeding had stopped.

"But—" I began, trying to tell Pilot Roy about my courageous acts in Kalpavriksha, but he interrupted me.

"I was never in favor of training Maruts or whatever. I don't like kids. They invite trouble. They disturb the balance in the universe," he said with a pout.

This is not about you, I wanted to scream, but I reined in my silhouette, which wanted to bite this stubborn man's head off. "Dakini Malini has my brother. He's not even a Marut," I said. Despite my best efforts to contain my emotions, my voice broke off a little.

Pilot Roy patted my shoulder, rolled up Kaleeni, and carried it to the house. I followed him. He halted at the doorstep, seemed to consider something, and said, "Red is a paladin with connections. He'll rustle up help to save your brother. I must save my own brother."

"Mothy Maddy isn't your brother," I said.

I realized at that moment that I was the only witness to the wager between the two paladins. Pilot Roy had come looking for an egg of a fire-breathing dragon. Did he know that Mothy Maddy had found it? That Mothy Maddy had hidden the truth from him?

Pilot Roy snorted. "Mothy Maddy? Who calls him that?"

Like, everyone I know? I thought to myself but instead said, "I'm sorry. I meant Madhav."

"Circumstances too can make brothers of people. Humans give too much importance to blood ties," Pilot Roy scoffed.

In the soft glow of outdoor lighting, he looked like a human-sized squeeze toy that had been pressed too hard, making his eyes bulge and his curly hair spring in all directions. He stood with his right arm akimbo, resting high on his waist next to his chest, and his left leg was bent slightly, like a dancer's. Lomri stood next to him. Pilot Roy had pocketed Mothy Maddy's ring earlier.

"Did you ever find the egg you came looking for a hundred and fifty years back?" I asked Pilot Roy.

His head jerked back as if he had been punched again. "How do you know about the egg?" he asked, showing a genuine interest in me for the first time.

"Never mind how but I know." I'd seen how Anku trusted Pilot Roy with her life, but something held me back from sharing everything with him. For me, he was a stranger. Naani's betrayal had made sure I would never trust anyone easily again.

"Wise people say knowledge brings misery," Pilot Roy said. "Stay ignorant. Remain happy, as your Naani intended."

"I have never been happy," I hissed. I couldn't stand anybody praising Naani for the way she'd brought me up. "Tell me, what does the triquetra have to do with the prophecy?"

Worry lines creased Pilot Roy's forehead, but only for a few seconds. "The triquetra is a totem that wakes up ancient shrapit, or cursed beasts."

"Do you mean Vasuki, the ancient snake spirit? Is he a shrapit silhouette?"

Pilot Roy stared back at me instead of replying. A window cracked open on the first floor, and Anku peered out. "What's keeping you, Adi?"

"What does Mohan have to do with it?" I asked as I looked up briefly at Anku. When I turned back to face him, Pilot Roy was gone. He didn't wait for me to tell him who had found the egg.

Red's living quarters were conveniently located above the restaurant. His cozy study contained a mahogany table, a chair, and a couch. A mantel shelf spanned the entire length of one wall. It held oddities like an ornate conch, a terrarium with a single plant inside it, and a peacock feather fashioned into a scepter. All were encased in glass and emitting a soft glow. The names of the artifacts were etched on small golden plates at the bottom. The large but plain conch was titled Paundrak Shankha.

Used by Bhima in the war of Mahabharata, the conch grants the user huge strength. Its echo fills the heart of enemies with fear.

The plant was called Holy Basil, and the peacock scepter was called Krishna's Pankh. The shelf also contained some photos of Red in his younger days.

The objects on the shelf were so mesmerizing that I only

realized there was anyone else in the room when someone cleared their throat. It was Anku. She sat fuming on the couch with her arms crossed against her chest. Someone was standing by the window. My heart lurched when I saw that it was the silent figure of Surp. Her appearance was so sudden that I wanted to talk to her and hide from her at the same time.

She was wearing the purple kurta, jeans, and boots she'd worn when I first met her. "Hello, Adi," she said.

I responded with a "Hi" as confidently as I could, but I felt my face heating up.

Anku shook her head in resignation. "Your precious Surp had been lying to you and me."

I must have blushed. I could tell because my face felt like a furnace. My precious Surp? Was she out of her mind?

"Thank you, Adi, for staying back in Wantra for me," Surp said, moving forward and hugging me. I froze, and my glance instantly went to Anku, who raised her eyebrows at me knowingly. I felt both angry and embarrassed.

"There's no need for thanks," I said. I should have told her that Patches was the main reason I'd stayed back, but I wanted the hug to continue a few moments longer, so I didn't.

"You helped me not once, but many times. But all of that later." She turned to Anku. "Look, I'm sorry I lied. Had I told you the truth, you would have never gone along with me."

"That's not true. There's nothing I wouldn't do for you. You're are like a…" Anku broke off, suddenly wary of my presence in the room. She didn't want to look vulnerable in my presence. I knew the feeling.

"Sister?" Surp said, finishing Anku's sentence with a smile.

"Okay, if I told you I wanted to visit Wantra to pluck the fruit off the weeping bough, would you have come along?"

"I would have told Mothy Maddy immediately!" Anku said, not helping her case.

"I've known all along where Dakini Malini has been holding Rudra and the boys," Surp said with a sigh.

"But why didn't you just confide in Mothy Maddy?" Anku asked.

"Because I received intelligence about a mole amongst us," Surp said. "My mother sent the message a few months back, but I did not believe her then. I thought she was just trying to get me to join her Dakini army."

"Who better than Mothy Maddy to help us find the mole?" Anku cried.

"Unless Mothy Maddy was the mole," I interjected.

"You don't know Mothy Maddy!" Anku snapped at me. "You stay out of this."

The Adi of a few days back would have snapped right back at her, but I'd come to understand Anku. Cats are socially clueless animals. The resulting indifference is generally misunderstood as disloyalty. Like her cat silhouette, Anku was unaware that her behavior came across as selfish. Also, like her silhouette, she was extremely loyal when she chose to be.

"He is right," Surp said, glancing at me.

Anku shook her head vigorously as if trying to shake off the thought. "Think of all the times Mothy Maddy has put his life in jeopardy for us," she said finally, her shoulders squared. "It's not possible. Mothy Maddy can't be the mole. Adi and I overheard Mrs. M and Fangless fighting. Fangless is the one who betrayed us."

"Mothy Maddy is the only one who knew that Rudra took the boys to visit the zoo," Surp added.

Anku's hand flew to her mouth as she gasped in disbelief.

"But what's the use of the fruit?" I asked.

"Rudra, Angad, and Bala will be recruited into Yech forces after they're stripped of their silhouettes," Surp said. "But the fruit from Kalpavriksha will restore them, bringing back their silhouettes. It's a universal panacea, a miracle cure."

She dipped her hand into her bag and brought out a small yellow mango with red flecks. The mango had shriveled skin and brown spots. The fruit was way past its juicy, ripe, edible stage.

One would expect the universal panacea to have some distinguishing features—a glow, or healthy skin free of blemishes, justifying the curative remedies it held inside. But this mango was so far gone that if it were lying on a pile with other mangoes, it would be the last to be picked, if it were picked at all.

"How did you escape the Panish?" I asked, referring to the bloodthirsty monsters that guarded the fruit on Kalpavriksha.

Before Surp could answer, we heard the doorbell ring, and Surp shushed us.

Red burst into the study, looking hassled. "It's Gargouille. Madhav gave away our location. You must hide quickly." He left to warn the guests in the restaurant.

"Not Mothy Maddy…" Anku moaned.

Surp beckoned us to the window. Two hooded men with spears were standing guard outside the back door. Just as a loud scream pierced the night, Surp leaped off the windowsill, snapping into a koel midair, and took flight.

On seeing her, the two guards at the entrance took to the skies after her. Outlines of a tiny koel and creepy Yech shapes with wings were visible for a few seconds before the night swallowed them.

Anku gripped my arm. "Where did you leave Kaleeni?"

"Near the door," I replied. "Vasuki upa—" I began, but Anku shushed me.

"Don't call Kaleeni now. You don't know what it might bring along with it," she said.

We heard scuffling outside the door of Red's study. Anku removed the guptikr from around her neck, and the two of us slipped under it just as the door of the study flung open and Gargouille walked into the room with three Yechs in tow. He was cradling Kaleeni in his arms. Anku was right. If I'd called Kaleeni, Gargouille would have flown in with it.

Gargouille lifted his head and sniffed the air. His death pike, hanging from his waist, rankled against the floor as he walked. "I can smell you, Naga boy. Once I've had a whiff, I don't forget. I won't have any Marut spoiling my lord's ascent to power today," he growled, then reached into the pocket of his jacket and withdrew a pouch.

"No, no, no. Not the spotting dust," Anku whispered to herself as Gargouille dipped his hand in the pouch and withdrew a fistful of shiny dust.

Mothy Maddy used that dust at the Haveli in my dream; Svarna dhool, he'd called it. At Haveli, the dust simply formed contours of bodies on the floor like outlines of dead people at a murder scene investigation. It was distressing to see so many overlapping outlines.

Gargouille flung the dust toward the chairs next to the table. It settled like silken snow on everything around it. Thankfully, we were crouching behind Gargouille under the ledge of the mantel.

Red's table, which had been empty and spotless, suddenly appeared cluttered and messy as the dust settled on it. Books made of papyrus, scrolls of paper, an ink bottle, and a glowing quill in a holder grew visible. Strangely, the table looked dusty, as if no one had used it for a while.

"Ugh. Valmiki's quill," Gargouille said. He took a step away as if afraid of the feather quill.

Anku and I inched toward the door, our sides pressed into the wall. Gargouille's eyes darted about. His dumb Yech followers looked around for valuables. One of them drew toward the mantel shelf, close to where we squatted, frozen. We flattened ourselves against the wall.

"Show yourself, Adi. Wouldn't you like to meet your brother?" Gargouille said, his face twisted into a malicious smile.

Anku placed her hand on my arm and shook her head at me. I took a deep breath. I surprised myself with how much better I had gotten at controlling my silhouette.

"Your grandmother brought you up to care for the boy who will bring about your death."

Well, I knew that already.

Anku and I started to inch toward the door. Gargouille growled again. He had come to stand right next to the guptikr. Oddly, despite the savage demands of his profession,

Gargouille smelled sickly sweet. I read somewhere that this was how mythical panthers attracted prey in the wild. "You will be happy to know that despite your Naani's best efforts to save your aunt, we have traced her in the hills," Gargouille said. He dipped his hand into the pouch once more, and this time, he aimed it toward the mantel shelf where Anku and I stood.

I stopped in my tracks. Was it possible that Naani was responsible for moving Aunty Padma to a secure location? After all, Dev Vidhata had fed me lies in his letters to grow close to me. Through my letters, had I inadvertently disclosed the truth about Aunty Padma's existence too? I couldn't be responsible for the deaths of so many people, people I cared about deeply.

"This time, we'll make a clean sweep of Nagas," Gargouille said.

Rage and helplessness started to take hold of my senses with every word Gargouille uttered. I couldn't think straight. I couldn't even feel Anku's hands on my arms as she tried to calm me.

Perhaps I would turn into my silhouette, and Gargouille would simply squash me. I flung the guptikr aside.

I may as well go down fighting.

"Aha, there you are!" Gargouille said gleefully. "With Durga's little kitten, too. Rahu will be so happy to meet you both."

"What do you need with me or Aunty Padma? You have the real Naga heir," I spat at Gargouille.

"Do I detect sibling rivalry? This is precious," Gargouille said, bursting out in loud guffaws.

Anku had already swung her challastra and was sporting her

club in her hands. But there was no way we could win against Gargouille. He suppressed his laughter and got his death pike ready to strike in case we made a move.

Without another thought, I smashed the case containing the Paundrak Shankha conch on the mantel shelf. Why that and not Krishna's Pankh or the Holy Basil? I guess my disillusionment with feathers was justified given Pavan, the Zephyr Rover's feather, hadn't helped me yet in any sticky situation. And the only use of basil I could think of was adding it to tea for flavor.

Paundrak Shankha felt smooth like marble but light as a feather in my hand. Its surface was carved with a battle scene, and I had no idea what would happen if I blew hard into it. My actions were simply based on the hunch that if a celestial quill could frighten Gargouille, then a warrior's conch was worth a try.

The sound of the shankha reverberated through the busy night and drowned the screeches and shrieks of the Yechs, who covered their ears. Even though Gargouille also covered his ears, he wouldn't let go of Kaleeni.

In the din of Yech screams, no one heard the tapping from inside the cupboard to our right. It was a standard wooden cupboard built inside the wall, common in older houses.

I stopped blowing the conch, but its sound continued as if waiting for a switch to be turned off. Gargouille put up his hand when he heard the knocking at the wooden cupboard. His Yech crew stopped screeching but kept their ears covered, their faces contorted in agony. Gargouille inched toward the wooden cupboard, his death pike in his hand.

Before he could reach the handle of the cupboard, the door broke, and fragments of wood flew in every direction. A shoe repeatedly kicked the remaining door from inside until its doors broke from its frame and fell. A woman in a black suit and oxfords jumped out. Behind her was a well-lit passage that resembled a metro train tunnel.

"Step away from Swahalok property," the woman said, taking a combat stance. She was as tall as Gargouille, and her facial features were so perfect that she didn't appear human. She looked at Gargouille, surprised. "You don't have the conch. Who summoned me?"

"Who are you?" Gargouille asked.

I still had the conch in my hands, but Gargouille and his Yechs seemed to have forgotten all about me and Anku.

"I can't hear you over this shankhadhvani," the woman said and snapped her fingers to shut the siren that the conch had launched.

"Who are you, and what are you doing here?" Gargouille growled.

"I am Apsara Tanya, and I work in the special commando cell of the Bank of Karma, also known as the BOK. There has been an attempt at stealing a high-security celestial object at this location."

"Commando?" Gargouille sniggered. "You'll break like a twig, little girl. Apsaras are good for dancing and serving food. Don't overestimate yourself."

Gargouille was correct in his information. According to ancient texts, apsaras were celestial dancers who worked at Indra's court. Yet here was an Apsara, a special commando soldier for the celestials, busting stereotypes just like the cupboard she had smashed through.

Apsara Tanya's body tensed, but her expression remained unchanged, unflappable as she studied Gargouille. "I know you. You are the panther ride of Rahu. You are the animal he promoted as the general of his army of dead souls," she said.

Gargouille jutted out his chin, pleased with his introduction.

"Given a choice, I would prefer to dance to music rather than jump around to a dark deity's tunes, Rahu's servant," she said as sweetly as possible to Gargouille.

"Iiiii… am not Rahu's servant!" Gargouille roared.

He threw his death pike at Apsara Tanya, who ducked. It landed on a Yech standing behind her. The Yech collapsed in a pile of ash. The other two Yechs, their death pikes at the ready, covered her from two sides as Gargouille advanced toward her, still holding on to Kaleeni.

I couldn't imagine how Apsara Tanya would defeat Gargouille and the Yechs without a weapon. The chivalrous part of me, which I didn't even know existed until a week earlier, wanted to help Apsara Tanya. But then I noticed there wasn't a crease of worry on her forehead. She didn't look like someone who needed help.

The Yechs reached out to catch hold of her arms. Apsara landed an elbow in the jaw of one Yech and scissor-kicked the other in the jaw. They now looked even more terrifying with their dangling jaws—yet they still stood with their death pikes trained on her.

Gargouille aimed his death pike again at Apsara. As he hurled it, Apsara flicked aside the flap of her coat and drew out a sword. She met the death pike with her sword, shattering it to pieces. But the cursed rasa from the death pike rubbed off on the sword. To Apsara Tanya's alarm and Gargouille's glee, the sword began to melt.

"You are no match for me, girl. You will pay for calling me a servant. Prepare to meet your future employer, Dakini Malini."

"Apsaras stand for perfection, and we make sure it reflects in our work," Tanya said, displaying a heartwarming and infectious pluck that seemed to irk Gargouille even more.

He held out his clawed hands and snarled, ready to shred Apsara Tanya to bits, when two apsaras dressed exactly like Apsara Tanya tumbled out of the cupboard. One of them cartwheeled to land in front of the window and blocked it. The other Apsara passed a sword to Apsara Tanya.

Despite the fixed evil grin on his face, Gargouille's manner changed. He stopped and grabbed Kaleeni instead of attacking the apsaras, barking commands.

"Fly, carpet! Open simsim!"

The rolled-up Kaleeni remained limp in his hands.

"Abracadabra! Go!" he added, cutting a pathetic figure.

Unsuccessful at getting Kaleeni to fly, Gargouille hurled it at Apsara Tanya, who ducked again and slashed her sword at Gargouille. Kaleeni hit the floor and unrolled to stop near our feet. I looked at Anku in disbelief.

"Vasuki Upakritam," I said.

One of the Yechs moved menacingly toward us as Anku and I hopped out of its reach onto Kaleeni. I pulled the invisibility tassel and vanished right before its eyes.

Anku ducked with a cry and pulled me down with her as the Yech flung its death pike like a yoyo and it whizzed past my shoulder. A second later, an Apsara pierced the papery body of the Yech, reducing him and his death pike to a pile of ash. To the thwacking of swords striking Gargouille's thick skin and the sound of his yowls, we floated out the study door.

I looked back. Red was nowhere to be seen. The apsaras were landing punches and kicks on Gargouille when suddenly Gargouille pulled the remaining Yech and used him as a shield. As the swords tore through the Yech, Gargouille toppled out of the window of Red's study and took flight.

"I think I know where he's headed," Anku said.

I checked my watch as Kaleeni landed outside a swanky, newly constructed building with shiny reflective glass exteriors. It was already eleven p.m. The hour of the blue blood moon was inching closer. The board outside the building read:

Mala Chaubey's Research Institute
Highest-quality clinical research services with
flexible tailored solutions.

A guard was fast asleep at the gates.

"Do you think Surp is here too?" I asked Anku.

Anku shrugged. "I don't know her as well as I thought I did."

"Why do you think she risked her life to get the fruit from the weeping bough?" I asked. I wasn't proud of asking so many questions. I could see my questions irritated Anku. But it also made her feel self-important to know more than me, which worked in my favor.

"Isn't it obvious?" she said. "Even if the Maruts are rescued, they would be stripped of their silhouettes. The fruit will remedy that. She prepared for the worst."

We climbed the steps to stand before a padlocked door.

"So for Surp, Rudra's lion silhouette is important," I said, more to myself.

"No, she knows that not having his silhouette will kill Rudra in a different manner," Anku said, removing a hairpin and using it to unlock the door.

Empty room upon empty room on both sides of the glossy marbled corridor greeted us. Terrifying thoughts about Mohan and Naani were swimming in my mind like sharks. These thoughts could devour my capacity to think and act, so I focused on the present.

We crept down a dingy staircase to a basement filled with silver cylinders marked Venvap. They all carried a logo: a panther's head. At least we were at the right spot. But there was no sign of life around. If Dakini Malini were running her dark operations from this spot, there should have been some bustle. Had we reached a dead end?

My spirits flagged. I backed into the wall of the corridor and slid down with my head in my hands. Mohan's death was turning into a certainty.

"I don't understand," Anku said, kneeling next to me. "Ludo and I followed her to this spot every day." She moved my hands away from my head and patted my shoulder. She sat next to me. "I won't say it's not all your fault. If you hadn't given the triquetra to Thauma…"

She had conveniently forgotten that we both had handed the triquetra to Thauma.

I kept my hands on the floor and propped my head on the wall. Had I snapped at Anku for blaming me or walked out in a huff, I would have never heard the faint sobbing through the floor surface.

"Someone's crying," I said, sitting up straight.

My stethoscopic hands had picked up and amplified the sobs of a child, soft scurrying, the grating of mortar and pestle, and faint chirping of insects.

"They're here," I said and asked Anku to follow me. I ran in the direction of the sounds, stopping every now and then to touch the ground until they grew louder and louder. Finally, I touched the outermost wall of the building. "They're definitely beyond this wall."

We peered out of the window to find an expanse of a fallow farm.

"It's like she is holding them inside the wall," I said, my frustration beginning to grow. "Do you think there's a ladder in here?"

"Akashi ladder?" Anku said. "We've checked all the rooms. There wasn't even a stepladder anywhere." She was right. Except for stacks of Venvap cylinders, there was nothing on the premises.

We sat, thinking, when I noticed a colony of spiders in the corner of the ceiling. Brown recluse spiders were not a social species, but they did live in colonies, and they weren't aggressive by nature.

A soft chirp from the spiders brought an idea to me. "Didn't Aunty Tara say she supplies blood to research labs?" I said to Anku.

"That's just another source of income for her," Anku said with a shrug.

"Yechs came for Surp while we were at Aunty Tara's shack. Do you think she could have alerted Dakini Malini?"

"She climbed the ladder in her shop," Anku said, sitting up. "But Aunty Tara's shop lies in Wantra, not Samsara."

"Didn't she say she'd been forced to hunt in the real world?" I asked.

Anku and I looked at the colony of spiders and said together, "The ladder."

"I think I know where Malini is hiding the Maruts," I said. "In fact, I doubt it was Gargouille or Dakini who abducted the Marut children in the first place."

CHAPTER 29

When we reached Tara's Attars, the door of the shack was padlocked and shut for the day.

"Are you sure about this?" Anku asked.

I knew what she meant. There was a lot at risk, and I was aware that my hunch about Aunty Tara's role in the blue blood moon ritual was far-fetched. After all, she was equal to an apothecary for the Maruts. If she wanted to harm Maruts, all she needed to do was slip poison into their tinctures.

I asked Anku to bear with me, but she badgered me for an explanation for visiting Tara's Attars. "Do you think she's a Dakini disguised as a Marut?" she asked. "Perhaps she's locked up the real Aunty Tara in a dungeon somewhere. What if an army of Dakinis attacks us?"

In a few days, I had trained myself to tune out Anku's musings. I studied the area all around.

In the narrow lane, Aunty Tara's living quarters constituted a single room located above the shop, accessed through the ladder. Barring one or two, all lodgings above the shuttered shops were dark with the occupants having slept off.

Through the window of the shop, we could see Aunty Tara moving about in the yellow light of a lone bulb. She was dressed like Ulupi, the Naga princess I met at Haveli—a long skirt and the traditional dupatta over her head. Her body was bent over with age; she moved slowly around the shop. I shuddered to think about the fate of innocent Maruts hunted and trapped by her, people who had probably wanted to help a fragile old lady.

I knocked on the door. She took some time to answer. She opened the padlocked door just a crack and peered at us with eyes clouded by cataracts.

"Shop opens at ten a.m. tomorrow. Go away," Aunty Tara said.

"We only need a minute of your time," Anku said.

"I don't have a minute." The words from Aunty Tara's mouth had a whistle-like sound from the absence of teeth.

"We have information on Maruts you could hunt for the blood," I said.

Aunty Tara stared wordlessly at me. My heart pounding, I returned her stare. Despite her frail, blind, and toothless state, she presented a frightening sight. While two of her hands held the door, another pair crept out and opened the lock.

"Which tincture do you need now?" she asked. "I don't sell them in Samsara. There are laws concerning controlled substances. But I could pop into Wantra and get it for you." Like the Underbridge, Tara's Attars spanned both worlds.

"Er, Kafamukt tincture," Anku said.

"You could have gone to the chemist for a cold!"

"It's for Mothy Maddy. You know human medicines don't work on paladins."

Aunty Tara groaned. "First give me the coordinates of the Maruts. I will check them in my Ichcha Darpan."

"Could you at least prepare the tincture first?" Anku stammered.

"Jantu House. First floor. Galleria," I said without hesitation. It was clear why Naani ran a shelter for animals. Jantu literally meant "animals." How had I not seen this before?

Curious herself, Anku joined Aunty Tara, who had moved before a small, chipped mirror. I searched for the jar of spiders on the shelves and finally found it under the cash counter. The jar contained plump and hairy spiders as big as my hand. We hadn't noticed this jar on our first visit due to the lack of movement in these spiders. They were sedentary, with legs so meaty that they could pass off as squishy toys.

Aunty Tara waved her long pointy nails before the mirror, and Naani's store popped up on the mirror's surface. While it was a pet shelter by day, at that moment and so late in the night it looked like a petting zoo. Kids sat eating or playing catch among freely moving animals.

Anku looked at me in alarm. I moved to stand behind Aunty Tara. I was closer to the jar of spiders now. Anku turned to watch the mirror in horror. I knew she would lash out at me for sharing the location of innocent Marut kids with Aunty Tara, but that bridge could be crossed later if we survived the evening.

"Five Maruts!" Aunty Tara said, clapping her hands.

With my hand behind my back, I could almost touch the jar

of spiders under the cash desk. I felt the cool surface of the glass but couldn't move it. It was a large jar that could only be picked up with both hands.

My fingertips grazed skin that was not my own. I looked down. A pair of Aunty Tara's hands were holding the jar tightly, and Aunty Tara herself stood over me, wearing an arrogant smirk.

"Leave my food alone, boy," she said, her old-lady act forgotten. She stood erect, her cataract afflicted eyes wide open, her manner sharp.

I had forgotten that spider silhouettes had extraordinary vision owing to more than one pair of eyes. Brown recluses had six eyes.

"Keep your end of the bargain now, Aunty Tara," Anku said. She had broken into a sweat. I could tell she'd figured out why we were here. The paladins and Maruts had been searching for Dakini Malini's lab all over the city. All the while, Aunty Tara had turned the Maruts into arachnid food.

"You think you can fool me? I know you are not here for Kafamukt tincture," Aunty Tara said, looking at me.

"Yes, we are not," I said. "You're holding the Maruts in this jar. What's your price for letting them go?"

Aunty Tara tittered. She drew the glass jar with spiders close to her. "You are right. These are Maruts, and you will join your friends in there to make a fine meal for winter when it gets too cold to go out hunting. This one will need some plumping up, though." She nodded to Anku.

She held our gaze while her arms lengthened toward the door and the window of the shop, drawing the shutters and locking the door. Two arms caught Anku's hands before she could swing her challastra.

"That's not possible," Anku said, struggling to free herself. "It takes months for humans in makadee webs to transmogrify into spiders."

"Not anymore," Aunty Tara said in a chilling voice. "Most makadee silhouettes were wiped out by humans and their god-forsaken pesticides. Indra and Amravati abandoned those of us left in Wantra. Finally, I found a well-wisher in Dakini Malini. She was worried about my declining health. She is developing supplements to strengthen makadees. And she delivered. All she asked for in return was help in procuring research subjects."

"You've been working for the Boors?" Anku whispered. I was surprised she hadn't figured it out on our last visit to Tara's Attars. I'd found Aunty Tara to be more Boor than the Yechs I met on my way.

"Why didn't you turn us in the first time we visited you?" I asked.

"I tried, but you injured me with this," Aunty said, producing the dagger that had gone missing from my bag in Kalpavriksha. Dusht Uchchaihshravas. "Surpanekha's daughter had it in her bag."

Surp had stolen the dagger from my bag?

"Boors are closer to you than you might imagine," Aunty Tara said with a chuckle. "In fact, too close."

She was talking about Mothy Maddy, but I doubted Anku got the hint. "Mothy Maddy will beat the pulp out of you," Anku said as if stating an indisputable fact.

"Nobody is coming to save you, girl. Snap out of it," Aunty Tara said, growing grim, and paused. "Since you are all set to be spider meat, I guess there's no harm in telling you. It was I who abducted newly discovered Maruts and delivered them to Dakini Malini. In fact, most times, it was Madhav who provided me with the information. Manasa's hoard has eluded me for a long time, though." She turned to look into the mirror again, a greedy glint in her eyes.

"That's not possible," Anku said.

I had to hand it to her for her loyalty to Mothy Maddy in the face of all the evidence that pointed to his betrayal. I was getting more and more convinced that Mothy Maddy was a Boor in disguise.

"It's easy," Aunty Tara said. "I knew a new Marut had been discovered every time Madhav visited me for tinctures."

"It's not possible," Anku repeated in a whisper.

"After Dakini Malini extracts the silhouette essences from Maruts, she hands the kids to me." Aunty Tara waved her hand before the Ichcha Darpan, and it returned to its original state. With a jerk, I moved forward as she started climbing the ladder, dragging Anku and me with her.

"Eating another Marut is unforgivable," Anku said, struggling to free herself. "You'll turn into a shrapit silhouette. You will go extinct. The paladins will not forgive you."

"But who will tell the paladins? Certainly not you," Aunty Tara said and burst out in chirpy laughter. She let go of us suddenly and clambered up the ladder with the glass jar.

Anku swung her challastra for her club, and together we followed Aunty Tara through the hole in the ceiling. We climbed into a room that had the feel of a tomb. The room was pitch dark. The light from the shop wasn't enough to dispel the darkness. The air was dank and permeated with the salty, acrid scent of brine, like in a pickle factory.

"Don't move," I instructed Anku.

The click of a switch was followed by light flooding the room. My voice stuck in my throat as a horrifying sight unfolded before our eyes. Thin gossamer webs had been woven in every corner of the room. Like ghastly Halloween decor, the cobwebs stretched between the ceiling and the floor. And roosting in these webs were figures—some human, others unrecognizable because cocoons had formed around them.

I heard Anku whimper and turned to find two webs that held the limp forms of Surp and Mohan. I tried to move toward them, but my feet wouldn't budge. I looked down. My feet were stuck in a thick tangle of spider silk. They sank into the material as if it were wet cement.

Anku clubbed the web around her feet, but it seemed to anger it more. In a matter of seconds, the web pulled our backs into its tight grip.

From its touch on my skin, I could tell that the silken web had the strength of metal and the sharpness of a diamond. If we struggled any more, we could end up without limbs.

"Welcome to my sanctuary," Aunty Tara said, emerging from behind Mohan. "Jaaldhatu—that's what Dakini Malini calls my silk—is impressive, don't you think?"

"Let us go," I said through clenched teeth. The pull of the thread grew harder, and my body grew taut.

"And who will feed me? Add another five Maruts from

Manasa's shop, and I will have enough fodder for the next few years. And this one will taste special since she still has her silhouette." She nodded toward Surp. "Dakini Malini sent her to me to hold as a prisoner, but I don't like stale food. I immediately put her on the spit."

She cackled loudly, and a light film of cocoon started knitting itself around Surp's feet and arms.

"And this one," Aunty Tara said, tapping Mohan's slack and still body with her forefinger. "Nothing is working on him. I need a stronger supplement to produce a web toxic enough to transmogrify him."

"You're right, Aunty Tara," I said. "No one will come looking for us here. But when Rahu finds out what you've done with Mohan, you're done for."

The pull of the web slackened in response to my remark. "What do you mean?" she said, narrowing her eyes.

"This boy's blood is meant to wake up the spirit of Vasuki that sleeps in the ring of Kundalini. Mohan is the last Naga heir." I paused between the last few words to let the implication sink in.

"Nooo, he's not," Aunty Tara said, discarding my words with an amused wave of her hands. "And Rahu will never have the ring of Kundalini. Shesh commanded Vasuki's spirit to vacate the diamond ring and possess three celestial relics. That was the riddle he had worked on all his life. Got bit by Vasuki a few times, too. It took quite a few tinctures from me to heal him."

Anku and I stared speechless at Aunty Tara, who went about adjusting the orientation of the cocoons. Anku recovered first. "You helped Shesh Nagaraj. It shows you are a Marut at heart," Anku said intent on appealing to the nonexistent emotional side of Aunty Tara.

Aunty Tara stopped arranging the webs. "Those times were different," she said with a faraway look. "The makadee silhouettes were not persecuted. We did not have to risk being trampled or swatted by humans in Samsara because there was no dearth of food. I had never used my webs to trap Maruts or humans."

She suddenly seemed like a different person, without the perpetual savage sneer on her face.

"But after Shesh died," she continued, snapping out of her nostalgic trance, her features hardening, "our kind had to flee Wantra to live amongst humans." She spat the word "humans" as if she'd accidentally ingested something unpleasant. "The tragic part is that most makadee Maruts were killed as silhouettes. We were the vermin no one wanted."

"What makes you think it will be better when Rahu rises to power?" Anku said.

"I am friends with Dakini Malini," Aunty Tara said self-importantly.

"Not for long, if you kill Surp and Mohan," I said. "Dakini Malini has political ambitions. She'll wipe out makadees if anyone comes in her way to power."

"Quiet, boy!" Aunty Tara said. "With my hoard of trapped Maruts, I can disappear without a trace for decades. Neither deities, Boors, nor Maruts will be able to find me." I shuddered to think about the number of kids she had turned into large juicy spiders to last her for decades.

The coconut chimes in Aunty Tara's shop clopped, announcing an arrival. I was sure the door was locked from the inside.

Aunty Tara's arms shot toward our mouths, and a string of gooey fluid oozed out of her nails, patching our mouths with a metal-like grip so we couldn't scream. She placed the jar of spiders on a table next to a mango with wrinkled skin and descended the ladder, her old-woman act back in place. The mango on the table was the same mango that Surp had shown us back at the Hungry Mongoose. Aunty Tara must have found it on Surp, unaware that it was the panacea.

Surp was already half covered by the jaaldhatu. It was beginning to knit in a thin film around my feet. The worrisome part was that if the jaaldhatu was self-generating, then the patches on our mouths would start spreading, too.

The patch on Anku's face began to creep downward. I felt the cold metallic touch of the web fan out over my cheeks and ears. How long would it take for it to cover my entire face and cut out the air?

I looked at Mohan's lifeless form with remorse. The yin-yang pendant he had lovingly made with his own hands was hanging out over his shirt. He was still in his school uniform. I knew Mohan and I had made decisions without informing grown-ups; we'd defied Naani's instructions. Still, I blamed Naani for this mess.

She had sown self-doubt and bitterness in me toward Mohan. She had deprived Mohan and me of a family. I wished she had never shown up at our doorstep on the day of Mohan's birth. Even I could have done a better job of bringing up

Mohan than she.

Muffled voices reached my ears. I caught snatches of the conversation. Anku made garbled and urgent noises, but I couldn't turn my head to look at her.

Just then, I realized that the jaaldhatu was knitting along my nostrils. I watched the forms of Mohan and Surp grow faint as the web moved over my glasses and covered my eyes.

A loud, hair-raising scream was followed by a refined drawl. "Mobbing mongooses!"

I gasped for the last few breaths of air, but instead, I ended up snorting in liquefied jaaldhatu.

When I opened my eyes, Red was holding a lit-up feather! Krishna's Pankh was aglow with iridescent blue, green, and yellow, causing the jaaldhatu to melt like plastic on fire and collect on the floor in puddles. In his other hand, Red held a jar with a large brown recluse spider in it.

As soon as Anku's feet were freed from the web, she rushed to catch the slack body of Surp while Red reached for Mohan.

Anku retrieved the shrapmukta tincture from her bag and applied it to Surp's hands and face. She did the same for Mohan. Surp stirred awake and sat up as if she were waking from a nap. She wasn't confused or physically hurt in any way.

Aunty Tara wasn't kidding when she said she liked her meat fresh.

I looked at Mohan, expecting him to bounce back as well, but he remained unconscious.

"I know what will help," I said.

I brought the mango lying on the table. Surp grinned in approval, but Red gasped when he saw the fruit. "Is that the fruit of Kalpavriksha?"

Surp nodded.

"But the Panish have never let anyone get near the fruit," Red said.

"They leave their post every time Gargouille puts on a show of power on Kalpavriksha. The day Adi was in Rahu's lair was when I got an opportunity to get to the fruit," Surp said, squeezing a few drops of the mango into Mohan's mouth.

Red was still holding Mohan's body. He looked at me, his eyes wide and his mouth round from surprise and awe. "You were in Rahu's lair?"

I brought the jar of spider Maruts to Surp.

"But the weeping bough would have wailed when the fruit was plucked. This can't be the real fruit," Red said. He regarded the still body of Mohan, seeming teary-eyed and spent from the act of storming Tara's lair.

Mohan's chest was heaving. At least he was still alive.

"Let's check it out, then," Surp said, doubt creeping into her voice.

She squeezed out the entire mango on the floor and emptied the jar of spiders around it. The spiders skittered toward the mango juice, and the moment their feet touched the juice, they transformed. One by one, kids popped up in Aunty Tara's sanctuary. With a cry, Surp hugged one of the boys while Anku hugged two boys closer to our age.

Some of the kids who snapped out of their spider forms were not even Maruts! None carried marks of physical injuries, but their faces looked lifeless, like fused bulbs with no hope of lighting up again. One of these children started crying for help.

"Get them out of here," Red said to Anku and the boys Anku had greeted a little too effusively.

"We'll take care of it," one of the boys said.

"It's not safe to go alone anywhere today, Angad," Anku said.

"We heard Dakini Malini say that now the Naga heir has been found, Yechs can wantonly kill Maruts," said the other boy, a lanky fellow with a mop of curly hair. Anku had called him by the name of Bala. He looked at me meaningfully.

I shifted uncomfortably on my feet, suddenly aware of my sodden sneakers and the fact that the floor was covered in puddles of liquefied jaaldhatu.

"I'm not the Naga heir," I said firmly to put a stop to any more questioning. Thankfully, just then, Mohan's hand stirred.

"Angad and Bala, take the human kids to the nearest police station," Surp said to the boys while Red picked up Mohan in his arms carefully.

Angad and Bala left with the human kids, practicing the story they would tell the cops: "We found them captive in a shop… Or we can say we busted a ring of human-trafficking goons."

"Even if these kids remember their time spent as a spider in the jar, it will only exist as a dream in their memories," Surp said.

"How did you know the Maruts were here?" I asked Surp.

"I didn't. When I reached the lab, I saw Mohan. She had been holding Mohan in," Surp hesitated, "a cage."

Red punched his fist in the air and said, "The nerve!" I squirmed at the thought of Mohan lying helplessly in a cage.

Surp continued, "I tried to rescue him, but she got me. Then she sent the both of us to Aunty Tara. She said no one would think of looking for Maruts here."

"It was lucky Anku and Adi figured out where to find you," Red said, flashing a sincere smile my way.

"Despite Mothy Maddy supplying blood from the butcher's, Aunty Tara owned jars filled with spiders. Brown recluse spiders live in colonies. They're not cannibals," I explained, making small of the compliment.

Surp nodded and got under the shoulder of a boy whose face was battered beyond recognition. That had to be Surp's boyfriend, Rudra. I remembered how back on Kalpavriksha, Dakini Malini had been ecstatic about catching a lion silhouette. Rudra must have fought back and paid heavily for his defiance.

Anku splashed water on Mohan's face, and I slapped him lightly. He blinked and furrowed his brows but sank into unconsciousness again.

"He'll come around by and by," Red said. "We must leave."

CHAPTER 30

We piled into Red's fancy Mercedes parked nearby.

"Even invisible, Kaleeni is not safe. Svarna dhool, or spotting dust, can be used to find you if you run into another ambush," Red said. "The skies are infested with Yechs."

"I wonder why Dakini Malini didn't post Yechs on guard duty near Tara's Attars," I said.

"She thought she had no use for these kids. The real mystery is how Mohan ended up here," Red said. "She should have never let him out of her sight, given his role in the rite of Rahu Amavasya. We are lucky to have found him."

"How did you know where to find us?" Surp asked Red suddenly.

"Searched up Ichcha Darpan for all the Wantra sites connected with Samsara. I saw nothing amiss at Tara's Attars the first time around. The room above her shop doesn't show up in the Ichcha Darpan. It must be located in Amravati and connected to this world through the ladder, just like the one outside the Underbridge."

"For what it's worth, I was right about the ladder being an Akashi ladder," Anku said, glancing at me.

I wanted to tell her that it was I who had figured out Aunty Tara's connection to this drama, but I kept my mouth shut. She liked to take credit for everything that went well. Challenging her was like poking an egoistic bear.

"But I heard voices at Dakini's lab," I said.

"You managed to pick up sounds of what already happened in the lab. Silhouettes can be marvelous and surprising," Red said, looking at me closely. "Anyway, when I saw the dagger, Dusht Uchchaihshravas, lying on her cash counter the second time I searched her shop for clues, I knew something was wrong."

He brought out the Dusht Uchchaihshravas from his jacket's inner pocket and stashed it in the dashboard.

"We can't afford a conflict with Apsara sleuths," he continued. "They're on a warpath searching high and low for celestial artifacts. They've wrecked my house already."

Red had made Mohan sit on the passenger seat next to the driver's seat. When Mohan's hand stirred, I rubbed his shoulder, my guilt for Red's smashed study forgotten. Mohan's eyes were open, and he was staring ahead through the windshield vacantly.

To my left, Surp was cradling Rudra's head on her shoulder. Her face was tearstained. I avoided looking at Surp and Rudra.

"Won't they find us easily here?" I asked Red as he stopped the car next to the Underbridge.

"The Akashi lamppost is under paladin protection. No

other place is safer," Red said.

Surp and I looked at each other. One of us should have spoken out our doubts about Mothy Maddy's loyalties as a paladin, but instead, Anku said, "We should help Mothy Maddy and Pilot Roy."

"The blue blood moon will take place in two hours. You must remain here and keep Mohan safe," Red said, promising to find Mothy Maddy and Pilot Roy.

Who would have thought that out of Mothy Maddy, Pilot Roy, and Red, it would be the dandy and delicate Red who'd save the day? I was more convinced than ever that heroism came from unexpected quarters.

Surp led Rudra to a cot inside. Mohan, who was physically unharmed, sat pensively on a stone stool, unlike his usual bubbly self.

Soon, Angad and Bala sauntered in too, and together we settled on the pavement adjoining the sack curtains, listening to the *plink-plonk* of the leaking tap outside. Surp started pacing the length of the road.

No one had any appetite for anything, neither food nor talk. Surp looked at the full moon from time to time. Anku got up to apply jambukita tincture on a few scratches that Bala and Angad had sustained as spiders.

"Thanks for saving my brother," I said to Surp after gathering all my courage. All of a sudden, I was conscious of my glasses and hearing aid. I knew I was closer to looking and acting like a hero in Wantra than in Samsara.

"This doesn't feel right," Surp said, halting suddenly. She

hadn't heard me.

"What do you mean?"

"This is too easy," she said. "Rahu has waited for hundreds of years for the blue blood moon. We must be missing something. It feels like a setup."

I was so relieved over finding Mohan that I hadn't thought about what could happen next.

"We must trust the paladins. They've protected us thus far," Anku said and sent Angad and Bala inside to catch some sleep.

"Mothy Maddy has changed ever since the night of the deadly storm ten years back," Surp said.

"You're imagining things," Anku said, shaking her head in disdain. She covered Mohan with a blanket and snuggled into a jacket, shutting her eyes.

"Do you think Mothy Maddy is on our side?" I whispered to Surp.

Surp shook her head. "I'm not sure. Mothy Maddy has been acting very secretive. That's the reason I decided to look for Rudra myself."

I glanced at Mohan, who was behaving like a stranger. He hadn't even acknowledged me or asked what was happening. I used to scoff at black magic, especially voodoo dolls, but Anku had shown me how celestials could snatch identities to get a taste of the real world from time to time. Could it be that a Boor had snatched Mohan's body? Mohan was a wastrel by celestial standards.

"I know who has the answers," I said, squaring my shoulders. I had made a decision that had been long coming. It was to talk to Naani. It was time for her to come clean.

I spread out Kaleeni and stood aside as it zapped into an airborne car. I could be mistaken, but every time I uttered the chant, Kaleeni's transformation seemed faster.

I looked at Surp. "Want to accompany me to meet Manasa Nagaraj?" I said.

Surp looked longingly toward the curtains. I read conflict in her troubled eyes and furrowed brows. She didn't want to risk leaving Rudra alone again.

"I can go alone," I said hurriedly, though I would have loved to have Surp by my side as I stood up to Naani.

In one last attempt to get a reaction from Mohan, I walked up to him and moved my face before his, but he looked through me. It was strange to see my brother so well-behaved and quiet. I hated his clinging and overenthusiastic behavior, but right now, I would have given anything to see him in his element: bouncy, bright, and protective of me.

I climbed onto Kaleeni and pulled the invisibility tassel. Kaleeni rose waist-high above the pavement, and I directed it away as quietly as possible.

Anku had urged me to talk to Naani at the night market, but I'd refused. Now that Mohan was safe, I was on a stronger footing to demand answers from Naani. I could have asked Anku to accompany me, but I couldn't bear the thought of smug satisfaction on her face saying, *I told you. You should have talked to her before.*

"You think you can do everything by yourself?" Anku's voice lamented in a spooky echo around me.

"Snake in the grass!" I cried as Anku emerged out of nowhere, the guptikr flung over her arm. Her face broke into a wide grin from having startled me.

"I am *not* a snake in the grass! I am here to help!"

"That is not why you came," I said wryly.

"That's right, I want to see you get an earful from your Naani," she said, cocking her head like a little miss know-it-all.

"Honestly," I said, raising my eyes to the heavens. There was no getting rid of her.

"I've always discounted Mrs. M. If only I had known she was actually Manasa Nagaraj, the powerful and famous ex-Marut with a dragon silhouette," Anku said and plonked herself next to me. "It's a pity Surp didn't come along."

Trust her to rub that in. "She agreed with my idea," I said.

Anku nodded. "Of course she did."

She infuriated me. It was like having a much younger Naani sitting right next to me.

Now that I had decided to face Naani, all repressed emotions came bubbling to the surface: her preference for Mohan, sending me to make deliveries to Wantra, denying everything when asked. Her web of deceit was too thick and messed up. Despite my indignation and anger, I was also a tad fearful of Naani's reaction.

Anku patted my arm and pointed into the darkness. I adjusted my glasses and looked hard. I could make out the darker shapes of Yechs that stood flapping their wings in the air. We checked the air around Kaleeni to find flapping wings of Yechs everywhere. The sky was a sea of Yechs. Thankfully, Kaleeni needed no maneuvering when it came to skirting the demonic forces.

It zigzagged through the Yechs and landed on the rooftop

of our apartment block. We hid Kaleeni on the roof and took the stairs down to apartment 701.

I knew something was amiss when I found the door ajar. Naani was so fond of putting locks on everything. She would never be careless enough to leave the main door open.

Anku swung her key ring and soon had her club in her hand. Every time she did that, I resented the Satya Pasha and wished my key ring weapon had been cooler than the silly truth loop. A part of me was glad that Satya Pasha had been left in the Maw hanging around the Deodar tree.

I nudged the door open with my foot and entered the apartment. In the light of the sole living room lamp, we found everything in disarray. The sofa had been upturned and its base slashed open. The cushioned seats had been cut open. Naani's locker-safe, dragged out of her bedroom, lay broken on the floor with the jewelry and cash spilled all around.

There were drops of blood on the floor. I felt a flutter in my tummy. I had imagined a scenario where Naani was dead many times in the past. But right now, the thought of her being gone forever filled me with a sense of dread.

I rushed to my bedroom to check on Patches. He was gone. There was no sign of any damage in my room. Was it possible that the blood on the floor belonged to Patches? I put the thought aside firmly.

Just then, a low whimpering reached me. It was coming from the kitchen pantry. I opened the door, and a white dove flew into my face. I batted it away, but it seemed to be protecting three cowering animals in the pantry: a dog, a hedgehog, and a kid goat. These must have been the pets that had taken temporary shelter in Naani's room. She often brought injured and dying animals home for hands-on care.

Anku's cry had me running back to the living room. In the dark shadow behind the balcony door was a rocking chair with the limp body of Naani on it. She had been gagged, and she was bleeding profusely from a wound on her forehead. But she was not dead.

Anku started untying the knots in the rope around the rocking chair.

"Yech?" I asked.

Anku nodded. "They didn't kill her. That's curious."

Perhaps they couldn't kill her, I thought wryly.

Anku dabbed shrapmukta tincture on Naani's wounds. I brought some water from the kitchen and sprinkled it on Naani's face. She began to come around.

"Adi," she cried, taking my face in her hands. "Thank God! You are alright."

This was the first time Naani had shown any concern for my safety. Given how much I'd bad-mouthed her, I felt embarrassed to have Naani embrace me as Anku sat there looking at us, judging me.

"What happened?" I asked her.

"Gargouille came," Naani said with a cry. "He took Patches. Said he wanted to present him to Dakini Malini for research. He also said," she broke down, gasping amid sobs, "Dakini has Mohan."

"Mohan is safe," I told her. "He's back at the Underbridge."

Naani's hands flew to her mouth as she looked at me with her eyes wide open. Was it admiration or disbelief? "You were with Mohan? Did you hurt each other?"

"What? We would never do that!"

"Take me to Mohan," Naani said, heaving herself up. She walked to the large bowl that held her precious potpourri and upturned it onto the floor.

I glanced at Anku. She was watching Naani with admiration, like a fan who goes speechless when they meet their favorite celebrity.

Naani held the bowl, its outer base facing us.

"Srivatsa!" Anku whispered when her eyes fell on the bowl.

"They came looking for this," Naani said. "It's funny how one overlooks the most obvious of places. I learned this lesson from Shesh. He would say, 'Mind creates lockers to store valuables. Mind also looks for valuables inside lockers.'"

"What is Srivatsa?" I asked.

"Srivatsa, the divine shield is the mark of Kalki, the last avatar of Lord Vishnu," Anku said, right on cue. "They say that Kalki will take birth when the physical world becomes too unstable to carry on."

"What do you mean by unstable?"

"Pollution, war, and exploitation of the vulnerable," Naani said. "Nagas were to keep Srivatsa safe for Kalki."

I had read about Kalki, the twenty-fourth Avatar of Vishnu, the preserver. Legend presented Kalki as a religious hero, but we all knew what actually ailed the societies. It was not religion. Naani knew mythology inside out, but I had never known her to be religious. Perhaps it was because she was part of the myth herself. She was a Marut. She respected celestial hierarchy. There was a difference between respect and devotion. Respect was grounded while devotion could be delusional.

"What does this have to do with the ring of Kundalini?" I asked.

"Before Fangless led Rahu to the ring of Kundalini, Shesh managed to split up its powers into three external objects." She pointed at the symbol in the center of Srivatsa. "The triquetra." Then she traced her finger on a band that ran through the petals of the triquetra. "Vasuki's body, the circle of Kundalini." Finally, Naani touched the dot on top of one petal of the triquetra. "The Nagamani."

I placed my finger on the jagged grooves that must have held the triquetra, a symbol I'd held in my hands a few hours back.

"To awaken Vasuki, the three symbols must be placed in this shield," Naani said, running her hand over the shield.

"But Srivatsa is in itself so powerful," Anku said, extending her hand to touch it gingerly.

"Each time a symbol is restored, this shield will grow in power," Naani said. "I heard one of the symbols has surfaced." Her eyes reflected both fear and confusion. She reminded me of a soldier who relies so much on preparedness that he crumbles in the face of a sudden attack, a shell-shocked warrior.

"The triquetra," I said, running my hand through my hair and assessing the mess in the living room. I couldn't look into Naani's eyes out of guilt for having gifted the triquetra to Takka. "What about the other symbols?" I asked.

"No one knows where Shesh hid the loop and the Nagamani," Naani said. "The night of the attack on Haveli, I was scared and confused. Even if Shesh did tell me where the three parts of Srivatsa are hidden, I have no recollection of it. My daughter, your great-grandmother, insisted on bringing Patches with her. We managed to escape just in time."

"*My* Patches?" I cried.

Naani nodded.

"He is that old?!" I exclaimed, noting that Naani had used only one "great" to describe her daughter. There should have been more.

"Age is relative," Naani said. "For pure Maruts, a hundred and fifty years is middle age. For celestials, it has no meaning at all. Patches is a celestial animal who comes from Shani Nandana."

Naani rounded her lips and gave a short, sharp whistle. The dove that had almost scratched my face flew down and perched on her hand. She whispered something to the dove.

"We may need Gandaks to fight for us," Naani said as the dove flew through the open balcony door.

"But they can't be seen in the real—" I began.

"Identity snatching," Anku said, supplying me with an answer.

Naani seemed to be muttering to herself as she hurried into her bedroom. She emerged a few moments later with some clothes, which she placed in the pantry with the rescued animals.

"Are these…?" Anku asked, but before she could finish her sentence, we heard the snapping and cracking of bones popping back together. The animals silhouetted into their human forms and emerged from the pantry.

"Hurt, abused, and hunted," Naani said, turning to me.

"That's the life of a Marut child."

Okay, but I had felt hurt too, and I was quite sure Naani's behavior amounted to abuse.

She brought out three amulets similar to the one I'd worn and tied these on the kids. She turned to the oldest, a girl of about ten, and said, "You must reach the Hungry Mongoose in Defense colony." Then she addressed them together. "Once the Yechs have your scent, these amulets won't work to protect you. Do not take them off."

They nodded in unison.

"Who will protect them from humans?" Anku said as the kids scurried out of the flat.

"Like you protect yourself," Naani said, pointing to the challastra on each child. Naani had provided these kids with weapons while sending me defenseless to make deliveries to Gargouille. Relieved at having let the kids go, Naani said, "Take me to Mohan now."

I felt a stab of good old jealousy. Great, there it was again. Mohan, her precious, needed protection.

"Vasuki Upakritam," I whispered. Kaleeni whizzed into the room through the balcony door. Now that everything was out in the open, what would she do? Give Kaleeni to Mohan? Declare him the Naga heir? Train him to fight with Srivatsa?

Perhaps, my heart replied to my mind. And maybe it would be okay if she did. But first I would make sure she answered my questions as soon as we were on our way to the bridge.

We took to the sky from the balcony. Naani directed Kaleeni to heights where Yechs couldn't fly. She sat hugging Srivatsa, and her sight was set ahead. Anku quickly narrated the happenings at Tara's Attars to Naani.

"Another Marut clan gone the Boor way," Naani said with a sigh. "Maruts are better off living in Amravati as second-class citizens rather than in Wantra or Samsara."

That didn't sound so bad. From what I'd read about Amravati, picture-perfect devas and apsaras lived there. Still, I wondered if Amravati was as dreamy as it was depicted in literature given the fact that Gandaks like Rinca and Gilli ran a pub there.

"Once I have Mohan, you must drop us at the northern gateway into Swahalok," Naani said. "Red will be waiting there for us with Apsara sleuths. All Maruts and paladins can leave this godforsaken place forever."

"Is that what you told the dove?" Anku said.

Naani nodded. "And also asked Red to get reinforcements."

"But how will Mohan travel to Swahalok with you? He's not a Marut. He can't even silhouette," I said. "And what about me?" Did she plan to leave me behind?

Naani sighed in exasperation. "Why must you always think about yourself?"

"ARE YOU KIDDING ME?" I screamed so loudly that I was afraid my voice would attract the Yechs in the sky.

As I checked through Kaleeni's windows and doors for any sign of Yechs, Anku showed a shaken Naani the map we found clutched in Surp's hands at the shivir. "Surp must have snatched it from Dakini," Anku said, holding it out to Naani.

Naani glanced at the message written in brahmi script on the map. "This is a celestial edict that shows the location of Kaal Stambhas or King Ashoka's time pillars. It says except for the Bare Stambha at the Qutb Complex, all other exits from the real world into Swahalok will be closed on the eve of Rahu Amavasya."

"Why would they do that?" Anku asked.

"Swahalok must be worried about an influx of Boors into their realm." Naani moved her hand up to cup her mouth. "What have I done? Red will bring all Marut kids to the North Stambha. If Dakini had this map, she must have surely stationed the Yechs here."

"If Swahalok was so worried, why would they leave the Bare Stambha open?" I asked, directing my words at Anku. I was still angry with Naani.

"According to legend, King Ashoka drove that Stambha into the hood of Serpent Vasuki, and Vasuki supports the earth from that spot," Anku said.

"That's where Kaleeni brought us the night of the delivery," I said. "Kaleeni answers to Vasuki."

Naani nodded. "That is also where Shesh's body was found. He must have tried to escape through the portal when Haveli was attacked," Naani said, her brow furrowed. "That portal can't be closed. What are we to do now?"

Even if Wantra, Swahalok, and Boorlok existed as parallel realities, how could Vasuki possibly be at all these places at one time, supporting the earth, sleeping inside a ring, and being responsible for the cycle of birth and death? I diverted my mind from the apparent absurdity of the thought to the present problem.

"There's a ladder in Aunty Tara's shack that connects to Amravati, which can be used for escape," I suggested.

"Who knows what lies beyond the ladder," Naani said. "We

must escape through the Bare Stambha. We must be in place when the lightning strikes the Stambha." She had still not clarified whether "we" included me.

Anku elbowed me and mouthed, "Talk to her."

I steeled myself and took a breath. Finally, I said, "Naani, why did you hide everything from me?"

Over the years, I wondered if there could be any answer to this question that I'd accept. If she would deserve my forgiveness. What excuse could she give me for subjecting me to years of neglect? In all my pondering, I'd never expected she would say what she said next.

"I wanted to protect you, Adi."

Another lie! my mind screamed. "You wanted to protect me, or Mohan?" I countered.

"I wanted to protect *you* from Mohan," she said.

I was surprised to see her eyes well up with tears. I was sick and tired of her riddles. "Will you please tell me the truth?" I said, trying my best to control the anger blazing inside of me, singeing my love for Mohan and everything I held dear. "Are you not the same Manasa Nagaraj who has connections with the fire dragons of the east?"

Naani shifted in her seat somewhat fearfully. She adjusted the neatly hemmed corners of her kurta every time they flew up, owing to the wind blowing into Kaleeni. "I am," she said, a tad defensively. "But I gave up my silhouette and celestial status."

"Why?"

"To save the Naga clan."

I stared at her, at a loss for words. Was her horrid behavior toward me because she was sore about giving up her Marut status?

"But I have no regrets," Naani said in a firm voice. "It was my choice, and I love you boys."

"Then why did you allow Batty to send me for deliveries to Gargouille?"

"Batty?" she said, confused, her brows furrowing.

"I mean Fangless." She hadn't expected me to be aware of her connection with Batty. And I didn't want to disclose that I'd eavesdropped on the two of them.

"Fangless was captured by Gargouille after the attack on Haveli," Naani said. "They tortured him for information about the Nagas. He agreed to work as an agent for them. But, thankfully, he remained loyal to us and provided us with information."

"You knew about the deliveries I was making for him?" I asked. I couldn't prevent the incredulity from creeping into my voice.

Naani nodded. "It was our plan all along. I mean, Madhav and mine. To gain Gargouille's trust. Before the blue blood moon, we wanted to know if Rahu possessed any part of the real ring, Srivatsa. For that, we had to locate the human identities that Rahu, Ketu, Dakini, and Gargouille had snatched. I used the Naga collection of celestial objects to lure Gargouille. Fangless hung out in the darkest corners of Chandni Chowk for years, and then one day, a Gargo D'Souza contacted him in the guise of an art collector."

"But why did you choose Adi for the deliveries?" Anku asked. "You could have asked one of us."

"It is true," Naani admitted, "but only a Naga can communicate with the ancient spirit of Vasuki that resides inside the parts of the ring of Kundalini. The talisman would have picked up on Adi immediately."

"And then what? I wouldn't have known what to do," I said.

"Why did you wait so long to tell Adi?" Anku interjected impatiently.

"Since Rahu believed he had the ring of Kundalini, we thought he would not hurt Adi, knowing that he needed a Naga heir for the transfer of the ring's powers to himself." She laid her forefinger on a tiny button-sized hole on Srivatsa. "We thought we had time." Her voice trembled.

"You sent me to my death without any preparation. Mohan attended karate classes and received kung fu and boxing lessons while you let me meet Gargouille without even a warning," I said. Unbidden tears streamed down my cheeks. I knew my chin was quivering. I clenched my teeth to keep myself from giving into full-on weeping.

"It was Fangless who sent you to meet Gargouille. When he got to know that triquetra had been stolen from the Bank of Karma, he jumped the gun. He knew I would have never allowed you to step into Wantra before the right time."

My fists balled up, and my breathing became slow and labored. "This is your last chance, Naani. Tell me the truth. You offered me as bait to Rahu. You were ready to sacrifice me just to save Mohan. Is that simply because he's the real Naga heir?"

Naani's face paled, and she looked at me, thunderstruck. "Mohan is not the real Naga heir, Adi. You are."

"Then who is Mohan?" I screamed. "Why is he so precious to you?"

My frustration was getting the better of me. Naani and Anku had gone still. Only the flapping of Kaleeni's curtains could be heard. Anku placed her finger on her mouth. Over the rustling of the curtains, a louder flapping was audible, the kind that the large wings of a bird would produce.

Then I remembered: In all our hurry, we had forgotten to pull the invisibility tassel! Even though Kaleeni's silk black exteriors merged seamlessly with the night, it was a flashy flying carpet that couldn't be missed.

Anku, Naani, and I ducked low. Anku put up three fingers for the number of Yechs she'd spotted.

Rage was still pounding my head, and I knew it wasn't from seeing the Yechs. Still, they would bear the brunt of Naani's revelations when I pummeled the living daylights out of them.

I heard a rasping sound close to the entrance of Kaleeni. I jumped up, taking the Yech by surprise. I lifted my leg and kicked the Yech in the middle of its forehead. Anku pounced on the Yech at the other entrance with her club. Naani moved to the center between Anku and me, her eyes fearful. *Some fire dragon!*

While we waited, alert, for the third Yech to attack, Naani lifted the flap of her kurta and brought out a dagger from around her waist. For a moment, I thought it was the Dusht Uchchaihshravas. Then I noticed the eye of the horse. It was made of a white pearl in contrast to the black onyx eye of the Dusht Uchchaihshravas.

"Shveta Uchchaihshravas!" Anku whispered.

While the hilts of both daggers were made of brass and the horses looked alike, there was something cold-hearted in the sharp glint of Dusht Uchchaihshravas, as if the dagger contained inside it would butcher gleefully, unflinchingly. The Shveta Uchchaihshravas gave out a faint glow. A zen horse, if it were possible.

Instead of unsheathing it, Naani extended her hand to me. I looked from the dagger to her.

"Take it. It belongs to your forefathers," she said.

I hesitated. If she thought this dagger could make up for her abhorrent behavior, she was mistaken. I would have refused the dagger had it not been for the complete lack of any weapon on me. It was too tempting, even for my highly bruised ego. Still, I wanted her to insist a little more.

Something made Kaleeni jerk as if it had just run over a huge boulder, and the dagger flew into my hand. Anku fell onto the silk seats, and I bumped my head against Kaleeni's roof.

As Kaleeni titled, Naani lost her footing and slipped out. This was a fatal design flaw in the flying carpet. If it could have a roof and windows, then it could also have done with two doors. Even flaps tied together would have been better than the gaping spaces that could suck a person out.

Before I could do anything to help Naani, two Yechs framed Kaleeni's doors. I could still see Naani's hand holding onto Kaleeni's edge. But a leering Yech was flapping its wings right above her.

I lunged at the Yech, slicing its neck with my newly acquired dagger. The Yech rasped and fell, its limbs flailing in the air at odd angles, like a wooden puppet let loose from a string.

I reached for Naani's hand, but it slipped before I could reach it. I was about to direct Kaleeni to follow Naani at full speed when a sight sent a chill down my spine. Dakini Malini rose in the air before us, sitting astride a vulture, and she held a petrified Naani by her collar.

Naani was by no means a petite or light person, but Dakini was holding her as if Naani were a dirty sock.

Dakini Malini reached toward Srivatsa, but Naani kept swatting her hand away as she called Dakini every unsavory name she knew. I now understood why Gargouille hadn't killed Naani but stationed Yechs outside the condo instead. He must have expected her to steal away with Srivatsa.

I heard a gravelly scream behind me. The Yech in the doorway, its head squished into his neck and green liquid dripping onto its body, fell into the night.

"How did you do that?" I said to Anku.

"I didn't," Anku said, her eyes fixed on a dark shape that grew visible behind the fallen Yech. A white dove in one hand and a death pike in the other, Kabeela grinned eerily at us, a patrol of Yechs behind him. He had killed a Yech simply to clear his line of vision.

He flapped his way around Kaleeni toward Dakini Malini. On seeing the dove in Kabeela's hand, Naani let out a heartrending wail. The dove was clutched in Kabeela's hand, writhing in agony.

Kabeela raised his hand and squeezed the bird until it stopped fluttering. Naani screamed, her face growing purple-red with rage and grief.

Once the bird stopped moving, Naani called me. I had

never seen her look so sure of herself. Her teeth were set together, and her eyes were narrow. She hurled Srivatsa toward me. "Catch it!" she cried.

Immediately, Dakini Malini let go of Naani and lunged toward the shield, but she was a second late.

"Look after your brother, Adi," I heard Naani's faint scream as she plummeted toward the ground. I caught Srivatsa, but my mind was in turmoil.

I wanted to dash after Naani, but as soon as I caught Srivatsa, my sight blurred and my head felt dizzy. My body was changing; my muscles grew heavier, and my hearing amplified so I could detect the sound of the cars driving on the roads far down below. I felt the same way I had the first time I entered Wantra the night of the delivery. I felt brawny and invincible. I snatched off my glasses and the hearing aid, tossing them out of Kaleeni.

The Yechs surrounded us like bees buzzing around a hive. I welted the face of one with Srivatsa and drove the dagger under the chin of another. I peered down after the falling Yech to look for Naani, but she had been swallowed by the night.

Anku was engaged in a battle with another Yech. One of them had burned a hole in Kaleeni's roof, releasing the invisibility tassel.

I ordered Kaleeni to zoom down after Naani, but Kaleeni did not budge. It floated in the air at one spot like a car whose wheels were entrenched in a deep, muddy pothole.

CHAPTER 31

I tried to guide Kaleeni away, but it remained floating in one place. Then I saw a Yech face looking at us through Kaleeni's back window. The Yechs had latched onto Kaleeni from all sides, making it hard for the carpet to move.

Kabeela and Malini were inching closer to us, their eyes fixed on Srivatsa in my hands. But something was different about them. The brazenness and arrogance had been replaced by caution. Malini was licking her lips nervously, and Kabeela looked almost human without his sneer. Both of them were looking from the dagger to the shield in my hands.

It was comforting to see Malini and Kabeela nervous, but I doubted Anku and I had any chance against the brutes, even with our weapons. Also, the loss of Naani had created a strange mix of emotions in me. I'd hated her all my life, and now that she was gone, I felt unmoored. It didn't make sense.

My watch read 1:00 a.m. One hour until the beginning of the blue blood moon. The evening had been so action-packed that I had lost all sense of time.

I glanced up at the moon and realized with alarm that a dark shadow was moving across its surface. Had the eclipse started already? Had Mohan been found? Was I too late? I looked at Anku, who seemed as confused as me.

With a sudden screech, the Yechs that were holding Kaleeni fell off, lifeless. I felt Kaleeni ripple as it floated free of the Yechs' hold.

Malini and Kabeela halted in the air and peered into the space around them, their weapons in their hands. In a few blinks, the moon became visible again. And just as suddenly, something black and satiny moved before Kaleeni's door, like a curtain cutting us off from Malini and Kabeela.

I extended my hand to the surface and felt soft, downy feathers. I was touching a gigantic wing. "I knew you were batting for the enemy," we heard Dakini Malini say spitefully.

"The first rule of battle is they don't harm our children, and we don't harm theirs," a female voice replied. It was Surpanekha.

"We're following Rahu's directions," Dakini Malini spat.

"Then let Rahu kill," Surpanekha said. "He is the deity of disease. He can get away with it. This monster next to you sold his soul to Rahu." I knew she was referring to Kabeela. "Dakinis are mothers. We're Boors, but we are not monsters."

"Surpanekha," Anku whispered in my ear. "Well done, Ludo!"

"You lied to me," an unfamiliar voice added to Surpanekha's.

I instructed Kaleeni to back away. As Kaleeni receded, the shapes of two giant birds, a koel and a raven, became visible.

The koel was larger than Surp's koel, and the feathers near its beak were graying. Her wings even had a few faded patches of feathers.

Once we were far enough, we saw that another circle of birds, a mix of koels and ravens, was streaming in to form a circle around Kabeela and Dakini Malini.

I wished I had enough time to watch the face-off, but I had a blue blood moon to attend. "Lodhi Road Underbridge," I whispered, and Kaleeni shot off toward the ground in the direction of the Underbridge. With the invisibility tassel torn, we would have to make our way in the shadows of the trees and dark streets.

"It's strange," I said, examining the Shveta Uchchaihshravas. "This dagger feels just right in my hands. Do you think this could be my actual challastra?"

Anku shrugged. She ran her hand over the hilt of the dagger. "The twin daggers of Uchchaihshravas are impossible to defeat when used together. But they belong to Lord Indra. I wonder how Manasa got to be in their possession."

Takka had said that if you used someone else's weapon, it could turn against you. But I could yield this weapon without any need for training.

"It feels like I'm in Wantra," I said, flexing my muscled arm.

"Adi," Anku said. "You are in your Marut form."

"But how does one know? It's true I can see without glasses, and I can hear voices from a distance, but you still wear your glasses," I pointed out.

"That's because I've never felt hindered by them. Maruts don't have any weaknesses. I don't consider my shortsightedness a weakness. These glasses work for me."

I studied Anku. I knew she used the glasses to hide just like I did. She and I were similar in many ways, and yet I had a long way to catch up with her in wisdom.

"What?" Anku said, waving a hand before my eyes.

Street smarts, not wisdom, I corrected myself as I caught myself staring at Anku. "I was just…" I stammered. "I was just wondering why it happened now. I silhouetted a long time back."

"Mothy Maddy left Surp and me in many dangerous situations to help us to overcome our fears before he handed us the challastras. I hated him at times," Anku said, hugging her knees. "This was probably why your Naani was being hard on you."

"But were you convinced that Mothy Maddy cared for you?" I asked.

"Of course."

"That's the difference. If Naani wanted me to learn, then why did she go out of her way to show she didn't love me?"

Anku had no answer to my question.

I knew what she was thinking. We had just seen Naani fall to her death. She expected me to grieve, but I couldn't bring myself to shed a tear for Naani.

It was 1:30 p.m. To avoid being detected, we cut through the Lodhi Garden adjacent to the bridge rather than the well-lit road to the Underbridge. The park was populated with towering Neem and Peepal trees, which would hide our movement.

"Apart from the banyan trees, Yechs don't like anything

green and alive," Anku explained.

Kaleeni skimmed over the untended grass and undergrowth, causing a slight rustle. Something dropped from a tree a few paces ahead. I glanced at my watch. We had no time to lose.

A human shape started running toward us, waving its arms, a shiny suitcase in one hand.

I cursed the Yech who had burned down Kaleeni's invisibility tassel and checked the approaching figure for a death pike or bat wings. When I saw the lush bushy tail of a fox running next to the figure, I relaxed. Even in the absence of light, I recognized the wild, frizzy hair of Pilot Roy.

Pilot Roy ran up to us and stood panting at the door of Kaleeni. Lomri jumped onto the carpet and sidled up to Anku.

"Yechs raided the Underbridge. Mohan and Surp are gone," Pilot Roy said amid pants. In his hand, he held a metal trunk, the same trunk that could unfold into a propellor airplane, the same plane that had been taken apart to erect the metal wall at the Underbridge. I wondered if Anku knew the truth about the wall. "I overheard Gargouille order the Yechs to bring them to the Bare Stambha," he said.

"Where's Mothy Maddy?' Anku demanded as Pilot Roy hopped onto Kaleeni.

"He is in Rahu's captivity," Pilot Roy replied. "When I reached Chaubey's house, I saw Thauma and Takka leaving. I guessed they had handed the triquetra to Chaubey. I silhouetted and scouted around the premises. My silhouette is especially strong at night."

I nodded. "Owls are nocturnal birds."

"How did you know my silhouette is an owl?" Pilot Roy asked sharply.

"This is not the time," I said, growing impatient with the distrust floating around the question of the mole amongst the Maruts.

"When I saw Chaubey leave with his lackeys in cars, I followed them to the Underbridge," Pilot Roy said, resuming his narration.

"But they couldn't have known unless a paladin led them there…" Anku said and stopped mid-sentence. "Mothy Maddy?" she said in disbelief.

Pilot Roy didn't nod, nor did he deny her words. "By the time I reached the bridge, they had Mohan and Surp in ropes."

"Why didn't you stop them?" Anku snapped at Pilot Roy.

"You know I can't fight to save my own life," he said sullenly. He looked unhappy about having had to confess his lack of skills in my presence. "Madhav is the muscle. I am the brain."

"We must leave for Bare Stambha," I said.

"What about Rudra and the boys?" Anku asked.

"Who?" Pilot Roy said, taken aback by the question. "Weren't Rudra and the boys in Dakini's captivity?"

"We rescued them from Aunty Tara," Anku said. "We left Mohan in their care and Rudra, Angad, and Bala would never allow anyone to touch Mohan. They would have fought the Yechs."

"To their deaths," Pilot Roy whispered.

"I have to check," Anku said, shaking her head in disbelief.

I was so occupied with keeping my own brother safe that

THE LEGEND OF TRIQUETRA

I'd forgotten that Rudra, Angad, and Bala were Anku's family. All my life, I'd felt cheated by my own family. I had given undue importance to blood ties. I had distrusted others and had slipped into the role of a victim. But, as pointed out by Pilot Roy earlier that day, circumstances made a family of people. Anku had to make sure her family was safe.

I nodded to her. She got off Kaleeni. Lomri decided to follow Anku. I directed Kaleeni to bring Pilot Roy and me to the Bare Stambha.

It was close to 1:45 p.m., and my nerves were frayed. On the way to Bare Stambha, to keep my mind from spiraling, I asked Pilot Roy if Gargouille had hurt Mohan.

Pilot Roy shook his head. I took that to mean that Mohan had been unharmed. I felt less sure, though, when Pilot Roy shook his head for every question I asked. I gave up when I asked, "Where do you work?" and he shook his head again, staring absentmindedly at Srivatsa and the Shveta Uchchaihshravas but not asking to touch them.

We crossed the forested Aravali Ridge. Some sort of carnival seemed to be going on in the middle of the forest. The Gandaks had mentioned the Wantra fair to celebrate the blue blood moon, or Rahu Amavasya. Fairy lights twinkled eerily under the forest canopy.

Had I been inducted into the Marut fold by Naani, I might have visited the fair. I may have ventured into the Kalpavriksha and met other creatures like the Zephyr Rovers and the Glitches. It was just my luck that I had to discover Wantra when the world was on the brink of destruction by evil forces.

As we approached the Qutb complex, I spotted a child tied

to the famous pillar of Ashoka in the main compound. Mohan looked frightened and was struggling to loosen the ropes tied around his body.

Gargouille, back in his jeans and jacket, watched Mohan. Apart from a few Yechs standing guard around the compound, there was no sign of anyone else.

"Where's Surp?" I whispered.

"Probably somewhere there," Pilot Roy whispered, pointing toward the scattered ruins in the complex.

"You look for her—" I began.

"We will free your brother first," Pilot Roy said, cutting me off mid-sentence. It made sense to stick together. The thought of facing Gargouille alone was daunting.

"Do you have a weapon?" I asked Pilot Roy over my shoulder. When he didn't answer, I turned to look at him and saw that he was holding a kitchen knife in his hands. I could have sworn I had seen a challastra dangling around his waist.

"You will get killed with that," I said.

"We shall see," he replied.

Pilot Roy reminded me of the careless buffoon-like characters in films who survived extreme disasters that the protagonists went to great lengths to escape. These comical characters were tough because they made light of everything. I mean, who would think of fighting Rahu and Yechs with a kitchen knife?

The moonlight lit up the entire ruins in a magical glow. Of the numerous empty lots around the Bare Stambha, I chose one that was submerged in the shadows of high walls.

The moment we landed, Pilot Roy bounded off, saying, "I will release Mohan from the rope." Without waiting to discuss the plan of action, he slipped behind a column on the periphery of the main compound.

CHAPTER 32

I guessed it was only fair that I take on Gargouille since I had the Shveta Uchchaihshravas in one hand and Srivatsa in the other. I hoped my surprise attack would prove to be enough distraction for the Yechs so Pilot Roy could cut Mohan loose. Rahu was nowhere to be seen, and with ten minutes left for the blue blood moon, I had a small window of time to escape with Mohan.

If we managed to escape, where would we flee? I couldn't think of any place. With Naani gone, we could live with Aunty Padma. The thought brought a spring to my step.

I slipped from column to column, getting nearer to Gargouille. The Yechs were facing outward and mostly stood on top of the wall. Blind as bats in the moonlight, they were straining hard to be watchful.

When I reached the column in the direct line of the Bare Stambha and Gargouille, I made my move.

Mohan saw me emerge from behind the pillar. I placed a finger on my lips, though I knew I needn't have. My brother hardly recognized me. I tiptoed toward Gargouille and pounced on him, driving my dagger into his back with all my power.

Gargouille roared, but not in pain. I was horrified to see that he seemed delighted with my arrival. My dagger had pierced the flesh of his shoulder, releasing spurts of blood, but he kept roaring in excitement without lifting a hand at me.

"What we heard about you is correct. You have moxie," I heard someone say behind me.

I pulled out the dagger from Gargouille's back and spun around to find Chaubey had walked into the compound. So Anku and I were correct in our assumption that Rahu had snatched Chaubey's identity!

Behind Chaubey, his crooks slinked into the compound. A bruised and battered Mothy Maddy was standing just behind Chaubey. His hands were tied, and a Yech held his collar. Next to Mothy Maddy, looking sheepish and shifty, was Thauma. And to Thauma's left was an unrecognizable Takka. This tall and young version of Takka bore no resemblance to the cobbler I'd met in Chandni Chowk.

"Naani has sent for the police," I said. I remembered Rahu mentioning in his lair that he didn't want the police around the sacrificial altar. "She knows you are Rahu."

Chaubey tittered. Mothy Maddy's body lurched forward, and he fell on his face on the dusty ground.

"Hear that, Madhav? Your students have made the same mistake. They think *I* am Rahu," Chaubey said.

"It doesn't matter if you are Ketu or Rahu," I said. I was sure this man was one of the two vile deities.

I gripped my dagger as Chaubey picked Mothy Maddy from his collar and pushed him forward so that they were both standing before me. I glared at Mothy Maddy. The paladin had told Chaubey about our location. He had betrayed the confidence of Naani and the Maruts, who had entrusted their lives to him. Even in my dream, he had double-crossed Pilot Roy by lying to him about the egg.

I could have driven my dagger through both of them. But then all hope of rescuing Mohan would be lost. I guess that was the reason why Gargouille had still not made any move to capture me or snatch my dagger or the shield. He knew I had nowhere to run.

"Gods are prisoners of their purpose," Chaubey said. "Rahu was created to spread death and disease, and Ketu to bring about despair and renunciation. In a way, they are on the team of the supreme destroyer." He paused and walked toward Mothy Maddy. "But I am not like them. I chose wickedness because it gives me pleasure. It's not a purpose I was born with. I chose this. I am god of my own world."

I was sure he was going to hit me. Instead, he turned around and whacked Mothy Maddy on the side of the head. Mothy Maddy didn't flinch as a wound appeared on his forehead. His lip was already cut and swollen, and his staff was gone.

"Make way," someone called, and Red scurried forward through the Yechs. A cry of relief escaped my lips.

CHAPTER 33

Red would have informed the police and notified the formidable Apsara sleuths. Chaubey, Mothy Maddy, and Gargouille were done for.

I looked over my shoulder at Mohan. Pilot Roy had still not moved in to free him from the ropes. The cowardly paladin must have split. I should have known when he hid his challastra from me. I would have to do the job with my dagger.

I began to step sideways but stopped short when Chaubey removed the triquetra from his pocket and held it out to Red. I knew that if I could place the triquetra in its rightful place on the shield, the powers of the shield would multiply.

"Red, give me the triquetra, quick," I said, holding up Srivatsa to show him why I wanted the triquetra.

Red looked at me, his eyebrows raised in surprise, and extended his hand instead. "Why don't I place it on Srivatsa for you?"

I was about to hand Srivatsa to Red when I saw Mothy Maddy give me the slightest shake of his head. Or had I imagined it? I wasn't sure. All I knew was that Naani had given Srivatsa to me with the words, "Save your brother."

"You don't understand, only a Naga can place it back," I said. Again, I don't know why I said that. It was a lie, but it felt right. Perhaps I'd learned to lie too well in Anku's company.

Red nodded repeatedly but didn't ask for Srivatsa again. "I can't ruin the much-awaited family union," he said, stopping before me and Mohan.

When he turned to face the audience, to my horror, Gargouille, Chaubey, Thauma, and the Yechs bowed to Red. Only Mothy Maddy and Takka remained standing. Mothy Maddy looked as shocked as I was.

A strong breeze picked up, causing Red's hair to blow into his eyes, picking up dust and gravel of which there was no dearth in these ruins. Red jerked his head every time to clear his eyes.

"It cannot be," Mothy Maddy whispered, like someone who had known the truth deep down but had fought it for a long time.

"The dove that Naani sent to you," I said.

"Yes," Red said, "I handed that pathetic bird silhouette to Kabeela. Funny how things work out. Now Manasa decides to take me into confidence after all these years of mysteriously hiding her identity and her family."

That meant that all these years, the only two people other than Naani who knew about Mohan and my existence were Mothy Maddy and Fangless.

"You are not our kind," Mothy Maddy said gruffly.

"Oh, but I was. Well, at least Anniruddh, better known as

Red, was. Everyone trusted him. Even more than Madhav."

"Red has never harmed a hair on any head. No one can match him in wisdom and heart," Mothy Maddy said fiercely.

"And that is why I had to take Red's place." The one who had taken Red's identity gave out a squeaky laugh. "But for all my goodwill, it's a pity Manasa never warmed up to me."

"You snatched a paladin's identity. That's a dishonor to your celestial position as a deity," Mothy Maddy said, spitting on the ground. He grunted and pulled at his handcuffs in an attempt to free himself but to no avail.

Red held up the triquetra toward Mothy Maddy. "Want to see what this little widget can do?"

Mothy Maddy stopped struggling and his face grew ghostly pale. His body went into spasms and flopped limply on the ground. Gargouille stepped off the platform and pulled up a helpless Mothy Maddy by the collar. Then he slapped Mothy Maddy hard on the face.

I looked up at the Yechs guarding the outer edges of the ruins to figure a possible way of escape by summoning Kaleeni. Could it fly us to safety with a busted invisibility booster? The Yechs were watching the scene as if they were spectators in an amphitheater. I shut my eyes and commanded Kaleeni to fetch Surp, Anku, and Rudra. I felt silly because it was akin to wishing for a miracle. But I was ready to look like a fool if only I could free Mohan.

Red turned toward me. "Without the ring of Kundalini to bridle it, the triquetra can be used for anything," he said with a satisfied smile. "It contains the powers of the creator, preserver, and destroyer. It's a potent totem but only second to what you are holding in your hand."

I wasn't sure if he was talking about Shveta Uchchaihshravas or Srivatsa.

"You can have whatever you want if you let my brother go," I said. "I am the Naga heir you want. He's just a wastrel."

Red stopped in his tracks. "Just a wastrel? She didn't tell you, did she?" he said, his eyes just about popping out of his thin face.

"Don't believe anything he says, Adi," Mothy Maddy rasped and glanced toward the sky.

The moon eclipse would begin any second. Gargouille slapped Mothy Maddy again. Mothy Maddy writhed and balled up his fists but couldn't break free of the ropes.

Gargouille roared with pleasure. Chaubey started laughing, and the Yechs screeched loudly, creating a mind-numbing ruckus. Red was still watching me.

"Anniruddh ji," Thauma said, using Red's formal name and stepping forward with folded hands through the din. "The deal was that you would perform the triquetra ritual, but there would be no violence."

"Thaumaaaaa," Red said. "The clever one. You knew Manasa would never let you have Srivatsa so you brought the triquetra to me, someone who was desperate for it. You should know better than to expect rational behavior from a desperate person. A desperate person will turn violent either on himself or the world."

"Technically," Thauma said, holding up a finger and tilting his head, "I brought the triquetra to Chaubey." Then, as an afterthought, he added "Ji," the word considered a symbol of respect.

"Forever the businessman," Red said, shaking his head. "Then let's get on with the ritual, shall we?" He held the triquetra toward himself and looked into it as if he were looking into a mirror.

Mothy Maddy's bloody and bruised body went limp as the triquetra lost its hold over him and he slumped on the ground.

Gargouille advanced toward me. I slashed my dagger at him, but he caught my hands in the air and twisted them behind me. I glanced at Mohan, who was watching Red with confused detachment. Every eye was fixed on Red with a mix of fear and awe.

"Watch, you snake," Gargouille whispered in my ear as Red's hair began to grow and twist into dark curls. Simultaneously, black fumes wafted out from under his collar, below his chin. Red's pale complexion grew darker and his cheeks more robust. A pair of long fangs came to rest on both sides of his lower lip just as smoke enveloped his head and body.

After a few seconds, his clothes flopped on the ground, leaving just a head kept afloat by a strong gush of sooty smoke. The triquetra remained suspended in the air next to Rahu's head. Had I not seen Rahu's real form on my visit to Kalpavriksha, I would have definitely screamed or fainted, but I had been inured to this sight. Mohan, on the other hand, passed out without a whimper.

"Why did I don the guise of Red?" Rahu said with a lisp, owing to his large fangs. "Many years ago, when pure Maruts existed, I snatched the identity of a plain Marut. When my wife, Chayya, a descendant of the Pakshi clan, got to know of my real identity, she deserted me." Rahu snorted. "She discovered that I planned to snatch the ring of Kundalini from Shesh Nagaraj. She bolted, spilling the whole story to the Nagas."

"I told you it wasn't me," Thauma said, snapping his fingers and pointing at Gargouille.

"Shesh Nagaraj involved himself with the freedom fighters and revolutionary Maruts. All the while, he held the source of universal power in his hands, the ring of Kundalini, a celestial totem that could regenerate souls," Rahu said, a faraway look in his eyes.

A Yech made loud clicking and rasping sound, pointing toward the sky. The neckless head of Rahu snapped out of its trance and regarded the moon, which had lost a sliver of its circumference to a shadow. The lunar eclipse—the blue blood moon—had begun.

"My wife, Chayya, was an idealist. You see, she believed in the goodness of humans and Maruts, especially Shesh and Manasa." Rahu paused and gave me a despising look. "I am told you are no stranger to the goodness of Manasa."

I glared at him with my jaws clenched. My newly acquired muscles were twitching with the need to lash out at someone from the anger I felt at both Rahu and Naani. I heard Gargouille grunt and hiss from the effort to hold me stationary.

"When Gargouille attacked Haveli, Manasa fled with her daughter. Thanks to Thauma's information, we caught Fangless with the ring of Kundalini." I noticed Thauma slink into Takka's shadow, a sheepish smile on his face.

Neither Rahu nor Thauma seemed to know that Srivatsa symbols were the new ring of Kundalini. Is spirit the home, or the circle it lives in? The circle in this riddle must mean the ring of Kundalini, and spirit was the ancient Serpent Vasuki. Since the real home is the spirit itself, Shesh could break the circle into three parts to secure the powers of Vasuki.

"It was a tragic day for the humans, Maruts, and the Boors," Rahu said, his voice soft and menacing. "My wife was expecting a child. She kept the news of her pregnancy from me, her own husband."

I caught a shadow in the sky that no one else had noticed. Large wings, perhaps.

"But Chayya had to learn a lesson, and learn she did when Manasa abandoned her on the night of the attack. In her silhouette form, Chayya delivered and fled Haveli, injured and heartbroken, leaving behind the egg with my child in it."

This was strange because one fact I had learned about Maruts was that they never delivered their babies in silhouette.

Chayya! It suddenly came to me that this was the same Dakini who had addressed the Yechs outside Rahu's den on Kalpavriksha. She was also the raven who had accosted Dakini Malini and Kabeela in the sky, along with Surpanekha. She had accused Dakini Malini of lying to her.

"Simmering with vengeance, Chayya came back to me. I loved her, and I accepted her with open arms," Rahu said. "I sent my boys every day for ten days to search Haveli high and low, but they did not find the egg."

I detected an ever-so-slight hint of grief in Rahu's voice.

"Chayya and I were together, but we were not a family. We would never be a family without our child. You should know, Adi. You lost your parents."

Rahu's lisping voice fell on my deadened senses. "You murdered my parents," I said through clenched teeth.

Rahu seemed to ponder this. "We believed we had lost our child forever. Even if he survived the battle between Boors and Maruts at Haveli, he would be squished as soon as he was born. Isn't that the fate of anomalous silhouettes?" Rahu said, looking at Mothy Maddy.

"Those were the old days," Mothy Maddy said. "All Maruts and silhouettes are loved and accepted."

"What about the silhouettes you consider cursed or shrapit?" Rahu smirked. Mothy Maddy looked on, speechless. "Change is an illusion imposed by the passage of time, my friend. Even today, my kind is treated with derision. Humans have their own reasons for persecuting their fellowmen. Oppression equals power and that will never change." He paused to allow his words to sink in, then went on. "Chayya and I swore to get back at the Nagas. I wanted a few drops of Naga blood to wake up Vasuki's spirit, which rested inside the ring of Kundalini. Chayya wanted a vendetta. She wanted a child's life for her child's life. And we were right on track with our plan. After years of searching for any clue, my brother suggested I snatch Red's identity. He suspected that Mothy Maddy was still in touch with the Nagas."

The moon was half covered in darkness now. The Yechs had started up a chant, "Rahu Amavasya," in their cackling voices.

"Then, ten years ago, there was a night of a great deadly storm, one that happens once in many blue moons, when an Ihamriga is born. We sent out scouts to find where my son had been born. We found your parents and murdered them, but Manasa gave us the slip and took you with her."

There was silence now. What Rahu was saying was simply unbelievable, an idea that belonged in the folk tales told within realms of myths and fairy tales.

"Then, one fine day, you wandered into Wantra yourself, bringing with you the news about another Naga boy."

My mind stopped looking for ways to escape as I caught the drift of Rahu's conversation.

"You see, your mother died in the hospital, as did your baby sister," Rahu said. "You had no sibling of your own."

I staggered as my head reeled from this information.

The smoke that carried Rahu's head like a soft fluffy bed got thicker at this point. He had floated toward Mohan as he spoke, and now he blew a breath of smoke that awakened him.

When Mohan's blank eyes met Rahu's, he seemed to snap out of the apathetic trance. "What's happening?" he cried.

I tried to free myself, but Gargouille held on. He had managed to wrangle Shveta Uchchaihshravas and Srivatsa from my hands in a weak moment.

Mohan spotted me and cried out my name. Once again, I struggled against the restraining arms of Gargouille, who grunted. I was so strong now that Gargouille was finding it difficult to hold me back.

"A deity and a Marut can never unite, and there's a good reason for it. The resulting child is destined to be a mutation, a shrapit silhouette, or Ihamriga," Gargaouille blustered.

I looked at Mohan in alarm. His chubby cheeks were tearstained now, and he kept shutting his eyes from the sand-laden winds and Rahu's body smoke.

With one massive heave, I managed to throw off Gargouille. I swept my leg to trip him and wrestled back my weapons from him.

I rushed toward Mohan. Holding out my dagger and Srivatsa, I covered his body behind my own and spread out my arms to shield him.

"I've got him," Pilot Roy's soft voice came from behind me.

The smoke from Rahu's body had created a haze around us, thus providing Pilot Roy with cover to sneak up to the pillar. I had to buy time for Pilot Roy to untie Mohan or cut him loose from the ropes.

"Mohan is ten. He can't even silhouette," I said. I looked over my shoulder. Pilot Roy was still struggling with the ropes that held Mohan, the kitchen knife doing a shoddy job of cutting through the ropes.

"After a gestation of more than a hundred and fifty years, a child was born, ten years ago," Rahu said slowly.

"No." I shook my head wildly. "That's impossible."

"You are right. Marut children are not born as silhouettes. But Ihamriga is half-human, half-animal."

I felt Mohan go still behind me, as did Pilot Roy. I wished Pilot Roy hadn't stopped. His job was to focus on cutting the ropes that tied Mohan.

"It was a cataclysmic event in the divine sense. It petrified the deities and stoked the elements of nature, causing storms, tsunamis, and earthquakes." Rahu paused. "The night of the Deadly Storm," he said with a faraway look on his face. "How was the world possibly going to handle two of me?" He grinned, revealing sharp, pointed teeth and a swollen, blood-red tongue. His mouth was like an opening into a never-ending abyss filled with smoke and death.

Mohan saw Rahu's face and screamed at the top of his lungs.

"After the child's birth, the evil omens that would have helped us track him down receded. We could not trace him. It was as if his brain had been washed of his purpose. It was the second time we gave up hope of ever being a family." Rahu shut his eyes as if drinking in the sound of Mohan's screaming, relishing it like a father who hears the first cry of his newborn. "But I still had the ring of Kundalini in my possession. The twist in the tale happened when the ring turned out to be a fake, planted by Fangless. And that, little Naga, is the reason why you are useless to me. At least for now," Rahu hissed.

I glanced at Mothy Maddy. He had saved the egg he found at Haveli, and he must have handed it to Naani in case it was a Naga egg. Anku had been right about him. Surp and I were proven wrong.

"This man," Rahu said, nodding his head toward Mothy Maddy, "never let Manasa get close to me or my brother."

Rahu's fanged face was within biting range of mine when Gargouille's cry sliced through the smoke. "It has begun!"

I looked up at the sky. The moon was completely under the spell of the eclipse save for a tiny tip that remained visible. For the remaining time of the eclipse, the few seconds when the moon was covered completely in shadow, the evil forces of Boorlok, Bhuvahlok, and Swahalok would be invincible.

"Brother! It's time!" Rahu roared as his head rose on the

billowing smoke.

"Hurry up, Pilot," I said over my shoulder, but I got no response. With my dagger held out, I braved a look behind to find Pilot Roy standing behind Mohan with a cleaver held against Mohan's neck. What was happening?

"Hand over the shield, Adi," Pilot Roy said.

"What are you doing?" I said. From the corner of my eye, I saw Mothy Maddy wince as Pilot Roy plucked the shield from my hand.

"By feeding the panacea to the puny Maruts, you have foiled my plan to expand Boor forces. But I will get humans on my side one day," Rahu said to me. "They're waiting for me to take over."

So the fruit from Kalpavriksha had rendered Venvap ineffective. Mohan screamed behind me when Pilot Roy pulled at the ropes that held him tied to the pillar.

"Pilot Roy!" Mothy Maddy cried, his face contorted with anger and hurt. "What are you doing?"

"Not Pilot Roy, but Ketu," Rahu said, relishing every syllable as he spoke.

"I don't care who you claim to be," Mothy Maddy said to Pilot Roy. "I've known you for more than a hundred and fifty years. You are better than that."

"You always maintained that family comes first," Ketu replied. "I'm just following your advice."

"What have you done to him, you brutes?" Mothy Maddy screamed at Gargouille.

"There was never a Pilot Roy, you ninny," Ketu said. "But you are right, a claim needs proof." He brought out a matchbox and struck a match. With the flame, he lit his own shirt.

Mohan began to weep loudly as he watched the immolation in horror. I turned around and hugged Mohan, covering his eyes and shutting my own. When we looked up, the thin, headless body of Ketu in a black kurta pajama stood before us. He was holding the triquetra in one hand, and his face was engulfed in flames.

Watching the visage of Pilot Roy burn, Mothy Maddy struggled to stand up. Huffing, he pulled and kicked himself free of the ropes. He lifted his hand to have his bony staff fly into his grip from the depths of the sky, nipping a few Yech heads on its way.

At the same time, the headless body of Ketu positioned the triquetra over the grooves in Srivatsa, and like a powerful magnet that finds its home, the triquetra flew into place.

The moment the triquetra settled in the shield, many things happened at once. Takka burst out in loud and triumphant laughter. His arms began to expand into large pincers, sending Thauma and the Yechs around him crashing to the ground.

Gargouille pounced on Mothy Maddy, who was advancing toward Ketu. Mothy Maddy registered a sharp thwack of his staff on Gargouille's bald head.

Gargouille let out a banshee-like shriek. Thauma, having fulfilled his side of a trade-off with Takka, slunk into the shadows of the ruins. Yechs swarmed all around us. Mohan shut his eyes again in terror.

We were surrounded by Yechs. I squared my shoulders. I'd heard stories about what adrenaline could do to bodies. I was sure one didn't have to be a Marut for that kind of bravery.

I, the most bullied kid of Shiksha High School, punched a Yech's chin from below and then drove my dagger into its chest.

From the shadows, Thauma emerged and launched his body at one of the Yechs. Together, Thauma and I slashed at them, turning them into piles of dust. I took to thrusting and stabbing the dagger at the Yechs in all directions as if making my way through a room bursting at its seams with balloons, but their number kept growing.

Mohan was still cowering, his eyes shut. This was when I saw five familiar forms standing astride Kaleeni, and a bushy-tailed Lomri behind a row of Yechs. The shadow I had seen before was Kaleeni and not a large bird, as I'd suspected. I had received the miracle I'd wished for.

Surp with her spear and Anku with her club landed behind a bunch of Yechs standing atop the uneven walls of the ruins. Rudra, Angad, and Bala dropped on top of the Yechs toward the other end of the periphery, causing them to scatter. Lomri ran toward Mothy Maddy and met him midair, transforming into a gigantesque warrior Lomri.

I slashed my dagger at the Yechs with renewed vigor and was soon joined by Anku.

"Go after Ketu. Get the Srivatsa," Anku said. "I'll take care of Mohan."

I sprinted after Ketu, but Anku's cry brought me to a halt. I looked around to find that Mohan's feet had lifted off the ground, and black smoke was billowing from under his clothes from the top of his collar and around his feet. His skin was turning red, the same shade as Rahu's. Mohan screamed and reached out to me.

I tried to catch his hand, but Ketu seized me in an iron-grip hold.

"Hang on, Mohan!" I cried as I stabbed Ketu with my dagger.

My blade met no resistance as it entered Ketu's body. It was like poking holes in an empty cardboard carton. I looked around wildly. Mohan had risen higher in the air. Love and familiarity left his eyes, and his hands came down by his sides.

"Let him go!" I pleaded to Rahu, throwing my dagger on the ground before him. "I will give you anything from Naga treasury. Naani is dead."

"He is my son," Rahu said. "Not a wastrel. He will come home with me."

Mohan was Rahu's son.

I tried to shake off what I'd just heard as if words were dust and they could be gotten rid of. This was the secret that Naani was petrified of disclosing. My past life and memories took on new meaning and color. On one hand, my long-held sense of persecution felt wrong, like a reflection that goes crooked when the mirror is shattered.

On the other hand, missing puzzle pieces fell into place by themselves. I now understood where Mohan and I fit in the prophecy and what Naani's silence had meant. Heirs, one Naga and one born of ash. She must have known that her grandchild was to eventually fight the Ihamriga.

She had decided to raise both heirs, but she had also decided to flip the prophecy on its face. A seed of self-doubt would make an all-powerful Marut wary of his actions, and unconditional love showered on the child of a monster would bring about a permanent change in his heart.

A terrifying future awaited both of us if we were discovered, so she'd kept us hidden from the world. Either one of us would die if we fought, so she had brought us up as brothers.

Had I been in her place, I would have replied to all my questions with silence too. I now also understood the conversation between the Fallen Ones at the Twelve Rhinos Café and Inn. Brahma had been talking about Mohan when he discussed how nurturing could trump one's nature. He had been right.

"Adi, move away!" Anku said as she vaulted to the platform, trying to pull me away from the smoke that was scorching everything it touched.

The Yechs and the Maruts stepped farther away. A blister formed and burst open on my hand, but I felt no pain.

The moon was in full eclipse now, just like Rahu was in complete control of Mohan. A bolt of lightning struck the pillar behind Mohan, cracking it open. The portal of Bare Stambha was wide open for Rahu, Ketu, and Mohan. This was what Rahu had planned all along by sealing the celestial gates. He intended to abandon the Maruts to death at the hands of the Yechs. Samsara would perish from Venvap, bringing new recruits into the Yech fold.

I shook off Anku's hand and rushed to Mohan. I removed the locket he presented to me on my birthday and held it up to him. "Mohan, we are brothers. Light and dark, good and bad. You have a family that loves you. Don't give in to him. Come back," I cried.

My skin was bubbling with blisters now, but the surge of adrenaline kept me hanging to the ropes around Mohan's feet. His body had started convulsing. A fresh wave of smoke now started to stream from his sleeves.

This was the end. All my resentment toward my brother melted when I saw that there was no bringing him back now. I wept, and I called out to Naani. I asked for Mohan's forgiveness and implored him to come back.

Then I saw Mohan's eyes move and rest on the locket. It was a flicker of the irises. The wave of smoke abated for a moment.

"Hold the triquetra closer," Rahu roared to Ketu.

Ketu brought Srivatsa closer, right above Mohan's forehead. But I already knew that Mohan had come back to me. The eclipse started to abate.

Just as the tip of the moon became visible, Mohan's eyes moved and settled on the locket in my hand. His body started to descend.

"Hold the triquetra on his forehead!" Rahu roared to Ketu, but no matter what Ketu tried, Mohan's body was reacting to the moon's light and not the triquetra's power. His skin started turning back to its original tone. Just as his feet touched the ground, he fainted, my locket clenched in his hand.

"Where are the Dakinis?" Rahu roared, but he got no reply.

I heard a loud thud and turned to see the shield drop on the ground. Ketu was running toward a grove of trees between the ruins and the boundary wall.

Yechs scattered in all directions as Rahu rose higher in the air, giving off vile fumes that made us cough and our eyes water. But it was clear we had won the battle.

The shrieks of the Yechs became fainter as Rahu and the smoke melted into the dark night. A propellor plane took off somewhere in a field nearby.

I sank to the ground next to Mohan and drifted into unconsciousness.

CHAPTER 34

I woke up to a repetitive beeping sound. I was in a hospital bed, and there was a drip connected through a needle that was inserted into my hand.

My face and body were in bandages. I tried to move my hand. A searing pain shot through my arm to my jaw and head. An image of Mohan hanging in the air flashed before my eyes. I tried to get up, but my hands slipped on the railings of the hospital bed.

A scuffing sound at the door announced someone.

"Nurse," I managed to croak.

"It's going to be alright," a lady said.

I could hear voices in the background. How could they have allowed so many people to visit? I heard hospitals were strict about visitors.

"He needs to know," a gruff voice said.

"Adi did splendidly. Rahu will stay put for a while. There's no need to rush," a singsong voice replied.

I'd heard these voices before.

The lady used a switch to lift the backside of the bed so I could sit and lean back. My eyes fluttered, letting in ripples of daylight, but the bandages on my face made it difficult for me to focus.

My body screamed in pain. As a Marut, I expected the agony to be less. But last night, when my mind refused to acknowledge my burning skin, I knew it wasn't a Marut thing because all Maruts and paladins had backed away from Rahu's acidic body smoke. I knew my body would wake up to the trauma later.

"Give him time. Let him get comfortable in his new skin, no pun intended," said a calm and composed voice.

The other two tittered. My eyes fully open now, I glanced at Dev Vidhata, who sat with a beatific smile on his face while the voices in his head jabbered endlessly.

The lady by my side was Apsara Tanya. As if unaware of the chattering between Dev Vidhata's invisible personas, she smiled at me. "I am here to collect this." She picked up Naani's dagger, the Shveta Uchchaihshravas, and the Srivatsa shield. "Don't worry. This will be kept safe for you at the Bank of Karma. Naga treasury has already reduced to half of what it was."

She placed the shield and the dagger inside a briefcase and snapped it shut. Naani and Fangless had squandered away the Naga treasures in an effort to sneak a look at Rahu's plans for the takeover of the three worlds.

Apsara Tanya peered at me. "Shrapmukta tincture has been acquired, and it is on its way. You'll be on your feet in no time. See you later."

She left the room. The sharp taps of her oxfords grew fainter.

"Had an eventful sleep?" Dev Vidhata asked me.

I'd just woken from another crazy dream about how Mohan had been born, but I was in no mood to dissect it for truth. Mohan was safe, and he would always be my annoying little brother.

"All these crazy dreams," I said. "What causes them?"

"My bet would be the triquetra," Dev Vidhata said. "Vasuki is connected to the Naga heir since he depends on you for protection."

But I had been having such dreams ever since I silhouetted at the age of ten. Perhaps because Srivatsa had been harmlessly lying in our living room, serving the purpose of a potpourri holder.

Dev Vidhata was watching me silently. He could carry a beatific smile on his face while the voices in his head argued.

I sighed. "You could have given the triquetra to Naani and prevented all of this."

"Deities can't affect changes for their own survival. It defeats the purpose of our existence," he said with a sheepish smile.

"Still, if Naani had silhouetted…" I said.

"In her emotional state, she would have fled. The future must be faced. You can't keep running from it."

"How can you be so sure?" I whispered, leaning back against the pillow.

"Everything turns out as it is meant to, Adi. 'Should haves' and 'could haves' are just ways of kidding oneself. The question is: What now?"

"I'm guessing Rahu won't give up on the ring of Kundalini," I said in the hope that Dev Vidhata might dismiss my worry as needless.

But Dev Vidhata nodded. "He won't give up. But for now, he is out of his depth. You did well."

"No thanks to you. Why didn't you tell me what the triquetra could do?" My body felt like it was on fire. I recalled the blisters that formed on my skin from the smoke that billowed from Mohan's body as I hugged his feet, trying to pull his floating body down.

"Adi, sometimes too much information can be a hurdle, not an asset. You used your instincts. Instincts are pure and powerful. Why did you not hand the triquetra to Manasa as directed by me?" Dev Vidhata asked gently.

I had feared this question, but he made it sound like proof, not an investigation.

"Naani couldn't hurt a mouse if she wanted to," I said.

"There you go. You used your instincts."

I couldn't tell if he was being patronizing.

"You knew the truth about Mohan?" I asked to bring the focus back on Dev Vidhata.

He pursed his lips. "The night of the storm, all celestials and Maruts were alerted to the birth of Ihamriga, but the omens vanished within a few hours. We, the Fallen Ones, believed the Ihamriga was killed. But…"

Dev Vidhata paused, his eyes glinting with excitement.

"Look at Manasa's brilliance," he continued, "the mark of Naga loyalty to their clan. By showering Mohan with love, she actually protected you. She expected the bond between you and Mohan to be so strong that it could withstand the lure of the dark." Dev Vidhata shook his head in awe. "And she was right."

"I'm not sure if you've heard, but Naani was killed last night. She fell."

My emotions regarding Naani were still in a muddle. Her excuse for being harsh with me was that she wanted to keep Mohan and me safe. I wished she'd confided in me. There was no way of undoing the hurt that Naani and I had caused one another.

"So I heard," Dev Vidhata said, shaking his head in disbelief. "Wherever her Marut soul takes her, she will know you and Mohan are in safe hands."

"Why didn't you fight Rahu along with Mothy Maddy and the Maruts?" I asked.

Dev Vidhata had been conspicuously absent the entire evening. Even Thauma had attacked the Yechs at the Bare Stambha last night, and in a way may have bought me precious moments to save Mohan.

"Of the three facets of the triquetra, creation has been forgotten. I don't have any divine powers left. Like the joker in a pack of cards, an informal replacement for damaged cards, I am best kept aside."

"Then why did you shadow me and keep in touch with me as my aunt?"

"Does an artist ever give up on his masterpiece?" Dev Vidhata said, shaking his head. "Indra, Varun, and Agni don't care about humans. They care only about themselves. Had I allowed them to interfere, this saga would have ended long ago."

"And not a very pleasant ending it would've been," Kalakar's singsong voice declared.

"A gruesome ending," Krodha growled in assent.

Dev Vidhata was the player in this game where humans and Maruts were the pawns, but he had me believing he wasn't important enough.

"Why are you here now?" I said, weary from all the dramatic revelations.

"I am here to congratulate you, and to thank you."

I was hardly in a celebratory mood, so I waited for him to continue, my eyes fixed on the foot of my bed.

"Adi, you brought a ray of hope to residents of Wantra when you caused uthaan in the Maw."

I looked at him in surprise. "I brought about uthaan?"

"The Maw has been spreading like cancer in the heart of Kalpavriksha. Uthaan literally means 'emancipation.' In the Maw, when you helped the tree reconnect with its true purpose, it left the Maw to enter the real world—its home, as it were. It brought you home as well, and everyone else who had entered Wantra with you."

"How do you know?"

"I got the story from a well-meaning Glitch with a lot of potential who goes by the name of Ludo."

The thought of Ludo lightened my weary heart. I wondered if I would ever meet him again.

"Therefore," Dev Vidhata continued, "I felt obligated to return this to you." He offered me a key ring with a small loop hanging from its end: Satya Pasha.

I had lost all the cool and deadly weapons and was back to being stuck with the loop of truth.

"Satya Pasha, the loop that brings out the good in the vilest of creatures," Dev Vidhata said, placing it on my bedside table.

"Even in creatures like Dakini Malini and Gargouille?" I asked.

Dev Vidhata nodded. "Even if there's not a drop of warmth left in them. Though they're likely to return to darkness the moment you remove the loop from them."

"How is that different from uthaan?"

"In the Maw, not only did you lasso this loop around a Chamruk tree, but you also sacrificed yourself to save your friends. Nature is very forgiving of selflessness. The universe comes together for such people."

A long yawn escaped me as Dev Vidhata collected himself to leave.

"If you're a forgotten deity, then why does the ring of Kundalini matter to you?" I said to him.

The voices that lived in him started chatting and whispering insults at one another.

Dev lifted his hand to quiet them. "They said I had done a shoddy job of creation, that humans would perish. I am just trying my best to prove them wrong."

That seemed fair. I was about to ask him who "they" were when someone knocked on the door. Dev Vidhata quickly bade me goodbye.

"Where can I find you if I need…" I paused to find the right word. "Answers."

Dev Vidhata flashed a smile. "I expect you will write many letters to an address in Shimla in the near future." With that, he gave a small bow to the entrants in the room and exited.

My eyes fell on Anku, who was flanked by Angad and Bala. She threw a suspicious look at Dev Vidhata as he left. "Who was that?"

I held up the Satya Pasha. "A messenger making a delivery."

Anku smiled when she saw the Satya Pasha. I had never seen her smile openly and sincerely before.

"Where's Mohan?" I asked.

Anku placed her hand on my shoulder and asked me to stay still. She made a cut in the plaster and studied the wounds. She held out her hand like a doctor in an operation theater. Angad and Bala placed cotton balls sodden in tincture in her hand.

Wordlessly, Anku dabbed the tincture all over my wounds. The touch of the tincture was cool and watery. It didn't sting, and it smelled of oranges and caramel even though it wasn't jambukita tincture.

She had not yet finished applying it, but I already started to feel better. Day was breaking. Anku put a finger to her mouth and gently replaced the dressing on my wounds.

"Best to give these a couple of days," she said. "We don't want the doctors to get suspicious. These tinctures only work on Marut bodies."

"Mohan is with Mothy Maddy. He sent this for you," Angad said, holding up the yin-yang pendant. I took it and wore it around my neck.

The nurse sleeping on her station outside the ward stirred. Angad and Bala made themselves comfortable on chairs in the room. Anku sat near my feet.

"So Rahu and Dakini Chayya are Mohan's parents," I said.

It was strange to accept a reality where Mohan was not my brother. I was not ready to give him up as a brother. Everything had changed, and yet none of it mattered.

"I still don't understand the story about the egg," Anku said.

I didn't tell them that I'd witnessed it all in my dream. It was Mothy Maddy who found the egg that Chayya's silhouette had laid.

They first thought it was a fire dragon's egg, for it grew to the size of a football. A hundred and fifty years later when Mohan was born as a baby with a beak and limbs of a bird, Naani reached out to my mother, but Gargouille had already murdered her and my baby sister. Naani switched the babies. She and Mothy Maddy were the only ones who knew about the switch. It was a horrifying story that had ended well, but hiding and lying had only postponed the facing of hard truths.

"I don't want to hide anymore," I said to Anku.

Her large eyes blinked at me through her eyeglasses. "Rahu and Chayya will not give up on getting Mohan back. Dakini Chayya is distraught about losing her son again."

I shook my head. "I don't care. If Mothy Maddy trains us, we can learn to fight the Boors in Wantra and Samsara." I thought of people like Chaubey, who was neither a dark deity nor a Yech. He was a demon in sheepskin.

"In that case," Angad said, grinning, his cheeks caving into dimples, "welcome to our band of Maruts."

With a sigh and a smile, Anku leaned back against the hospital bed.

TARA REWA

I was discharged from the hospital after two days. The nurses were astounded by the speed at which my wounds healed. I could also tell they'd grown tired of Anku, Angad, and Bala hanging around me constantly.

Surp didn't visit me. Her role as a Marut was more important, I told myself. I couldn't imagine Mothy Maddy sending Anku, Bala, and Angad on any missions.

I was surprised to find Mothy Maddy waiting at the reception for me. "We underestimated you, Adi," Mothy Maddy said and hugged me warmly.

I hugged him back awkwardly. Between Naani's lack of affection and Mohan smothering me with it to the point that I tried my best to avoid being hugged by him, I didn't know that a hug could stand for acceptance and security.

"Mohan is waiting for you at the Underbridge," Mothy Maddy said.

"But Rahu," I said, alarmed at the thought of a defenseless Mohan sitting in the middle of a road under a bridge.

He held up his hand. "Manasa managed to pull off an impossible feat. She nipped Mohan's silhouette in the bud. The Ihamriga in him didn't get an opportunity to grow."

I didn't care for Mothy Maddy's admiration of Naani. It's not easy to forget years of neglect and nagging.

"Anyway, as long as Mohan has us, no Boor can step close to him," Mothy Maddy continued. "Moreover, even if we try to place him somewhere safe, he refuses to leave his brother."

"So I can live with you and the others?"

"Your grandmother's strict instructions were for you and Mohan to finish your education. I welcome you boys to live with us, but Marut work will happen after school."

I nodded and pursed my lips to hide my smile.

"I hope you know it's not easy," Mothy Maddy went on to say. "You must use the public toilets and survive on tea and omelets."

Though I had never explored it completely and wondered how we would fit into a tiny space, I couldn't imagine any other place than the Underbridge where I could be happier.

We walked to the two-wheeler parking where Mothy Maddy's motorbike was parked. "Do you think Rahu will come after the ring of Kundalini again?" I asked.

"We can expect all kinds of Boors, celestials, and even humans to seek it out. A scavenger hunt has begun, and the only way Maruts can come out unharmed is if we get there first."

"I want to meet Gargouille and Dakini Malini again," I said.

"That's a wish I thought I would never hear anyone express," Mothy Maddy said, raising a questioning eyebrow at me as he sat astride his bike and asked me to ride pillion, handing me Anku's pink and flowery helmet.

"They can't go around pinching people's pets," I said as I vowed to get my buddy Patches back home.

You Write. We Publish.

To publish your own book, contact us.

We publish poetry collections, short story collections, novellas and novels.

contact@thewriteorder.com

Instagram- thewriteorder

www.facebook.com/thewriteorder

Made in the USA
Monee, IL
03 May 2026

49455733R00245